CROWN OF POWER

THE HIDDEN MAGE SERIES

Crown of Secrets

Crown of Danger

Crown of Strength

Crown of Power

And set in the same world:

THE SPOKEN MAGE SERIES

Voice of Power

Voice of Command

Voice of Dominion

Voice of Life

Power of Pen and Voice:

A Spoken Mage Companion Novel

CROWN OF POWER

THE HIDDEN MAGE BOOK 4

MELANIE CELLIER

For Rachel and Greg
for providing both inspiration and support

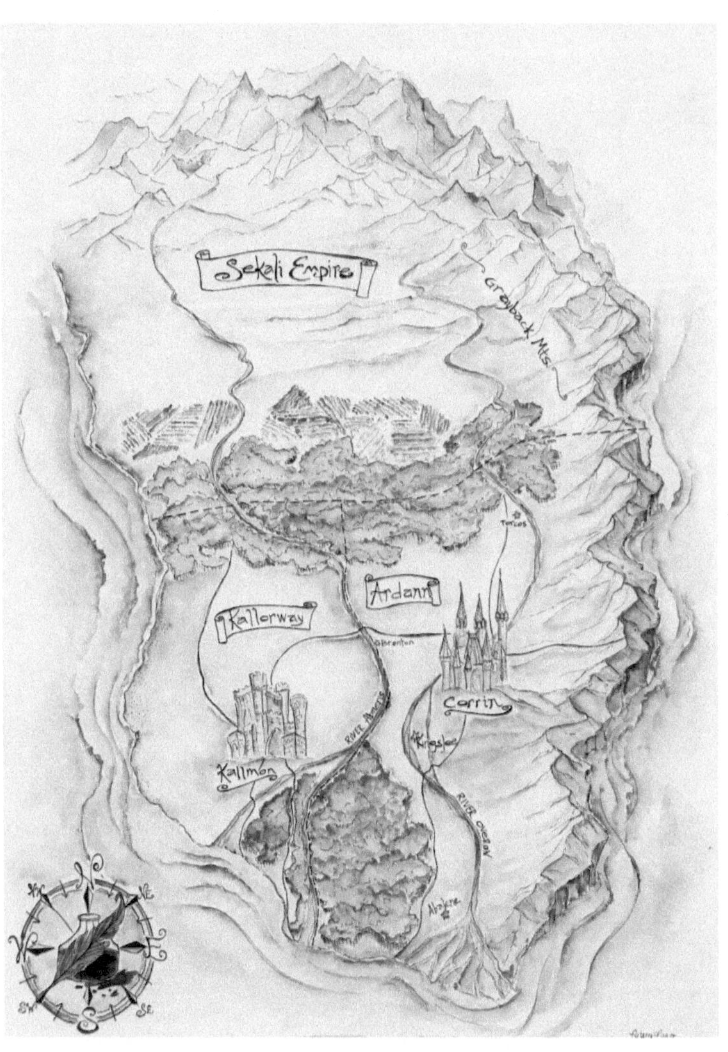

Sekeli Empire
Greyback Mts.
Torles
Ardann
Kallorway
Brenton
Corrin
River Ardelis
Kingslee
Kallmon
River Cherav
Abiskra

CHAPTER 1

My golden skirts swished around me as I slipped behind a large potted plant and contemplated the ballroom. Somehow I had been in high demand all evening, despite everyone in attendance still considering me the family disappointment—born without an ability when everyone had hoped for so much.

My Aunt Lucienne had insisted someone must represent my family at her end of summer ball, and with both of my parents away until the morning, the task had fallen to me. Apparently I was here to answer a myriad of inquiries about my parents' opinions on various recent policy decisions along with almost as many questions about the new king-elect of Kallorway. Even now, when I finally had a moment to myself, I couldn't decide which kind of question I disliked more.

A few kindly souls had asked about my studies, but even they hadn't been able to muster much sincere interest. Of what significance were the studies of a girl—however well-born—without power?

Of course, if they knew the truth…

The long window behind me—closed in an effort to keep out

the late summer heat—rattled slightly. I spun around, but not in time to block the hand that caught me around the wrist and tugged me outside.

I stumbled into the gardens, trying to restore my balance so I could wrench myself free. My darting eyes looked for Captain Layna, my usually alert personal guard, but there was no sign of her. Instead my eyes fell on someone far more chilling. Castor, my aunt's personal guard.

The experienced and powerful mage had stood protectively at her back since before she ascended to the throne. What possible reason could he have to attack me now?

And I couldn't doubt it was an attack. Although he let me go as soon as I was clear of the ballroom, he whipped out an entire pile of compositions, showing no hesitation as he ripped them all. I couldn't tell specifics, but I sensed the vague intent of the unleashed power as it rushed toward me. It was coming to wound and to bind me. What he intended after that, I could only guess. I had expected boredom and irritation at the ball but not physical danger.

I had a shield around me—both a habit and an expectation for a royal at court—but I could already tell it wasn't strong enough to withstand the onslaught of such a powerful mage. Not that I needed a shield to protect myself. But for a precious second, I wavered. If I acted, it would reveal my true abilities.

The power hit my shield, dissolving it instantly and rushing for me. As soon as it hit, my arms and legs became rigid. I toppled and fell to the ground.

Pain lanced through me before I even hit the gravel beneath our feet. The burning sensation cleared the fog of indecision in my mind. I might not understand why, but this was an attack with serious intent, and I couldn't afford to hold back.

"Take control." I gasped the words through another wave of pain. I was gripped by multiple compositions, but my mind seized on the one causing my agony.

"Send it back," I muttered as soon as it came under my direction. The pain immediately fell away.

The composition flew back toward my attacker, but the power fueling it beat itself out uselessly against his shield. I frowned. What was Castor—a personal guard—doing with such a strong shield? But then what was he doing attacking one of the members of the family he had sworn to protect?

He pulled out another composition, so I stopped thinking and ground out four more commands to take control. One by one, the compositions attacking me faltered and twisted beneath my words. I sent them all back toward their creator in a steady stream that beat against his shield.

The third one broke through his protections, and the fourth one felled him just as he was reaching for yet another parchment. I slowly stood, testing my trembling muscles, and schooling my face into granite. I gave my skirts an extra shake, frowning down at the dirt now clinging to them.

I had purposefully sent the binding composition last. So as I strolled toward Castor, he lay rigid on the ground before me, his reaching hand stilled.

I stood over him, staring down at his prone form with knit brows. An involuntary shudder ran through me as my body remembered the way his composition had set all my nerve endings on fire. Turning his own compositions against him no longer felt like enough.

"Connect," I growled.

Instantly I was inside his energy, with full access to his ability. Knowledge and compositions unfurled before me, organized and concise. Curiosity edged out some of my anger as I sensed open connections of power trailing away from him.

For half a second, I thought of my old year mate Tyron, and his father Conall—the energy mage who led the Tarxi. His ability to steal and keep small pieces of the energy of others—thus binding them to his will in some way—was the stuff of nightmares. Was someone controlling my aunt's personal guard? I was in even more danger than I had feared if so.

But a moment later I realized that these threads originated with Castor himself, and their flavor was one of protection not control. I pushed deeper, only to be brought back to an awareness of my surroundings by a new voice.

"Enough, Niece."

I pulled back, severing the connection instinctively. Queen Lucienne of Ardann stepped forward out of the shadows. The deep gold of her dress glittered as it caught reflected light from the ballroom. The material had been embroidered with flecks of obsidian, darkening the gold and allowing her to blend into the shadows or shine under light.

"Aunt." I dipped into the shallowest of curtsies, regarding her with a hard eye.

I should have known Castor wouldn't be far from the queen. I just hadn't considered that a member of my own family might be behind the attack. But as silence stretched between us, my confusion grew deeper. My aunt knew the truth about me and my abilities, and she had no shortage of resources to draw on. Castor's attack seemed designed to capture or harm me. But my aunt must know she would need more than a single guard, however powerful, to stand a chance of succeeding.

I wanted to accuse and question her, but I had never been more conscious that my parents were away and my aunt was far more than just my aunt. So we continued to stand in silence, facing each other.

Movement behind us shattered the stillness, making me start. My muscles clenched in anticipation of another attack. But the person who burst through the long window calmed at the sight of me. Captain Layna—my own personal guard—faltered, her eyes flicking between me and the queen before dropping to the bound man at my feet. She frowned and looked back at me.

"I'm sorry, Your Highness, I was distracted..." Her frown

deepened as her eyes lingered on the face of her superior—now lying helpless before me.

"I think that was arranged on purpose." I forced myself to keep my voice light. "You couldn't be expected to know your own commanders might be a threat to me."

Layna shook her head. "On the contrary, Your Highness. It's my job to see everyone and everything as a potential threat."

My aunt gave a soft laugh. "They told me you were a bright young star among the guards, and I can see they were right." Her eyes swung in my direction. "And that's why we needed you distracted."

"I'm afraid I don't understand," Layna said, her tone hesitant given she addressed her queen. But as she spoke, she moved to stand behind me, a comfortingly solid presence at my back.

A small smile slipped across Aunt Lucienne's face. "They told me you were loyal to your charge as well. It's good to know that some, at least, of my information isn't faulty." Her voice hardened on the last line, her gaze dwelling on my face.

I flushed slightly. "So it was a test."

"Of course. You can't think I'd actually harm my own niece."

I barely kept the scowl off my face. The pain of the attack compositions had been real enough, as would be the bruises from where I'd hit the ground.

Aunt Lucienne glanced down at her guard. "I don't suppose you'd care to release him?"

I shrugged. "The power has to go somewhere. Would you prefer I transferred it to you?"

Her eyes flashed, but she said nothing in response to my impertinence. The restraint was probably all the acknowledgment I was going to get that she had wronged me.

Layna looked between us. "Perhaps it could be redirected to bind his speech, or some such."

I sighed. "Take control." As soon as I connected with the power, I directed it to bind his speech.

He immediately jumped to his feet, his eyes flying to his queen. He looked chastened, as if he thought he had failed. But she smiled and nodded at him.

He bowed low. "Your Majesty."

All three of them looked at me, obviously wondering why he could speak.

"I bound only your ability to speak of me," I told him. "You poured a lot of power into that composition, so with such limited parameters, it should last a long time." I shrugged. "You might have a better idea than me of how long since it was your composition to start with."

A look of respect crossed his face along with something less welcome—fear. I didn't want to be feared, not even by him. At least not now I knew he had been attacking me under orders from the queen. I couldn't blame him for obeying her.

But when his eyes moved from me to my aunt, I stiffened. He wasn't afraid for himself, he was afraid for her. He thought I was a threat to his queen. And if she thought the same thing, then I was in deep trouble indeed.

"And now, dear niece," Queen Lucienne said, "we need to talk."

With a wave of her hands, my aunt indicated for the two guards to draw back out of earshot. They both hesitated. With an arch of her eyebrows, the queen sent her own guard bowing and hurrying to withdraw. Layna stayed obstinately at my back for another second before I also waved her away.

She stepped back to join my aunt's guard, the two of them studiously ignoring each other and keeping their eyes on us, although they were too far away now to hear us.

"That was an impressive performance," my aunt said.

"Are you aware your personal guard is maintaining some open workings?" I asked. "That seems dangerous."

"How do you—" She cut herself off. "You needn't be concerned about him. They're not of sufficient energy draw to put his reserves at risk."

"Did you send my parents away on purpose for this?" I asked. "Or were you just taking advantage of the opportunity offered? You must know how they would react if I was attacked in their presence."

"My dear brother and his wife failed to tell me about their

daughter's unexpected discovery of a new and powerful ability," she said, not answering the question.

I shook my head. "You can't blame them. They didn't know."

She raised a single eyebrow, watching me in silence as if waiting for me to catch on.

I gasped softly. "You mean they didn't tell you when we returned from Kallorway? But you've known all summer. I assumed…"

"Your brother recognizes his duty."

Of course. Of course it had been Lucien. Why had I not considered that possibility? Even after weeks, Lucien was still furious with me for keeping my abilities a secret. Raised as our aunt's heir, he considered my silence a betrayal not only of our family but of the entire kingdom.

I had tried to explain to him that I never meant for events to unfold in such a way, and that I had always intended to tell my family the truth myself—eventually. But he wasn't interested in what he called my *pathetic excuses*. He couldn't see that his reaction was the entire reason I hadn't told anyone for so long.

In retrospect, I should have known he would run to our aunt with everything he knew.

And so, when the opportunity arose, my aunt had sent my parents away in punishment. And then she had used their absence to test me—to see if the unbelievable report could possibly be true.

"But surely you can't doubt my parents' loyalty to you or Ardann," I said, unable to completely keep the heat from my voice. "They've devoted their lives to this kingdom."

"If you mean do I suspect them of having greater loyalty to Kallorway or the Sekalis, of course I do not." She watched me with a keen eye. "What I think is that—like so many before them —there is something they place above me. Or rather, *someone*. Their children."

Affection for my parents filled me at the suggestion, but I

shook my head. "How can you say that when they gave you their firstborn?"

My aunt's face softened for the first time. "Lucien is still your parents' child and your brother. Never doubt that he cares for you, Verene."

I snorted, and a slight smile crossed her face.

"For all he tries to hide it behind a controlled facade, Lucien has much of your mother in him." When I frowned, she continued. "You didn't know her when she was your age, but your mother used to have quite a hot head. She appeared from nowhere and blazed so brightly she burned our whole world down."

"You say that like you disapprove of her."

My aunt shook her head with a faint air of surprise. "Not at all. She helped us build a better world in place of the old one. But you cannot blame a monarch for being wary of such firebrands."

"And you think I might be like my mother as well," I said, full comprehension blooming. "You're wondering if I intend to burn down your world anew. And if maybe I have the power to do it."

"Do you?" she asked, her eyes boring into me.

I shook my head emphatically. "I have no desire for such a thing. All I ever wanted was to prove myself to you—to be worthy of the family I was born into."

She raised an eyebrow. "And yet you told us nothing."

I sighed. "I was naïve before. I didn't understand how much it would change everything to discover I possess a power others would covet."

"That a crown would covet, you mean," my aunt said in a flat tone. "And now the future crown of Kallorway has requested that we relinquish you to a marriage alliance." She paused. "Or rather, he has asked for your parents' blessing on such a union."

I watched her carefully. Was this another reason my parents had been sent away? Did my aunt resent that Darius had applied to them and not to her for permission for our betrothal? Did she fear their silence on the topic meant they were putting their love for their child above the good of Ardann as they made their decision?

If so, it was a surprise to me. They had said nothing all these long weeks to suggest they meant to consider my wishes as paramount. I had been open about my feelings for Darius, but it hadn't seemed to lessen their concerns. And Darius had made it clear he wouldn't ask me to marry him if he had to do so in the face of my family's disapproval. From his perspective it was an act of love to refuse to steal me from my first home and family.

"I didn't tell Darius either at first," I said to my aunt, my mind dwelling on the Kallorwegian prince and the history between us. "Not for a long time. Not until I had to."

Aunt Lucienne's astute eyes flashed to mine.

"I love Darius," I continued. "I won't deny it. And I believe in what he dreams of achieving in Kallorway. I believe that Ardann and Kallorway can be true friends and allies one day." I straightened. "But I have no more desire to be his pawn than yours."

One of her eyebrows arched, and for a moment we stared at one another. Then a small smile crept across her eyes.

"Yes, you have parts of both your parents in you, there's no denying that. So you do not wish to be pawn to a crown." Her stance relaxed slightly. "I can hardly blame you for that."

She looked me over. "Winning a crown for yourself is certainly one way to avoid being a pawn, but are you sure it's a future you're prepared for?"

I grimaced. "Is it ever possible to be prepared for such a thing?"

"Perhaps not," she said, her voice soft. "And yet those of us cursed with such a fate must do the best we can. I admit it would be advantageous to Ardann to have Darius on the throne and you beside him. Just as long as..."

"Just as long as I retain loyalty to Ardann and my family," I finished for her. "My loyalty to my roots is exactly what has kept me apart from Darius for so long. But I can see now I was mistaken in him. He would never try to use me against Ardann or my family." A slight note of resentment crept into my voice. "He won't even make a formal proposal without my parents' approval."

Amusement filled her eyes. "I find it hard to remember the impatience of youth, and yet I'm sure I must have been young once. You must give your parents time, Verene. They fear losing you, and they fear the revelations made by Kallorway's young king-elect."

"But you approve?" I asked, unable to keep the eagerness from my voice. "You'll give your consent?"

The shadow returned to her eyes. "It is not my consent that has been sought. And as I said before, in one area your parents do not defer to my authority."

I winced.

"But," she continued, "I trust that your Darius's honesty will weigh with them as it has with me. It is rare to receive unvarnished truth from one crown to another—and even rarer between Kallorway and Ardann. His actions do much to confirm your claims."

"Then you believe in the danger we all face from Conall?" I stepped forward in my earnestness, and both guards stirred. But I ignored them. My concerns about Conall had been eating at me all summer.

In the ballroom, only a short stroll from where we stood, the elite of Ardann—mages, sealed commonborns, and merchant families alike—danced and laughed because they knew nothing of the threat hanging over us all. And the royalty of two kingdoms and an empire had done everything possible to keep them in ignorance—just long enough for us to find a way to counter the threat.

Conall had used his evil ability to build an army. And if he discovered we knew his secrets, he would command that army to march against us ahead of schedule. And then all of us would either be engulfed in deadly conflict or forced to kill unknown numbers of innocent commonborns and mages who only fought against us because of his control.

My aunt sighed. "I wish I could disbelieve the existence of such a threat, but I have sent trusted mages of my own to question Tyron. And the emperor has finally admitted to what we have long known—that there have been strange goings on in the north of his empire."

"The emperor will ally with us?" I asked.

She nodded. "For once, he's the one in more immediate danger. And it is his people who have been imposed upon by this Tarxi warlord. He has already requested our aid." She paused. "In particular the Spoken Mage."

I bit my lip. Of course they wanted my mother—no matter how much she herself might not wish it. And she did not. This summer I had overheard her talking to my father about the return of her nightmares from the battles they had fought years before my birth. And I had seen the haunted look in her eyes for myself.

As the great Spoken Mage, able to draw unlimited energy from others in order to work compositions of unimaginable strength, she knew who everyone would look to if it became necessary to stop that army before it could overwhelm us.

I shot a glance at my aunt. Hers was a complicated relationship with my parents. If she had sent them on this trip as punishment, then it was the only action she could take against them. She needed them, my mother in particular.

"I will admit," my aunt said softly, "there are moments when I wish I could leave the emperor to deal with the problem himself. So far Ardann has been the least targeted by this Conall."

I looked at her in alarm, and she gave a brief chuckle followed by a sigh.

"Oh, you needn't look at me in such a way, Verene. I know

better than to engage in such short-sighted thinking. If these Tarxi remnants take over the Empire, then we are all lost. We must stand together."

Relief filled me. The summer break had slipped away with constant meetings and discreet emissaries sent between Ardann, Kallorway, and the Sekali Empire. But after generations of conflict between the two southern kingdoms, and almost as many years of a closed border with the northern empire, neither our monarchs nor their people were used to the kind of coordination required for such a joint undertaking.

"So you have a plan?" I asked, once again wishing I had been permitted to take part in some of the many meetings. "You mean to act together?"

A wry look crossed the queen's face. "Ah, the optimism of youth. We have agreed we must stand united. Coming up with a plan, however…"

She looked at me, weighing me with her eyes.

I held my breath. She had already said more than anyone had been willing to tell me all summer. None of the select few permitted into the secret of Conall and his threat would have expected to see me in the meetings—not when they thought of me as the powerless second child of a younger son, and one who was not even yet an Academy graduate. But my family knew of my secret abilities and the crucial role I had played in uncovering the threat. So they knew my exclusion was a punishment.

Only my younger brother, Stellan, had forgiven me for the secrets I had kept. And even his acceptance had been begrudgingly given. But since I had not only befriended the commonborn girl he loved but had promised to support them as a couple, he could hardly hold on to his hurt at my reticence.

But as a third child who had only completed one year at the Academy, he had even less position at court than me. With everyone else who knew the truth having closed ranks against me, I had been forced to spend the summer without any knowledge of the combined efforts being made against Conall. If my aunt was finally willing to share them with me, then I didn't want to say anything to jeopardize that unexpected openness.

But her next words took me by surprise.

"I cannot force your parents to give their blessing to you becoming the future queen of Kallorway, but I know they will not hamper our efforts to combat this immediate threat. Which means you will get to see your prince again. You will return to your Academy in the fall as normal. We cannot risk giving any unnecessary sign that we are alert to the true situation."

A knot of tension that had been sitting between my shoulders all summer lifted.

"I'm to return? Truly?"

"The year is about to begin again, and we will not have formulated an effective strategy by the time classes commence. Conall does not mean to act until closer to your graduation, and we must use that time."

"I want to help," I blurted out.

She eyed me again, and I tried to read what might be lurking behind her expression.

"You are only nineteen and not even a graduated mage. We need you to spend your year dutifully attending lessons at a remote Academy. So ordinarily I would dismiss the suggestion that you could be of assistance. But the king-elect must also return to the Academy—it is necessary for him to complete the year if he wishes to be crowned. So, with him there, you will be central to unfolding events—whatever I or your parents think about the matter."

She paused. "If you and Darius think of some way to bring us a bloodless victory, I hope you will not hesitate to share it with us all."

"Of course we would share it," I said, not entirely sure if she was gently mocking me with her final line or if she truly thought

I might keep something of such import to myself. Or was there something else entirely behind her inscrutable manner?

My aunt took a step back, the air about her changing subtly to one of cool command. "I will continue to assign your loyal guardian to you. Her superiors tell me she has indicated her willingness to return to Kallorway. But for now, I think it might be best if you withdrew from the ball. If anyone inquires, I shall inform them you are fatigued and need to rest before your upcoming journey back to the Academy."

I frowned, but a glance down at my dirty gown, torn in one place, made me nod in agreement.

"Very well, Aunt. As you wish." I turned to go but paused and looked back. "You know, if you'd asked, I would have been happy to demonstrate my ability for you."

"I find more is revealed in the heat of battle than in a dry demonstration," she replied, her face once more inscrutable.

I considered answering but ended up merely dropping a shallow curtsy and departing, Layna at my heels. If I succeeded in convincing my parents to give their approval to Darius, I might one day need to remember that the world looked different when you wore a crown.

I didn't see my parents until lunch the next day, and by then they must have spoken to the queen because they seemed resigned to my imminent departure. Stellan, however, looked disappointed. My return to Kallorway meant Elsie's return as well.

Lucien arrived late for the meal, sliding into his place without looking in my direction. I gave him a hard stare.

"I find myself suddenly suspicious about your inability to attend the ball last night, Lucien," I said. "It's not that I minded representing the family, but I'd hate to think you knew about the planned attack."

Both my parents swiveled to stare at me. Whoops. I guess their conversation with my aunt hadn't been entirely comprehensive.

"Attack?" my mother asked sharply.

"Someone attacked you?" My father leaned forward. "Why weren't we informed of this?"

"Probably because it was Aunt Lucienne who attacked her," Stellan said caustically.

Lucien gave me a reproving look, and I sighed.

"Well, not personally. But ordering her personal guard to attack me is basically the same thing."

My parents exchanged an outraged glance before my mother turned narrowed eyes on Lucien.

"And you knew of this plan?"

"Verene is the one who chose to keep secrets from us all," Lucien said. "She has to expect to be challenged."

I snorted. "Challenged? Is that what you're calling it?"

"Don't be such a baby," he snapped. "You look fine to me."

"Lucien." My father's tone was the sort that brooked no opposition. "It is time for this to stop. We have always supported you in spending time with your aunt and encouraged you to focus on your duties as crown prince. But I will not permit you to forget your family."

"You mean like Verene did?" Lucien met his gaze with fiery eyes.

I held my breath, my eyes flicking between them. What would my father say to that? Did his defense of me mean he and my mother had moved past my deception?

"Verene did not attack one of her own family members," Mother said. "Or condone such a thing."

She sighed. "For all you've graduated now, you're still young, Lucien. You'll learn the value of family—it is not something to be overlooked or underestimated." Her eyes swung to me. "And your sister is younger still. We all—young and old—make mistakes. As family, we must be first to forgive."

The tension across my shoulders eased. But something drove me to challenge her statement, even while I relished her words.

"But did I make a mistake?" I asked. "Or has Lucien proven my exact point? I never set out to deceive *my family*. It's the queen and crown prince of Ardann who made me wary—and it seems to me with good reason."

Lucien stiffened. "Don't try to blame this on me, Verene."

I sighed. "I'm not trying to blame it on anybody. I'm saying it's a complicated situation without clear right or wrong. I wanted the freedom to explore and develop my new abilities before I became a tool to be fought over and bargained between crowns. That's why I kept it a secret from *everybody*. You can't blame me for having a different path from yours, Lucien. But I would *never* betray Ardann or my family."

"Not even if your precious prince ordered you to?" Lucien muttered into his plate.

"Darius would never order such a thing," I said, heatedly. "Do I have to remind you he's the reason any of you even know of my abilities? I think if nothing else, Darius has proven himself there."

Lucien opened his mouth, but I snapped at him before he could speak.

"And don't say that a crown changes people—that would just be proving my original point."

Lucien closed his mouth and looked at me. And for the first time since my parents had dragged me back, his gaze was more considering than angry. I drew a long, trembling breath, preparing to turn to my parents and address them next. But before I had a chance to do so, the door to our private dining room burst open, and Elsie tumbled into the room.

CHAPTER 3

*H*er eyes swept over us all, not even pausing on Stellan before they fastened on me. My younger brother leaped to his feet, but I gave him a stern look, and he reluctantly sank back down.

"Princess Verene," she gasped, panting slightly as if she'd been running through the palace to reach me. "I need you."

My father's eyebrows rose, and Lucien gave her an astonished look, but I ignored them both. Pushing my chair back, I hurried around the table to join her at the door. Glancing back over my shoulder at my family, I instructed them to continue the rest of the meal without me.

"More secrets, I suppose," I heard Lucien mutter as I closed the door, but his voice held less rancor than it had previously.

As soon as we were out in the corridor, I pulled on Elsie's arm, ushering her into an alcove to one side of the thoroughfare.

"What is it?" I asked. "What's happening?"

After a year of living in close quarters with the servant girl, I knew she wouldn't have sought me out in such a manner unless it was something urgent.

She had regained her breath, meeting my eyes now with

earnest concern. "Someone's been talking. I don't know who. But one of the servants knows about—" she dropped her voice before finishing the sentence, "Conall and his army."

Fear gripped me. "You mean a servant with a position like yours? Someone's trusted personal servant?"

She bit her lip. "If a senior mage trusted them enough to tell them, then their trust was misplaced. Oscar is a notorious gossip. He must have only just found out, or it would be all over the palace by now."

I slammed my palm into the marble wall behind us, groaning in frustration. But a moment later, I straightened, my mind racing.

"It sounds like we don't have any time to lose. Can you take me to him?"

She nodded, already starting to move down the hall. I hurried to keep pace as we raced along several corridors and down two flights of stairs. We crossed into the servants' back halls, Elsie only coming to a stop when we reached a wooden door that failed to hold back the loud babble of many voices.

She looked at me uncertainly. "This is the dining hall for the upper servants. We don't usually get visits from any of the royals." She grimaced. "In fact, I suspect we've never had such a visit."

I bit my lip. If the news was about to spread, we didn't have time to waste. But, on the other hand, if he'd already started to talk about what he knew, would my appearance lend credence to the story?

"Who has he already told?" I asked. "How many of the servants in there will have heard the story?"

A look of discomfort spread over her face. "I don't think he's told anyone else. At least, I'm hoping he won't until after he gets a drink or two in him later tonight."

I stared at her in horror. "He talks freely when he's in his cups?" That was even worse than I had been imagining. We would have no choice but to lock the man away.

"Oh no," she said quickly. "He's just a storyteller. He likes to have an audience once he's had a drink of an evening. But he's not out of control or anything. He wouldn't be a senior servant if he was."

"Oh good." My shoulders slumped in relief, before I gave her a curious look. "So how did you come to find out about the situation if he hasn't spread the story yet?"

Her look of discomfort returned. "Last year I didn't realize…it all happened so quickly…"

I continued to stare at her in perplexity, her confused words doing nothing to explain matters. With a wry look, she spoke more clearly.

"It's just that there aren't many members of the royal family. It turns out that despite my age and inexperience, being your personal servant has raised my status immeasurably. Lots of servants who wouldn't have given me the time of day before are friendly now."

I narrowed my eyes, reading between her words. "Just friendly? Or do you mean they try to ingratiate themselves with you?"

She grimaced. "Both. Oscar clearly assumed I already knew, and I got the impression he was wanting to impress me by showing he had inside information as well."

I raised an eyebrow. "Let me guess, is Oscar by any chance young and single?"

Elsie flushed. "Yes, he is."

That explained a lot. Elsie said the other servants now flocked to her despite her youth, but I suspected her age might actually be exacerbating the situation—given it was paired with remarkable beauty. I frowned.

"This Oscar has never harassed you, has he? Or any of the other servants? You'd tell me if they did?"

"Oh no," she said quickly. "They wouldn't dare given I'm your personal servant. They would be too scared of my reporting their behavior to you."

My frown remained. "What about before you were my servant?"

She shook her head. "Her Majesty doesn't have patience with such goings on. There's a reason there are rigid hierarchies among the servants. Even the most junior servants have someone they can go to if they have any complaints. I don't know how it used to be, but in the first year of Her Majesty's reign, a mage was forced to conduct a sealing ceremony and seal his power because he attacked a kitchen maid."

Her eyes were enormous as she told the story. "Queen Lucienne insisted Duke Soren use a truth composition on the mage to prove his guilt. I wasn't here then, of course, but I've heard the tale told often enough. The servants still remember it, and its message is clear. The royal servants are under Her Majesty's protection—no matter who you are."

I raised an eyebrow. Somehow I had never heard this story about my aunt. "I'm guessing the servants are fiercely loyal to Her Majesty," I said, keeping my voice neutral. I was pleased my aunt had acted in such a way, but I also knew she never did anything for only one reason.

Elsie nodded.

"We need to talk to my aunt about this rumor getting out," I said. "But I also can't risk leaving this Oscar on the loose where he might decide to try to impress someone else with his knowledge." I drummed my fingers against my leg as I considered my options. "We need to isolate him until I can gather more information."

"Do you want me to go in and bring him out?" Elsie suggested.

I narrowed my eyes. "No, I have another idea. You said he wanted to impress you, and that he's a storyteller who likes to have an audience. He wants to be important, so I think I'll give him a chance to be just that. You wait out here."

I pushed open the door and swept into the large room beyond. The men and women lining the long wooden tables inside fell silent, the hush spreading out in waves starting with those closest to the door. I had expected my arrival to be greeted with curious whispers, but instead I received total silence.

I kept my back rigid, and my expression haughty.

"I am come in search of Oscar on important crown business."

Now the whispers did break out as people twisted in their seats, all looking toward a table in the middle of the room. A surprised looking young man, attractive enough if you liked the smooth, slick type, rose slowly to his feet.

"I'm Oscar, Your Highness." He bowed deeply.

I looked him over from top to toe. "Excellent. If you would please come with me."

A tremor of nerves crossed his face before he squared his shoulders and pasted on a confident smile. He kept his gaze on me but didn't actually meet my eyes as he crossed the room to meet me at the door.

I smiled at the astonished crowd. "I apologize for disturbing your meal. I trust I will only need to borrow Oscar for a short time. As always, the crown appreciates your loyalty and discretion."

I swept out of the room, Oscar trailing behind me. He started slightly when he saw Elsie waiting for us, a nervous crease appearing on his brow. But he didn't speak.

When the door had closed firmly behind us, I addressed him.

"What is your position here in the palace, Oscar?"

He blinked, seeming startled by the simple nature of the question.

"I'm a junior steward, Your Highness. I'm in charge of the team who look after the rooms used by visiting officers of the Armed Forces."

I held back a groan. It would have been much simpler if he'd been the personal servant of a particular mage. Naturally a number of the senior members of the Armed Forces were involved in planning our defense, and his knowledge could have come from any of them.

"And you're sealed, I see." I indicated his wrists with my eyes, and he nodded.

"Yes, Your Highness." A note of pride crept into his voice. "For five years now."

"You're needed on a matter of great importance," I told him, making my tone serious and more pompous than usual. "But I'm afraid we'll need to enlist your patience. If you could please wait with Elsie in here."

She had been leading us as we talked down yet another corridor and now opened a door with a flourish. A small, empty meeting room was revealed, furnished simply and with a slim window looking over the palace grounds. I gave her an approving look. Perfect.

"I will be back to fetch you both as soon as can be arranged," I said.

Oscar bowed deeply. "Of course, Your Highness. I am always happy to serve in whatever way the crown desires."

I exchanged a speaking glance with Elsie, who gave me a decided nod, a stern look in her eyes. I could trust her to say nothing of import and to keep him here until I returned.

I once again hurried through the corridors of the palace, this time heading for the wing occupied by my aunt. Unless she was entertaining dignitaries, she usually ate a simple lunch in her study, so I directed my feet there first.

When I turned the corner and saw the two guards stationed outside her office door, I breathed a sigh of relief. I hadn't relished the idea of having to search the palace for her.

I gave the more senior of the guards an inquiring look when I arrived at the door. They would know if she was currently available to visitors—as long as they were of sufficient rank, of course.

"She's not to be disturbed, Your Highness," he said, a regretful note in his voice.

My lips tightened into a thin line. That complicated matters, but the situation couldn't wait.

"Is she in a meeting?" I asked.

"No, Your Highness," he said. "But she left strict instructions."

A sudden memory flooded me of pain ripping through my body after Castor dragged me from the ball. I narrowed my eyes.

"I'm afraid this can't wait." Catching them both by surprise, I gripped the door handle and twisted.

I had the door open and was halfway into the room before someone grabbed my arms from behind, jerking me to a stop. I ignored the guard's hold on me, my eyes focusing on my aunt. She sat at her vast desk, a groove between her eyes and a pen in her hand.

She met my gaze, a hint of surprise crossing her face before she waved her free hand to signal to the guards. They let me go, and I continued forward into the room without looking back.

"I'm sorry, Your Majesty," the more senior of them said, and I could hear the faintest anxiety in his voice.

"A visit from my favorite niece is always welcome," she replied. "My family do not fall into the same category as the Mage Council."

I heard the rustle of their uniforms as the guards bowed again before retreating from the room. Part of me screamed the lie at her words, still remembering the night before, but another part remembered my mother's words from lunch. Perhaps Aunt Lucienne did recognize the value of family—even if she wasn't always the best at showing it.

"I'm sorry to barge in on you in such a way, Aunt. But it couldn't wait." I nodded at her desk. "I hope I didn't interrupt you mid-composition."

If she was halfway through composing, then an interruption could be more than unwelcome, it could be dangerous.

She laid her pen down with a quick shake of her head.

"Nothing of such import. I merely wished some mental space." She directed a conspiratorial smile at me. "To tell truth, the Head of the Creators has been hounding me all week, and I merely sought a few moments of peace. I trust you are not here to upbraid me for our previous interaction."

I almost laughed at the idea that I might have dared push into her office in such a way if that had been my purpose.

"No, indeed. Although I wish for all our sakes it was something so simple."

She raised an eyebrow. "You see me rapt with interest."

"The junior steward in charge of the visiting officers from the Armed Forces has somehow found out about Conall. And he's been boasting about it to my personal servant. I thought everyone who knew about this knew it needed to be kept utterly quiet?"

She drew in a long breath through her nostrils before saying in an icy voice, "They do."

"Well, someone is being careless. And we can't afford for someone to be careless."

"How did he hear it?" she asked.

I shrugged. "I don't know. I got him out of the servants' hall and have isolated him with Elsie to keep watch, but I haven't told him why. I wasn't sure what approach you'd want to take, and I didn't want to let him know that the information is correct—or how important it is."

My aunt nodded in approval. "You did the right thing. We will have to be careful in how we deal with him." Her eyes narrowed. "Although I will be less careful with whoever told him."

"It's possible he just overheard it."

"That is only marginally more excusable. Everyone involved in the meetings should know better than to let themselves be overheard." She stood up, her manner brisk. "We need to know how he heard and who he's told. And then we need to make sure he doesn't tell anyone else. I will deal with the careless mage who divulged the information."

"Do you want to use a composition on the servant?" I asked.

She looked at me for a moment. "You should do it. It makes sense for you to be the one to talk to him, since you already have. You can use your ability to connect with your mother, and then you can speak a composition without him ever knowing anything about it."

My mouth fell open. "You want me to steal my mother's ability?"

"Why not?"

I shook my head, struggling for words. "Because she's my mother. Because her ability is incredibly powerful, and I've never tried to use it before. Because there's no urgent need—we could just ask her to help us directly. She doesn't have to be in the room."

A slight smile broke across my aunt's face, and I realized her words had been yet another test. I relaxed.

"You can ask for her help if you like, Verene, but I think you should consider asking her if you can borrow her ability and do it yourself. You need to practice, and it's a good opportunity."

My mouth nearly dropped open again. Use my mother's ability? The thought sent an uncomfortable, shivery feeling down my spine. But lingering behind it was a curiosity I couldn't deny. What did my mother's unique ability feel like? And what would it be like to wield it?

CHAPTER 4

$\mathcal{M}$y aunt sent me away with specific instructions on how to deal with Oscar. She intended to waste no time in confronting the officers herself.

On the way back to Elsie, I stopped at my family's private dining room. They were just finishing the meal, Lucien having already disappeared. Stellan fixed an anxious look on me, glancing behind me in search of Elsie, but I ignored him.

My eyes focused on my mother, and I licked my lips, trying to think how to start.

"Could I speak to you for a moment, Mother?"

She exchanged the briefest of glances with my father before getting up in a single fluid motion.

"Of course, Verene."

She joined me out in the corridor, waiting patiently while I tried to work up the courage to pass on my aunt's suggestion. Finally I gave up on finding a diplomatic way to phrase it and just blurted the words out.

"I need to interrogate someone, and Aunt Lucienne thinks I should ask if I can borrow your power to do it."

My mother's eyebrows flew up. "You mean you want me to come and assist you?"

I shook my head, not quite able to meet her eyes. "I mean using my ability. Aunt Lucienne thinks it would be good practice."

"How very interesting," Mother murmured. "I didn't realize she was so invested in your education."

"I don't have to if you don't like the idea," I said hurriedly. "You could come and do it yourself. You'd just have to stay out of sight."

"Actually," Mother said, "I think you should do it."

When I gave her a shocked look, she chuckled. "I'm as human as anyone else Verene, and I've been full of curiosity ever since Darius told us the truth. He said the people you connect with can't feel it, but it's hard not to wonder if maybe…"

"You might, actually," I said. "Tyron could. We think it's because he's such an experienced energy mage."

Mother's brows lowered slightly. "But Bryony couldn't feel it?"

I shook my head. "Tyron's training is far beyond ours, though. And, unlike us, he was trained by actual energy mages."

"I'm no energy mage, remember," my mother said.

"No, but you can feel energy." I shrugged. "That might be enough."

"It sounds like we need an experiment." Mother gave me a smile that looked almost excited.

"Are you sure about this?" I asked, unable to believe her attitude after the disapproval I'd been receiving from her all summer.

She sighed. "Verene, you're my daughter. I want you to train and explore and master your abilities. I'm happy to help you. I just wish you'd given me the opportunity to help you from the beginning."

I bit my lip. "I know, Mother. And I wish I could have told you and Father. But I didn't know how to tell you and not Lucien and my aunt. I didn't want to pass on the burden of my secret to you."

"Oh Verene." She wrapped her arms around me. "I'm your mother. I always want to help carry your burdens."

"I know," I said, my voice muffled against her robe. "But that doesn't mean you can. I'm an adult now. I can't shelter behind you and Father forever."

She sighed again, pulling back from me. "And I know that. In my head, at least. But it takes some adjustment for your father and me. To us, you're still our little girl."

It felt good to talk to my mother like I always used to do, and to feel her strong arms around me. It reminded me of the love I had always received from my parents, and it filled me with hope.

"Does this mean you're going to give Darius your blessing?" I asked, unable to keep the question from spilling out.

She stiffened. "You may be an adult—just—but that doesn't mean we're willing to lose you to Kallorway. You've never envied your brother his future crown. You know what a burden it can be. And that's the Ardannian crown. Your father and I want a better future for you than being bound to the Kallorwegian one."

"You're right I have no interest in a crown," I said. "But I believe in Darius completely and in the vision he has for Kallorway. We can forge a better kingdom together. It's important work. Can't you see that?"

A stern look came into her eyes. "Your father and I wish you'd told us the truth about yourself, Verene, but we understand why you felt torn. And we respect that it was your secret to tell. But that wasn't the only secret being kept at that Academy during the last three years. Both you and that prince hid from us the fact that someone was attempting to assassinate you—*for two years*. You were just a child when you started, Verene, and you were in danger. You hid it from us—and he helped you do so. You could have been killed. How can you expect your father and me to trust your safety and your future to him after that? We're worried about the influence he exerts over you."

Her voice softened. "I remember what it was like to be young and in love, Verene. But I know it doesn't always lead to the best of decisions. It's my duty to protect you."

"But keeping the attacks a secret was my decision. It had nothing to do with Darius!" I cried. "I didn't tell you about that because I knew you would react like this. I was afraid you would pull me out of the Academy."

"Exactly." She gave me a knowing look. "And why didn't you want that?"

"Ugh!" I threw my hands into the air. "It wasn't because of Darius—it was because of you!"

She frowned. "What's that supposed to mean?"

"I wanted to prove myself to Aunt Lucienne and to everyone. I wanted to prove I was worthy to be your daughter. And I knew that if you found out I was in danger, you would pull me out of the Academy before I achieved what I was sent there to do."

My mother stepped back slightly, shock in her eyes. "You've never had to prove yourself to us, Verene. You've always belonged in our family."

I deflated. "I don't have to prove myself to you or Father. But the rest of the court doesn't feel that way. And don't try to deny it," I added quickly.

She shrank a little, weariness seeming to suddenly weigh her down. "We always tried to protect you from that."

"I know you did, Mother," I said, my voice soft. "And I've always loved you both for it. But there are some things even the Spoken Mage can't protect me from."

For a moment I thought I had reached her, but then she straightened. "You're right—we can't protect you from everything. But this is something we can protect you from. One day you'll understand, and you'll thank us."

All my frustration from the summer wanted to burst out of

me, but I didn't have time to rage at my mother. Elsie and Oscar were waiting for me, and I didn't have any more time for a family argument.

"Very well," I said coldly. "But I have an interrogation waiting. If you still intend to assist, then we need to get moving."

My mother arched a single eyebrow but fell into step beside me without comment. After we had walked for a short distance, she asked, in a meek voice, if she was permitted to know who I would be interrogating.

"I rather thought law enforcement and the Royal Guard would have such matters well in hand," she said.

My lips twisted. "Except that no laws have been broken, exactly. And the matter is too sensitive to bring in unnecessary people."

"Conall?" she asked, her voice barely a murmur. "Is that why Elsie came tearing into our dining room?"

I nodded. "One of the other servants found out about what's been happening and didn't have the wits to keep his mouth shut."

My mother sucked in a worried breath.

"As far as we know it hasn't spread yet," I said quickly. "But that's what I need to confirm."

"You've been to Lucienne?" she asked, but it wasn't really a question.

I nodded. "She's going to deal with the mages he works for." I grimaced. "I wouldn't want to be them right now."

"So you know who it was who was indiscreet?"

I shook my head. "Not exactly. But the servant in question is junior steward to the Armed Forces' officers."

Mother winced, obviously thinking much the same as I had when I found out. We fell silent, me concentrating on finding my way back to the room where I had left the two servants. I almost sighed with relief when I recognized the door, coming to a stop outside it.

"Aunt Lucienne doesn't want him to see anyone but me. We don't want to alert him to how serious a matter this is."

My mother turned to me. "So how does this work then? Do I need to do anything?" She immediately corrected herself. "No, of course not. So I guess I just stand here?"

I opened the door one down from the one we wanted, pulling back when I found a cleaning cupboard. I tried the next door along and revealed another meeting room, almost identical to the one occupied by Elsie and Oscar.

"You come in here," I told my mother. "You'll easily be close enough. And I'll come and get you when I've finished."

She followed me into the room, seating herself in a chair near the single window. When she fixed her eyes on me, the curiosity showing in her expression, I forced myself to swallow. I had done this enough times for it to come easily now, but I still hesitated. This time felt different.

"Connect," I finally managed to croak out.

My ability didn't share my hesitancy, connecting with her energy as easily as it had always done with others. Knowledge and understanding flooded my mind, and for a moment, I lost myself in it.

I had connected with powerful mages before but never like this. My mother had adjusted to her ability, learning to tune out her awareness of the energy of everyone around her, just as I had done. But that was where the similarities in our senses ended. Now that I was connected to her, the presence of a palace full of people sprang to my mind in a stronger, more acute way than I had ever experienced before. It took every bit of my self-control not to reach for them, greedily draining their energy. How easy it was for my mother to do such a thing.

I had experienced taking the energy of others, but even connected as I was now, it was hard to fathom what it would be like to take energy from so many at once. It was one thing to know my mother was more powerful than any other, but another thing again to experience it for myself.

Only my brothers and I could control our abilities with spoken words as our mother could, but I couldn't pull power from the air as she could and shape it any way I willed. With my own ability, I was limited in ways she was not. Wearing her ability as if it were my own, I had to bite down on my tongue to keep from speaking and unleashing the vast power that now stirred so readily to my command.

I broke the connection, gasping, and staring at my mother with wide eyes.

"How do you contain it?" I asked. "It's so…much. I was terrified to say a single word."

She smiled a little ruefully. "Practice, of course. My ability didn't come to me all at once any more than yours did."

I took a shaky breath. "Did you feel anything?"

She nodded, a thoughtful look in her eye. "I felt a connection between us. But I can't be sure I would have felt it if I hadn't been prepared and paying attention. I certainly couldn't have guessed, just from the sensation, that you had accessed my power." She shook her head. "Yours is a remarkable ability, Verene."

"Mine?" I gaped at her. "What about yours? I've never felt anything like it. Mother, you have so much power."

Her lips twisted into a somewhat mocking smile. "And yet I seem to encounter so very many problems that can't be solved with brute power alone. It's funny how that works."

I rubbed the side of my head. "Yes, I used to think if only I had an ability, everything else would be so simple…It seems naive now."

"I wish you could have stayed so youthful and innocent," my mother whispered with a wistful look.

I bit my lip. Could I wish such a thing? Did I? If I could go back to before any of this and wish it all out of existence, would I?

I only had to think of Darius and the looming threat to my friends, family, and kingdoms to know I could never wish my ability away. If I could help defend them, even in some small way, then it would all be worth it.

"I don't feel the connection between us now," Mother said. "Don't you need to maintain it during the interrogation?"

I winced. "I'm afraid of what might happen if I speak while I'm connected to you."

"You can do this, Verene." She met my eyes, her own warm and encouraging. "You're a spoken mage yourself, remember. I'm certain you can control my power. You just need to believe in yourself."

I barely refrained from rolling my eyes at her motherly encouragement. But at the same time, I drew strength from her short speech. She was right. I knew what it was to speak empty words and what it was to speak words that could slice through anything. My mother's ability wasn't as foreign to me as it had felt at first contact.

I drew a deep breath and once again connected with her. For a moment I let it wash over me, and then I withdrew a little, holding myself apart from her.

"You stay here," I said, not so much as a wisp of power escaping. "I won't be long."

I slipped out of the room and into the next one. Oscar had relaxed considerably in my absence. He sat on the corner of one of the tables, one leg braced on the ground, looking down at Elsie where she sat in a chair.

But at sight of me, they both sprang up, bowing and curtsying in unison.

"Truth," I whispered almost silently to myself.

Connected with my mother's power, it was a simple matter to shape the one-word composition. If Oscar lied, it would show a flash of light in my eyes only, rather than the more traditional approach of a visible light in front of us both.

"Oscar," I said, making my tone serious. "I understand that you are a loyal subject of the crown, and that is why we need your special assistance."

He drew himself up to his full height, his chest puffing out.

"There is none more loyal than I, Your Highness. And I am ready and willing to perform any service of which the crown might be in need."

I nodded gravely. "As you know, Her Majesty deals constantly with matters of great delicacy—matters which must be kept quiet from the general population."

"Of course," he said, nodding just as gravely. "And you can rely on my discretion."

For the second time in only a few minutes I had to suppress an eye roll. But no light flashed in front of my eyes, and some of my tension relaxed. Oscar believed in his ability to keep a secret. And from what Elsie had told me, he had enough control that if I handled this right, he might prove true to his word. I would have to thank her later for the valuable insight into his character.

"Yes, I am sure I can trust you," I said. "But I have been tasked by Her Majesty with identifying anyone lacking in such discretion. And that is where I believe you can help me. Naturally, I know you would not spread false stories around, but some others lack such wisdom and circumspection. False rumors can be dangerous, but they also serve a purpose. They allow us to track down leaks before the people involved can do true damage."

His eyes widened as I spoke, and I could almost see him turning over my words in his head and applying them to the outrageous story he had so recently heard.

"Elsie is the most loyal of servants," I continued, "but, of course, she spends most of the year in Kallorway with me. We need someone here in Corrin who has their ear to the ground and a canny sense—someone who can keep alert for such tales and report them back to us along with their source."

He straightened, a look of importance transforming his face.

"Of course," I said hurriedly, "such an important and trusted role would need to be performed in secrecy."

"Naturally." His eyes shone as he said it. This was what he wanted more than anything—to be on the inside. I was offering him something more valuable than holding the other servants enthralled with a good story. And it wouldn't matter in the least if he let drop hints that he was involved in important work for the crown.

"Who should I report to?" he asked.

"Elsie—and through her, me. At least initially," I said. "But once we've departed, you can report directly to Leila."

His eyes widened slightly at the name of the sealed commonborn who had worked for my mother for more years than I'd been alive. I had always liked Leila—she was irrepressible, a force to be reckoned with. And Oscar was clearly in awe of her. As one of the Spoken Mage's most trusted officials, she wielded more authority around the palace than many mages. An association with Leila would increase his standing among the servants without any need to compromise his promised discretion.

"I have something to report now," he said eagerly. "I've just heard a story so outlandish it couldn't possibly be true. It must be one of those false tales you're talking about, to flush out those with loose lips."

"Oh?" I tilted my head inquiringly.

He quickly outlined the threat from Conall and the unwilling army massing in the north. It took all my royal training to keep an amused and slightly incredulous expression on my face. I had hoped that at the very least the story might have grown and changed in the telling, but it was accurate in all its particulars.

"Gracious," I said mildly when he finished. "I would certainly like to know who would spread such a tale."

The thread of energy still connected me with my mother in the neighboring room, and I waited tensely for a flash of light behind my eyes. If he had been listening at doors, this would surely be the moment for him to start the untruths.

But no flash came when he named Captain Matthis, one of the most senior and trusted mage officers.

"Captain Matthis?" I asked, unable to help myself. "Are you sure?"

"I'll admit," Oscar said in the face of my disbelief, "that I didn't immediately recognize the tale as a falsehood, given the source."

"And he told you this story directly?" I asked. "You didn't overhear it somehow?"

Oscar frowned at the suggestion. "Certainly not. Although," he admitted grudgingly, "I was surprised when he spoke to me at all, let alone to relate such a tale. I took it as a sign of great trust due to my excellent service to the officers."

He frowned for a moment before brightening. "But that must be it. He no doubt intended it as a test, knowing you were looking for a trustworthy individual and believing I was such a person."

"Captain Matthis could certainly be trusted with such a task," I said cautiously. "He has served the crown faithfully since before the war ended."

Oscar nodded solemnly. "He's a legend from the war years. And, of course, the expedition that discovered the energy mages. I am honored by his efforts."

I nodded. "Thank you for undertaking such an important task." I paused. "You said that the credible source made you at first believe the story. I hope such an outrageous tale is not spreading through the servants' halls as we speak."

"No indeed!" He looked desperate to reassure me of his reliability. "I've told no one!"

A flash of light in front of me made my stomach clench. Was I already too late?

His eyes slid to Elsie. "Except for Elsie, I mean," he added in a rush. "I knew she would know the truth of it."

The light, which had already faded, didn't reappear, and my muscles relaxed.

"Elsie can be trusted, certainly," I said, keeping my face calm and my voice steady. "And now you had better return to the servants' hall before anyone grows concerned that you're in trouble."

He bowed low to me and smiled at Elsie and was still murmuring his thanks as he hurried from the room. As soon as he was gone, I collapsed into a chair.

"Captain Matthis! It seems impossible!"

Elsie was still watching the now-closed door. "Do you think he was telling the truth?"

"I know he was," I said firmly, letting my connection to my mother end.

She raised her eyebrows but didn't question me. "You managed that very adroitly. He won't be spreading the story further—not now he thinks it isn't true."

"We're just fortunate he was so quick to come up with his own explanations for everything. I wouldn't want to be the source of a rumor that Matthis is disloyal. Not until we can get to the bottom of what's going on here. He's always been one of my grandfather's most trusted officers."

The door opened again, and I shot to my feet, but it was only my mother. She was frowning as she joined us.

"I heard him leaving. Did you get the answers you needed?"

I worried at my lip. "We got *an* answer. But it's a little hard to believe. He named Captain Matthis."

"Matthis?" Both my mother's eyebrows rose almost to her hairline. "Now that *is* hard to believe." She frowned. "But perhaps it explains why I just received an urgent summons from your aunt."

"She wants to see you?" I asked.

"No." My mother shook her head. "She wants to see you."

CHAPTER 5

My aunt awaited me in her study, Captain Matthis standing rigidly before her. I would have taken both of my companions in with me, but my mother shook her head, saying the queen had asked only for me. After getting an inside glimpse of the vast power that lurked inside my mother, it felt utterly strange to think that anyone would prefer my assistance over hers. But not even family could ignore such a summons from the queen of Ardann.

Matthis stood in silence, his gaze fixed on the far wall. He had been a fixture of the Armed Forces my entire life—as solid and unmovable as my grandfather, General Griffith, himself. It was as impossible to believe he had been careless and over-talkative as it was to believe him a traitor.

"What did you discover from the servant?" my aunt asked as soon as the door closed behind me.

I could read the trouble in her eyes. If Captain Matthis proved to be untrustworthy, we were in greater difficulty than we had realized.

"He named the source of his information as Captain Matthis," I said slowly.

"As in he overheard him talking to another officer about it?" the queen asked, but not as if she expected a positive answer.

Reluctantly I shook my head. "He told him directly. The servant thinks it was a test. And has been tasked with looking out for and reporting other such outlandish rumors. He won't be a problem from here. But all the details he had on the matter were correct, and he wasn't lying when he said where he heard it." I met my aunt's eyes, trying to convey silently that I had used my mother's power as she suggested. I couldn't say it aloud with Matthis in the room.

She nodded slowly, although she didn't look happy, and I forced myself to look directly at Matthis. His face had tightened, his muscles tense, but he still stood at attention, his eyes fixed on the wall.

"All of the officers currently at the palace submitted to questioning under truth compositions," my aunt said. "When asked, Matthis agreed he had told the servant, although he seemed unaware of having done so until directly questioned on it. And he cannot tell us why."

"Cannot? Or will not?" My brow furrowed.

"Cannot. I myself placed him under a working compelling him to talk. But he had nothing to say."

"I've seen something like this before." I frowned, trying to remember the exact details of my long-ago conversation with Prince Jareth. "On that occasion the person seemed unsure if they didn't know the answer or couldn't speak it."

Matthis gave a small start, his eyes flying to me. I addressed him directly.

"Is that how it feels for you?"

He nodded. "I have assured Her Majesty that I have never experienced such a thing before in my life. And I cannot account for having spread such sensitive information."

"If it was anyone else," Aunt Lucienne said, "or if I hadn't used my own composition…" She met my eyes. "That's why I called for you. I need to know what's going on here."

I could now understand why my aunt had wanted me and not my mother. For all her power, there were some things only I could do.

I nodded once, not waiting for any further invitation.

"Connect," I whispered under my breath, and dove into Matthis's energy.

His ability was ordered in a way I had rarely seen, everything controlled and regimented—and focused on knowledge and compositions relating to the Armed Forces. He was in every way a career soldier.

His discipline assisted me in my task. In some mages, the chaos was overwhelming, but amid such order, it was much easier to pick out a wrong note.

I feared finding signs of the sort of control Tyron wielded, terrified of how much damage might already have been done by such influence in the heart of our defense efforts. But I could feel no trace of my traitorous year mate, nor any sign of such an energy link to anyone else, either.

Instead, I found a dark spot. Buried deep, it might have been hard to notice in someone else, but in Matthis it drew my attention instantly, a sharp contrast to the rest of his ordered energy. I homed in on it, trying to understand what I was feeling.

On closer inspection, it was more an absence than anything else—a hole in his energy that felt black and cancerous. The rest of his energy swirled around it, trying to pull it back or tug it closed or cover it up. But it sat there, unchanging.

My eyes focused on his face, which hadn't changed in any way while I invaded his energy and ability.

"Can you feel that?" I asked him.

He frowned. "Feel what?"

"That…that hole in your energy. Can you feel that some of your energy is missing?"

He blinked. "My energy? Missing? I haven't noticed any decrease."

"You wouldn't. It's only the smallest piece."

A swift indrawn breath drew my attention back to my aunt. When I met her eyes, I nodded.

"I have no experience with any of Conall's compositions, so I can't guarantee it, but it certainly sounds like what he can do."

"Conall?" Matthis jumped in. "You think I'm being controlled by Conall?" He sounded horrified.

I shrugged. "It's the only thing that makes sense. We know he takes a small piece of someone's energy and uses it to control them, and it looks like a small piece of your energy has been forcibly removed. But there's good news in that. The control Conall exerts is much more limited than what Tyron's ability can do. It has to be extremely focused."

"Can you tell its purpose?" my aunt asked.

I grimaced. "I can try." Unlike other mages, I could often sense the vague purpose of a composition, but I had never encountered one like this before.

I concentrated on it again, trying to gain a feel for it, although everything in me wanted to pull away from its unnatural sensation. My overwhelming sense was one of contradiction—something hidden and something open.

I chewed on the inside of my cheek before meeting my aunt's eyes. "It's hard to tell with any specificity. I could take control of it, though. That would tell us everything. But do we want it removed?"

"Of course!" Matthis said, the words bursting out of him, his face instantly reflecting shame at his loss of control.

Aunt Lucienne regarded him for a moment with narrowed eyes before nodding.

"Yes, I think we must. While there is some small risk of alerting Conall to a change, we must trust that he holds so many people in thrall, he will not notice the loss of one. And at such a distance, for all he knows, Matthis might have died."

"Take control," I whispered, forcing my ability toward the hole in his energy, even as my inner self tried to pull away from such a connection.

The working unfolded inside my mind, its purpose and shape instantly clear. Only now, when I wielded it myself, could I detect the faintest trace of a connection between Matthis and the mage who had composed it, like a tube or pipe holding the hole open and maintaining the link.

The energy used to form the composition—which I now controlled—wanted to hold on to the energy it had stolen from Matthis with a tenacity I had rarely experienced. I let it cling to its shape for a moment as I considered the best way forward.

"Extract with care," I eventually whispered, doing my best to layer in more meaning than I usually needed to employ.

The working I had taken hold of was strong and focused—let it use that level of focus to recover Matthis's stolen energy without alerting Conall that it was being ripped away.

For a moment, I thought the working meant to defy me, and then with a feeling akin to an audible pop, a small sliver of energy rushed back into place within Matthis. I could feel the way the rest of his energy swirled around it, almost as if welcoming it back home. The angry feeling hiding deep inside him smoothed over until no sign remained there had ever been internal division.

"Disconnect," I whispered, withdrawing with relief.

"It's done?" my aunt asked.

I nodded. "You're free," I said to Matthis.

He blinked and then blinked again. "I told the junior steward all about Conall and his plans." He sounded utterly shocked. "I felt compelled not to keep it to myself, and he was there, so I told him." He frowned, as if searching further back in his memory.

"And I met someone strange on my last trip to the Sekali Empire."

He focused on the two of us, his eyes widening. "I think I encountered Conall himself."

"That's a relief," my aunt said, sinking down into the chair behind her desk.

When I looked at her, she gave me a strained smile. "I was having nightmarish visions of Conall being able to reach across such a vast distance and ensnare any one of us."

"Oh! No. I'm sorry, I could have relieved your mind on that. Tyron said he needs vicinity, just like Tyron himself does. And Conall actually implanted two commands into Matthis with the energy he was controlling. One was to keep silent on his encounter with Conall, and the other was essentially the opposite. He couldn't use any particular finesse, but he built in an undirected element of…indiscretion, I suppose. I think he must have known Matthis was privy to important information, and he wanted to make sure Ardann's secrets became known."

"I suppose he has a way of ensuring any rumors that start circulating make their way back to him," my aunt mused. "Although we've seen from Tyron that he's as interested in causing chaos here as he is in directly advantaging himself. He must have seen the situation as beneficial either way."

She nodded briskly as if a weight had lifted from her mind. "I will have everyone who has been in the Sekali Empire in the last few years gathered together." She steepled her hands, her face considering. "I will throw a party. Just an intimate gathering of a trusted few." She gave me a wry look. "That will ensure no one misses the occasion. With any luck, none of them will notice that all the invitees have been part of various delegations or trade ventures."

"You're worried Matthis isn't the only one." I could understand her concern. It was a valid one.

"You can check them all, Verene. Which means you'll have to

delay your return to Kallorway. But if I move quickly, we should still be able to get you back in time for the start of classes."

I looked at Matthis. "Do you remember anyone else from your delegation being there when you encountered Conall?"

He shook his head. "It was a chance meeting, or so it seemed. He was a hulking man, with white-blond hair which he wore in a number of thick braids."

"He wasn't at court, was he?" I asked, a new worry rearing its head.

"No, we had traveled up north at the invitation of one of the clan heads who wished to host us at his estate."

"Thank goodness for that." The situation we faced was bad enough without imagining the emperor already in thrall to Conall.

"We must turn this to our advantage," the queen said. "Now that you have been given free access to all your memories again, Matthis, you must dredge up every tiny detail you can recall about Conall himself and his methods. Who knows what valuable information may have been lurking inside you all this time?"

"Certainly, Your Majesty. I am eager to be of service in any possible way after being used in such a manner." Matthis sounded angry, and I couldn't blame him. But when he turned to me, there was only gratitude in his eyes. "And while I don't understand precisely how you assisted me, Princess Verene, I am deeply grateful. If I can ever be of service, please let me know."

My aunt nodded her approval and dismissed him before turning back to me.

"You needn't worry about him saying anything about your ability—or asking any awkward questions. This aberration aside, he is far too disciplined a soldier for such a thing."

"Yes, I could see that inside him. I'm not concerned." I bit my lip. "What I am concerned about is what happens if you gather everyone at this party, and I discover they are all similarly afflicted. It is reasonable enough to hope that Matthis's liberation will go unnoticed by Conall. But if every seed he has in Ardann is suddenly cut off at the same time…"

My aunt sighed. "It is a valid concern. I don't wish you to disconnect any of them. At least not initially. Let's begin by discovering how far the rot has spread. We can decide a course of action from there." She paused. "And you must accept my own gratitude—to both you and your servant. Your intervention has prevented what could have been a disastrous breach."

I dropped a shallow curtsy. "I just hope it goes some small way toward proving to you that I have loyalty enough for both my family and Darius." And seizing the moment, I added, "And no one could be more loyal or trustworthy than Elsie."

My aunt nodded absent-mindedly, her attention already turning to the papers on her desk and the tasks before her. I hurried from the room, hoping that Elsie's name would at least stick in the recesses of my aunt's mind somewhere. Every little thing I could do to prepare the ground for Stellan's announcement could only help.

I saw little of my parents or Lucien over the next few days, all three of them spending long hours closeted with the queen discussing the latest development and all the possible ramifications. I knew from their reports that the invitations had been sent and acceptances were pouring in.

I, meanwhile, prepared to return to the Academy the morning following the queen's soiree. I gave Elsie several rest days, knowing how desperate Stellan was to spend time with her, and she accepted them gratefully. I just wished, after all my promises, I could have done something more significant to help them.

But when I encountered the two of them in my family's otherwise abandoned sitting-room-turned-library one afternoon, we discussed the matter and came to a reluctant conclusion.

"You're going to have to wait," I told them, letting my regret tinge my voice. "Mother and Father are refusing to budge about Darius and me. They believe we're too young to be trusted with such a momentous decision about our own future." I gave them both a significant look. "And I'm nearly two years older than you, Stell, with only one year to go before I graduate. And Darius is even older with responsibility for an entire kingdom."

Stellan grimaced. "If they think that about you, I can only imagine how they would react to us."

"I have hope, though," I said. "I'm going to find a way to turn their minds around about me and Darius. And when I do—once I've softened them for you—that will be your moment."

"It's so ridiculous!" he burst out. "As if they weren't exactly the same at our age! Falling in love with someone they shouldn't and running off to try to save an entire kingdom."

"Don't think the irony has escaped me," I said. "But I'm told that no matter how grown up and responsible you felt in your own youthful days, you don't think that looking back at yourself. And it doesn't make it easier to watch your children caught in the same *youthful passions*."

Stellan burst out laughing. "Did Aunt Saffron and Uncle Julian tell you that during their recent visit?"

I grinned. "No, Aunt Saffron provided a much more sympathetic ear. That was Uncle Jasper. He accompanied them back from the Empire, remember? Aunt Clara is insisting they spend a couple of years in Corrin before returning since she's hoping to get both of our cousins accepted to the University."

Stellan rolled his eyes. "Of course Uncle Jasper would defend Mother. He always does."

"Naturally," I said with a straight face. "He's her brother, after all. Just like you would always defend me."

Stellan snorted, but Elsie slipped her arm around his shoulders. "He would defend you, Princess Verene. He's very loyal."

I smiled at her, wondering if she was thinking of herself or me. I knew how nervous she had been at the thought Stellan might have forgotten her in their months apart, her place in his heart taken by a mage girl from the Academy. But she needn't have worried.

"Now that I've committed to supporting your cause, I think it's time you dropped my title," I told her. "Just Verene is fine." I hesitated. "At least when we're in private. If others are around, it would be better to maintain protocol."

"Oh, but—"

Stellan squeezed her to his side, cutting off her words. "I intend to make you Verene's sister, Elsie. You can't keep using her title forever."

Elsie, ducked her head, unsuccessfully trying to hide her flush. "Very well, then…Verene."

"I just wish you didn't have to disappear back to Kallorway," Stellan sighed, burying his face in her hair.

I took that as my cue to escape and did so as unobtrusively as possible. If I only got to see Darius for a few short weeks each year, I'd want to make the most of our time as well, without one of my brothers hanging around.

Our carriage rolled out of the palace three days later. Stellan came to see us off—although I didn't remember his having done so my first two years at the Academy. The thought made me smile, although it was easy to smile after the good news of the night before. It had been an exhausting evening, but I had hidden myself away in a small antechamber and checked every guest at my aunt's soiree. None of them had carried the taint infecting Matthis. I had even checked him for good measure, seeing no sign that the working had reestablished itself.

Either Conall had been concerned we would pick up on a pattern if he infected numerous delegates and had picked

Matthis as the most influential, or else their meeting truly had been a chance one. Either way, it didn't matter, and we were spared the difficulty of deciding how to deal with a whole host of infected Ardannians.

My parents had also given me an affectionate send off, reminding me that they stood in opposition to Darius and my relationship only because they loved me. Knowing I was leaving them and returning to him for an entire year made it easier to accept their gestures of love. I couldn't help the hopeful feeling that a year was long enough to find a way to change their minds.

But by the time we passed through the western gate, my smile had disappeared. Did I really have a year? Who knew how long any of us had with Conall bearing down on us? But the thought didn't make me regret my parting with my parents. Now wasn't the time to be leaving anyone in anger. I just hoped that finding a way to save the future of both kingdoms wouldn't require throwing my own away.

CHAPTER 6

We pulled into the Academy courtyard the next morning, and I had never been so glad to see the austere stone building. After three years living within its walls, it gave me a pang to think I might never see it again after this year. At least if my parents had their way, and I was forced to return to my old life in Ardann.

Elsie looked less enthused about our arrival, but Layna smiled almost as affectionately at the old gray stone as I did. While we were inside the Academy, she didn't act as my personal guard in the same way she did outside its walls. But she had never seemed to mind being posted here all year anyway.

When I climbed out of the carriage, she swung down from her horse and approached me. Her smile dropped away, and she looked as serious as she had during any of the attacks we had weathered together. I gave her a concerned look but didn't have the chance to ask her anything before she began talking.

"We're back in Kallorway now, and this is your final year." She paused. "I'm not going to pretend I don't know you intend to remain here."

"Hope would probably be a more accurate word," I said, trying not to sound too dejected.

A ghost of her earlier smile returned. "Princess Verene, you honored me with your confidence at the beginning of the summer, but I know you didn't tell me everything that has been going on for the last three years. But I've always been observant. Since the age of sixteen, you've survived multiple assassination attempts, installed a new—and better—king on Kallorway's throne, mastered an unheard-of new ability without proper training, saved an entire kingdom's harvest, and stopped a killer storm. I have full confidence in you."

I flushed. It did sound impressive when she listed it like that, but it didn't reflect the reality of what had happened. I hadn't done those things alone.

I shifted uncomfortably. "Layna, I—"

She held up a hand to stop me. "I'm not asking you to confirm anything. I'm just trying to tell you I'm behind you. Fully. After what my own superiors did at that ball back home—using their position to take my attention away from my charge while she was in danger..." Layna shook her head. "Well, they made it easy for me. I want you to know my loyalties are no longer divided. As long as you want me protecting you, I'll be at your side."

My eyes widened. "Layna, I don't know what to say. Are you sure? Ardann is your home."

She shook her head. "I think you're forgetting you're not the only one who's spent a lot of time here in recent years. Homes can change."

"I...thank you." I didn't have a chance to say more before a small blur catapulted out of the Academy and threw herself at me. Before I had time to take a breath, she had spun toward Elsie and was embracing her as well.

"You're here! You made it!" Bryony cried. "I was beginning to think they were going to keep you locked in your room back in Corrin."

"I wrote to tell you I was allowed to return," I said, casting a final speaking glance at Layna as Bryony tugged me up the Academy steps. "I'm sure I did."

"Yes, but then you didn't arrive."

"There was a delay." I gave her a significant look, and her eyes widened.

"How very intriguing." She gave a satisfied smile. "I'm so glad you're back. Think how awful and boring the year would have been without you."

"I want to hear all about how your summer went back home in the Empire." I gave her another look, but she just shook her head despairingly.

"Far, far less interesting than it should have been, everything considered. I actually had high hopes, but my parents' town is just as small and boring as it ever was."

"That's a good thing, remember," I said in a low voice, but she shrugged off my words.

"I just wish I could have been in the thick of the excitement, like you were."

I sighed. "It wasn't at all exciting for most of the summer. Everyone seemed determined to shut me out."

"But then something happened to make them realize they're all fools?" Bryony asked.

I laughed. "Something like that. I'll tell you all about it this evening." We crossed the entranceway and started up the main stairs. "I suppose I'm in the same suite as usual?"

Bryony nodded. "And I'm only two floors above you this year." She puffed out her chest in a dramatic pose. "Now that we're important fourth years, we've all moved down in the world."

I laughed again. "I missed you, Bree!"

"Not as much as I missed you," Bryony assured me fervently. "I even missed this place—astonishingly. Why, I even missed those arrogant faces." She pointed down the corridor to where both princes waited outside the door to my suite.

Suddenly I couldn't hear her words anymore. All of my attention focused on one face alone. How could he look more vivid and breath-taking than I had remembered? His face had already been enough to haunt my dreams.

"I heard you were here." Darius's eyes were only for me, the warmth in them setting me on fire.

"I meant to arrive earlier," I said. "But I was…delayed."

"And yes, that's just as intriguing as it sounds," Bryony said, opening my door for me. "So if we all hurry her inside, we might manage to pry an explanation out of her before the evening meal instead of having to wait until after."

Jareth followed her inside my suite with a chuckle, but Darius lingered, holding the door open courteously. As I walked through, he spoke in a low voice, just for my ears.

"It was a long summer. I missed you."

I flushed, unable to help myself. "I missed you, too."

I gave him a long examination, trying to ignore the way my heart pounded faster at the sight of him, still as good-looking as ever, despite the shadows around his eyes. "You look tired. Have they all been running you ragged?"

He shrugged. "I can rest when Kallorway is safe from this maniac."

I shook my head. "If you don't look after yourself, who's going to protect the kingdom?"

He smiled down at me as he shut the door behind us. "Did I already say that I missed you, Verene?"

I smiled back. "You might have mentioned it."

Now that we were safely in the suite, I stepped toward him, my arms reaching for an embrace, but he stepped away, the shadows around his eyes deepening.

"I haven't heard anything from your parents. Have they changed their minds and sent their blessing?"

For one wild moment, I wanted to tell him they had, but I couldn't bring myself to speak the untruth. I shook my head, and the light went out of his eyes.

"I was hoping they might have reconsidered with so much time," he said softly.

"I still have hope they will." I bit my lip, watching him carefully. "And I'll admit I also had hope you might have changed your mind and be willing to put aside this plan of yours. Our happiness shouldn't be reliant on them."

He straightened, the unyielding prince I had first met visible again. "I gave them my word, and I won't go back on that. I won't steal you away like a thief, Verene. You deserve better than that."

I sighed. "I just wish you would trust yourself, Darius. I trust you completely—I know you won't betray me. You don't need my parents to reassure you of that."

His voice dropped even lower, a haunted look filling his eyes. "I wish I had your confidence in me. But I've made too many mistakes."

"That's quite enough sighing over one another," Bryony interrupted briskly from the other side of the room. "Jareth and I are waiting over here with less than patience, may I remind you."

For a moment I couldn't move, still held in Darius's intense gaze, unable to pull my mind back to the world around us. But then he turned to the others, his face closing off, and I shook myself.

Bryony and Jareth stood shoulder to shoulder, giving me such identical looks of curiosity and reproach that I had to laugh.

"Fine. But I'll make it as quick as I can."

I outlined everything that had happened from my aunt's attack through to her soiree the night before I left.

A quick indrawn breath from Darius at my first mention of the attack made me pause. It was hard to interact with him like this—pretending everything was normal between us. I wanted to point out to him that there was danger for me everywhere, not just in Kallorway. But Bryony and Jareth's presence stopped me, and I continued with the story.

The shadows were back around Darius's eyes by the time I finished.

"And yet I've heard no word of this from Queen Lucienne." He sighed. "I only wish our months of preparation had opened more effective avenues of communication."

I shrugged awkwardly. "I'm sure she assumed I would tell you."

Darius turned and strode up and down my sitting room. "I'll need to check my own people as well, of course. But stuck here at the Academy, I can hardly call a soiree to gather them all together."

My eyes wandered over to where Jareth was watching his brother with concern.

"Actually, about that," I said. "I've been thinking. Jareth, you went on a delegation to the Sekali Empire just before we all started at the Academy, didn't you? Did you go any further than the capital?"

All three of them fixed their eyes on me.

"Actually, we did." Jareth sounded a little sick. "We received a tour of several of the regions. But I thought you were confident Tyron no longer had any hold on me?"

"I am." I paused. "But it's not Tyron I'm concerned about now. The way Captain Matthis talked…it reminded me of you. You couldn't explain why you had two competing and contradictory opinions alongside each other in your mind, just as he couldn't explain his own actions. But there was something else as well. Something separate."

"What do you mean?" Jareth asked, his eyes intent on me.

"Even when you broke through the false thoughts, and Tyron was no longer renewing his control over you, you couldn't tell us who you were working for. You remembered which attacks you had been involved with, but you couldn't name Tyron himself. It was like you'd forgotten his identity entirely."

"You think Conall got hold of Jareth on that trip?" Darius asked.

I shrugged. "It's at least possible. He may have laid the groundwork for his son's efforts."

Jareth stepped forward, his face angry, although I knew the emotion wasn't directed at me. "Well, have a look and see! Don't waste any more time."

"Connect," I said, with strength, not having to keep my voice down for once.

For some reason I had expected Jareth's ability to feel like a less powerful version of Darius's, but it didn't. He had far less order and control despite his natural strength. In comparison to Matthis, in particular, his energy felt like a giant mess, and it took me a moment to find the hidden hole, snarling the energy around it.

"Yes, it's there!" I said. "Shall I cut off the working?"

"Yes!" Jareth said with a shudder before Darius could answer.

I glanced at Darius, but he nodded swiftly.

"Take control." I seized the composition still latched on to Jareth, working more quickly than I had with Matthis since this was now my second attempt at the same thing. Within moments, I disconnected again.

"All done," I said.

"Just like that." Jareth shook his head. "Your ability really is incredible, Verene."

"I'm just glad I could help," I said.

"And were you right?" he asked. "When you take control of a composition you understand its nature, don't you?"

I nodded. "Yes, Conall's control was what kept you from naming Tyron."

He growled, clenching his fists and looking as if he longed for some sort of physical outlet for his feelings.

"How carefully they laid their plans." Darius looked black. "And how close they came to succeeding. They would have, if it hadn't been for you and your ability, Verene."

"We all played a part," I said swiftly. "And it isn't over yet."

"No." Darius sounded deeply weary. "It's very far from over." He sighed. "I suppose there's no need to send an urgent warning to the emperor of the dangers just discovered by Queen Lucienne and myself. The emperor will be well aware of the risk Conall already poses to his people. We were the fools for thinking our distance protected us for now."

I looked around the familiar sitting room, the green sofas looking comfortable and inviting. But something was missing. I had been so pleased to see Darius again that I had forgotten something important.

"Where's Tyron? Have you had him transferred to a cell in the capital? I thought we still needed to maintain appearances?"

"He's still here." Jareth sounded grim. "More's the pity."

Darius shot him a look. "He's actually been less trouble than I expected. Almost cooperative, in fact. I didn't even have to use a composition to compel him to speak when we questioned him about his summer plans."

"But you used a truth composition, I hope." Bryony sounded concerned.

"Of course. And he said he never had any intention of returning home over the summer. The journey is too far, and he didn't want to risk any connection between him and the increasing rumors in the north. He intended to secretly stay in Kallorway—as he did last summer—and look for ways to cause trouble. So we haven't had to worry about his failure to appear rousing Conall's suspicions."

"I'm glad that worked out so smoothly," I said. "But what's your plan for the year? Are you going to have to keep him bound again all year?" I couldn't quite keep the worry out of my voice. Maintaining the binding—first on Jareth and then on Tyron—on top of all his other responsibilities had been a significant strain on Darius in third year.

"Actually Vincent has been working on that all summer," Jareth said. "He's worked out a simpler version that his own team can oversee. That's why Tyron isn't here now."

"Is that a good idea?" Bryony's skepticism was clear in her voice. "He's caused a lot of trouble."

"He has," Darius agreed, "and his ability is very powerful. But it's also limited compared to the abilities of a power mage, especially one as powerful as Jareth. And without his ability, Tyron has a lot less influence than a Kallorwegian prince. He doesn't need the same bindings as Jareth did."

"Of course, he'll still have to be with us constantly." Jareth sounded sour. "He needs to be watched at all times, and there's no other way to explain guards in his classes other than having them pose as guards for Darius and me."

I winced. Spending my days with Tyron, pretending for the rest of the Academy that we were still friends, wasn't how I wanted to spend my final year.

"Duke Francis and Zora have had my suite expanded over the summer break," Darius said. "The rooms next to mine were empty, and they've now been joined to make a three-bedroom suite. That way Jareth, Tyron, and I can be close together and well-guarded at all times."

I glanced around my own untouched suite, foolishly grateful they hadn't taken it to use in the expansion. It felt far more like home than I had ever imagined it could. My eyes flicked to the tapestry on the wall. And I wasn't ready to give up my connection with Darius—even if it was now a connection with Jareth and Tyron as well.

"So he's in there now?" Bryony also stared at the tapestry, distaste in her voice and on her face.

Jareth nodded. "But he's watched at all times. He will never be allowed to be a danger to either of you. I hope you know that."

"He's a danger to my temper," she muttered. "Because all I want to do is give him a swift kick."

Jareth laughed. "Well, if he causes any trouble, you have my permission to do just that."

Bryony grinned at him. "I'm going to hold you to that. If he attempts to escape or wiggle out of his bindings, I want a piece of him."

"After three years of watching you fight with that sword of yours, I would be far too terrified to get in your way," Jareth said solemnly.

"Are we going to be late for the evening meal?" I asked. "I'm sure I'll deny it strenuously in about three months' time, but I miss the bells, telling us where to be, when."

Bryony shot upright. "We can't miss the meal! They always have something nice the night before classes start." She grabbed Jareth's arm and started towing him toward the door, glaring at Darius and me as she passed by. "Come on, you two."

I followed reluctantly, feeling foolish when I realized I had been hoping for a moment alone with Darius after their departure. Was this what it was going to be like all year? Had we returned to pretense in public, punctuated by stolen moments together? I wanted more from Darius than that.

We almost collided with Elsie as we all filed out of the door. She had two other servants with her, all of them laden down with bags. Darius and Jareth both greeted her by name, and the other two servants looked impressed. Something told me it wasn't only in Corrin that Elsie had status beyond her age. I smiled as we hurried along the corridor to Darius's door. She deserved all of it. After all, it was only thanks to her we had discovered Conall had his hooks in both Matthis and Jareth.

Tyron strolled out of the entrance to Darius's suite, looking neither chastened and downcast nor particularly confident. He looked, in fact, almost entirely normal. For a moment, it felt unutterably strange, and then I felt a wave of relief. As strange as it was, it would make the coming year a lot easier if we could all pretend everything was normal.

The hum and bustle of the dining hall certainly helped with that impression, washing over me and bringing as much pleasure as the smell of the food. We had made our way from the far right of the room in first year to the long row of tables on the far left. There were no older trainees ahead of us this year. We were not just the highest-ranking group now, but also the oldest and most experienced.

Glancing up and down the tables, I saw we were the last to arrive. With a whisper, Bryony pointed out that Frida and Armand were openly sitting together.

She grinned at me. "Good for them. I was wondering if they would find their courage over the summer."

"Ashlyn doesn't look happy about being forced to sit with Wardell," I said with a chuckle. "I wonder if they'll manage to last the year, or if Ashlyn and Wardell's disapproval will drive them apart?"

"I don't think Wardell disapproves." Bryony indicated the smile on his face as he spoke to Ashlyn. "I think the bigger question is how long it takes for Ashlyn to lose her temper and whack him."

"I wouldn't lay you any odds on that," Jareth said, joining the conversation. "She's never had much patience for him."

"She has my sympathy." I chose a seat in a long open section of chairs and sat down. "He's been obnoxious to her since the first day."

The others all slid into seats around me, the two guards who accompanied us taking up positions behind Darius's chair. They clearly knew their part well. I didn't think anyone unfamiliar with the situation could have guessed they really guarded Tyron, who had taken the seat beside Darius.

I realized with an internal start that we would likely all be sitting together every day now. Tyron had always sat with us, and Darius and Jareth now needed to stay close to him.

Glancing down the table, I saw that a number of eyes were turned our way. Dellion called a lazy greeting, a smug smile on her face when she met my eyes. I smiled back. I didn't care how obnoxious she wanted to be about Darius and me—her choice to support us was enough to make me disposed in her favor.

Ashlyn looked interested, leaning over to whisper something to Frida who nodded back, wide-eyed. Even Royce was watching us, although he did so with the glare that now seemed permanently ingrained on his face. Apparently the summer had done nothing to sweeten his attitude toward King Cassius's removal from power.

Only Isabelle seemed not to notice us, distracted by her food and lost in her own world. The sight of her made me smile. I loved that even after all these years she maintained her independence.

"Royce looks as sour as ever," Jareth said quietly to Darius.

Darius grimaced, showing more concern than I had ever seen him display toward his second cousin.

"With what's coming, we're going to need everyone united. Even those who still support Father."

I bit my lip. In the rush of nostalgia at being back at the Academy, I had almost forgotten we had far more important things than classes to occupy us this year.

"Is that even possible?" I asked.

Darius's expression didn't change. "We will have to make it possible."

"Not asking much, are you?" Bryony muttered into her soup.

Jareth grinned at her. "We've missed you over the summer, Bree. Both this place and the castle at Kallmon were dark and gloomy without such a ray of sunshine."

She rolled her eyes at him, but I couldn't help grinning. Who would have predicted that Jareth of all people would be calling my friend Bree, and poking fun at her? And that she would be letting him? She had always been the one most staunchly set against him.

Their banter was proving Darius's point. Opinions could change. Allegiances could shift. And at some point, the truth about Conall's threat would have to come out. When that happened, everyone would have a significant inducement to put pettier squabbles behind them.

But glancing down the table at Royce, it was hard to maintain the optimistic feeling. Jareth was one thing. But Royce?

CHAPTER 7

The first morning of lessons started with the same sense of familiarity as the meal in the dining hall the evening before. Bryony greeted me at breakfast with a cheeky twinkle, asking how I had liked the longed-for bell when it woke me from sleep.

I answered the only way I could—with a dignified silence.

Isabelle had finally noticed my arrival, greeting me warmly, although her biggest smile was reserved for Darius. Apparently the king-elect was still in high favor among the farmlands. Isabelle arrived in the dining hall after we did, and actually selected the empty seat beside Bryony at the table, chattering away about various bits and pieces of news from home.

"What happens for you after this year?" I asked. "What sort of training will the wind workers give you?"

"They don't have a formal training center like the healers, or law enforcement. We prefer a less centralized method given the importance of being out in the elements for training. So I'll be assigned an older mentor. After everything that happened last year, our discipline has a large number of mages posted alongside growers, watching over the harvest fields, and I imagine that will be the same next year as well. So with any luck, I'll be posted near home from the beginning."

"Wouldn't you prefer to be down by the southern beaches?" Dellion asked, taking a seat across from us. "That's where I'd want to be if I was a wind worker."

Isabelle wrinkled her nose. "And have to deal with entitled mages complaining that the weather isn't perfect for their beach-side holidays? No, thank you."

I laughed, and Dellion surprised me by chuckling along.

"Clearly you've met my great-aunt," she said. "But I can assure you my grandfather would have put any of us young ones in our place for even suggesting such a thing. Our family knows the weather isn't something you tamper with for such frivolous reasons. But even Grandfather has yet to find a way to suppress his sister." She grinned across the table at me. "If you think he's fierce and forbidding..."

"Gracious, she sounds terrifying!" I said, trying to imagine how the powerful and imperious General Haddon could have a more imposing sibling.

"Thankfully she never leaves the estate. She considers all other parts of the kingdom to be inferior to the south coast and not worth her time or effort."

"Even the capital?" Bryony asked.

Dellion tossed her hair. "Didn't you hear me say she's utterly impossible?"

Jareth laughed. "I love Great-Aunt Mildred. She always makes me laugh."

Dellion wrinkled her nose at him. "That's because you're her favorite. She isn't half as pleasant to the rest of us."

Darius looked over, smiling. "Don't even try to deny it, Jareth. You've been her pet since the beginning. And you encourage her in it shamelessly."

"I can't help it if she knows superior quality when she sees it." He winked at the rest of us. "They're just jealous."

I grinned, delighted to see Darius entering into the banter. I couldn't remember ever seeing him so relaxed in the dining hall —aside from those too short days between his winning the position of king-elect and Jareth's attempt to kill him. Even the specter of a coming attack didn't weigh him down as his brother's betrayal had done.

Tyron never spoke at all, but neither Dellion nor Isabelle seemed to notice. And it certainly made it easier for the rest of us to ignore his presence. But I knew we couldn't continue that way indefinitely. If he intended to suddenly render himself mute then someone would eventually notice.

We all walked to combat class together, Dellion and Jareth still laughing over various family stories, with Bryony egging them on. I lingered behind a little, watching them and enjoying the smile they put on Darius's face.

Even Mitchell's dour expression couldn't kill my good mood.

"Does he look even more unhappy than usual?" Bryony asked me in a carrying whisper.

Jareth looked around, not very successfully suppressing his grin, so I glared at them both.

"Don't let him hear you say that, or who knows what he'll do?"

"So you agree he looks grumpier than usual?" Bryony watched him with narrowed eyes. "He's always been shockingly uninterested in teaching us on training yard days, but this seems like a whole different level."

I shushed her again as our instructor drew close. Although I had to admit he did have more of a glower than usual.

After a short lecture about our responsibilities as fourth years and our upcoming graduation—an event he seemed to view with disapproval, as if we were not yet ready to leave his mostly lax tutelage—he set us to our regular individual bouts and actually left the training yard.

"Well, that's new," I admitted. "Maybe because we're fourth

years we don't even need the most superficial supervision anymore?"

Bryony snorted. "Too bad we've still got those two to stop me stabbing Tyron 'by accident.'" She indicated the two guards who stood at attention just outside the yard.

"Do you think they would stop you?" I asked, weighing them up. "They're not here to *protect* him."

When I saw the gleam leap into Bryony's eyes, I groaned. "No, pretend I didn't say that. Don't you dare. And remember Tyron might well be a match with a blade even for you." I glanced around, suddenly guilty, before dropping my voice lower. "And we really shouldn't be talking about this out here."

Bryony accepted my caution with only a slight huff and moved away to challenge Jareth. Dellion appeared in front of me, asking with only the lift of an eyebrow if I wanted to bout. I shrugged acceptance, and we moved into position.

"I'm hoping you've let your skills slip over the summer," she said. "I'm sure you were much too lovesick to practice."

I rolled my eyes, but she had said it with a smile and without the mocking tone of the past. Somehow Dellion and I had arrived at a more comfortable place than I would have imagined possible.

It didn't stop her from attacking with full force, however, and whatever she thought I had done with my summer, she certainly hadn't been allowing her own skills to grow rusty. Unfortunately for her, my summer had consisted mainly of free time. Allowed to do little else, I had been determined not to return to the Academy at a disadvantage after my early withdrawal from third year.

We both fought hard until I managed to catch her off guard with a new trick I had mastered over the break. She yielded, slightly out of breath, and we saluted each other.

"I've never seen that one before," she said. "Will you teach me?"

I agreed, pleased to be asked, and we spent the rest of the lesson working on the difficult move.

"When do you think they'll let us in the arena this year?" she asked as we strolled back to the Academy after the lesson. "Mitchell seems to be increasingly unpredictable on that front."

"They can't keep us out of the arena." Ashlyn approached us from behind. "We're fourth years now. If they don't give us enough opportunity to practice, we might fail." She gave an exaggerated shudder.

"What do final exams involve?" I asked.

"They don't tell us exactly," Frida said, joining the conversation. "And graduates are forbidden from telling trainees what the final exams involved. But it's definitely in the arena."

"What? No tales from your ridiculous brother?" Ashlyn asked.

"Hardly." Frida looked disdainful. "I know better than to listen to him on such things now."

"Unless those monsters he told you about—the ones that never showed up in second year—are actually part of fourth year exams," I said.

The two girls looked at me with wide eyes and gave such identical shudders, that I couldn't help laughing.

"I'm sorry, I'm teasing you. I'm sure they're not."

"They'd better not be!" Ashlyn said. "They can't throw something at us that we've never had the chance to study or practice against."

"I suspect they can do what they like." Dellion lifted one shoulder in a careless gesture. "But considering how rare it is for anyone to fail the Academy, I'm guessing we can all rest easy on that front at least. It's not as if they want us to fail."

I remembered back to first year when that was precisely what some of the Mage Council had wanted for me. How long ago that seemed. I wished my only problem now was someone wanting me to fail the Academy.

After lunch, we all filed into composition class, taking our same, familiar seats. Our classroom hadn't changed in four years, and we still sat with the same desk mates we had chosen in first year. Back then I had felt sorry for Tyron, forced to sit with Royce. Now I felt sorry for Royce. Almost.

Instructor Alvin was usually waiting for us when we arrived, but this time there was no sign of him. I wondered idly if that meant we were to have a junior instructor for the lesson, as we sometimes did. As senior composition instructor, Alvin would normally have been with the first years in these first few weeks, but we had always had more time with the senior instructors than seemed equitable—a consequence of having both princes in our year.

However, we were still settling into our seats when Alvin came bounding into the room, his usual good-natured grin on his face.

"Welcome trainees!" he said. "Apologies for running late. I hope you've all come ready to learn."

I gave him a weak smile in return while a few of the other trainees muttered less than enthusiastic responses. Alvin always seemed to think we had forgotten everything we ever learned over the summer and started each year with a series of basic lectures.

Darius already had his nose buried in an enormous pile of reports, and I had settled myself in for a boring lesson, when Alvin surprised me.

"This year, as fourth years, I'm sure you don't need any revision. I trust you all spent your summers practicing and honing your skills in your various disciplines. It's not long now until you will be a fully qualified mage, contributing to the well-being of the kingdom in your chosen career."

I sat up a little straighter at his unexpected words. Not that any of my instructors knew of my actual abilities. Almost no one did. But I had still learned a lot from Alvin over the years.

"This year, I am going to challenge the creativity of your

minds," he said. "You never know what problem might confront you as a mage, and sometimes it is necessary to come up with new and creative solutions. So I will be presenting you with a series of problems that you're not likely to have encountered in your discipline studies."

Darius put down his reports and fixed slightly narrowed eyes on Alvin. Whatever the instructor was intending, Darius hadn't been given forewarning of it.

Alvin rubbed his hands together as if about to present us with a special treat. "The first problem for you all to consider is what compositions you might use if you needed to incapacitate someone for an extended period of time."

"I can think of a few ways," Royce said, with an unpleasant look in Darius's direction. I bridled, the guards behind the rows of desks stirring slightly as well, but it was Alvin who answered.

"*Without* hurting the person being bound, Royce. I should have specified that at the beginning. By now after three years of arena battles, you are all familiar with how to bind someone. But such a composition requires too much power to be maintained for a long time."

"I would hand the person over to law enforcement and have them placed in a mage cell," Ashlyn said.

"And if one was not available to you?" Alvin asked, losing none of his good cheer at his class's apparent disinterest in engaging with him on the exercise. "Perhaps it would be helpful to imagine a specific scenario. Let us say, Ashlyn, that you are in the far northeast of the kingdom examining some crops with a fellow grower. You discover saboteurs tampering with them and incapacitate the villains."

I raised my eyebrows. This scenario was sounding less than fanciful.

"But there is a whole gang of them. And you and your grower associate are alone without mage reinforcements and without access to a carriage. It is a long journey to the capital and those holding cells you have mentioned. How do you either transport the criminals there yourself, or hold them long enough for law enforcement officials to arrive and take them in hand?"

Darius stood to his feet, his reports gripped in one hand.

"Excuse me, Instructor, but I need to consult with Duke Francis."

Both of Alvin's brows arched, but he nodded permission. Darius strode from the room, indicating as he passed the two guards that one should accompany him while one remained stationed behind Jareth. I watched Darius go with narrowed eyes, but I could hardly question him in the middle of the classroom.

Instead I considered the question Alvin had set us. We had been confronted with a gang of attackers in the fields the year before, but on that occasion we had been surrounded by well-trained and equipped guards. It had never entered my head that it might be left to me to restrain them. But if it had been—or more accurately, if I had been a regular power mage like Ashlyn and it had been—how would I have approached the problem?

"If sending for law enforcement is an option, then it isn't a necessity that we travel with them," Armand said, surprising me by speaking up in class without being addressed directly by an instructor. Apparently his relationship with Frida was giving him confidence. "So that means we just need to incapacitate them for a substantial length of time. Like you said at the beginning."

"The problem, of course, is power," Wardell said. "You're almost completely limited to the kind of compositions you're likely to already have on hand. I can't imagine I'd be carrying anything of relevance as a matter of course. And I wouldn't want to prostrate myself to write a new one—not out in the fields surrounded by a gang of saboteurs."

"Obviously." Ashlyn rolled her eyes. "The question is what you would do, not how difficult it would be."

"It's not the sort of thing that comes up among the wind

workers," Isabelle said thoughtfully. "I can't think of a single weather phenomenon that might be helpful."

Conversation continued as various suggestions were made and discarded. In the end, the most popular suggestion came somewhat incredibly from Royce. He said, in a bored voice, that he would use a regular binding composition but only apply it to their hands and feet.

"They won't get far without their feet, and they can't work a composition without their hands," Armand said. "That might actually work. And it would take a lot less power than a full binding composition."

"But how much less?" Alvin asked, contributing for the first time. "That is the sort of experiment we must undertake. I would like you all to compose a few such workings, and I will see about finding some volunteers for us to test them on. We must see how long they might last."

"Volunteers?" I frowned at Bryony as we all hurried from the room following the sound of the bell. "I hope he doesn't mean servants who have been forced into it."

She shrugged. "I could imagine worse work than sitting around waiting for a painless composition to wear off. I'm sure if it is servants they'll be compensated for their troubles. You can be sure Zora will see to that."

"Yes, of course." I relaxed. Bryony was right. With Zora in charge, I needn't fear the servants being misused.

"What's going to happen with discipline class?" I asked, suddenly wondering how Darius intended to ensure Tyron's supervision in a class that included neither prince.

"At the end of last year, after the storm and your departure, we didn't have lessons at all," Bryony said. "I don't think anyone knew quite what to do after Amalia's unexpected betrayal. So I have no idea what they're planning for this year."

"Darius has it all organized," Jareth said from Bryony's other side. "You lot spend the year moving between the disciplines anyway, so you're just going to do that from the beginning and come under the instruction of the various discipline-specific instructors. And Duke Francis has agreed that Darius and I can both already perform at a satisfactory level for law enforcement fourth years, so we're to move around with you. Darius says as king-elect, he needs to have knowledge of all the disciplines, and no one is going to dispute that."

"What's your excuse?" Bryony asked.

He grinned at her. "I'm the heir, you know. Until Darius starts procreating, I have to be kept vaguely knowledgeable."

He wasn't looking at me, but I flushed anyway. As hard as I was fighting for a future for Darius and me, I wasn't ready to think about being responsible for producing future Kallorwegian heirs.

"So where are we to start?" I asked hurriedly, trying to ground my thoughts back in the Academy.

"The healers, I believe," Jareth said, bringing a smile to my face. It would be nice to see Raelynn's motherly face again, even if I would have to avert my eyes from half of the healings done in the class.

"I've always liked working with the healers," Tyron said, giving us all a shock. All three of us turned to look at him. "We don't have any healers of our own in the mountains, and my father has often railed against the injustice of our being denied access to their powers."

He said it all in a neutral voice, but after his studied silence, it felt as if he were shouting aggression in our direction. The guard who trailed us moved closer, his manner threatening.

"I suggest you watch your tongue when we're in public," Jareth said in a quiet voice that was laden with even more danger than the guard's movements.

Tyron shrugged. "Sorry. I just meant that I'm glad we're to start with the healers."

Jareth's eyes narrowed. "Don't think you'll be working any compositions other than those to give energy."

"Of course not." Tyron's eyes flashed briefly in the direction of the guard. "But I can still watch the healings."

I frowned the rest of the way to class, watching Tyron's back as he walked ahead of me. I had almost grown used to Tyron as a silent prisoner, present but mostly forgotten. But his words made it sound as if he were still one of the trainees, and that thought wasn't comfortable at all.

CHAPTER 8

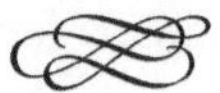

Darius didn't make an appearance at the evening meal, and the next morning at breakfast he was almost as inscrutable as when I first met him. Even Jareth commented, his words making it obvious Darius hadn't returned from his meeting with the duke until late. But Darius gave a noncommittal answer, keeping his focus on his food.

I began to seriously worry, too busy watching him to eat properly or listen to Jareth, Bryony, and Dellion discussing the upcoming day's lessons. I only relaxed when Darius looked up and, seeing me watching, gave a wink.

Surprise replaced concern, my curiosity almost over-whelming me as we finally finished the meal and strolled out toward combat class. When we reached our normal training yard, Mitchell was waiting for us.

"Fourth years will be in the arena today," he said, before marching off in the direction of the large structure.

Excited whispers broke out around me as I looked toward Darius. But he was absorbed in quiet conversation with the two guards, so I couldn't see his reaction to the news. Last year, the duke had adroitly managed to keep all of us royals out of the arena, but there had been no mention of our exclusion now. If Darius disapproved of the development, he certainly wasn't making any protest. And from his manner over breakfast, I had to assume he was aware of our instructor's plans.

We all moved from the yard to the arena much faster than we had from the dining hall to the yard, the conversation continuing all the way. But when we filed into the arena, everyone fell silent.

In third year, Mitchell had arranged for the trainees to form groups across the year levels to battle each other, so it wouldn't have been surprising to find another group of trainees already in the arena seating. But the people awaiting us were clearly not trainees.

We sat grouped together in an empty patch of seating, some way around the curved wall of the arena. Mitchell stood in front of the other group, talking to them in words too low for us to catch. Once we were sitting, conversation broke out again, quieter than before.

"Who are they?"

"What are they doing at the Academy?"

"Well, obviously they're Armed Forces," Dellion said. "Just look at their uniforms."

"But why are they here?" Ashlyn frowned across at them. "Are they going to be assessing us? Shouldn't it only be the Armed Forces trainees in here, then?" She glared at Royce—the only fourth year studying to join the Armed Forces—as if the situation was somehow his fault.

I couldn't quite suppress a shiver. The commonborn soldiers wore black uniforms, alleviated only by the red of the hems which looked as if they had been dipped in blood. Sprinkled among them were several mage officers, their robes bearing a similar pattern. Even after more than twenty years of peace, the colors inspired fear and dislike in the heart of every Ardannian.

But I sternly reprimanded myself for the instinctive reaction. If I truly believed in Kallorway, I would have to put such feelings aside. And if we were all to survive the threat from Conall, then the Ardannian Armed Forces would have to find a way to fight alongside the Kallorwegians.

Mitchell spun suddenly, marching across the arena to confront us instead of the soldiers.

"This year you will be engaging in a new type of combat. Rather than fighting each other, you will work together as a team. Your opponents will be them." He pointed across the arena at the soldiers, a group easily four times our number.

"What? All of them?" Royce asked.

"All of them," Mitchell said coldly. "You will note that you are all mages and therefore at a significant advantage."

"Except we didn't know anything about this exercise, so we're not exactly prepared," Wardell muttered.

"The battle will last for one hour," Mitchell continued, drawing gasps and squawks of protest at the astonishing length. "To succeed, you need to incapacitate them all and keep them incapacitated until the end of the battle. But you must do this without harming them in anything more than superficial ways. Unlike with your bouts against each other, you cannot assume that a healer will be standing by ready to assist. There are too many of them."

"What's the point of a battle where no one's allowed to hurt each other?" Dellion asked.

Mitchell regarded her coldly. "I didn't say *they* weren't allowed to hurt *you*. Merely that you are not permitted to harm them. Raelynn will still be available for any injuries sustained by trainees."

"What?! That's hardly fair," Royce exclaimed.

Mitchell's eyes narrowed. "At the end of this year, you will be fully qualified mages, and it is time to leave the fantasy world of children behind you. Life is not fair, and it never has been. Get used to it. And learn to be creative." He looked around at us all. "You have five minutes before the battle commences."

He strode back over to the soldiers as our section of the stands erupted in excited chatter.

"Well, of all the outrageous things," Ashlyn gasped.

"We certainly couldn't have predicted this," Frida said. "I don't think it's ever been done before."

Bryony leaned toward me and said quietly, "At least you don't have to worry about servants being used as forced volunteers. I'm guessing you don't feel quite the same compunction about soldiers."

"What?" I blinked. "Oh, right, of course."

"At least we know why Alvin moved straight to composition in the first class of the year," Jareth said, mirroring my thoughts. "And why he gave us such a strange assignment."

Several of the others stared at him.

"Of course," Isabelle said. "And we should all be thanking him. If it hadn't been for yesterday's lesson, how many of us would have compositions in our arsenals for an exercise like this?"

It wasn't only Alvin's speed that now made more sense. Put into the context of the arena and the soldiers, it seemed beyond obvious that Alvin's lesson had been about Conall's current threat, not the dangers we faced in third year. I glanced at Darius. Unlike me, he had clearly recognized the scenario Alvin was describing immediately. Had he gone racing to Duke Francis to demand why the trainees were being given assignments related to fighting Conall's army? Or had he already known about this plan and merely wanted to question the timing and details?

"I think it's past time we moved on to a discussion of strategy," Darius said, cutting across the other conversations.

Everyone fell silent, looking to him as they usually did in arena battles.

"Exactly how many of these simplified binding compositions do we have between us?" he asked.

Everyone started calling out numbers, and within moments

we had ascertained that between us we had thirty. I looked across the arena, making a rough count of about fifty soldiers.

"That's not going to be enough."

"Some of them might be able to double up," Jareth offered. "We were supposed to make them to hold as long as possible, so I'm fairly certain mine could bind two people if it's only for an hour. It will depend how specifically everyone worded them."

Dellion nodded, as did Royce and Ashlyn.

"And we must have some other options," I said. "It's only for an hour, after all." I looked to Ashlyn and Frida. "What about wrapping some of them in vines? You and Isabelle have mastered that composition combination effectively."

"We would do best to keep solutions like that for the end," Darius said. "We don't want one of their comrades hacking them free with a knife. But if most others are already bound, it could work for a few."

"We must only have about a minute left." I glanced at Mitchell who was already moving back in our direction. "How do you want us organized?"

"Pass around the compositions equally," he instructed, talking fast. "None of the energy mages will have any, so anyone who produced multiples should share. I don't know how our opponents will organize themselves, but we need to scatter quickly, so we don't present too easy a target. We should circle around them if we possibly can."

"Swords?" Bryony asked.

"Surely we're allowed to use our swords," I said. "We have to protect ourselves. Mitchell said they wouldn't be bound by the same standards as us, and they're all carrying weapons."

Darius nodded. "Swords out. Just be careful how you use them."

"We need attack compositions," I said. "The kind that can batter down shields. They have mage officers, so we can expect their forces to be shielded, and we don't want to waste any of our binding compositions until we're sure they'll be able to reach our intended targets. We don't have enough to be letting any of them burn themselves out against a shield."

Darius nodded. "Verene is right. Draw your swords and get out any compositions you might have designed to break down shields. We go for their shields, and if they go down, even for a moment, be ready to act."

"Once we manage to bind a few, we'll need to find a way to keep our prisoners secure," I added. "Darius mentioned the simple task of hacking them free of vines, but they may also have a way to release our binding compositions."

"Please make your way to the center of the arena ready for the battle to begin," Mitchell said in a stentorian voice.

We all shuffled to our feet and down from the seats. The mass of black and red awaiting us on the arena floor almost made me stumble. There suddenly seemed far more of them than when they had still been seated.

"Remember to go for their mage officers first," Darius said in a hurried voice.

I counted the robes. Five. So one mage to each squad of ten soldiers, just like normal for the Armed Forces.

Jareth thrust two rolls of parchment toward me, and it took me a confused moment to realize they must be binding compositions. As soon as I understood, I grabbed them from him, slipping them into my most accessible pocket. Darius pushed another parchment into my hand, but when I went to add it to the same pocket, he shook his head.

I glanced down at the words as I drew my sword. A shielding composition.

"Shields out and ready, everyone," Darius said quietly, and a flurry of movement surrounded me. Between our swords, various attack compositions, and now shields, every trainee's hands were full.

Even Tyron had his blade in one hand and a parchment in the

other. I eyed it uneasily, but I couldn't see how he could do any harm with a shield.

Last year Duke Francis had rearranged the entire arena training program to assist Darius in keeping Jareth out of it. But apparently either the duke or Darius himself hadn't felt it necessary this year with Tyron. I resolved to ask Darius about it at the earliest opportunity.

I forced myself to examine our opponents with a calm eye. They all held weapons, but only the five mages held parchments in their hands. I caught the swirling pattern that marked sealed commonborns on a small handful of necks, but they were scattered among the other soldiers without any other distinction.

I shook my head. It was foolish of them not to make better use of their sealed forces, but it would give us an advantage. If they had armed them with compositions written by mages, they would have been nearly as effective in battle as an actual mage, lacking only the ability to sense power.

"Go for their mages," I said, repeating Darius's earlier words. Without their mages, their numbers advantage wouldn't do them much good.

I drew a deep, steadying breath. I needed to do my part in this battle, but I also needed to refrain from using my own ability. I could already tell how tempting it would be, and how easily we could gain victory if I did intervene. But this bout was too highly scrutinized for me to risk it.

Instructor Mitchell called for us to begin, and I immediately stuck one side of my parchment between my teeth and tore it in half. A bubble of power sprang to life around me. I could hear tearing on every side as my year mates did the same, and from the rush of power that enveloped the soldiers, their mages had lost no time in activating their own shields.

By the feel of the power around them, it was clear each mage had created a single large bubble of power around their squad, rather than shielding each soldier individually. It was an efficient use of power but gave another advantage to us since it meant they would have to cluster together while we were free to spread out.

Darius barked an order which spurred us all into motion, scattering in different directions as we remembered his commands. But the soldiers were already surging toward us, spreading out into five separate groups. A quick glance showed there weren't enough of us to make any sort of circle around them. The best we could hope for was to make ourselves elusive targets.

With that in mind, I took off ducking and weaving while I endeavored to observe their formations. The commonborn soldiers formed themselves into rings, with their weapons facing outward in all directions and their mage in the middle. They knew we would be targeting their mages and intended to make it as difficult as possible.

Of course, with compositions at our disposal, we didn't need direct physical access to the center of their circles. We did need to bring their shields down, though, and I wasn't going to be much use for that. I had powerful compositions in my pockets, but they had been provided by my family for my personal protection—not for use in arena battles.

I itched to reach out with my own ability and turn the shield of the closest squad of soldiers against them, but I refrained, tightening my grip on my sword instead. Movement to one side drew my gaze in time to see two soldiers dart forward from their formation, their focus on Isabelle.

My year mate was distracted, her eyes scanning a number of parchments in her hand. Was she trying to decide which one to use?

I took off running, angling so as to approach from behind the soldiers. They had briefly left the protection of their squad's shield, so I would have to be careful when confronting them or risk injuring them by accident.

Isabelle looked up, shock twisting her face when she saw the racing soldiers closing in on her. But I leaped forward, thrusting my blade between them in time to stop the first wild thrust in the wind worker's direction. She fell back, gasping a little as I jumped in front of her.

"If you've found the composition you were looking for, I would suggest using it," I panted between ringing clangs as my blade met that of my opponents. My skill level far exceeded theirs, but I was holding off two at once while hampered by the stricture not to harm them.

Isabelle gasped again, closely followed by a ripping sound behind me. A rush of pure power swept past us both to batter at the shield protecting the squad these two soldiers had abandoned. The power pulled at me again, my ability longing to take hold of it, and the half-second distraction created an opening I couldn't afford.

One of the soldiers managed to land a hit, a glancing blow up my arm that drew blood, although it wasn't deep. Isabelle squeaked and ripped a second composition. This time her power attacked the two soldiers fighting me, both of them stumbling and dropping to the ground as their feet and hands sprang together.

Isabelle rushed forward to collect both of their swords from the ground. But before we could celebrate even such a minor victory, power slammed into us both. My shield, provided by Darius, held against the force, but Isabelle's sputtered and died.

Instinctively I leaped toward her, but I was too late. She fell hard, hit by the wave of shapeless power.

CHAPTER 9

"*I*sabelle!" I fell to my knees beside her, relieved to see she was still breathing as I heard a second voice call her name. It took a moment for me to realize it was Mitchell, declaring her "deceased" for the remainder of the battle.

I glanced toward the stands and saw Raelynn directing two green-clad servants to hurry across the arena in our direction. Apparently they would be collecting injured trainees for the healer.

"I'm sorry," Isabelle said in a weak and miserable voice.

Knowing she was well enough to speak relieved me enough to turn my mind back to the ongoing battle. I glanced again at the servants who had nearly reached us, and then held out my hand.

"Quick," I said in a low voice. "Give me whatever you were planning to use."

For a brief second she blinked at me in confusion before understanding filled her eyes and one of her hands dove into her pockets. The servants were kneeling beside her as she thrust a collection of compositions at me.

"Thank you," I whispered, clambering to my feet and looking quickly around. I had never stripped a "dying" trainee of their compositions before, but this was a different sort of battle—one which felt much closer to how I imagined actual combat. And in war a mage wouldn't hesitate to make use of their fallen comrade's supplies.

The two bound soldiers still lay where we had left them, unable to move, but their squad had crept closer, appearing intent on reclaiming and freeing them. I stepped up to stand over the bound men, my sword raised. This was what Darius had been talking about. We needed somewhere safe to guard our prisoners once we captured them, or we'd soon run out of compositions.

Now that I was so close, my shield would protect them too, a fortunate thing since their mage launched another attack. Once again, Darius's shield held. For an uneasy moment I wondered just how powerful a shield he'd given me before I forced my mind to more pressing matters. The squad were getting closer.

Movement on my other side made me spin around to confront Tyron. Every nerve in my body shot into full awareness, my instincts screaming that here was the real threat. But he merely stooped and pulled one of the bound soldiers over his shoulder with a grunt.

When he straightened, he nodded toward the edge of the arena. "We're collecting them over there."

To one side of the battle, Bryony stood, sword and teeth both bared, a small pile of bound soldiers behind her. Sadly I could see no mage robes among the prisoners under her guard.

Apparently Darius had assigned the two energy mages to play the guard role—a wise allocation of resources since they were unlikely to have many useful compositions of their own. But what they did have in abundance was energy, and from the feel of them, they had both made use of Bryony's stored compositions and were brimming with extra energy. No wonder Tyron could carry another man over his shoulder.

Whirling back to the advancing squad, I found they had picked up their pace. I looked down at the compositions in my hand. The one on top was one of Isabelle's specialties—a working that would send vines erupting from the packed dirt and twining around their victim.

I tore it, flicking my fingers toward the approaching soldiers. Despite knowing they sheltered behind a shield, they faltered when thick ropes of green burst out of the ground in front of them.

Their mage officer urged them on, however, and they pressed forward again. The vines writhed and squirmed up the invisible barrier of the shield, searching for a way in. Out of the corner of my eye, I saw Tyron return for the second bound soldier, carrying him out of the squad's reach.

The advancing soldiers didn't slow, continuing to approach me, and I took several steps back. They had now swept past the point where the vines had emerged from the dirt, their shield crushing them completely. But their protection felt weaker now than it had before.

I took a second to glance around the arena floor. No further help was coming for me. With Tyron and Bryony guarding the prisoners, and Isabelle out of action, no squad had more than two trainees fighting to keep it contained. And as I looked back toward the squad approaching me, I heard Mitchell calling Armand's name.

I winced. I had seen him fighting alongside his cousin, and I didn't think Wardell could take on an entire squad on his own. But even as I thought it, a shout rang out. I glanced involuntarily toward the noise. Thankfully, so did the soldiers advancing toward me.

For a moment I couldn't tell what had happened, and then an entire squad went down—blown to the ground by a sudden, heavy wind. Darius shouted something, and Royce darted forward, scooping the obviously bound mage from the midst of the fallen soldiers. He dragged him away, seeming to struggle with the burden until Tyron ran forward to assist him. The two of them managed to remove the mage before the first of the soldiers struggled back to their feet.

A grin spread across my face. With their mage gone, Darius would have no trouble taking care of the rest of his squad.

But I had taken too long looking, and I obviously wasn't the only one. As I heard Mitchell shout Frida's name, a new force slammed into my own shield.

Overstretched, my shield at last gave way, and the attacking composition latched on to me. With a lurch, I recognized its purpose. As it pulled at my energy, my mouth spoke before I could think better of it.

"Take control," I muttered.

The composition that was attempting to drain me instantly came under my control. But still my energy drained away while I stood frozen with indecision, failing to redirect the working. I needed to do it fast before I lost too much more energy, but I couldn't just wrest control of this mage's composition in the middle of the arena.

A rustling from my clenched fingers reminded me I still held a stack of compositions. Glancing down at them, I identified a shield. Ripping it, I muttered, "reverse" at the same time. The drain on my energy cut off just as a cocoon of power surrounded me. Hopefully the mage would think it was the shield that had cut off his working.

I had directed the energy draining composition back against all the soldiers in the squad. I expected it to burn out against their shield, but in case their shield was close to giving way, I hoped to mask the effects of the composition by dispersing it among so many.

To my surprise, although I could still feel the shield, the working passed straight through it, hitting each of the remaining soldiers equally. So their shield was only for attacks with either power or physical objects. They weren't shielded against energy attacks.

A single moment of reflection explained this omission. As far as the soldiers knew, no one currently in the Academy had an offensive energy ability.

Without stopping to think it through, I whispered, "Connect," and reached for the mage at the center of the squad.

I reeled back as I sank into his energy, pulling free immediately. He was an energy mage. I cut the connection, not wanting to risk his sensing my presence as Tyron had done. Before he had been nothing but a black and red robe, but now I noticed he was young—especially compared to the other mages in the battle.

My mind raced as I realized what his being an energy mage meant. He couldn't sense power. If I did use my ability, taking down his shield and reassigning it to myself, he would have no idea anything had happened.

I risked another glance around the arena. Dellion and Ashlyn had also succeeded in taking down their mage and were busy mopping up the remaining soldiers of their squad. The others were too absorbed in their own battles to be paying attention to me.

I moved back further again, giving myself more room as I picked another attack composition, almost at random, from the stack Isabelle had left me. I needed the mage and his soldiers to see me working a composition, that was all.

I ripped the parchment, sending a weak wave of power toward the shield around the squad. But the mage had already torn a second composition, shoring up their defenses. The working I had used would never be enough. It didn't matter, though. No one in front of me could sense power which meant they had no way of measuring the attack against their defense.

"Take control," I whispered, seizing their fresh layer of shielding and pulling it toward myself, whispering the words to reshape it into a shield for me instead.

"Take control," I whispered again, seizing on the remaining remnants of the shield beneath. But instead of pulling it toward me, I sent it back against the mage, reversing its purpose so that instead of shielding him, it shielded everyone else from him. For a moment the power tried to buck against me before it accepted the binding as a close enough substitute to its original shielding purpose.

As the power tightened around his limbs, he stumbled and then fell. A ripple swept through his soldiers as they turned toward him in confusion. But none of them—not even the one with a sealed pattern around his neck—stepped forward to recover the mage's store of compositions, as I had done with Isabelle.

I pulled out the binding compositions Jareth had given me, adding the ones Isabelle had left me and tearing them all at once. I flicked my fingers toward the soldiers in front of me, the power rushing out from the compositions to overwhelm them. Six of the eight went down to lie beside their mage.

But the remaining two recovered quickly, letting out loud yells as they charged me with their swords raised. I barely pulled my own blade up in time to counter them, stumbling backward yet again. I had nearly reached the edge of the arena and had nowhere else to go.

I had used all of Isabelle's specific binding compositions, but it was possible she had something else of use in the couple remaining from the stack she had passed me. If there was another one to create vines, the soldiers were now unprotected.

But with two opponents, I had to focus on their swords and didn't have time to check the parchments I had left. I could already barely keep up with the ferocity of their double attack.

Mitchell had said the battle was to last an hour, and it must still be far less time than that. A trickle of sweat ran down my back. I wouldn't last in an extended fight against these two.

I stepped back again, my foot catching on a loose rock and nearly slipping out from under me. I thrust my sword out as I stumbled, desperately hoping to hold them off long enough to regain my footing. But one of them slipped his blade under my weak defense, its length reaching for me.

Before it could land, however, another blade appeared, protecting me. Bryony darted in front of me, her sword moving almost too fast to be seen as she took the offensive, now driving both my attackers backward.

I gasped a relieved breath and started after them. But a moment later I stopped myself, instead looking down at the parchments in my hand. One was a shield which I hardly had need of now, but the second was indeed another vine composition. Ripping it, I gestured toward the two soldiers now fighting my friend.

Vines sprouted from the dirt at their feet, and they had time to do no more than shout in alarm before the greenery had wended its way up their bodies, wrapping both their arms and legs. Their swords dropped and a moment later they toppled over to land beside them.

"Yes!" Bryony shouted, pumping the air.

I took a moment to catch my breath, my own blade trailing in the dust as I bent over and sucked in deep lungfuls of air. But I had soon recovered enough to straighten and take a look around the arena.

I had missed Mitchell calling Tyron's name, along with Jareth and Ashlyn. But that still left Bryony, Darius, Royce, Dellion, Wardell, and me. Half of our force still stood, and they were the only ones left upright on the arena floor. The pile of soldiers Bryony and Tyron had been guarding looked enormous now, and several other groupings were scattered in different locations—including the two directly in front of me, and the seven prone bodies I had left some distance away after I felled their mage.

Bryony and I walked toward the middle of the arena floor, approaching Darius where he consulted in low tones with Dellion. He looked up at our approach, a smile breaking across his face at sight of me, although it darkened when he saw the blood still seeping from the slight gash on my arm.

"I'm fine," I said quickly.

"We won!" Bryony announced, looking like she was about to start dancing on the spot. Had she topped up her energy yet again? She certainly looked ready to take off from the ground.

"Not yet," Darius said, an edge of fatigue to his voice. "We still have to last an hour, remember."

Dellion had walked away while he was speaking, heading toward Royce and Wardell. I followed her with my eyes as did Darius.

"She's passing on my instructions for the three of them to write out some more binding compositions," Darius said. "We need to patrol all the prisoners. Some of the bindings are stretched to cover two, and some of the soldiers have…less traditional restraints." His eyes rested for a moment on the two bound with Isabelle's vines.

I nodded. "We can help keep an eye on them all, even if we can't write more compositions." I paused, pointing back toward the location of my particular fight. "But when the hour is over, we need to talk about the fact that the mage over there is Amalia's old student—the one who can take energy."

CHAPTER 10

We survived the hour, refreshing several of the bindings and fighting off a couple of soldiers who managed to leap to their feet and attack before we realized their restraints had worn off. When the specified time elapsed, Bryony gave a loud cheer and embraced Dellion who was closest at hand.

I stood nearer to Darius, but instead of turning to me, he turned in the other direction. Clapping Royce on the back, he smiled broadly at him.

"Victory, Cousin," he said.

To my surprise, Royce grinned back at him. "We showed them, right enough. They won't go underestimating us next battle and writing us off as mere trainees."

"Next battle?" I asked.

He glanced my way, hesitating for a moment before shrugging. "I can't imagine they brought five whole squads of the Armed Forces to the Academy for a single bout."

"No, I suppose not." I hadn't given the matter any thought, but he was likely right.

"Come," Darius said. "We've all well and truly earned our meal this morning."

For the briefest second, Royce hesitated again, before he bowed slightly and gestured for us to precede him. He gave me a sour look as I passed, but I forced myself to smile in response.

When Darius fell into step beside me, I glanced back at Royce, walking just behind us. His eyes were fixed on Darius's back, and he wore a thoughtful expression that looked out of place on his face.

My eyes slid sideways to Darius, catching his smile. When he turned toward me, I raised an eyebrow, and his grin quirked up on one side.

"I had a great deal of difficulty making sure he survived the battle and made it to the moment of victory intact," he said in an under voice. "But I think the effort is already paying off, don't you?"

I remembered the two of them had been fighting side-by-side when they took down the first mage. So Darius had placed himself beside his second cousin on purpose.

"A clever move," I acknowledged, my voice equally quiet. There was nothing like fighting side-by-side to create a sense of camaraderie. It wasn't the first time I had seen the arena have such an effect on my year mates. And if Royce was right, Darius would have plenty of opportunities to strengthen the current fellow feeling he had managed to create between them.

I glanced back again. So far Royce's new warmth didn't seem to stretch to me. But at least it was progress.

When we reached the seating where the defeated members of our year awaited us, Mitchell congratulated us all in his usual dour voice. But I detected a note of pride beneath his expression.

The trainees, even those who had "died" early in the battle, had an air of energy and excitement as we all walked back to the Academy for lunch. Dellion and Wardell were both voluble in their agreement that we would face similar challenges in combat classes to come. And everyone seemed willing enough to enter into a debate about what compositions they would prepare and how we could refine our strategy.

I walked slowly, letting most of the group surge ahead. A slight clasp on Bryony's arm made her stick to my side, and a significant look in the direction of the princes caused them to slow as well. Tyron glanced back at us, matching his pace to ours until Darius sent him a cold look. Shrugging, the energy mage fell even further back to walk beside Darius's ever-present guards.

"You knew that battle was coming," I accused Darius.

He smiled slightly. "Only from yesterday afternoon. Duke Francis and I had discussed the possibility of such an exercise, but we weren't sure when soldiers would actually be able to arrive. When Alvin arrived late to our first composition class and then announced our assignment, I realized the forces must have arrived after all."

"I'll admit I didn't grasp the significance of Alvin's assignment," I said. "But when Mitchell announced the parameters of the bout, it was impossible not to recognize the parallels with our situation with Conall. How to incapacitate his army without harming them is exactly what we've been trying to work out all summer, and I was a fool not to realize as soon as Alvin explained the lesson."

Darius nodded. "The duke felt it would be the best approach, and I agreed with him."

"But what was the point?" Bryony asked. "Surely they're not thinking of sending the trainees out to face that army?"

"No, of course not," Darius said. "This will all be over—one way or another—before even the fourth years graduate. But what our armies will be facing this year in the north is an unprecedented situation. We have mages who have spent their whole lives in the Armed Forces and know far more about battle strategy than me. But that very experience is working against them now when we're facing a different kind of enemy and a different kind of war. We need new thinking, flexible thinking."

"Creative thinking," I murmured.

He nodded. "And I'm told that young minds are the best for that."

"Plus," Jareth added, "there are other advantages. It's not enough to develop new strategies in theory—we need the chance to experiment with them. But we also have to keep pretending everything is normal. The Armed Forces wanted to start war exercises immediately, but there's no way to hide something of that scale."

"That's why I suggested the Academy," Darius said. "Combat training is a normal part of life here, so it's the perfect place to hide real war exercises."

I raised an eyebrow. "And it has the added benefit of allowing you to be present."

He smiled. "That is certainly a positive side effect as far as I'm concerned."

"So what did you learn?" Bryony asked.

"Perhaps it's more important what our year mates learned," Darius said. "We're hoping that as they continue to engage in these mock battles, we'll see effective strategies start to emerge."

"Not that the various luminaries of the Armed Forces won't have their own opinions," Jareth said. "I'm sure they'll be debating it hotly over lunch in the barracks."

"So they're going to be here a while?" Bryony asked.

Darius nodded. "The Armed Forces is to be stationed here long term, but they'll rotate the specific soldiers to give as many as possible the chance to be involved."

"I hope one lesson is already abundantly clear," I said, thinking about the completed battle.

Darius looked at me inquiringly, and I shrugged.

"I wouldn't have succeeded in taking down the squad I was facing without Isabelle's compositions. And even then, I might not have managed it if the sealed commonborn soldier among them had taken his mage's compositions when the mage himself was incapacitated. It was a serious advantage to us that only the five mages were using compositions. And it's not an advantage we can necessarily expect when we're facing the Sekali forces Conall is controlling."

Bryony winced. "No, definitely not. Back in the Empire every single soldier will be sealed, and they don't have the same barriers between mages and commonborns as you do here in Kallorway. We'll be the ones with that disadvantage in the actual war."

I looked at Darius. "I know you've promised to change the law about sealed commonborns being able to wield compositions after you're crowned, but I don't think we can afford to wait that long."

"They're right," Jareth said quietly, also looking at Darius.

A crease marred Darius's forehead, and his eyes looked stormy. "I would have already made the change if there weren't certain political complications. But you make a good point—and one that will hopefully be strong enough for me to push this matter through as soon as possible. I thought I would have years to heal the rifts in Kallorway and bring us together as a kingdom —but now with this threat, we have only months."

"But you also have a common enemy to unite you," I said softly. "And there is nothing else so effective."

Darius gave a grim smile. "I never thought I would have something to thank Conall for."

Jareth clapped him on the shoulder. "Maybe wait until we actually win for that, Brother."

Despite our slow pace we had nearly reached the Academy doors, so I came to an abrupt stop. Our year mates had already disappeared inside on their way to the dining hall, but the other three all stopped a stride or so in front of me, looking back with raised brows.

"You said the soldiers will be at the guard barracks?" I asked Darius.

He nodded, and I glanced over at the large outbuilding that housed the Academy's guards.

"We still haven't addressed the issue of that energy mage," I said. "Is it really safe to have him here given his close association with Amalia?"

"His name is Cooper, and I know Tyron and I used some of his compositions against you," Jareth said, "but it wasn't with his knowledge. I got them from my father."

"That may be," I said, "but Amalia went rogue even after Tyron's influence was withdrawn. It's true that she might not have tried to destroy the Academy without him pushing her over the edge, but she's always hated the royals of both kingdoms. Are we sure her protégé doesn't feel the same way?"

"He's been thoroughly examined," Darius said. "He was checked under truth composition by his superiors in the Armed Forces after Amalia's attack, and then again by Captain Vincent when he turned up at the Academy with this group." He looked at me. "Did you want to check him yourself?"

I bit my lip. "Not really, if I can avoid it. He's a trained and experienced energy mage, so there's every chance he would sense me in the same way Tyron can. I did connect with him briefly during the attack—that's how I realized who he was. And I didn't notice anything untoward."

Jareth raised an eyebrow. "You used your ability during the battle?"

I raised an eyebrow back. "Did you notice anything amiss? I am a trainee, after all, so my ability is as valid as any of your compositions." I glanced at Darius. "I was careful, though. And I only used it after I realized I was facing an energy mage who couldn't feel power. It makes it much harder for someone to tell what I'm doing if the person can't sense anything of what's going on."

"I trust your judgment," Darius said. "If you think it was safe, then I'm sure it was."

Bryony made a disgusted noise in her throat and pointed to the Academy doors. "Lunch is waiting, remember? If we've devolved to the gazing-at-each-other-longingly phase, can we move on to the eating one instead?"

I covered up my flush by rolling my eyes and starting to move again.

"I'd like to meet him," I said. "The energy mage—Cooper."

"I thought you would." Darius fell into step beside me. "And he's actually offered to teach some energy mage classes."

Jareth glanced back at Tyron who had been lingering out of earshot with the guards. "Is that wise?"

"It's a valuable opportunity for us." Bryony looked interested enough to have forgotten about the food we were missing. "I've been saying the Academy should get an energy mage on the instructing staff."

"If they could find one interested in taking up a position, they would offer them a permanent position in a heartbeat," Darius said. "Ardann has the advantage of the Spoken Mage and her sons to lure other energy mages to join them, and yet even they don't have an energy mage on permanent staff at the Academy."

"My parents pushed quite hard to try to find one before Stellan started last year," I said. "But the instructor they found would only sign on for one year, so they're back to looking again."

"It's nice to be in demand," Bryony said with a grin. Darius opened his mouth, and she quickly added, "But don't waste your time trying to convince me to stick around here after this year. You don't have a chance."

I grinned. "I think Darius knows that. We all know your feelings about the Academy's remote location."

"It's not that I dislike Kallorway," she told Darius and Jareth in a kind voice. "But since I intend to help you defeat Conall and save the entire kingdom, I think that's quite enough service to cover the next few years."

"If you can think of a way for us to defeat Conall," Darius said dryly, "then we'll give you a medal and a position next to all the choicest shops."

"Now that is a more appealing offer." She laughed. "I'll let you know if I have any flashes of brilliance."

As we passed into the entranceway of the Academy, Darius leaned over to speak quietly to me.

"I insisted on meeting Cooper myself yesterday afternoon. I really don't think we have anything to worry about."

I smiled up at him. "Thank you."

His eyes looked warmly back down into mine, and I felt my flush returning. Thoughtful gestures and moments like this only made it more frustrating that Darius could ever doubt himself. He had proven his love over and over, and if it was enough for me, then why couldn't it be enough for him too?

The noise from the dining hall washed over us, breaking the moment, and he drew back, entering the room several steps behind me. Tyron had caught up now, so we entered as a group of five, as we so often did, the guards trailing behind.

When we sat down at the fourth year table, we found our year mates still discussing the battle and potential future strategies. I loaded my plate, listening idly to their conversation.

I envied them, in a way. None of them had any idea why the instructors had assigned such a peculiar exercise and thought it merely a new method of testing and training us. I envied them the light-heartedness afforded by their ignorance.

In composition class, Alvin asked everyone to reflect on the performances of their binding compositions, leading the group in a discussion of how to refine this new type of working, as well as other options that might be effective.

I raised an eyebrow at Bryony. "The senior instructors are obviously throwing their full support behind this effort," I murmured.

"Can you blame them?" She shook her head. "If I let myself

stop and think about any of it for too long, it's completely terrifying. I just wish I could do something to help."

"You can, and you do," I said firmly. "I have no doubt that when the time comes, your energy will be incredibly valuable."

She sighed. "I hope so."

Despite the interesting topic, the class passed slowly thanks to my preoccupation with the upcoming discipline studies class. Apparently we were to have one lesson with Cooper in our old classroom, and then he would join us back with the healers. It made sense given his own experience using his ability for healing purposes, and I could imagine Raelynn's class were almost as interested to meet him as I was.

When I reached our old classroom, I paused for a moment on the threshold, taken by surprise. I had braced myself to once again be confronted with the black and red robe of the Armed Forces, but those colors were nowhere in sight.

The young man at the front of the room grinned at me. "I recognize you. You were my opponent this morning. Princess Verene, I believe?"

With a blink, I continued on into the room, now recognizing Cooper despite his new silver robe. Bryony came in behind me, with the others trailing some way after her.

"Duke Francis has convinced my superiors to lend me to the Academy for a period," Cooper said. "Apparently you're short an energy instructor. And they've decided I'm not much use for the exercises anyway."

Jareth raised both eyebrows as he slid into an empty seat. "I would have thought with your rare ability you'd be more valuable than a regular mage."

"In actual battle, perhaps," he said, although he didn't look particularly pleased at the idea. "But these are meant to be exercises to develop strategies for the troops as a whole. Rare abilities aren't helpful for that purpose."

I immediately felt a brief stab of guilt. He was right, and it meant I really shouldn't be using my ability in the arena battles either. I didn't want to give the impression that the trainees' strategies were more successful than they actually were.

Cooper glanced around the classroom. "It's strange to be back here. Especially without Amalia."

All of us except Tyron stiffened at her name.

"I still can't believe she attacked the Academy," Cooper continued, apparently oblivious to our reaction. "She was always bitter, of course—she didn't exactly try to hide it—but I never dreamed she would do something like that."

"I hear you've had to endure some inconvenience because of your connection with her," I said, watching him closely.

He shook his head. "That's understandable enough. I mean if she could lose it like that…" He fell silent for a moment. "She was a good teacher, though. I learned a lot from her. And I can't help but still be grateful to her for helping me find a use for my power that wasn't only about stealing others' energy. Because who wants a power like that?"

I bit my lip, looking at him in a different light. I knew that feeling all too well. And I, too, had rejoiced at finding a way to use my powers that didn't just feel like stealing from others. If a single instructor had dedicated four years to helping me achieve that goal, how would I feel about them?

"From what I understand, she had a hard life," I said softly, earning a surprised look from Bryony.

Cooper sighed. "Yes. She told me about it once, when I was in fourth year. It wasn't like her to open up about personal things, but it was the anniversary of her brother's death, and she wanted someone to remember him with." He sighed. "I guess she didn't have anyone else to fill that role. Maybe if she had, she never would have gone over the edge."

I couldn't help glancing at Tyron, my emotions mixed and confused. If he hadn't tampered inside Amalia's head, she likely never would have snapped either. But with a father like Conall, had Tyron himself ever had anyone to sympathize with him?

Cooper looked at Darius. "If I'm permitted to ask, Your Highness, what has happened to Amalia? My superiors either didn't know or wouldn't tell me—I'm not sure which."

Darius didn't say anything, but my moment of fellow feeling made me speak up. "She's being held securely for now, but she'll be completing a sealing ceremony soon."

Cooper whistled softly. "She'll hate that, I'm sure. She worked so hard to refine her power and control."

"But then she chose to misuse it," Darius said in a hard voice. "She should be grateful the consequences aren't more severe. If she had succeeded in her aim, they would have been."

I sighed. "At least some good will come of it, whether she believes in the cause or not. She's strong, so she'll be able to seal a great many."

"And I intend to contribute an energy composition to make sure it's even more," Bryony said.

"As will I," Tyron said, as if the idea had been his own and not one forced on him by Darius who had said it was the very least he could do to start making amends for his many crimes.

Cooper nodded his approval at them both and then began to ask questions about their studies so far. He and Bryony were soon involved in a highly technical conversation, and I could see my friend's delight at having an instructor who actually had experience as an energy mage—even if he didn't have exactly the same ability as her.

I found it hard to concentrate on their words, my attention shifting sideways to Darius. For once he hadn't buried himself in a pile of reports but was instead watching Cooper with narrowed eyes. I examined his face, wondering about the source of his animosity given his earlier approval of Cooper.

Only when Cooper turned, smiling at me as he included me in the conversation, did I understand. Darius stiffened beside me as I answered our temporary instructor, although the gesture was so slight I doubted anyone else noticed it. He glanced rapidly from Cooper to me, his eyes lingering on my face with an expression that made my heart hurt.

Darius had turned cold toward Cooper because of Cooper's interest in me. For a moment I wanted to shake him. Surely he knew he had no need for jealousy? I had made my feelings for Darius clear, and Cooper's interest in me was purely academic.

I shook my head in impatience, drawing Darius's gaze again, and I read the truth in his eyes. He was the source of his own jealousy, and he knew it. It must make the sting even worse. He had been the one to put barriers between us, driving himself to the point of resenting the smiles I gave other people, even when he knew there was nothing romantic between me and Cooper.

Everything in me wanted to reach out and reassure him—touched to discover he felt like I did. Despite our constant close proximity, we both yearned for more. But I forced myself to turn away. Darius was the cause of the distance between us. He was the reason we remained no more than year mates, allies, and friends. I didn't want to see him hurting, but I couldn't save him from this. I couldn't save either of us from this pain.

My eyes, seeking anything other than Darius's face, latched on to Tyron. He sat there as disengaged as always, calm rather than rebellious. He had said he was going to help with the sealing ceremony in the most nonchalant way, and it hit me suddenly that he might be able to help in other ways as well.

Tyron's ability, although different from his father's, was closely linked. Certainly more closely linked than any other ability. Tyron had explained how his father was able to wield energy, but explanations weren't the same as experience. Bryony and Cooper's enthusiastic conversation only demonstrated that.

But I had a unique ability myself—one that would allow me to experience Tyron's ability as closely as if it were my own. And I didn't even need Tyron's willing cooperation. I just needed to convince Darius to give me time with Tyron in a private location.

CHAPTER 11

We all soon settled into the new rhythm of lessons. Alvin still worked with the power trainees on their stamina and control, but he tailored his lessons to compositions that would help them in our ongoing arena battles against the Armed Forces. Despite our initial victory, we didn't win every bout. The soldiers were learning, too, and I kept my resolution to refrain from using my ability to intervene on our behalf.

I still didn't mention my true powers to my year mates or instructors. The crowns of both Kallorway and Ardann knew the truth now, but with the specter of Conall hanging over us, we needed to hold on to any possible tactical advantage, no matter how minor.

Cooper soon became a fixture at the Academy, alternating between giving us dedicated energy lessons and accompanying us to the other discipline classes. Raelynn held on to him for as long as she could, but we eventually moved on to the Royal Guard class whose instructor wanted the opportunity for his trainees to work on their shields to block energy-stealing compositions. If the Armed Forces wanted Cooper back, then

Duke Francis was holding his own against them because there was no talk of the energy mage returning to his usual role.

It took me several weeks to convince Darius to let me experiment with Tyron. I could understand his reluctance—I wasn't eager to spend prolonged time in such intimacy with Tyron either. But eventually Darius had to accede. The threat that faced us was too big not to throw every possible tool at it.

The first evening Darius invited me into the sitting room of his now enlarged suite, he had not only Jareth hovering nearby but both guards actually inside the room. I wanted to roll my eyes but refrained. I knew he did it out of love, even if it was misguided. I would be inside Tyron's ability—he could hardly use it against me, and if he tried to attack me physically, it wouldn't take four people to restrain him. It probably wouldn't take any, since I could turn his own power against him.

As soon as I appeared at the door behind the tapestry, Darius hurried over to join me.

"I won't be leaving your side the whole time," he promised.

I smiled up at him. "So that's the key to keeping you close. What a pity it took me so long to discover it. I should have started experimenting with Tyron the day I arrived."

He gave a low growl, but to my surprise it sounded almost playful. For a moment, hope surged in my heart. Maybe the pain of our separation had grown too much for him.

"I miss you," I said, in an equally low voice. "And I don't care whether or not we can convince my parents."

He sighed, the humorous light dropping out of his eyes. "You say that now, and I'm sure you believe it now. But a lifetime is a long time to be separated from the people who love us. Family— if it's a good, loving family—is important. You don't just throw that away, Verene."

"But what if we can never convince them?" I asked despairingly.

"Then maybe they have an insight into our situation unclouded by emotion," he said. "Maybe I really am bad for you."

I shook my head. "I don't believe that."

His face softened. "And some days I still can't believe you feel that way. I spent half the summer convinced that if you came back, you would come back hating me for betraying you to your parents."

I sighed. "I'm not saying I wasn't angry. I was. Very. But I also know you didn't mean to betray me. I just wish you hadn't let your faith in yourself be so shaken by what happened with Jareth and Tyron."

I shook my head. "But how could I claim our love was true enough and strong enough to be worth the sacrifice if I couldn't forgive you? Especially for a mistake made without ill intentions."

Jareth cleared his throat, breaking our quiet moment. I grimaced at him, struck for an odd moment by the strangeness of being so comfortable with him after spending so long mistrusting and then fearing him.

My eyes strayed to where Tyron sat on one of the sofas, an expression of distaste on his face. My expression hardened. Jareth was one thing, but no one had been controlling Tyron's mind.

I strode fully into the room, ignoring the guards, and took one of the remaining seats. My anger was useful, overriding the revulsion that made me shrink from connecting so closely with Tyron. I didn't look at him because I didn't need to for my experiments. Instead I dove straight into his energy.

Despite my anger, I flinched at the connection with his insidious ability. From the corner of my eye, I saw him give a matching flinch, and I used it to whip up my outrage. He had given up his right to privacy when he set out to destroy our kingdom.

In the past, I had been focused on speed—or in our final

confrontation, on the revelations he was making. This time I went for depth and a thorough examination of exactly how his ability worked. And that first evening I didn't do anything except immerse myself in it.

I emerged feeling dirty, although I had never moved from Darius's pristine sofa. Without my own surprise and fear to color my response to his ability, as it had in the past, I experienced it much as he did. And it left me shaken and uncomfortable to see just how natural it could feel to reach into the sanctity of another person's mind.

I returned to my own suite slowly, grateful to find that with the connection broken, his ability seemed as revolting to me as it always had. But as I attended classes the next day, I realized the return to my own perspective had negative consequences as well. While we were connected, every aspect of his ability was laid bare to me, making as much sense to me as it did to him. But that knowledge had faded all too quickly once the connection was broken.

The next time I came to Darius's suite to continue my study, I brought parchment and pen and made copious notes. At least they would remain once the session was over.

As I explored Tyron's ability over a number of evenings, curiosity grew in me. I wanted to attempt one of his compositions for myself. The desire scared me, though, and I hesitated. Again and again I asked myself if it was only the desire for understanding that drove me, or if it was something darker. After each session, I trod back to my suite with heavy steps, desperately testing my emotions in the wake of the broken connection. Did his ability still disgust me as much as it always had? Or had too much exposure started to twist my thinking?

I thought I retained the same feelings as I ever had, but the look on Jareth's face when I tentatively mentioned the idea—keeping my words and tone as casual as possible—made me question myself again. And, of course, I couldn't attempt one of Tyron's compositions on my own. But how could I expect anyone to volunteer to be the recipient of such a working?

I could understand Jareth's reaction, and I would never have considered asking him to be involved. Darius had confided in me some time ago that his brother still had nightmares about the years he had spent under Tyron's control.

Darius himself was out of the question as well, of course. Not even in the name of defeating Conall could I place Kallorway's king-elect under any kind of mental control. And even Bryony, usually so reckless and eager to assist, looked horrified at the idea.

She had started accompanying me to the princes' suite, although I told her my efforts weren't in the least interesting to watch. But she seemed to have taken Tyron's actions as a more personal affront than anyone else other than Jareth. Perhaps because she and Tyron had spent so long as the only two energy mages at the Academy. She informed me that his betrayal wasn't just one against Kallorway, but against the energy mages too.

"My mother was one of the Tarxi who came down from the mountains," she told me hotly one day. "Which means his father has held a piece of my mother's energy captive for twenty-five years. And he's been controlling her with it! For twenty-five years! Tyron claims the rest of us are the traitors to the Tarxi, but they're the ones who betrayed the energy mages. They're the source of all our troubles."

In the end, it was Elsie who volunteered. I hated to do such a thing to her, but I didn't have any other options, and Darius at least was enthusiastic about the idea.

"Have you ever connected with a commonborn before?" he asked.

I frowned. "No, I don't think I have. I've never had a reason to do so."

"Many of the people Conall has entrapped are commonborns.

So experimenting with how Tyron's workings interact with them makes excellent sense. We might learn something of relevance to his father's ability as well."

"I'm happy to be of assistance, Verene," Elsie said quietly.

Darius gave me a curious look at her use of my first name, but she didn't see his expression, her focus on me as she continued on.

"I know you won't make me do anything of significance, and that you won't leave me trapped for long. I trust you."

Somehow her trust only made me feel worse. But I forced myself to remember that the threat we faced was too great to allow such delicate considerations. If our allies wanted to help, we had to let them—whoever they might be. Just as Darius had been forced to put aside his feelings and let me connect with Tyron's ability.

I didn't bring Elsie into the room with Tyron, though. I didn't want him knowing she was involved. Instead I wrote out the composition while connected to him, naming Elsie specifically in the wording, but merely slipped it into one of my pockets when I was done.

Tyron usually made no comment during our sessions, but he watched me closely while I wrote. When I finished, a strange smile twisted his face.

"So even the great Verene isn't immune," he said quietly.

Darius stood swiftly, looming menacingly over Tyron, but he didn't break eye contact with me. My pulse sped up.

"What's that supposed to mean?" I asked, my voice coming out breathier than I had intended.

"Power is meant to be used," he said. "It's inescapable."

I rose to my feet, pushing the parchment deeper into my pocket. "We are *meant* to help and protect those around us. And certainly any power we possess should be used in such an effort. But we are not slaves to our abilities, Tyron."

A wave of some emotion crossed his face, but I didn't try to understand what it was, already turning away toward the door behind the tapestry. But my ears could still hear the whispered words that accompanied me from the room.

"Are you sure about that?"

~

I worked the composition the next evening when Elsie and I were alone in my suite. The parchment had been burning a hole in my pocket all day, and I was grateful to be rid of the awful thing.

Ripping it quickly, I watched her eyes change focus slightly before her expression returned to normal. I had experienced Tyron's style of composition once before, from the other side. It hadn't prepared me for how it felt now, though. Even when I had turned Tyron's composition against him, it hadn't acted in a normal way since it was his own working used within his own mind.

The energy I had released from my composition latched on to Elsie, tugging until a piece of her energy broke free and flew back to connect with me. In many ways it reminded me of the tube of energy that had connected Conall and Captain Matthis. But that had been whisper thin, tucked deep in his energy. A small, dark, hidden corner.

Tyron's ability seemed overwhelmingly strong in comparison, my connection to Elsie more like a tunnel than a tube—an opening wide enough for me to send any thought or compulsion I liked. A large chunk of her energy was now attached to me, and I could implant it with any thoughts I liked, the impact flowing back down the connection. Her mind was like malleable clay, shaping itself under the directions I had written into the composition. And now that we were directly linked, I could refine those thoughts and push her to act on them.

Despite myself, I was both fascinated and slightly exhilarated.

I—more than any other—had been given the chance to sample many types of power. But I had never felt anything like this.

For a moment Elsie and I just looked at each other, and then she launched into action. Flinging herself around the room, she knocked over chairs, threw cushions on the floor, and even upended my desk.

"It's too tidy in here," she said in a frenzied voice. "We need to make a mess. A bigger mess." She looked around, as if trying to find a more destructive target.

I had been caught motionless while she wreaked her destruction, trapped in an internal battle of my own. Alongside the heady sensation of control, I fought against the queasy feeling of her energy. Ripped from its rightful owner by force, it roiled inside me, wanting to be free. I had felt something similar before, when reversing energy stealing compositions, but this was even stronger.

Every part of her stolen energy rebelled against my control. But her outward appearance gave no sign of this struggle as she acted on my implanted thoughts without hesitation. The battle was being waged inside me, not her, and it was all I could do not to lose the contents of my stomach.

Is this how Tyron had lived all the time? If so, I could hardly wonder at the strange calm that had gripped him since his capture and binding. He might hate us for discovering his ability and stopping him—he might hate us just for being mages from the flatlands. But there must be at least a part of him that was relieved to have his mind to himself again, to be free of this constant unsettling discomfort.

The crash of another falling chair made me start and refocus on Elsie before my room could be completely torn apart. I had only completed one half of my experiment, and I needed to hurry with the rest of it. I murmured the words to connect with her.

For a moment I felt a strange emptiness, the sensation throwing me off so badly that I nearly pulled free of her energy.

But a moment later, I realized all I was feeling was an absence of ability. Elsie still had energy—as every person did—but she used it for her regular tasks and not as fuel for any sort of ability. So when I connected with her, I didn't access a store of knowledge or compositions. I felt only a connection to her life force itself.

As soon as I adjusted to the sensation, I recognized where my composition had sunk into her, stealing a chunk of her energy. I could feel the link between us from both sides.

It would be easy to let it go from my side. Too easy. I fought the burning desire to do just that. But I was not the one who had enthralled an army. It would do us no good to know how the person who created the link could remove it. I wanted to try freeing her with my own ability from her side, as I had freed Captain Matthis and Jareth from Conall's workings.

Having identified the link in her energy, I took control of the working.

I froze for several seconds after I did so, my mind whirling. This wasn't like a normal composition—even one I had worked. This was an open working which maintained a connection between me and the composition—and I had now connected with it again in a different way. My mind was rapidly starting to lose control of the complicated situation.

But this ability of mine to seize a working was the most comfortable and familiar, and after a moment, I could see what I needed to do. I released her energy, cutting it free. It sprang back to her, and we both took deep, gasping breaths. Instantly my mind felt clearer.

The composition I had worked was finished, the connection it had created between us gone. But the direct connection I had made with her using my own ability remained. And through it, I could easily see that her mind and energy were once again her own. I pulled free of that connection as well.

But the exercise was not yet over. Tyron's energy, released from my written composition and now no longer being used to hold Elsie's stolen energy, surged back toward her, trying to reforge the connection. It had not yet been expended.

I grimaced. I had written it too strong, using Tyron's usual allocation of strength as a guide. And now that energy needed to go somewhere, just as the power did when I took control of regular compositions. The longer I hesitated, the more it pulled at my control until at last it pulled completely free, flying back to Elsie. As it did so, I whispered some hurried words.

"Sorry about this in advance," I said, wincing as the energy latched on to her. Completing its original purpose, it stole some of her energy, sending it to me, only for me to release it again. The cycle repeated over and over until the energy from the composition I had written had burned itself out, and I released her for the last time.

Elsie put her hand to her head. "I don't know what that was, but it was the strangest sensation. And I feel exhausted suddenly."

I winced again. "Sorry, that was poor planning on my part. But your mind is your own again at least."

She looked around the room in dismay. "Look what I did!" she wailed.

"Look what I made you do, you mean." I moved to stand in front of her. "You aren't responsible for your actions while you were under my control."

She wrinkled her nose. "It was the strangest thing. I was utterly convinced the room was disgustingly tidy and that I needed to create chaos. Why didn't I recognize the strangeness of the thought? I always keep your room completely tidy."

"That's part of the working," I said. "It separates out your thoughts and hides the inconsistencies. It's an incredibly powerful ability, and you would need to be shocked with something much more central to your core beliefs and emotions than the tidiness of a room to have any hope of breaking free on your own."

"Then it's lucky we have you," she said, ignoring the part

where I was the one who had worked the composition on her in the first place.

I worried my lip between my teeth. "But that's just the problem, isn't it? All those poor people under Conall's control don't have me to free them. They're helpless. And many of them probably don't even know they've been captured yet."

"You'll find a way," Elsie said, the complete faith in her voice overwhelming me.

I was a fourth year Academy trainee stuck in a remote region of Kallorway. How could I possibly free vast armies of people in the northern Sekali Empire?

The next morning, Bryony wanted to know how I had gone with Elsie. But fourth year had finally broken down the last of the barriers between our year mates, and we usually ate in a big group now, the better to discuss classes and strategies for our next arena battle.

With Dellion on one side and Isabelle across the table, I couldn't answer any of Bryony's questions, no matter how quietly she tried to whisper them. I could see in Darius's eyes that she wasn't the only one wanting answers, but since the fourth years had been assigned to the arena that morning, I couldn't take them aside to discuss it. Instead I resolved they would have to wait until we had a proper chance to talk in the evening.

When I finally slipped into Darius's suite after the evening meal, I found Bryony already there, hotly debating something with Jareth. But as soon as she saw me, she broke off and demanded I give them a proper update.

I described everything from the evening before, and after a short discussion—in which Darius was pleased there had been no barrier to my connecting with a commonborn—he asked if he should have the guards bring in Tyron.

"Were you needing to study him further?" Darius's voice made it clear he hoped I had already wrung all the information from the energy mage that I could.

I frowned. "I don't know how much more I can learn by connecting to him, if that's what you mean. But I need to talk to him. I have some questions."

"Questions?" Bryony wrinkled her nose. "I thought there was no way for him to hide any part of his ability from you when you connect with him."

"There isn't. I now have a good understanding of the limits of his ability and how exactly he controls his victims. But his ability isn't identical to his father's, remember. And I haven't had a chance to connect with Conall. There might be crucial differences in how they operate, and Tyron is the one most likely to know about those differences."

Darius and Jareth exchanged a glance.

"I'll go and fetch him and the guards." Jareth turned to leave the sitting room, but I called after him.

"Maybe leave the guards behind this time? We don't know what he's going to say."

Jareth sent a questioning look at Darius, but he nodded his agreement, and Jareth left the room.

"I'll put a truth composition on him," Darius said without my having to ask.

"Thank you." I hadn't liked to demand he use such a complex composition, but neither did I want to trust anything Tyron might say without one.

When Tyron came into the room and saw Darius standing ready with the parchment in his hand, a curious look came over his face.

"What's that for?" he asked.

Darius stiffened, so I jumped in to answer for him. This would be easier if we didn't antagonize Tyron. "It's a truth composition. I have some questions for you."

Tyron met my eyes for a moment, a strangely solemn look on his face. "You don't need to use that. I'll answer your questions."

"I'm sure you'll understand why we're not willing to take you at your word." I kept my voice calm.

Tyron shrugged. "Suit yourself. I suppose when you're king-elect, you have an endless number of compositions."

"Not endless," Darius said. "But enough."

Tyron sat on his usual sofa and spread his arms wide. "Well, then. What are these questions?"

I slowly sat down opposite him, waiting until Darius had ripped the truth composition and a golden glow had appeared above the torn strips of parchment. I focused my attention on Tyron's face, leaving it to Darius and the others to watch for the glow to turn a poisonous black if Tyron lied.

"Is it a relief?" I asked. "Even a little bit? To be free of it."

Out of the corner of my eye I saw all three of the others frowning at me, but I ignored them.

Tyron looked thoughtful, taking a moment to consider the question.

"Yes," he said at last. "I haven't been alone in my own head since I turned sixteen. It's…peaceful."

He leaned forward suddenly. "You ask that like you know, Verene. Am I right then? About your ability? I've had a great deal of time to think about what it might be, and—"

"Verene asks the questions," Jareth barked, stepping forward with tense muscles, the threat palpable.

"And she's Princess Verene to you," Darius added, his icy tone and face somehow even more unnerving than Jareth's more overt reaction.

Tyron shrugged and sat back.

I cleared my throat and continued. "I want to understand more about how your father's ability works. How could he possibly hold on to the energy of so many and for so many years? The enormity of it, the discomfort…" I shivered. "Your mind and energy always at war. So many always trying to break free. Never a moment of peace. It couldn't be borne."

"My father is strong," Tyron said, and my eyes flew back to his.

I had heard him make such statements before, but always with a tone of pride. This time he sounded more thoughtful—almost weary.

"But it's also the difference in how his ability works," Tyron continued. "He takes only the tiniest sliver of energy, not the chunks that I must steal."

I nodded slowly. I had seen the difference in the minds of Matthis and then Jareth. The size of the missing energy was what made it easy to miss at a cursory inspection.

"But still, so many people," I said.

Tyron frowned. "Time is also a factor. The longer he holds the energy, the more it blends with his own."

"You mean he gets to keep it permanently?" Bryony asked, disgust in her voice. "It increases his energy stores?"

Tyron shook his head. "No, not like that. It's not energy he can use. It's just that it becomes used to him, blended with his own energy to the extent that it stops fighting him, it stops trying to get free. There's a reason his plan has moved so slowly. He can't gather too many people all at once. To hold so many people, he has needed to spread his efforts out over years. Many said it couldn't be done, but my father is nothing if not determined."

I rubbed the side of my head. I had been afraid of something like that. Having experienced the pull and tug of it for myself, I had concluded it would be impossible for someone to hold even the smallest sliver of energy from thousands of people. At least, not without an effect such as Tyron was describing.

But if the energy blended with Conall in such a way, then I could only imagine what happened to the controlling thoughts he had bound within it. And the energy stopped fighting to be free, he said. That was the bit that truly scared me.

I held Tyron's eyes with mine, wanting to read every nuance of his expression as I asked my next question. "So he no longer has to consciously maintain his control? That tiny segment of their energy is…permanently tainted?"

Tyron shrugged. "I suppose you could describe it that way."

"Has he ever let someone free?" I asked.

Tyron frowned. "In training exercises, he has. He was the one to train me after I turned sixteen. But other than that?" He paused. "I don't know. Possibly not. He isn't the sort to let go."

I swallowed, massaging my temples again. But when I looked back at Tyron, I paused.

"He has no more hold on you, Tyron. I've examined every cranny of your energy, and you are free of his control."

A strange look came over Tyron's face, but he replied coldly. "Why would he need to control me? I'm his son."

And yet, I thought, *here you are, freely answering my questions.*

I looked up at Darius. "Was all of that the truth?"

Reluctantly, Darius nodded.

"As he knows and understands it," Jareth added quickly. He glared at Tyron although he continued to speak to me. "If you're finished, I'm sure Tyron is feeling ready to retire for the night." He pointed at the door that led to Tyron's bedchamber.

Tyron looked at me with a raised eyebrow, and I forced a vague approximation of a smile.

"Thank you for answering my questions. I think I have enough information for now."

Tyron stood in a single, fluid movement and disappeared through the door without a further word.

"Why are you being so kind to him?" Bryony put her hands on her hips. "Thanking him? Really?"

"Because you get more flies with honey," Darius said, although he didn't sound like he liked the necessity. "She's being smart instead of emotional."

Bryony rolled her eyes but didn't argue.

I looked around at them all, realizing from their calm that I was the only one to have grasped the significance of my line of questioning.

"Never mind that," I said. "What are we going to do about the fact that we can't kill Conall?"

CHAPTER 12

"Of course we're going to kill Conall!" Jareth's hand moved to his sword hilt, as if he meant to stab the Tarxi warlord on the spot.

Darius, however, watched me with concern in his eyes. "What do you mean?"

"If Tyron is right, then we can't afford to kill him."

Bryony frowned. "I thought that's what Kallorway, Ardann, and the Empire have been trying to do all summer—find a way to get through those armies he hides behind and kill him. Without killing the armies," she added as an afterthought.

"As far as I know that's exactly what they've been trying to work out how to do." I looked to Darius for confirmation, and he nodded. "But we can't let them do it."

"Why not?" Darius asked. "We can't let him continue on unchecked."

"No, we need to stop him," I agreed. "We may even need to kill him in the end—I can't imagine how warped his mind must be after using his ability for so long. But we can't kill him until we've freed all the people he's entrapped."

A slight crease appeared in Darius's forehead, and I could

almost see him running back through the whole conversation with Tyron.

"You think if we kill him, it won't free their minds from his influence," he said slowly.

"Maybe his most recent captures," I said. "But not the majority."

All three of them looked horrified.

"But surely when he dies, all of the energy he's stolen will return to the true owners?" Bryony asked. "There would be no reason for it to die with him since it isn't truly a part of him."

"To be honest, it would be easier if it did," I said. "Clearly those people can live without that small piece of energy. But I believe you're right—their energy will return to them."

"So what's the problem?" she asked.

"Verene believes that it will return to them, but it will still be tainted by Conall's control," Darius said. "That he's held it for so long, that it no longer needs any active link to him to be maintained. Which means he can keep controlling them past his death."

Bryony made no reply, looking slightly ill.

"But what else can we do?" Jareth asked. "We have to kill him."

I drew a deep breath, not looking at Darius. "First we have to go in and free their minds. We have to actively undo his working before releasing it. Then we deal with Conall himself."

"But there's only one person who can take charge of those workings and dismantle them from within," Darius said in an awful voice. "You."

"Yes." I nodded. "Unfortunately, that's true."

That wasn't the end of the matter, of course. Bryony argued almost as passionately as Darius that I was mad to think of going after Conall myself. Only Jareth watched the debate silently, a thoughtful expression on his face.

"I have no more desire than anyone to see Verene in danger," he said at last. "But she has a point. And we might not have a choice. If killing Conall will lock in his commands permanently, then it's the last thing we can afford to do. We would end up forced to massacre all those innocent people. And those of our own troops to survive would come home with the kind of mental scars that never go away."

"So you just want to sacrifice Verene instead?" Darius asked, his voice tight.

"No, of course not." Jareth held his ground against his brother. "We're not talking about sending her off alone and unequipped to go wandering around the Empire in the hopes she stumbles over Conall. All she's saying is that we need to pivot our strategy. And that she can't be left out of it—as much as we would all like her to be." He grimaced. "And we're not going to be the only ones who wish she didn't have to be involved."

I winced. He was right. I could easily imagine my parents' reaction to the suggestion that I should physically lead the search for Conall. But there was no other option. He had already taken control of too many people for me to free them all individually.

"You're right," I said. "Which is why we have to be in agreement if we're to have any hope of bringing Ardann on board with this plan. We need the Spoken Mage fighting on our side. And since she just happens to be my mother, that means we have to convince her that this is the only way."

Darius held my gaze for a long moment, neither of us speaking. I tried to convey to him the strength of my conviction, and something in my face must have convinced him because he deflated slightly, his tense muscles relaxing.

"So what exactly is your plan?" he asked.

Bryony threw herself onto a sofa. "That we storm the Tarxi

stronghold, I suppose." She looked in my direction. "Or were you thinking of a stealth approach?"

"We?" I asked with some alarm.

"Of course." She sounded matter-of-fact. "If you're going, so are we." She glanced between the princes. "Or, well, I am, at least. I suppose Kallorway might not be so enthusiastic about their king-elect charging off into battle. Or his heir either."

Darius opened his mouth, and I could read his hot refute on his face, but slowly his expression changed, and he closed it again without speaking. Crowns carried chains as well as privilege.

I considered arguing that Bryony couldn't come either but decided it would be a futile effort. And probably unnecessary, anyway. If the three crowns agreed I must go, then they would no doubt insist on choosing who accompanied me. And I doubted an Academy trainee would make their list.

"The moment it comes to open conflict, some of our element of surprise is gone," I said. "But not all of it. Conall won't know how far our knowledge extends, and he certainly won't know we have a way to counter his ability. So I think we need to use that advantage. We send our armies as a distraction while a small group attempts to infiltrate his front lines and find him. If I can get close enough to reverse his workings and free his army, the entire war will end immediately. And with our armies in the field, it will be easy for our forces to defeat the few who are truly loyal to him—regardless of their abilities."

"So we just have to get you close," Darius said slowly.

I nodded. "I'm not suggesting I duel Conall to the death or anything. I'm more than happy to leave that sort of thing to those better equipped for it. If we manage it well, he won't even have to know we're there until after I connect with him."

"That doesn't mean getting you close is going to be easy," Jareth said, his tone regretful. "There will still be danger."

"I know." I met his look with a steady one of my own. "And I'm willing to accept that danger given the severity of the threat.

How could I do anything else?" I bit my lip. "It may sound foolish, but it feels like I was given my ability for this purpose. No one else can do this but me. I wanted to have power, and I wanted to use it to help and protect the people I love. I'll never get a better chance than this."

"But only if we can convince Ardann and the Sekalis," Darius said. "Not to mention my own Mage Council."

Bryony bounced back up off the sofa. "She just convinced you, didn't she? We'll convince them."

I grimaced. "Maybe. But remember Darius is familiar with my ability, and he trusts me. That can't be said for everyone else on that list. How many of them are going to be excited about giving that level of responsibility to a nineteen-year-old girl?"

"So we make it convincing," Jareth said grimly.

Darius stepped closer to me, dropping his voice lower. "Are you sure you're ready for this, Verene? It will mean a lot of people finding out about your ability."

I looked up at him. "I've survived more than three years at the Academy of my kingdom's traditional enemies, with constant assassination attempts, attacks, and killer storms. I think I've been preparing for this since I was sixteen, even if I didn't know it. I've grown stronger than I ever thought I could be. I'm ready to be open about who I really am."

"I wish there was another way," he said.

"So do I." I sighed. "It's not as if I relish the prospect of facing Conall. But at the same time, it's something I have to do. I can feel that down to my bones."

For another moment his eyes weighed me, and then he gave a decisive nod. "Then we convince them all, we defeat Conall, and we bring you home. Whatever it takes."

"Hear, hear to that," Bryony said.

~

We all agreed it wasn't the sort of plan Darius could pass on through a communication composition. He would need the chance to argue our case in person to the various representatives. And they would almost certainly want to talk to me as well—and likely see a demonstration of my ability. Which meant we needed them at the Academy.

We debated at length about how to bring them to us without raising suspicions that might make it back to Conall. In fact, we debated far longer over the issue than we had over the idea of sending me after Conall in the first place.

While we debated, the weather turned. Winter had truly taken hold, making the frequent battles in the arena even less pleasant than usual. None of us suggested halting them, though.

Somehow my new personal stake in the situation made them feel all the more important. The longer I took to find Conall and dismantle his workings, the longer our armies would need to hold off his army—preferably without either massacring them or being massacred themselves. Every strategy that might help them achieve that goal had become even more valuable in my eyes.

However, Darius no longer always took part. He claimed he didn't want his strength to unbalance the exercises, but his absence also gave him time to meet with Duke Francis and communicate with his Council.

Sometimes Jareth stepped up to take his leadership role among the trainees, but other times it was Dellion.

"You might have missed your calling," I told her one day after she led us to a particularly resounding victory.

We stood on the sidelines of the arena, watching the soldiers pick themselves up from the pile we had made of their bound bodies, some of them groaning and rubbing at various bruises.

"What?" She cocked her head with its regal crown of braided hair. "You mean join the Armed Forces? And wear black all day while tromping around battlefields and sleeping in a tent?" She gave an exaggerated shudder. "Hardly. I have bigger plans."

"My mistake," I said solemnly.

She looked sideways at me and laughed. "Admit it, Verene, you don't find the thought any more appealing than I do."

I broke into a grin. "Well, when you put it like that, I most definitely don't. My only surprise is that Royce picked the Armed Forces."

My eyes dwelt on him thoughtfully. He had become almost friendly toward Darius since he had begun his campaign to win Royce over. And it hadn't escaped me that Dellion had followed Darius's lead—giving Royce an important role in the battle she had just led.

Dellion laughed again. "Royce lacks foresight. Among other things. He'll realize his mistake at some point, and I shan't feel the least sorry for him when he does."

I glanced at her in surprise. Her words belied her behavior toward him during the bout.

She saw my expression and rolled her eyes. "Royce always believed in his own importance far more than it deserved. When King Cassius lost power, Royce's father also lost the last of the power he was clinging to. And our own dear Royce couldn't handle that loss. At least not with any grace. But I'm no simpleton. I can see the way everyone in our year adores Darius—and more and more of the kingdom seem to be joining them. And I can see the effort Darius is making with Royce. I may not understand why he thinks Royce's opinion is important, but I'm willing to take it on faith that it is."

She shrugged. "If the king needs Royce's support, then maybe it behooves me to ensure I'm not on the outer myself. With either of them."

I couldn't help one of my eyebrows raising slightly and was surprised when Dellion responded to it with a grin.

"Oh, you don't have to say it out loud, I know what you're thinking. You think I'm not so different from Royce—that I have a strong belief in my own importance, too. The difference is I've never sat back and expected it as my due. I'll use my connections, it's true, but I also expect to work for it—even if that means breaking away from my family's opinions and pursuing the path I can see leads to the future." She wrinkled her nose. "Even if that path includes Royce."

I nodded slowly. I couldn't dispute anything she'd said.

She shifted slightly, looking out across the arena. "And don't think I'm unaware there's something going on I don't know about—something big. And that the five of you are at the heart of it." She grimaced. "Back in first year, that would have infuriated me. But now..." She shrugged. "Call it age or wisdom, but I'm starting to realize there are some headaches it's not an advantage to be part of."

I sighed. "You have that right," I murmured.

She fixed me with another piercing look. "But I still believe you and Darius are the future for Kallorway, Verene. So if you need me, I hope you know I'm here for you."

I blinked, but she merely waved a lazy hand and sauntered away. That had felt and sounded like an offer of friendship and support—if I overlooked the fact she had stated quite openly that her goal was her own advancement. I shook my head, a slow smile spreading across my face. In the world of court and politics, there was something to be said for someone who was open about their motivations and intentions. And if Dellion believed allying with us was her best path forward, I was more than willing to accept her assistance, even if it didn't have the value of Bryony's true loyalty.

The next day, Darius informed us all at breakfast that he would be missing some more lessons in the coming days due to preparations for his coronation.

"As you all know," he said, "the Mage Council has decreed it take place immediately following graduation. So we will graduate as normal here at the Academy, with our friends and family in attendance, and then proceed as a group to the capital for the coronation and surrounding celebrations. You are all invited to attend, of course."

"Ooh, yes please," Ashlyn said. "I'll be there."

"As will I, and my family." Isabelle surprised me with her prompt response, but I was glad for it.

Obviously the summer break had done nothing to destroy the new opinion Isabelle's family held about the court. I just hoped Darius's assistance with the harvest had resulted in an equally sustained change of heart across the whole farming region of the kingdom.

"I'll check my schedule," Jareth said in a serious tone. "But if I can possibly squeeze it in, I will."

Ashlyn and Frida both laughed while Bryony rolled her eyes. I joined in the chuckles, though. This was the plan we had come up with to get the relevant officials to the Academy, and I wanted to help sell it as a normal and natural thing.

"I'm not surprised they want to start preparing and organizing now," Dellion said. "It will be the largest ceremony and festivities we've had in Kallorway in years. Adding in the graduation ceremony here first complicates planning enormously."

I couldn't help looking at her with faint surprise. She hadn't been involved with any of our conversations, but we could have scripted her words, they were so perfect. She gave me a faint return smile that only increased my curiosity. She had claimed she wanted no part of the headache we were dealing with, but it almost seemed as if she realized we were hiding something and was trying to help.

"Who do you have handling planning at the capital?" she asked Darius.

He gave her a name I didn't recognize, and she responded with a satisfied nod. "He's more than capable and won't forget any of the important details. And, of course, Zora will oversee the graduation ceremony, so we need have no fears there. I don't think the woman has ever mismanaged a job in her life."

"No, I have no hesitations where Zora is concerned," Darius agreed. "But the entire Mage Council as well as a number of other officials will be involved in the coronation, and of course they all want to meet with me in person to discuss the importance of their role." He sighed like it was an imposition.

The conversation continued for a few minutes with talk moving to graduation and life afterward. Even those with close relatives as discipline heads seemed to feel some uncertainty about what life in their chosen disciplines would really be like.

As the talk flowed around us, Darius met my eyes and smiled. I smiled back, buoyed by our year mates' ready acceptance of our ploy. But a moment later my mood crashed. The first stage of our plan had been successfully implemented, but every stage from now on would only get harder. And I knew I was fixated on convincing the various delegates only because I was avoiding thinking about what would come after we won their agreement.

Because while I might be the only mage with the ability to stop Conall, I felt far from ready to face him—let alone find a way into the heart of the Sekali Empire to do it.

CHAPTER 13

*a*shlyn was cheerful the next day, informing us all that her mother was coming to visit the Academy. I took this information in stride, Darius having already told me that Duchess Ashten was to be among the first of the summoned officials to arrive.

I didn't see the Head of the Wind Workers until three days later, however. Intent on taking advantage of an unusually sunny rest day, I exited the Academy building to the sight of a carriage being led away by two grooms. Instantly all thoughts of relaxing in the sun fled my mind, tension taking their place. After so long keeping my abilities a secret, it still felt wrong to think of openly sharing them with so many. But I knew it had to be done.

I considered turning back into the Academy but forced myself to continue on toward the gardens. The duchess would want to visit her daughter first and recover from the travel. I wouldn't be needed immediately. And I still wanted a glimpse of the exercises being undertaken by the current group of soldiers residing at the Academy.

When trainees were involved, all combat exercises had to be done inside the safe enclosure of the arena. Since we were still learning, our compositions couldn't be trusted. But on our rest day, the officers often took the chance to have their forces train outside the Academy walls. Today, I had heard they intended to take advantage of the different terrain of the training yards and gardens, and I was curious to see how they trained when we weren't involved.

I didn't make it far from the courtyard, however, before the quiet murmur of voices caught my attention. I would have passed them by if the sound of my own name hadn't reached me. A moment later I recognized the voice.

Royce.

"Verene is dangerous," he was saying.

"Dangerous?" Dellion's lazy tones made me slow. Who exactly was gathered out here, talking about me in such terms?

"Yes." Royce sounded defensive. "She's dangerous because she's so weak. Darius has my full support, but now, more than ever, Kallorway needs strength not weakness. We cannot afford for our king to be shackled to a powerless Ardannian." He said it like the words were the greatest insult he could imagine.

"The general believes…" My mind froze at the next voice, not catching the rest of the sentence.

Royce was talking to Duchess Ashten. This wasn't idle talk among the trainees. Royce had the temerity to attempt to poison the Mage Council against me.

Had he been lurking at the Academy windows, waiting for her arrival, ready to hurry out and intercept her? He must have known he was unlikely to have a chance for such a conversation once she had made it inside the building.

Anger filled me, eliminating the last of my nerves. Instead of Royce's voice, I heard the voices of my childhood—whispers behind hands and around corners, veiled insults and mocking turns of phrase.

For nearly four years Royce had insulted and derided me, but he had finally gone too far. I was no longer the unwanted princess, an embarrassment to her family line. And I was done hiding my true self. I would be an asset to Darius's rule, and it was time his court knew it.

"Do you really think her so weak, Royce?" Dellion asked, her tone impossible to read.

"Of course I do," he scoffed. "She may have powerful parents, but Verene herself is utterly useless. Can we risk her future children being equally so?"

I stepped around the bushes that kept Royce and his companions out of sight. Several audible breaths sounded at my appearance, and vaguely I took in that the group included not only Dellion, but also Duke Gilbert, the impressive young Head of Law Enforcement. But most of my attention was focused on Royce.

He paled at sight of me, glancing uneasily at his companions.

"You were saying?" I asked in my iciest voice.

For a second, no one so much as breathed, everyone waiting to see how Royce would respond. I could see the war in his eyes. He could back down and apologize, giving the lie to his own words about my weakness and lack of importance, but everything in him rebelled at the idea. What was it Dellion had said? He had never been able to let go of the idea of his own importance.

I could see the moment he decided to stand by his words, his back straightening. He met my eyes defiantly.

"I only want what's best for my king and my kingdom. And that's not you. I won't apologize for being the only one willing to say what we all know is true."

For a brief moment a pang of sadness shot through me. I knew in that moment he believed his own words. He couldn't see how it was his own arrogance and pride that drove him. He had always seen himself in far brighter hues than he truly deserved. He was the hero of his own story, and no matter how badly he behaved, he wouldn't be convinced otherwise.

"You're wrong, Royce," I said.

But something of my sadness for his warped thinking must have sounded in my voice. He seemed to swell a little, buoyed by my apparent weakness.

Before I could set him straight, shouts interrupted us. A soldier crashed through a nearby clump of bushes, several other soldiers in close pursuit.

The soldier nearest us pulled out a composition and ripped it, a shield springing to life around him. One of those chasing him also pulled out a parchment. Both of them had the elaborate pattern around their necks that marked them as sealed, and I wasn't the only one in our group distracted by their conflict.

Although it hadn't been widely publicized, Darius had just enacted an emergency edict allowing sealed commonborns to use compositions. And this was all of our first opportunity to see the new law put into effect by the Armed Forces.

The attacking soldier withdrew a second composition without having yet ripped the first, and the pursued soldier glanced back at him in concern. He dodged, running in our direction and swerving at the last moment to dive into a denser bush to one side of our group.

His attacker ripped both compositions, and a rush of power swept toward the hidden soldier. We all continued to watch, our conversation suspended. But out of the corner of my eye, I could see Royce's focus was still on me. Just as I swung back around to look at him, he staggered, stumbling into me and knocking me into the path of the oncoming attack compositions.

My earlier anger whipped into fury. Royce had no way to know what those compositions were crafted to do. He knew only that they were likely to stop short of killing. With only the thinnest pretense of an accident, he was attempting to humiliate and demean me in front of two members of the Mage Council.

Duke Gilbert shouted a warning and lunged forward, pushing me out of the way and placing himself in the path of the attack instead. Royce called a horrified protest as the first of the compositions hit the duke. I could feel its intent—to disarm through pain—but fortunately the duke was shielded. The composition was a powerful one, however, and it left his shield insubstantial and weak.

Unheeding of our drama, the soldier erupted from the other side of the bush and took off across the garden. With a shout, the other soldiers followed, not having noticed who it was who had intruded on their field of combat.

Before any of us could speak, the second composition hit the duke. It broke through his shield, and invisible bonds wrapped around his hands and feet.

I shouted, "Take control," just as he toppled to the ground.

"Go to Royce," I said, redirecting the power toward the person who had set it on the duke. The binding composition left Gilbert to race toward Royce instead.

"I don't know what you're playing at," Royce said, sounding less confident than before, "but I'm shielded."

At some point during my distraction, driven by some instinct for danger, he had worked a shield composition. He had attempted to thrust me into unknown danger while hiding from any possibility of harm himself.

"Take control." I let the fury sound in my voice.

I seized his shield and directed it toward the duke, righting the last of Royce's wrongs by replacing the one the duke had just lost. The power streamed across the small gap between them and wrapped around him, just as he climbed back to his feet.

As soon as Royce's protection disappeared, the binding composition—which had not yet exhausted its power beating against his shield—hit him with its remaining force. He shouted a disbelieving protest and fell to the ground, his hands and feet clamped together as if tied with invisible rope.

Fortunately for him, the composition had little power left and quickly burned out. He scrambled back to his feet and stood staring at me.

I stepped toward him, not breaking eye contact.

"Do you still believe I would weaken Kallorway, Royce?"

He shook slightly, fear in his eyes. "How…how did you do that?"

"Not everything is always as it appears," I said. "You should know that by now."

Duke Gilbert audibly swallowed, reminding me we had an audience.

"You took his shield," he said. "And you gave it to me."

I nodded without looking away from Royce.

"You took his shield," the duke repeated. "How did you do that? No one can do that. And you did it with a spoken composition."

In my peripheral vision, I saw him exchange a shaken look with Duchess Ashten.

"You have power after all," she said. "Power like your mother's."

"No," Gilbert said quickly. "That wasn't like the Spoken Mage. She could break through a shield easily enough, but not steal it."

"Verene can't steal a shield," Royce said, but his voice wobbled. "No one can do that."

"And yet," Dellion drawled, "she just did."

I finally looked away from Royce to glance at my other year mate. She regarded me with shock lurking in her eyes. But she didn't allow it to shake her voice. "I knew there was something going on with you, Princess."

"You took his shield and gave it to me," the duke repeated for the third time.

"You keep saying that," Royce snapped, finally losing the last of his calm.

"Yes, Cousin," Gilbert said in a stern tone.

I raised an eyebrow. I hadn't realized they were related. It must be a distant connection, or Royce would have boasted about it. But it went some way toward explaining Royce's outrageous audacity in chasing down two members of the Mage Council and attempting to turn them against me.

"I don't think you understand what it means," the duke continued. "It appears Princess Verene has a new ability we haven't yet encountered. And if it can steal a shield, then I don't see how anything can stop it. Such a power would make the wielder not just powerful but literally unbeatable."

I flushed. Trust the Head of Law Enforcement to leap straight to that aspect of my ability.

"How extremely fortunate for us." Duchess Ashten was watching me with a greedy, hopeful light in her eyes. "Since we are in desperate need of saving."

"Stop right there." Dellion put up her hand. "Royce and I do not need to hear whatever is behind that statement."

I raised an eyebrow at her, but she just shrugged. Apparently she had actually meant her words about wanting no part of what we were involved in.

I nodded. "You're right, you don't." I looked back at Royce. "Obviously Their Graces will receive a complete explanation from Darius himself. That's why they've been summoned here. But why are you here, Royce?"

"I…I didn't know. I still don't understand."

"Oh come, Cousin," Duke Gilbert said with impatience. "The princess has an ability she hasn't yet made public. It doesn't take great intelligence to understand that much."

I stepped toward Royce. "You said you care about the good of our kingdom. Can you believe me—can you believe your cousin here—when we tell you there is a great danger to Kallorway and all of us? You may not understand, but can you keep what you just saw to yourself?"

I held out my hand. He eyed it, hesitating. I knew him well enough to know he had no desire to take it. But neither was he a traitor. And with Duke Gilbert and Duchess Ashten watching, he couldn't declare himself one by refusing my overture.

Sullenly, he reached out his own hand and clasped mine. With a glance at his cousin, he bowed quickly over it before letting it fall.

"That is gracious, Your Highness." Duke Gilbert gave me a deeper bow. "And on behalf of my graceless young relative, I offer my apologies and my gratitude for your forbearance."

"Come," the duchess said, impatience in the word. "Let us return to the Academy. I want to hear this promised explanation."

I hesitated, my eyes still on Royce. I believed in his new loyalty to Darius, but I had read his hatred for me in his eyes. I had done what I had to when I forced him to recognize my strength, but he would never forgive me for it.

Dellion stepped up beside me. "Don't worry," she said quietly. "I only came out here because I thought someone had better find out what Royce was up to creeping around. I'll talk to him and make sure he knows exactly what will happen if he ever breathes a word about any of this to anyone." A hint of amusement entered her eyes. "Somehow I don't imagine this is a story he'll be eager to tell, anyway."

I nodded my thanks and turned to go, the duke and duchess keeping pace beside me. I had grown up watching my aunt, and I knew that no queen could win everyone over. With some people, all you could do was teach them to respect the power you wielded.

After that, it seemed as if the stream of officials arriving at the Academy was never-ending. They came alone or in twos and threes, and all of them began by meeting with Darius. But all of them finished by wanting to meet with me.

Or, at least, the ones who came because of Conall did. A few had legitimately been invited to discuss the logistics of the coronation, but most had bigger worries.

Darius didn't agree for all of them to meet with me, and at first I worried he was once again trying unnecessarily to protect me, especially after the confrontation in the gardens. But when I challenged him on it, he denied it.

"I don't doubt you, Verene. But while I have a reason to stay locked away in meetings, you don't. And if you were meeting with everyone who came here, someone would be bound to eventually notice."

Somewhat sheepishly I admitted that made sense.

"It's more than that, as well," he added. "I have a delicate balance to strike here. For certain people—those important enough and influential enough—it's crucial we ensure their full support through an open demonstration. But with others..."

"You need to reinforce your authority by requiring them to take your word for it," I finished for him. "That makes sense. I'm sorry I doubted you."

He shook his head. "No, never apologize for questioning me. I need people around me who I trust and who will call me out if they see me making choices that don't make sense. No one is infallible—least of all me."

"Are any of them angry with Ardann?" I asked. "Do they believe that I came here not knowing about my ability?"

He gave me the ghost of a smile. "If they don't believe it, they would hardly dare say as much to me. Not when I have just told them that I watched you discover your ability myself." He hesitated. "If anything, I think they're impressed to hear I knew of it before your own family."

I nodded, hiding my dismay. When he put it like that, it seemed clear it would be the Ardannian officials and not the Kallorwegian ones who would have reason for anger and offense.

There was nothing I could do about that, however. It would take time for my aunt to send an official of her own, and in the meantime, the Kallorwegians kept coming.

After the unexpected exhibition in the garden, demonstrating my ability no longer felt strange. In fact, the whole process became almost routine.

Darius would have the visitor work a simple composition that I would then seize control of and twist in some visible way. After that, he would have me connect with them and produce the composition myself. There were always questions, of course, but I kept my responses as basic as possible. These were smart men and women, and they would no doubt work out the various ramifications of such an ability for themselves—but not all of them grasped my strength as quickly as Duke Gilbert had done, and I felt no responsibility to point it out to them.

By the time everyone on the Kallorwegian Mage Council had seen me perform, Darius had their full support for his proposed strategy for tackling Conall. Only General Haddon asked to question Tyron to confirm my theory about the consequences of killing Conall.

I assumed it was a power play on his part since he and Darius had yet to mend relations between them. But when I mentioned it to Bryony, she shook her head.

"Not according to Jareth." She gave me a sideways look that made me uneasy.

"Well, out with it, then. How does Jareth interpret his grandfather's suspicion?"

"Apparently there's one consequence of your demonstrations that we should have foreseen but that Darius seems determined not to mention to you."

My brow lowered. "And what's that?"

"Every single member of the Mage Council is now joined with the old general on one matter, at least. They're all pressuring Darius to secure a marriage alliance with you as soon as possible. If the general thought you were a valuable consort before, he's practically foaming at the mouth to get you now. Jareth says that wasn't mistrust of Darius that prompted the general's interrogation but due diligence as the Head of the Royal Guard. He's already thinking of you as one of his charges, and he doesn't want to send you into danger unnecessarily."

I almost choked, spluttering for a moment as I stared at her. "General Haddon questioned Tyron because he wants to protect me?" I shook my head. "My goodness, how everything has changed."

"It's good and bad news for Darius," Bryony said. "Basically depending on whether he comes to his senses and proposes to you or not. If he does, it sounds like any remaining opposition to his rule will disappear. As a couple—given your powers, as well as your connections to Ardann—you're just too powerful. Even the general is starting to view a King Darius reign differently,

Jareth tells me. But if Darius doesn't propose, he'll find the general isn't the only one questioning his readiness to rule."

I groaned. "I don't want to cause Darius trouble. But neither do I want him to marry me because his Mage Council forced him into it."

"Whyever not?" Bryony asked. "You know he loves you and is only hesitating due to noble—but misguided—principles. If I was in your place, I'd be cheering the Mage Council on."

My laugh turned into another despairing groan. "Somehow I believe that is completely true. But it's not me. Maybe it's because my whole life has been so dominated by court and intrigue and politics. I want this one thing to be different."

She sighed. "In that case, we'll just have to hope that either Darius or your parents come to their senses."

My aunt sent Captain Matthis as Ardann's representative. Darius invited me to participate in the entire meeting, saying it made sense that an official from Ardann might be here to see me as well as him. When Darius finished his explanation of my ability, Matthis didn't ask for a demonstration, saying he'd already had one—he just understood what had happened better now. He did, however, have a great many questions about our proposed plan.

I didn't know the captain well, but I could still read his face.

"You think the plan is solid and might be our only hope," I said quietly. "But you're not sure you can convince my parents to accept it."

He looked at me and grimaced. "I'm a soldier, Your Highness, not a politician. But I do know your parents." He sighed. "I expect Her Majesty will see the wisdom of the proposal." He held up a hand. "I'm not saying she'll like it, but I think she'll accept it. But this is a difficult situation. I don't see how we have any chance of holding back that army without a massacre unless we have the Spoken Mage's assistance. She can perform feats no one else has a hope of achieving. And she knows it, too. When it comes to planning, we can't risk going against her wishes. And I don't know if even a direct order from Queen Lucienne would be enough to convince her to agree on this matter…"

I winced. Causing political turmoil in Ardann and potentially driving a wedge between my parents and my aunt was the last thing I wanted to do.

"I need to talk to my parents myself," I said. "I might be the only one who can convince them that I'm ready for this."

Matthis raised an eyebrow. "With all due respect, Princess Verene…*are* you ready for this?"

I squared my shoulders. "I have to be, don't I?"

He continued to look at me, and I met his eyes firmly.

"Somehow I don't think this is the kind of thing anyone is ever truly ready for," I said. "But my parents were my age when they ended the decades-long war between Kallorway and Ardann. I suspect, if you'd asked my mother at the time, she wouldn't have felt ready for such a task either. But they succeeded. I have to believe I can do the same."

Matthis nodded. "I was around back then. Your mother was always impressive, there's no denying that, but you're right that she was barely more than a child." He grunted. "Not that she ever let that stop her. But maybe she could do with some reminding."

"You can't go to Ardann now, though," Darius said. "Not in the middle of the year. And even if we could come up with a reason for you to need a short visit home, my Mage Council would never consent to you traveling without an extensive guard. Not now they know you might be our only hope of ending this threat without a large-scale disaster. How would we explain you suddenly traveling between kingdoms with a heavy escort of guards?"

"But I need to speak to my parents in person," I said, frustrated. "And Midwinter is coming up. I know I haven't gone home for the holiday in previous years, but maybe—wait! Midwinter! That's our chance!"

"A ball?" Darius asked, instantly grasping my train of thought. "It's a good idea. The Sekali representative has taken our plan back to discuss with the emperor, but if we actually want agreement, we'll need to get someone more senior here. If I host a ball, I'll have an excuse to invite any number of important dignitaries and royals."

Matthis grunted. "Balls aren't my specialty, but I can carry an invitation back to Corrin for you. And while I don't know if you'll get agreement from them, I think your parents will come to speak to you at least."

I nodded. "I know they will, if I ask for them. After all, that's the problem—they care about me too much."

Darius shook his head. "Your parents can't care about you too much. Or at least, I can assure you that the opposite is worse."

I squeezed his hand beneath the table. I wished with all my heart Darius had grown up with at least one loving, involved parent. Sudden insight hit me. Was his own lack—something I could sympathize with but never truly understand—part of the reason he was so insistent we win my parents' approval to our betrothal? He valued what I had even more because he had been denied it.

I sighed. "You're right, of course. I appreciate my parents' love. But that doesn't mean their care can't be dangerously misguided."

"Aye." Matthis levered himself to his feet. "And they wouldn't be the first parents to fall into that trap. But at least they want what's best for you. We can just hope they'll give a little thought to what's best for the rest of us as well."

Zora took the news that she was to organize a formal Midwinter Ball as well as a royal graduation calmly in stride. Elsie informed me the next day that Zora had requested her assistance and asked if I would give her permission to help with the preparations.

"In truth," she admitted, "while you're still a trainee here, there isn't enough work to keep me occupied all the time. Zora has been letting me accompany her at times—mentoring me, I suppose, which is amazingly kind of her. But this would be a more substantial time commitment, so I didn't want to say yes without your agreement."

I gave it gladly, privately pleased that Zora had followed through with my request that she mentor Elsie. It reflected well on her, since Zora had promised only to consider the matter. Obviously Elsie had impressed the older woman.

I regarded Elsie with curiosity. Did she know the truth about Zora and Duke Francis yet? I had been under the impression it was something of an open secret among the servants. Although, given their loyalty, I doubted they would have revealed the information to Elsie when she was newly arrived from Ardann.

If she did know, she gave me no indication of it, merely entering into the Midwinter preparations with enthusiasm. Dellion and Ashlyn showed similar interest, saying that as fourth years and Darius's year mates, we should take some ownership of the event.

Zora accepted their assistance as graciously as ever, allowing them to help with decorations and with corralling the other trainees. I kept expecting to hear word of my parents' acceptance of the invitation, but instead I was alone in my suite one evening when a rush of power swept in to hover in front of me in the shape of a ball.

I barely had time to leap to my feet before my aunt's voice emerged from the communication composition.

"Are you alone?" she asked.

"I am." I wished I could see her face. She must have the report from Matthis by now. Had she called to reprimand me for developing such a plan without first consulting her?

"Your parents aren't happy with your proposal. They fear for you."

"Have you been able to convince them of its necessity?"

"I have instructed them to attend your ball."

I frowned. That wasn't exactly an answer. "Will they speak for Ardann as well as themselves at the talks?"

"Certainly. For the purposes of this matter, they speak with my voice. Convince them, and you have Ardann's full support."

I leaned forward. "I will convince them. This is the only way to victory."

"So you and Darius say. Convince my brother and the Spoken Mage, and you convince me."

I repressed a sigh. I had hoped for more active support from her.

"Very well, Aunt. I look forward to their arrival."

"As I look forward to their report." She hesitated. "Keep safe, Niece."

"And you, Aunt."

The power cut off, but I remained in place, staring at the empty air. That had been…strange.

I had feared her anger, but instead she had been oddly formal. I wasn't even sure of the purpose of her using such a valuable composition. What had she really told me? It had been almost as if…

I slowly sat down on the nearest chair. We had titled each other *aunt* and *niece*, but that hadn't been a conversation between family, like our talk at the ball before fourth year began. That had been the queen of Ardann, calling to make sure Kallorway knew that Ardann presented a united front.

If my aunt was angry that I had proceeded with this plan without her, she was never going to tell me so. A shiver ran up and down my spine. I had come to this Academy as a first year, grateful for the chance to serve my queen and kingdom. And now Queen Lucienne spoke to me as an equal.

My aunt believed I would sit on a throne in Kallmon before long. Did that mean she knew my parents had relented?

If my parents had changed their minds, they were obviously waiting to see us in person to say so. I received no direct communication from them. The silence made it hard to feel excitement at the prospect of their change of heart. I would have to wait until I heard it from their mouths to believe it could be true.

At least Zora reported their official acceptance of our invitation, along with the acceptance of Princess Kalani of the Sekalis.

"She's the sealed princess, isn't she?" Elsie asked one evening in our suite. "Is that an insult from the Sekalis, then?"

Bryony shook her head. "Not at all. She's a highly regarded diplomat. The Sekalis consider her actions in being sealed to bring great honor to her family, not shame."

"I wasn't raised in the Empire like Bree," I said, "but from what I understand, they view their sealed—both mages and commonborns—completely differently from here in Kallorway. Different even from in Ardann. Sealed commonborns in the Empire are even able to win the right to wear robes, like mages. They have a whole branch for them."

Elsie's eyes widened. "It sounds impossible."

"You still sometimes hear Sekalis referring to people from the two kingdoms as southern savages," Bryony said. "Now that the borders are open, opinions are changing. But changes like that take generations. Still, they're slowly realizing that with so many fewer mages, it just isn't possible for you to seal all your commonborns the way they do."

I sighed. "Although they're not wrong it's our own fault that we decimated our mage numbers through pointless wars. But then, those wars happened so many generations ago now that they can hardly hold us directly responsible for our ancestors' foolishness.

"But it is one of the reasons the Empire has had closer relations with Ardann since opening their border than with Kallorway," I added. "They don't approve of Cassius's approach to his sealed population—they consider it uncivilized."

"And they'd be right," Bryony muttered.

I nodded my agreement. "It's something I'm hoping Darius and I can change."

Elsie shook her head. "The Empire sounds like some fairyland."

"Hardly," Bryony said dryly. "It's uncomfortably hot for much of the year, and they have an unfortunate tendency to think everyone should be happy filling the roles the Empire assigns to them. Personally, I prefer a little more individual freedom."

"In short, they're different from Ardann and Kallorway," I said. "In some ways, they seem superior, and in others, they seem foreign and hard to understand. But I can only assume we seem the same to them."

"A diplomat's reply," Bryony said dryly.

"I'd like to go there one day." Elsie sounded a little wistful.

"As my personal servant, I imagine that's within the realm of possibility." As I said the words, a thought crept into my head. It was only the seed of an idea, but I could feel it taking root.

"If Verene doesn't take you, I'll invite you," Bryony said cheerfully. "You can come and visit my family. My parents are a little eccentric, but the Sekalis in general have an amazing sense of hospitality. I think you'll like the Empire."

Given her curiosity, I suggested Elsie join the crowd in the entranceway for the formal welcome of the Imperial Princess. She stood with the group of servants to the left of Darius and Duke Francis, grinning broadly when I caught her eye.

Kalani was a good friend of my Aunt Saffron, and I had met

her several times before when she visited Corrin on diplomatic missions. She looked just the same as always, her golden skin smooth and unlined, and her sleek hair still black and unmarred by even a single strand of gray, although she was at least as old as my parents.

After greeting Darius, Jareth, and Duke Francis, she gave me a warmer smile, and a bow. "It is good to see you again, Princess Verene. I look forward to further conversation between us."

I bowed back and agreed. I knew enough of the reserved Sekali to know her comments represented great interest and curiosity. She had once been the emperor's heir and had been raised to exercise even greater control than my brothers and me.

Darius wasted no time in organizing a demonstration of my ability for her, and even the well-trained princess couldn't keep the gleam of excitement and interest from her eyes when she saw my work for herself.

"My father sees the wisdom in your plan," she told Darius. "But there are many details that must be discussed before a formal agreement can be reached."

Darius inclined his head in her direction. "I look forward to successful discussions. But we must wait for the Ardannians to arrive before we embark upon them."

"Ah, yes, we must not leave the Spoken Mage out of any such conversation," she agreed, and I bit my lip.

In the subtle language of Princess Kalani, that was a warning that the Sekalis would not enter into any agreement that didn't include my mother.

We all gathered again the next day to greet the delegation from Ardann. I saw Elsie slip in to join the crowd as she had done the day before. But this time she didn't look in my direction, her attention riveted on the great gates. I could almost feel her tension despite the crowd between us. I hoped no one else noticed her discomfort at the anticipated sight of my parents or heard her gasp when the Ardannians finally came through the great gates.

But then I followed her gaze and almost gasped myself. I had been expecting my parents, but not my younger brother.

CHAPTER 15

I moved forward to embrace each of my family members, not waiting for them to exchange formal greetings with the duke or Darius first.

"Stellan! What are you doing here?" I asked. "Shouldn't you be back at your own Academy? Are you even on Midwinter break yet?"

"We can discuss this later." My father gave a significant look toward the Kallorwegian officials still waiting to greet the new arrivals.

I nodded and stepped back but could hardly contain my impatience as the formalities were completed. When Zora appeared to show my family to their suites, I trailed behind, pulling Stellan into our parents' sitting room with me.

"Well? What's going on?" I grinned. "Did you miss your big sister too much to stay away?"

It wasn't me he had likely missed, but I couldn't mention Elsie in front of our parents. After Darius had inadvertently revealed my secret to them, I wasn't about to do the same to my brother.

"I'm not just here for Midwinter break," Stellan said, a note of triumph in his voice. "I'm here on an exchange."

"An exchange?" I stared at him.

"A short-term exchange," Mother said in a firm voice.

"But what does that mean?" I asked.

She sighed. "We still haven't been able to secure a full-time energy mage instructor for our own Academy, so Stellan has been without one since the start of the year. When we heard Duke Francis had managed to secure Cooper's services, Stellan asked if he could come here to study under him for a period."

I raised an eyebrow at my brother, my face angled away from our parents. That had been brazen. He just grinned back at me.

"You seem to like it here," he said. "I thought it would be a good opportunity to learn more about our neighbors and new allies."

His face took on a more serious expression. "It seems the time has come for us to put old differences aside, regardless of our individual feelings on the matter."

I sighed and nodded. "I hold on to hope that if any good is to come from this sorry business it is a new beginning between Ardann and Kallorway. And between our kingdoms and the Empire," I added as an afterthought.

"But not at the expense of our daughter," Father said in a hard voice.

I winced.

"I have no intention of sacrificing myself," I said. "But that doesn't mean I'll let other people die just so I don't have to take any risks."

"We don't have to talk about this right now," Mother said. "We could have one pleasant evening together first, surely."

I sighed. "Then you mean to oppose our plan?"

"Verene, it would be incredibly dangerous to send you into the Empire ahead of the army," Father said. "Surely you can understand our hesitation."

"Of course I can. It's not exactly a prospect that excites me either. But that doesn't mean it isn't necessary. You heard everything Matthis reported? You understand why I need to do this?"

My parents exchanged a look.

"Your ability is powerful, Verene, we're not denying that. But there must be another way for you to use it to help the efforts other than charging off into the middle of Conall's army."

"I wouldn't be going alone," I said quickly. "And of course we expect both you and Kalani will want to have input into who makes up my team. Remember I'm not going on some assassination attempt. Stealth will be our main aim, and with any luck we'll be able to keep away from Tarxi notice altogether until after our mission is accomplished."

"Except that on missions such as these, you can never count on luck," Father said grimly.

"Which you would know from experience," Stellan said, unexpectedly coming to my defense. "Since you basically did what you don't want Verene to do—and at the same age."

Our parents exchanged another look, and Mother surprised me by bursting into a low laugh.

"Well, we can't deny that one, Lucas."

"We were driven by desperation," he said.

"And we're not now?" I stared at him, willing him to see the necessity of this plan. "This isn't something I want to do—it's something we all need me to do. You know how important Mother is to everything. If you use her participation as a threat to force them to exclude me, then countless people will die. We can't have those deaths on our heads."

Mother shuddered. When she leaned into Father, he wrapped his arm around her shoulders.

"This isn't what I wanted for my children," she whispered into his shoulder, her voice anguished.

I slumped back onto one of their seats. I knew her well enough to recognize the significance of that tone. My parents understood the situation and the sacrifices that needed to be made. It wasn't me they were fighting, but themselves. And deep inside, the battle had already been won. This was just a brief moment of rebellion, a final chance to deny that they could not stand against a plan that involved their daughter throwing herself into the middle of a looming battle.

I watched them in silence, a second realization settling into my bones. Just as they were too sensible to prevent my inclusion in the fight, they were too loving and reasonable to keep denying their blessing to Darius and me. It might not be today, but eventually they would agree.

My aunt knew them well enough to recognize the same thing. Her new attitude wasn't because they had already relented, but because she knew they eventually would. And I realized suddenly why I had been feeling discomfort instead of joy since my conversation with my aunt.

At the first hint of my parents' agreement, I had found I didn't want their blessing. I certainly hoped they would eventually approve of my marriage, but I didn't want them to be the cause of it. In the same way that I didn't want Darius to marry me because of his Mage Council, I didn't want him to marry me because of my parents, either.

We weren't children any longer, and when we graduated, Darius would rule a kingdom. How could he do that unless he trusted in himself? And how could we have a future together unless he trusted in us?

And, worst of all, how long could I wait for him to realize that before I had no choice but to walk away?

Assuming, of course, I made it back from the Sekali Empire intact. At the start of the year, I had been desperate to win my parents' agreement. Now they seemed like the smallest of the obstacles that stood between the two of us and a life together.

The next morning was Midwinter, but I didn't get to spend the day with my parents. I didn't even spend much of it with my brother.

Darius had my parents, Princess Kalani, General Haddon, and the Head of the Kallorwegian Armed Forces sequestered in a meeting for most of the day, and Stellan commandeered my sitting room so he could spend the day with Elsie.

Bryony burst in on us, insisting on teasing him endlessly on his exchange plan until I eventually had pity on the young couple and dragged her into my bedchamber.

"My parents brought a gown for me from home." I twisted my lips. "You'll be astonished to hear it's red and gold." All of my formal dresses were in the royal colors of Ardann.

Bryony rolled her eyes. "Of course it is. So what are you going to do?" My friend knew I had already commissioned a Midwinter dress of my own.

I bit my lip. "I'm going to wear mine."

She whooped. "Good for you!" Grinning, she added, "Darius is going to love it."

"He'd better," I muttered.

I had designed the gown with him in mind, my choice of color a small act of rebellion. Darius always wore black to formal parties—alleviated only by his golden circlet and his gold and purple sashes. The gown I had ordered was purple—the color a perfect match for both Darius's sash and the purple flowers he sometimes left me as a secret token of love. Combined with the golden embroidery, we would look like a matching pair. Exactly as I had intended.

When I surveyed myself in the mirror that evening, I had to admit to a feeling of satisfaction. The purple suited me, and the gold glints brought out the gold in my eyes.

Given the rebellion of the coloring, I had opted for a simple design. Seeing it now, I was glad of my choice. The fitted bodice and flaring skirt looked regal and classic.

When Bryony bounced into the room in her own gown, she was all smiles. "It's nice to see you in something other than red and gold for once."

I nodded, my earlier doubts gone. "It feels liberating." I paused and smoothed my hand over a thick patch of embroidery. "Although I'm glad it still has gold. I don't want to forget—or reject—my old home. I'm just ready to embrace a new one."

Bryony nodded. "If your parents can't see that tonight, then they're completely blind."

I sighed. "I hope you're right." I hesitated before confessing in a rush. "I don't want to go off into the Sekali Empire, leaving things with Darius as they currently stand. I want to know that if I come back triumphant, I'm coming back to a future with him."

"When," Bryony said sharply. "When we come back triumphant, you mean."

I smiled at her. "Yes, that."

This time she was the one to hesitate. "I wish I could tell you that he would relent tonight. Or that your parents would, but…"

"But you're too honest." My mouth twisted to one side. "I do appreciate that, Bree—much more than empty platitudes."

She nodded. "But that doesn't mean there's no hope." A wicked glint came into her eye. "There's always the chance Darius will see you in that dress and decide he has to have you, no matter what."

I smoothed my hand down the dress one more time, examining myself in the mirror. "At the very least, I want to enjoy one night of festivities before the final meetings tomorrow. Because somehow I suspect that after they're completed, I won't have much reason to smile for a good long while."

Bryony slipped her arm around me. "The only person who hasn't hesitated to sacrifice you for the good of everyone is you. You deserve one night of celebration."

I reminded myself of her words when I stepped into the

dining hall which had once again been transformed into an unrecognizable ballroom of festive elegance.

"I will never know how Zora does it," Bryony said in a wondering voice.

"Elsie could give you all the details," Stellan said from behind us.

Bryony wrinkled her nose. "That would kill all the charm."

"They both did an incredible job," I said. "And I love that they incorporated the red Ardannian berries again." The traditional holiday decorations from my home looked as effective as ever against the dark green Kallorwegian garlands.

Darius stepped into my line of sight, and I forgot all about the decorations.

"Come on," Bryony whispered behind me. "That's our cue to leave." She tugged Stellan away, but I hardly noticed their departure.

"You look…" Darius didn't seem able to find words.

I grinned up at him. "And you look the same as ever." I hoped my words covered the way my heart beat just as hard as it ever had at the sight of him in his formal garb, every inch the future king.

He shook his head. "You shouldn't have worn that."

"Why not?" I held his gaze. "I belong here. You know I do. It was past time for me to stop wearing red."

He glanced across at the refreshment table, the direction of his gaze showing me my parents' location.

"But it hardly seems like the time to be antagonizing your parents."

I gave a soft sigh. "If they didn't capitulate in the meeting today, they will tomorrow. I can read them. They know I have to do this."

His lips twisted. "They agreed. It's just the details we have to determine now."

I considered telling him about my recent certainty that they would agree to our betrothal as well. But the earlier perversity held me back. I didn't want him to know that yet.

"I look just as I should look—as if I belong with you." I stepped closer to him. "I know you've been in meetings all day, but can't you put aside your political self and just be Darius? For one night?"

"For one night..." For a long moment, Darius looked down at me. Then he closed the remaining distance between us, sweeping me into his arms and into the dance. "As Darius, I think you've never looked more beautiful. And that no dress could suit you better."

"Can we pretend, just for tonight, that there's no Conall to fight and no parents between us?" I whispered.

Darius stared down at me as if mesmerized before nodding his head. "If there are no such considerations, then I intend to dance with you for most of the evening."

"How funny," I said with a little smile. "That's just what I was intending."

And so we did. We talked of Kallorway—how far it had already come and how far it still had to go. We talked about the dreams and hopes we had for it, and what Darius's life might look like in Kallmon after graduation. It was like spending the night in an enchanted dream.

Most of the members of the Mage Council came to speak to us at some point, every one of them looking satisfied. Even Kalani had an amused glint in her eye as she gave us Midwinter greetings. Only my parents looked displeased, but they didn't voice their disapproval, and that was enough for me. At least for this one night.

Bryony and Jareth danced past several times, both of their faces showing delight and a little amusement as they watched us. I ignored them. I knew well enough they felt impatience with our normal restraint, but I also knew neither of them had ever carried the weight of a throne. Was it any wonder Darius felt more pressure than either of them? And that, sometimes, under the exterior he had to show the world, he questioned himself?

Late in the evening, I wandered over to the refreshment table, picking at the various holiday delicacies that still remained. I was just reaching for a particularly alluring confection when a quiet voice at my elbow made me start and nearly drop it.

I glanced back at Frida and shook my head. "You gave me a fright."

"Sorry." She sounded distracted, glancing over her shoulder to the dance floor. I followed her gaze to see Ashlyn circling in the arms of a young man whose robe had the high collar and elaborate embroidery that marked him as a Sekali.

"Is something wrong?" I asked.

She bit her lip, focusing her attention back on me. "I just wanted to ask you something."

I waited, an encouraging expression on my face, but it still took her several long moments to speak.

"Is it worth it?" she blurted out at last.

I frowned. "Is what worth it?"

This time her eyes picked out Darius who was deep in quiet conversation with Duchess Ashten.

"A secret, forbidden romance. Is it worth pursuing love when it's so complicated?"

I raised an eyebrow, and she gave a small chuckle. "None of us are stupid or blind, Verene. You've captivated Darius since you arrived back in first year. I don't pretend to know anything about your relationship, or what's keeping you apart now, but clearly you haven't given up on each other."

I regarded her thoughtfully. "I won't pretend not to be aware of what you're talking about either. And I can't tell you if Armand is worth it. Only you can decide that."

She started slightly at his name before relaxing.

"But I will say this," I continued. "If your love isn't strong enough to face some disapproval from your friends, then I don't see how it will survive the ups and downs of life. Love doesn't mean everything will be easy—not even between the two of you. You need commitment to make it work, and if you don't even want to admit your relationship to your friends…"

"It's not just them," Frida said quickly. "They're not even the main issue. I can handle Ashlyn." She said it in the half-amused voice of long friendship, and I found I believed her.

"What is it, then?" I asked.

She sighed. "It's our families. Here at the Academy, it's different. We all support Darius and the new regime that's coming. But back at home, our families are still fixed in their old ways. Armand's family support General Haddon, and his father is also sealed—a double count against them as far as my parents are concerned. And Armand's parents would be no more welcoming of the match since my parents have always supported the crown. Ever since Armand's father was sealed for his support of the old king, he's hated Cassius."

I sighed. "Family. Yes, that's a more difficult problem." I stared unseeing at the table, wondering how much I could say. "I don't know either of your parents, but if that's your biggest hesitation, then I would say to have hope. We all know times are changing, but I think you're going to find events are coming that will make them change much faster than you might guess."

Frida's eyes widened. "What is it? What's coming?"

I shrugged. "I suppose you're afraid if you tell your friends about your relationship, word will get back to your families. But maybe you should start by trusting Ashlyn and Wardell. And for the rest—give it to graduation to make any big decisions. Who knows how our world will look then?"

"Graduation." Frida still looked intrigued, but she didn't push me for further information. "I can manage that."

"I really do hope it works out for you." My eyes lingered on Darius across the room. I hoped it worked out for both of us.

Frida thanked me, disappearing back into the crowd as I once again surveyed the refreshment table, although this time I wasn't seeing the food. What *would* our world look like at graduation? What would my world look like?

Another figure approached me, coming to stand silently beside me in a comforting way that reminded me of my childhood but also how far I was from those times.

"We need to talk tomorrow morning," my father said. "Before the meeting."

My mood plummeted, my enchanted evening over. Real life had intruded again.

I nodded. "I'll come to your suite."

He hesitated before embracing me. "You look beautiful, Verene. More grown up than seems possible."

I held my breath, my heart filling with hope, but he merely shook his head and turned away. His words hadn't been an agreement to let me choose my own path, but merely the pride of a loving father. I sighed. Once again, my perversity was rearing its head. I wanted Darius to choose me even without my parents' approval, but at the same time, I wanted affirmation from my parents as well. I wanted them to see Darius's value and to truly recognize I was no longer a child.

I couldn't find Bryony, so I slipped out of the ball alone, in a trail of sleepy guests heading for their beds. The time to be a fourth year, to dance with my prince and pretend the only thing in our future was graduation, was passed. When I woke up in the morning, I would have to face reality. A madman threatened us all, and I seemed to be the only one with any hope of stopping him.

~

I expected to be greeted the next morning with recriminations on my choice of dress for the ball, but neither of my parents so much as mentioned it. Instead my mother wrapped her arms around me, tears in her eyes as she murmured an apology.

I pulled back, frowning. "What for?"

"For giving you such a unique and powerful ability that you have to go racing into danger. If your father had married someone else—like he was supposed to—then you would have been an ordinary power mage, and no one would expect you to carry this burden."

I laughed. "If Father had married someone else, I wouldn't be me." I paused. "I've wrestled with the nature of my ability in the past, it's true, but I'm not wrestling with it now. If I was an ordinary power mage, we would have no clear path to defeating Conall and his coerced army. We can all thank Father for his excellent choice."

My father chuckled. "That's what I keep telling her. I don't like this situation—of course I don't—but how could I be anything but proud that my two girls are going to save my kingdom? Again."

My mother pulled back, wiping her eyes and then rolling them at him. "We'll see if you're so blasé about it when we actually have to send her off."

A darkness flitted through my father's eyes that made me throw my arms around him next.

"I really will be careful," I said. "I promise. I'm just as eager to make it back as either of you."

"You'd better be," he said gruffly. "But for now, we have a meeting to attend."

The negotiations lasted all day. But by the end of it, an agreement had been reached. Each kingdom had nominated several of their most powerful mages to form the team who would accompany me. Most of them were guards and soldiers, but a skilled healer had been included by my parents.

As the host, Darius led the meeting, and my heart filled with pride to watch him. He might be young, but he came across as no less royal or authoritative than my parents or Kalani. I kept glancing at my parents, wondering if they were taking note. And could they read in his eyes that he hated having to send me as much as they did?

Once the team had been chosen, potential plans for how we might attempt to find Conall were discussed in detail. But even then, our business wasn't complete. For our part of the plan to succeed, everyone else had to take on an even more challenging task. They needed to distract Conall's army—drawing them out to leave him as little protection as possible—all while trying to keep as many of their opponents alive as possible.

Zora herself brought us trays of lunch, and the talk continued until the early evening. A basic plan was eventually agreed on, although many practical details would still have to be discussed between the various Armed Forces. The Spoken Mage would lead the combined Ardannian, Kallorwegian, and Sekali armies in a great show of force. They would march into the north of the Empire and face the army Conall had managed to ensnare.

The Head of the Kallorwegian Armed Forces banged his fist on the table, his face red.

"In an ordinary battle, we would crush them easily."

"Of course we would," my mother said, the faintest hint of impatience in her voice. "If this was an ordinary battle, none of this would be necessary." She nodded at Kalani. "I'm sure the emperor wouldn't even need our help if this was some sort of regular rebellion."

Kalani nodded. "Certainly the Empire would not seek assistance in such a case. My father's strength is unsurpassed in our history. But he will not turn that strength against his own people—not when they are unwilling slaves to a power-hungry warlord."

"Precisely," my mother said crisply. "Which is why we need the full might of our own armies—and in particular all the mage officers we can find. Even with my powers, it will not be easy to keep so many restrained for what might be a long time."

She glanced quickly at me and then equally quickly away.

"We will endeavor to find Conall as quickly as possible," I said. "But I cannot even hazard a guess as to how difficult the task might be."

"You are the most important element in this puzzle," my father said. "And it is not worth you taking unnecessary risks in the name of speed. If we lose you, the entire plan falls apart."

Everyone around the table nodded, even the gruff old general of the Armed Forces. I took a deep breath and nodded as well. I needed to keep my focus on my one role in this, or I would get overwhelmed. They had all assigned their most elite mages to accompany me, and I would have to leave it to them to discover Conall's whereabouts and get me close enough to do my part. Because if everything relied on me, then I feared we were all doomed.

CHAPTER 16

Midwinter had felt like the end of my time as a trainee. Difficult as it had been, I had accepted that reality. And yet, when the break ended, classes resumed. It felt surreal to sit at a desk and hear the instructors talk of exams as if life as I knew it weren't about to end.

And yet, it didn't end. We had no specified time for our mission to begin, but no one thought the middle of winter an ideal time to set out. And the armies needed time to arrange the logistics. Never in all our long annals had all three armies come together to fight a single enemy before. We had no established precedents to use.

I received word that Ardann had sent a small contingent of soldiers to the Kallorwegian headquarters, and they had sent their own group back. The whole process felt glacially slow, but I reminded myself of my own reaction to the black and red robes of the soldiers in the arena during our first battle. And I had never fought against Kallorwegian soldiers like some of the older veterans of the Ardannian Armed Forces.

I didn't even notice the robes now, and I could understand why the leaders of both kingdoms wanted a chance for their troops to reach the same level of familiarity. Nothing could be more disastrous than our combined forces turning on each other during the campaign.

But still, it felt almost unendurable waiting out the cold winter days at the Academy, knowing what was to come.

Royce seemed to have found peace with our interaction in the gardens by ignoring me. He still sought Darius's favor, though, and he now avoided showing me any overt disrespect while he did so. It was a situation I could accept. We needed Royce—and those like him—to work with us; I didn't need him to love me.

Having my brother present provided one spark of interest at least. Stellan had been assigned Royce's old suite on the royal level, and he joined the five of us for our daily energy lessons. Cooper seemed as interested in him as Stellan was to learn from Cooper.

The instructor who had taught Stellan the previous year had been able to give energy, the most common of the energy mage abilities. But giving energy was only half of my brother's ability. Stellan—a spoken mage like our mother, but an energy mage instead of a power one—could both give and take energy. He was the only known energy mage to be able to do both, as well as the only spoken energy mage.

It was easy to understand why Cooper found Stellan's unique ability intriguing. And my brother had never before had such easy access to a mage who could take energy. He was especially fascinated by the medical uses Cooper had found for the ability, and in their enthusiastic conversations on the topic, I received an insight into the fears I had never heard my brother voice.

Stellan had also wrestled with the aggressive part of his ability. Reading between his words, I could tell he felt a pull to use it —and that the pull scared him. Often as they talked, I found my eyes straying to Tyron. He leaned forward in his desk during the lessons, following the conversation closely, although he always remained silent.

Only once did he look over and meet my eyes, and for that moment I forgot myself, sharing a brief flash of understanding and fellow feeling with him. It lasted only seconds, and yet it left me shaken for the rest of the lesson.

Tyron believed that I alone knew how he felt. That I, too, had felt the irresistible urge to use his ability. And in my deepest heart, I had to admit I had felt that urge. First with my own ability, and then with his. When Cooper and Stellan spoke, I knew the struggle that lurked beneath their words all too well.

But I refused to accept Tyron's unspoken message. I refused to believe we were mere captives to the abilities we had been dealt. If we were given power, it was to do good with it.

And yet, Tyron's eyes haunted me with their unspoken questions. What possible good could come from such an ability as his? And was it truly possible to live with it and resist using it?

The questions scared me most of all because they suggested Tyron wasn't to blame for the path he had taken. And if his path had been inevitable, what path would my own abilities lead me down when I no longer had Conall to fight?

Determined to drive out the haunting questions, I threw myself into our arena battles, once again allowing myself to use my ability. The time was coming when my life might depend on my ability to operate at full capacity in mid combat. The effort often left me tired, and I usually headed in the direction of my bed early. I knew Stellan appreciated my doing so since it left my sitting room free for Elsie's use in the evenings. His days were taken up with lessons, and Elsie continued to spend her free time during the day with Zora. But I could usually hear them talking quietly after I had withdrawn for the night.

The days had finally started lengthening again—although winter still had us in its grasp—when I encountered Dellion one morning coming out of her suite.

"Are you all right?" I asked, stopping her with a hand on her arm. I had never seen the other girl so pale or her eyes so blank. "What's happened?"

"Great-Aunt Mildred," she said in tones of shock.

"Oh." I dropped my hand. "Did she pass away? I'm so sorry."

"Pass away?" Dellion stared at me blankly before giving a short laugh. "I suppose she is old, when I think about it. But somehow I feel sure even death itself is too terrified of her to come calling. I assure you I wouldn't be half so discomposed if that were all."

"Oh," I said again, not sure how to respond to that.

"She's here," Dellion said, her voice holding the hint of a wail. "At the Academy. She's already been to my rooms since she likes to begin her day with her favorite activity—criticizing me and bemoaning the degenerate youth of today."

I glanced back at her suite door, my eyes wide. "She's in your suite right now?" Had she heard our comments about her death?

"Oh no," Dellion said, and I relaxed. "She's moved on to find her favorite." A tone of disgust entered her voice. "I bet Jareth's room is messy as well, and she'll merely say she's glad he's managed to feel at home in such an inferior place. Mother tells me Aunt Mildred has always had a soft spot for handsome and charming young men."

"I thought you said she never leaves the south coast," I said.

"She doesn't!" Dellion cried.

"It's always best to keep one's relatives on their toes," said a voice from behind us.

We both spun around, Dellion looking horrified, to confront Jareth, emerging from his suite with an elderly woman on his arm. He was grinning at us, clearly only just holding back a laugh, but my focus was on the infamous Great-Aunt Mildred.

Her wrinkled skin and gray hair betrayed her age, but her keen eyes and straight back dared anyone to challenge her.

"My fool of a brother might think I'm as foolish as he," she said, "but nothing could be further from the truth."

Dellion choked slightly, and I almost laughed at the sight of my self-possessed year mate so disconcerted. Jareth didn't restrain himself, letting out a delighted chuckle.

"I wish Grandfather were present to hear you say so," he said.

Mildred looked up at him, a twinkle in her eye. "He wouldn't dare. If he hears I'm at the Academy, you may be sure he'll keep his distance. He knows I would soon put him in his place."

"I somehow feel sure you would," I said, adding silently that I would dearly love to see it. For all he supported me now, General Haddon had caused me plenty of pain in the past.

The full force of Mildred's piercing gaze turned on me. She had the same dark eyes as her two great-nephews and looked as if she must have been a great beauty in her day. She certainly carried herself with the confidence of one.

"So you're the Ardannian girl everyone's making a fuss over." She looked me slowly up and down. "You look well enough, I suppose." Her compliment sounded reluctant.

"Thank you," I said, the faint trace of a laugh in my voice.

"Great-Aunt Mildred!" Darius stepped out of the other door to his expanded suite. Obviously he hadn't encountered his aunt while she was inside visiting his brother. "I didn't know you were here at the Academy."

"Darius." She turned toward him. "Come and give your great-aunt a kiss."

He raised a brow but obediently dropped a quick kiss on her upraised cheek. "You should have informed me of your impending arrival. We would have been more prepared for you."

"Ha! Don't try to bamboozle me. Zora was never unprepared for anything in her life."

My interest in the old lady increased even further. How did a recluse from the south coast know Zora?

"She is certainly a capable manager for the Academy," Darius said calmly. "But what brings you so far? I hope your journey wasn't uncomfortable."

"My journey was a nightmare as you are no doubt aware," she said acerbically. "There is a reason I don't like to travel."

"Then I'm sorry you put yourself to so much trouble," Darius said. "I hope it wasn't for my sake."

His aunt's eyes narrowed. "I have just finished telling this lot I'm no fool, and I would appreciate not having to repeat myself. I may choose to live in a somewhat retired way, but I have my sources of information. I know that something is afoot, and I have no doubt my brother will bungle the matter if left to his own devices."

"My grandfather is not the one who rules in Kallorway," Darius said stiffly.

She raised her brows, her expression depressing his pretension as if he were any recalcitrant youth and not her future king.

"No, I understand that is you, my boy. And I must say the business was handled with more neatness than I looked for, all things considered." She folded her hands over her stomach. "No doubt I may attribute it to Zora's efficient intervention."

My eyes widened, and her sharp gaze flashed to me, a satisfied smile crossing her face as if my expression was affirmation of her words.

Internally I shook my head at having allowed myself to be so easily played. I would do well not to underestimate Mildred. I had been well-trained, but she had been playing this game a great deal longer.

"You will do well enough, Nephew," she continued. "But I could not allow my brother to push yet another unqualified queen onto the throne. Since he seems to have sweet-talked the rest of the Council into supporting him, I had to make sure he wasn't leading us all by the nose once again."

Dellion coughed, and Jareth snorted. For myself I could barely keep the shock from my face. That unqualified queen was her own niece and the only reason she claimed kinship with the current king-elect.

But I had already seen that she showed no great respect toward her family. Had she always been like that, or had age removed her inhibitions? I suspected that just a little time in Mildred's company would rob me of the ability to be shocked by anything she said.

"Neither your opinions nor your intervention are welcome, Great-Aunt," Darius said, showing none of his brother's amusement. "Just as my grandfather doesn't rule, he also isn't responsible for choosing my bride." He gave her the full force of his closed, icy mask. "Whoever she might be."

I tried to keep my face equally impassive, fighting an unwelcome surge of tears. After everything we had been through, it hurt to hear Darius repudiate me publicly, even if I knew he was only thinking of our privacy. Even knowing he didn't mean it as a rejection, his words hit me harder than I had expected.

Mildred, however, continued as if he hadn't spoken.

"Oh, I mean no disrespect to my niece," she said with a wave of her hand. "Endellion was always a nice enough girl. But much too weak to be queen—especially to Cassius. She didn't have the gumption to stand up to either her father or her husband. Kallorway wouldn't be in such a mess now if someone had kept their hands on the reins and kept those two idiot men in line."

"No, I can't say my mother was the one for that task," Jareth said thoughtfully.

"Of course she was not! That's what I've just been telling you," Mildred said. "And we can't afford another five decades of such inanity. And so I have come to inspect our proposed future queen for myself."

Darius straightened, his eyes flashing, so I spoke quickly, cutting off anything he might say.

"Future queen or not, I'm curious." I forced my voice to hold only amusement. "Do I pass muster?"

"Ha! You don't seem spineless, I'll give you that much." She looked me over again. "You've an air about you I like. But I don't give out my approval as easily as that, mind."

"Of course not," I said, my voice grave, but my eyes laughing despite myself.

"And don't think I'm unaware there's something else going on at this Academy," she said abruptly, causing my spark of amusement to instantly fade.

No one replied, although Dellion gave the rest of us a curious look.

Mildred sniffed. "It's good to see you at least understand when discretion is needed. It's more than I usually look to find in youth. Now, Jareth, be a dear and escort me to His Grace's private dining room. I'm sure Zora has arranged an exemplary breakfast, and I don't approve of letting good food grow cold."

Jareth chuckled and offered her his arm again, leading her away down the corridor as she scolded him in an affectionate voice.

"Well," I said when they had disappeared from sight. "I now see what you all meant." I carefully avoided meeting Darius's eyes, and he appeared to be doing the same thing, turning to his cousin instead.

"What in the kingdoms is she doing here, Dellion?"

"Don't look at me as if I invited her." Dellion shuddered. "That's the last thing I would do. You think you're shocked—imagine if she barged into your suite before you were even dressed for the morning. I'll need the whole day just to recover." She glanced in my direction. "At least she seemed to like Verene. And for that we can all be thankful."

Darius frowned, but Dellion continued before he could speak. "Oh, don't bother giving me the same speech you just gave our beloved great-aunt. I've spent years living beside the two of you, and if you can't fool her, you certainly can't fool me."

"Dellion," he said, the warning clear in his voice.

"Relax," she said. "I'm not going to say any more. I have Great-

Aunt Mildred to contend with, I don't need to be fighting with you as well." She shook her head. "And now I need some breakfast."

She started off down the corridor toward the stairs, but neither Darius nor I moved to follow her. After several breaths, I made myself turn to face him, only to find him looking at me with such intense emotion, I caught my breath.

"Verene," he said in a low voice. "You don't need anyone's approval. You're above every one of them."

I swayed toward him, tears springing to my eyes again. But at the last moment, I squeezed them back down and held myself rigid. The empty air between us seemed unutterably cold, a distance that loomed far larger than the mere handspan of actual space.

"You're right that it shouldn't be your grandfather that chooses your bride," I said. "But you're also right that you haven't chosen her yourself."

"Verene." The word seemed wrung out of him, my hurt clearly causing him pain.

But I hardened myself against it. "Apparently you know it isn't your grandfather's role to choose your queen. So why are you so determined to give that choice to my parents?"

"I..."

I waited for him to continue, but the silence stretched on. I drew a shuddering breath and pulled myself together. I had told myself that the day might come when I would have to walk away, but I wasn't ready for that day yet. And if we were to face what was coming, we needed to be able to work together.

With all my strength, I made myself bury my emotions and speak in a normal tone.

"What do you think she knows? Not about us, but about the other matter..."

Darius stared at me for a final heartrending moment, his love and his inner turmoil clear. And then he, too, pushed his emotions away, turning instead to gaze down the hall in the direction his aunt had taken.

"I don't know. I'll admit to feeling some unease. She's always been a canny one with far more information than she has any right to, but she shouldn't have word of this."

I nodded. We had gone to so much effort to keep our preparations secret. It wasn't reassuring to know a recluse from the other side of the kingdom had heard of them—whoever that recluse might be. Her brother knew all of our plans, of course, but it was clear from her manner that she didn't receive confidences from the general.

"I'll look into it," he said. "For now, we shouldn't miss our own breakfast."

For a brief moment I thought he meant to say something more, but instead he started down the corridor. With a soft sigh, I followed him.

The day passed in a normal fashion with no further unexpected appearances from Mildred. Dellion remained on edge, though, always looking over her shoulder as if she expected her aunt to appear at any moment.

But it wasn't Mildred who ended up disrupting the day. We had made it as far as discipline studies without anything unusual happening, and we were all in our old energy studies classroom, as we were once or twice a week now that we had both Cooper and Stellan with us. I wasn't paying much attention to their discussion of a complicated healing Cooper had assisted with, and Jareth and Bryony had gone as far as starting up a whispered conversation. Darius, as usual, was engrossed in another one of his endless stacks of reports, and even Tyron, who continued to find healing a fascinating topic, had slumped in his seat and appeared to have fallen into a half-doze.

My brother was halfway through a lengthy question when Tyron suddenly sat up straight, his eyes flying fully open. We all stopped what we were doing to stare at him.

"Bryony, did you just give me energy?" he asked, his voice sharper than I had ever heard it.

"What? No, of course not." She stared at him.

He shook his head, gripped by some strong emotion. "No, of course you didn't. It doesn't feel like you at all."

For a moment he sat frozen, his eyes wide but unseeing, staring at the opposite wall. Then he nodded once and turned to Darius.

"My father knows. He's gathering his army already. We're out of time."

CHAPTER 17

"What?" Darius stood up. "What do you mean? How can you know that?"

"I just received energy," Tyron said grimly. "Energy from home."

Bryony's mouth dropped open. "That's impossible. It's so far!"

"Actually, I don't think it is impossible." Cooper was watching Tyron with a crease between his eyes. "Sending energy as a prearranged signal is a system my mother and uncle developed years ago. They were so familiar with each other's energy that my uncle could send a boost to my mother across any distance—at least the way he tells it. That's how he let them know it was safe to come down from the mountains."

"Your uncle is Amias?" Bryony asked, startled. "You never said that."

Cooper shrugged. "It never came up."

"So you were raised at the Sekali court?" Bryony sat forward before quickly shaking her head. "No, never mind. That's not important right now." She turned back to Tyron. "So you're saying you had a prearranged signal with your father?"

Tyron nodded. "One of his people can give energy. Her family are the only ones with that ability who stayed with the Tarxi, and my father always kept them close. He said that if anything happened to make him move before the prearranged time, he would have her send me energy as a signal that it was time for action."

My stomach roiled, and I gripped the desk in front of me. "But we're not ready. The Armed Forces haven't gathered. My team hasn't arrived. We were supposed to have the element of surprise."

"I'm sorry," Tyron said, and to my surprise he actually sounded apologetic. "The only thing I can think of is that my father has somehow discovered you know of his plans. So he's going to move before you have time to act against him."

My eyes flew to Darius. "This is a disaster."

"If it's true," he said grimly.

"All I know is that I just received familiar energy from home, and that receiving such energy was a prearranged signal," Tyron said. "I can't guarantee anything else."

Darius rummaged in his pockets, pulling out a composition. "Then you won't mind my asking you to repeat all that under a truth composition."

Tyron shrugged. "If you like."

It only took a few minutes to ascertain Tyron had been telling us the truth.

A small part of my mind was surprised at his ready assistance, but most of my attention was taken up with thinking over the various ramifications of his revelation. Front and center was one recurring and terrifying thought. If Conall was moving, then we needed to be moving, too. The time had come for me to go after him, and I had none of the supports the three monarchs had so carefully planned for me.

~

We ate the evening meal from trays in Duke Francis's office. All of us had gone straight from our classroom to meet with him, even Cooper trailing along. He had already provided valuable knowledge, and we couldn't afford to miss even the slightest advantage now that we were scrambling to catch up.

"If we assume this is true, what will Conall's first move be?" the duke asked.

"We have to assume it's true," Darius said grimly. The duke nodded his acquiescence, his focus on Tyron.

Tyron frowned. "He'll gather his makeshift army, and then he'll start moving south for the Sekali capital."

"How long will that take him?" I asked, trying to think past the clock that had begun ticking down in my mind.

Tyron shrugged. "To reach the capital? To overrun the capital? To gather his armies? Or to start wreaking havoc in general?"

I gulped. "The last two, I suppose."

"I couldn't say for certain, but he should have some forces gathered by tomorrow. And more will come together over the day or two after that. Once he has a sizable enough force, I expect he'll start the march, even if he's still gathering stragglers. And he'll set his army to destroy everything in their path."

"Everything?" I stared at him. "But doesn't he want to rule in the emperor's place? Surely he doesn't want to gut the Empire first."

Tyron's lips twisted. "The Empire is a large place. It isn't all within his path, and my father doesn't care if half the people starve or go homeless after he takes the throne. He thinks all flat-landers are traitors, fit only to be ground beneath his boot. There will be plenty of wealth and power left from other parts of the Empire for him and all the Tarxi."

"Plus the southern kingdoms," Darius said in a grim tone.

Tyron met his eyes, nodding. "Plus the southern kingdoms. For now, my father will be most interested in sending a message."

For a moment I thought I might be sick, but I ruthlessly suppressed the sensation. Now wasn't the time for emotion.

"Then we really are out of time," I said. "I can't wait for my team to gather, I have to leave immediately. Even if I left now and moved at speed—and knew exactly where to find Conall, which I don't—I wouldn't be able to reach him before the destruction begins. Not without our combined forces to slow him down and protect the Sekalis in his path."

"It's not just an issue of time," Bryony said, and I had never heard her sound so worried.

"What do you mean?" I stared at her.

"If it was just the need for immediate action, we could always send word for them to meet you at some prearranged spot on the road, except…"

"Except we can't do that," Darius finished for her. I frowned, and he continued. "Somehow word has reached Conall of our plans, and we have no way to know how that happened. Without the team here to be examined and tested, we can't be sure none of them are the traitor. If we leave word of where you can be found, you might walk straight into an ambush."

I swallowed. "But surely there are many ways Conall could have found out? Now that planning is underway with the Armed Forces, the circle of knowledge is growing unmanageably large."

Jareth groaned. "Yes, just look at Great-Aunt Mildred." He shook his head. "But that doesn't change anything. We can't send out the information of where you're going to be. In fact, there's some value in your leaving as soon as possible for your own security. If Conall knows how important you are, we don't want you somewhere as obvious as the Academy."

"He doesn't know everything, though," Duke Francis cut in. "We can be grateful for that, at least. Wherever he got his knowledge, it's incomplete."

Tyron nodded. "That's true, or else he never would have contacted me."

"As soon as we've finished here, I'll send word to Ardann and the emperor, as well as to my own officers," Darius said. "Our armies must gather and begin a forced march into the Empire. The Sekalis will have to hold the line alone until we can arrive to bolster their forces."

"My mother will go immediately," I said. "She can travel much faster than an army."

"Yes, let us be grateful for that," the duke said. "With her powers, we may still have a chance. But there is no denying our situation just became a great deal more precarious."

I stood up. "So I have to leave. Now."

Bryony pulled me back down into my chair. "Don't be ridiculous. We're not sending you out there alone without so much as a bag."

I frowned, trying to think clearly over the beating of my heart and the ticking in my head. How many people would die for every minute that I hesitated?

"Certainly not," Darius said. "Kallorway, Ardann, and the Empire combined intended to send you out with the best they had to offer. Instead you will have to go with the best the Academy has to offer. And we will just have to hope it's enough."

Duke Francis raised an eyebrow. "I hesitate to point out that you, Your Highness, may be the best we have to offer."

"Precisely," Darius said, meeting his eyes.

I gasped. "You can't go, Darius. You're needed here!"

"Am I?" he asked. "They didn't intend to let me join the armies on the front lines, and I have far less experience with battle or strategy than half my officers. Everything has changed, and I can't afford to sit back here in safety while Verene goes to try to stop Conall without adequate protection."

"You mean you don't want to," Jareth said quietly.

Darius met his brother's eyes. "And what of you, Jareth? Do you intend to stay behind? I'm sure Bryony doesn't."

All of our eyes flew to my petite friend, who just rolled her eyes. "Well, naturally not. But then I was always going."

I narrowed my eyes. "Funny, I don't remember seeing your name on the list chosen by the delegates."

"I wasn't intending to ask permission," she told me with the ghost of a smile.

"Of course I'm going as well," Jareth said quickly. "But I still think you should stay behind, Darius. The Mage Council will never agree to it."

"I don't intend to ask their permission." Darius's voice and face were like granite.

"Bravo," said a new voice from just inside the office door.

We all swung around to face Mildred and Zora, who was calmly carrying the enormous tray of food to the duke's desk.

"It is about time we had a king who is neither a lily-livered coward focused only on his own aggrandizement nor a pushover to that useless Council."

"The Council is hardly useless, Aunt," Darius said. "But this is not a moment for consultation or committees."

"Precisely." She nodded her head and advanced into the room. "It is time for action and courage, and I am glad to see my nephew has the stomach for both."

"If you leave without consulting them, they're not going to like it," Jareth said, trying for a final warning, although I could hear the fight had left his voice.

"You leave my brother and the rest of them to me," Mildred said in tones of steel. "I will soon set them straight if they try to quibble."

She directed a quelling look at the duke, who looked like he was trying to suppress a smile. "You may count on my support, Lady Mildred."

"I should hope so," she snapped. "Especially since I came all this way to prevent you and your wife running headlong into catastrophe."

I started at her casual mention of the duke's marriage, and Francis himself raised a disapproving eyebrow. But Zora merely clucked and began distributing the food.

"We've no need of your intervention, Mildred, as I suspect you well know. It's been a long time now since I needed your protection."

Mildred narrowed her eyes, although her expression still held surprising hints of affection and respect as she looked at Zora.

"Ha! I'm not so confident about that."

Zora straightened and looked at her with a direct gaze. "I'll not forget all you've done for me. But I'll go my own way. I think you know me well enough to know that."

"So you truly mean to do it, then?" Mildred asked.

"I do." Zora calmly returned to handing out the food.

My eyebrows had climbed so far up my head they were in danger of disappearing into my hair. I expected a cutting response from Mildred at this defiance, but she merely sniffed.

"I can see I was right in thinking my guidance sorely needed. But now is not the time for that." She wheeled suddenly on Darius. "We must ensure you return to find your throne still waiting for you. The kingdom has spent quite long enough in this limbo. So I assume you've already discussed the matter of an instructor?"

We all stared at her blankly. My curiosity was caught on the strange conversation between her and Zora, and it took some effort to remind myself that I had no time to wonder about such things.

"An instructor?" Bryony asked, recovering more quickly than me.

Mildred tsked, looking around at us all with a judgmental eye. "The Mage Council requires Darius to complete his four years at the Academy and graduate before he can be crowned, do they not? It is the reason for this farce we have all been enduring for a year and a half now. If you intend to undermine their authority,

Darius, then you had best not give them an avenue to claim you have not fulfilled their requirements for your coronation."

"Yes, you have to stay here, Darius," I said. "I'm sure—"

"He has to do nothing of the sort." Mildred stomped over and sank elegantly into a free chair. "I believe field trips from the Academy are not unheard of—or at least that's the impression I received from your little jaunt to the coast last year."

She bent an inquiring eye on the duke who nodded stiffly.

"Indeed, Lady Mildred. Although rare, it is established tradition, both in Kallorway and Ardann, that trainees may spend time away from the Academy under the supervision of an instructor on trips judged to enhance their learning."

"Precisely. And I'm sure my nephew will learn a very great deal on this particular trip," she said wryly. "So there is merely the matter of an instructor. As I said."

We were all silent for a moment, considering her words.

"The healing instructor would be the most ideal choice if everything were equal," the duke said at last.

"Ha!" Mildred crowed. "Unless Raelynn has changed a great deal, you won't be dragging her halfway across the peninsula chasing down some maniacal warlord. She may not be as ancient as me, but she's still too old for such an undertaking."

"No, I don't think in the circumstances that she would be the best choice," Duke Francis said with dignity.

I leaned forward. "What about Cooper? He's been wearing a silver robe and instructing classes for months now. Would he count?"

"Cooper?" The duke stared at me blankly before a slow smile spread across his face. "Why, yes, certainly. He is currently an Academy instructor, even if it is only a temporary assignment."

Everyone turned to look at Cooper.

"You would be perfect for the role," Stellan said, speaking for the first time since we had entered the duke's office. "You're not only a trained Armed Forces officer, but you were raised in the Empire and know it well."

"And you have a rare and powerful offensive ability," Jareth added. His gaze swung to me, and I could read the unspoken other half of his thoughts. Cooper had been checked so many times since coming to the Academy—including by me—that he was one of the most trustworthy people here. After his own experience, Jareth had developed a tendency to mistrust everyone, so it was a matter of great importance to him.

"You'll come, of course, won't you, Cooper?" Bryony spoke with certainty. When I directed an inquiring look at her, she just shrugged. "He's one of us, an energy mage. Which means this is personal for him. And you heard what he said earlier—he's Amias's nephew. I would bet a fair amount of gold he's eager for the opportunity to assist." She turned back to Cooper, waiting for him to confirm her words.

Cooper nodded. "Bryony is right. I will serve in any way I can."

"That's decided, then," Duke Francis said. "I admit it will give me some small amount of extra peace to know you are one of the group, Cooper."

"I don't think we'd manage to escape the Academy grounds without Captains Vincent and Layna in tow as well," Darius said. "Even if we wished to do so, which I do not. But in the meetings over Midwinter, there was clear agreement that the group must be kept small. We will be traveling a long way, at speed, and attempting to remain concealed while we do so. Numbers will hinder that."

Duke Francis didn't look convinced, so I spoke up in Darius's support. "If we end up in the middle of Conall's army, it won't matter how many guards we took with us, they won't be enough to protect us. Our best hope lies in secrecy and concealment. And one mage is worth a great many commonborn soldiers when it comes to the type of combat we may encounter. We will be seeking to run, not stand our ground if it comes to conflict."

"With eight of us, our number is high enough already," Jareth said.

"So many?" I murmured, counting people in my mind. Darius, Jareth, and Bryony were determined to accompany me, so that made four of us. Then the two captains and Cooper. "I'm only counting seven."

"That's including Tyron," Jareth said.

"Tyron?" Bryony stared at him. "I understand why he's had to stay close to us at the Academy, but surely we're not planning to drag him into the Empire?"

Tyron had looked up at the mention of his name, but I couldn't read his expression. I regarded him thoughtfully.

"We wouldn't know anything about this if it wasn't for him," I said slowly. "And he has a wealth of information about his father and the Tarxi that no one else could possibly have. He might prove useful."

"In other ways, too." Something about Jareth's voice made me look at him sharply. "With Verene along, we have access to his ability. And that could prove incredibly valuable."

I sucked in a breath. "You want me to use his ability against people? To coerce and control them?"

"We don't want you to," Darius said quietly. "But if it comes down to a life or death situation, then I trust you would use every tool at your disposal."

I swallowed the hot words I had been about to speak. He was right. If the lives of my friends and my team were in the balance, I would use Tyron's power to get them free in a heartbeat.

"We lose that power unless Tyron comes with us," Jareth said. "Thankfully we have only recently finished restocking his binding compositions. We have a fair number stashed away. We can keep him bound."

"Well?" I looked across the room, meeting Tyron's eyes. "Will you come? Will you assist us?"

A tense silence settled around me, and I didn't have to look at the faces of the others to know they felt varying levels of disapproval. Tyron was a traitor and a prisoner, not a willing participant. But he had shown himself to be strangely helpful of late. And even with the binding composition, it would make a significant difference if he came willingly or was dragged along against his will. Whatever advantages he represented could be outweighed if he made our journey difficult enough.

He looked steadily back at me, and once again I had the impression of a silent conversation passing between our gazes. His eyes seemed to press me, accusing me of the admission I had just made. I would use his power to help my friends, so how was I any different from him? *Can you really blame me?* his eyes seemed to say. *Are you sure you wouldn't have done the same in my place? Am I really your enemy?*

But all his mouth said was, "I will come, and I will help you."

Bryony snorted. "And why should we believe you would ever do that?"

"Other than that he just did by telling us about Conall's message," I murmured.

Tyron himself just shrugged. "Likely you won't. I understand that." He looked at me. "Verene understands on the vaguest of levels because she's the only other one who's experienced it. I hated you all and wanted to destroy you, as I'd been trained to do, but then you gave me the greatest possible gift. A gift I didn't even know I needed."

"What gift?" Jareth asked suspiciously.

"The gift of silence," I said, not looking away from Tyron.

He nodded. "Silence and solitude inside my own head. It feels…I cannot describe how it feels. I had forgotten. It's hard to stay angry in the midst of so much…peace."

"So, just like that, you're willing to turn on your father?" Darius also sounded skeptical.

"If you mean have I been converted to your cause," Tyron asked dryly, "then no. I have no loyalty to Kallorway. But I also just saw Verene's reaction to the suggestion that she use my ability. I know what life under my father's rule is like—I'm expected to use my ability in his cause at all times. But you seem to feel differently about its use. I suppose I've realized I'd rather be a prisoner in Kallorway, but at peace inside my own mind, than be a prince in his world without it."

His words reminded me of Dellion. Their cases were far from the same, but the principle still applied. In a situation as desperate as this, I would accept help from wherever it was forthcoming, whether selfishly motivated or not.

I stood up. "That's settled then. We need to leave immediately."

"Certainly," Zora said. "If by immediately you mean in two hours, which is how long I estimate it will take for you all to be properly supplied and provisioned and the necessary messages sent."

"It will be dark by then," Darius said, "but I still want us out of the Academy. Even if we don't make it far tonight." From the way his eyes lingered on me, I knew it was me he wanted safely away.

We scattered to our rooms to pack, with Duke Francis's reminder that whatever we took we must carry ringing in our ears. Zora told us she would send packs to each of our rooms, along with some basic supplies.

I hurried to my suite, hardly noticing my brother trailing behind until he slipped into my sitting room after me.

"Have you come to help me pack, Stellan?" I asked absently, my mind still occupied with what to take. "I'll be relying on you to smooth things over with Mother and Father. They'll be furious."

"I'm afraid you'll have to find someone else to do that," he said with such seriousness that it broke through my distraction.

I frowned at him. "What do you mean? You aren't angry at me for going, are you?"

"Of course not. I just mean I'm going with you."

"Stellan! You can't come with us. You're not even eighteen yet."

He scoffed at that. "I'll be eighteen in two weeks, and you know it. I'm not staying behind while you run off into danger."

I groaned. "I appreciate your care for me, but you really can't come, Stellan."

"Cooper will be valuable to have along," Stellan said. "But the truth is I'm more valuable. And as Jareth pointed out, anyone who comes is essentially a tool you can draw on. You double the ability of anyone with you. And I have something none of the rest of them do—a spoken ability. Mother has shown how valuable the flexibility of speaking compositions can be—especially in emergencies."

"But if I use your ability, Stell, I do it with your energy, remember. So it isn't really double."

"Except in the case of taking energy," he said with a serious expression. "That increases my energy, not decreases it, so we could both be using my ability at the same time."

I winced at his reminder that we would be likely to need offensive abilities the most on this venture. "Yes, I suppose in that case…"

Elsie appeared, her arms piled high with items which she dumped on one of the sofas. I saw my most practical travel clothes on the top and smiled my gratitude at her. I didn't bother asking how she already knew what was happening. Zora had taken her under her wing, and Zora always seemed to know an impossible amount about everything that was going on.

I continued to argue with my brother, but when he said that he would simply follow me—with or without my permission—I had to capitulate. I didn't have time to argue any more, and he was right that my ability to draw on his unique skills might come in useful for us all. I certainly didn't want to risk the danger of him trailing us at a distance.

Zora entered the suite without knocking, depositing three cases on the remaining free sofa. Elsie immediately grabbed one and promised she would be back in just a moment before disappearing behind the screens that sectioned off her part of the room.

I followed her, frowning as I watched her pull clothes from a large chest. "What are you doing?"

She looked over at me. "Packing. Would you prefer I finish your packing first? I understood we were in a significant rush…"

"I'm not worried about my packing, I'm just…Elsie, you're not coming with me on this trip. This isn't a journey home to Ardann for the holidays."

"Of course not." She calmly continued loading items into her pack. "You're going after Conall, and I'm coming too." She shoved a final item in and pushed defiantly past me back into the main sitting room.

"Elsie, no!" Stellan cried, horrified. "You can't come. It's going to be dangerous."

She gave him an unimpressed look. "So you've decided to stay behind, then?"

He winced. "No."

She nodded knowingly. "If you and Verene are both going, then I'm going too."

"Elsie, we have to keep our numbers down," I said. "Darius was very insistent on it."

A bark of laughter reminded me Zora was still in the room. "Yes, I had an internal chuckle at that when you all listed those making up the party. You say you don't want Elsie going, but who, may I ask, will be preparing your meals on the trail? Setting up camp? Do you have a lot of experience in such areas, Princess?"

"I'm sure the captains..." I started to say weakly, but Zora spoke over me.

"The captains will be entirely occupied with keeping you all alive—as they should be. But I don't know how far you're going to get on empty stomachs and no sleep."

I sighed, realizing for the first time that Zora had brought three packs to my room. As far as she was concerned, the decision had been made, and it was never a good idea to argue with Zora.

"Very well. I don't have time to argue anyway. If you're coming, Stellan, you'd better run and pack."

He grabbed one of the remaining two packs and dashed from the room as Elsie assisted me in loading up mine.

"Are you sure about this?" I asked her as we worked.

"Entirely sure, Verene," she said firmly. "I may not have your ability, but I'll do my part."

When we gathered a short time later in Darius's suite, he didn't look happy about the two new additions. But when I summarized their separate arguments for attending, he didn't bother fighting over their presence.

Both Vincent and Layna had arrived before us, despite not having been at the meeting. For a brief moment I almost didn't recognize them without their gold robes, but none of us would be wearing robes for such a trip. Instead they wore practical clothes in thick leather, looking serious and prepared, their eyes alert. Beside them, I felt like a child playing at being an adult.

But I forced myself to draw a deep breath and straighten my spine. Child or not, both my kingdoms needed me, and the time had come for action. Within minutes, Bryony had also joined us, and finally Cooper, who exchanged a serious nod with the two captains who looked relieved to see him. We set out without further discussion.

Elsie led us for the first few minutes, her suggestion that we leave the Academy via the tunnels having found immediate favor with Darius. Walking the tunnels used by the servants and climbing the rickety stair, it seemed impossibly strange to think I had made this exact trek less than a year before, in the aftermath of a storm. Everything felt different now.

But none of us paused for reminiscences. In a matter of minutes, we were outside in the cool evening air, the moon providing ample illumination as we finally left the Academy behind us.

$\mathcal{A}$s soon as we were out in the open, Vincent took over the role of leader, leaving Layna to take the rear. We were ten now, and the other eight of us walked between them in loose pairs, although few words were exchanged.

I had seen the landscape around the Academy many times, but it looked eerie in the moonlight, and I jumped at even the normal rustle of small nocturnal creatures. I had expected to avoid the nearby village, bypassing it completely, but Vincent led us right along its edge.

When we reached a small but dense copse of trees, he bid us wait there for his return. I expected Darius to protest, but instead a look of understanding passed between them, and Vincent disappeared into the night.

"Where is he going?" I asked in a whisper, moving closer to Darius.

The rest of the group followed my lead, huddling around the prince with expressions that ranged from curious to anxious.

"The fastest and easiest way into the Empire is up the Abneris River," Darius said quietly. "Who knows how long it would take us to trek through the forests along the border on foot? But to take the river, we need a boat. Vincent had already been making arrangements to procure one for your expedition, Verene. Now he's just seeing if he can appropriate it early."

A boat. Of course. I should have thought of that myself. I knew it had been the original intention for me to use the river to gain access to the Empire. Kallorway sent nearly as many expeditions up the Abneris as they did along the coast.

Vincent reappeared suddenly, making me jump and proving his skills for stealth and silence.

"It's all arranged." He signaled for us to fall back into line, and we did so without further comment. Everyone present was aware, in their own way, of the enormity of the moment, and all of us were processing it in the privacy of our minds.

Despite the sense of urgency that drove me on, weariness began to make my steps drag, and I had to concentrate to keep from slowing to a crawl. Bryony, beside me, looked tireless, and every time I started to flag, I looked at her and felt my determination boost.

Although it felt like a long time, we reached the river before even half the night had passed. Somehow Vincent must have known the exact angle to take to intercept the flowing water at the correct point, because when the river appeared before us, glimmering in the moonlight, a dark shape sat on the bank beside it.

Vincent grunted. "That's the barge, Your Highness. It should be big enough for us all."

A rough covering lay draped over the wooden hull, but Vincent pulled it aside with a single movement. Whoever had organized this boat for us had clearly left it in an out-of-the-way spot, meaning there wasn't so much as a simple dock to help us get it into the water.

Somehow the ten of us managed to launch the barge, Jareth and Vincent holding it steady in the shallows along the shoreline while the rest of us clambered inelegantly aboard. We perched on the rows of benches, our packs tucked beneath us. The basic vessel didn't include a proper cabin, but it did have a simple timber canopy to give us some protection against the coming sun.

As soon as we were all settled, Darius signaled for Jareth and Vincent to jump aboard. He tore three compositions as they did so, and a strong wind sprang up behind us. With a jolt and a lurch, the barge began to move upstream against the current, picking up speed as it went.

For a long moment I was mesmerized by the water lapping and foaming against the hull as we moved against its flow. Fractured splashes of moonlight reflected back from the churning surface, and the rocking of the vessel was unexpectedly comforting.

But Elsie's voice broke me from my reverie.

"I suggest we try to get some sleep while we can," she whispered to Bryony and me. "We might be needed later."

Layna, overhearing, nodded. "Everyone who can do so should sleep now. We don't know when we'll have such a good opportunity again."

Diligently I lay down on one of the bench seats, but sleep seemed unlikely in such a situation. Or so I thought for the brief moments before my eyes drifted closed and the waves rocked me to sleep.

I woke abruptly, jolted awake by a violent lurching as I squinted with confusion into full sunlight. Another jerk sent me rolling off the bench seat. I crashed against the wooden floor of the barge, wincing at the pain.

Shouts made me sit up abruptly, peering over the side of the hull. The shouts hadn't come from any of my companions, I was certain of that.

Flashes of movement along the shoreline resolved into a number of figures, grouped on both sides of the river. They were still a way upriver from us, but most of them were pointing in our direction, shouting and—in two cases—pulling out compositions.

I gasped and hauled myself fully upright, my eyes flying around the barge. Stellan had shoved Elsie to the floor between two of the other bench seats and was hovering protectively over her. He seemed to be arguing with Bryony, and a moment later I realized he was telling her to get down as well.

She looked mulish, and I fully expected her to refuse, but to my surprise after one exasperated look, she threw herself down beside Elsie.

"You too, Stellan, Tyron, and Cooper," Layna ordered from her position at the back of the boat, and I finally realized what was happening.

Someone had been waiting to ambush any boats coming up the river, and the captain was getting anyone who couldn't help out of the way. Being able to take energy was useful, but it wasn't the sort of combat composition we needed now.

I looked back upriver, the ambush approaching far too rapidly for my comfort. Someone on the left side gave a loud shout, and several people on both sides rushed forward in a coordinated movement. They appeared to be pulling on something, and a moment later, ropes appeared above the water.

The thick cords looked serious and sturdy, and a number of them had been lashed together to make a sort of lattice. They must have been lying slack in the water before, secured on both sides of the river. But now that they were pulled taut, they stretched just above the waterline, extending up a couple of feet.

It was a trap. Our forward momentum would dash us against the ropes within a minute.

Even as I was processing what I was seeing, Vincent had already ripped a composition, sending a wave of power racing along the top of the water ahead of us. But it crashed against a bubble of power that surrounded the ropes and protected them. The ambush had been set with both physical means and compositions, to ensure its victims couldn't easily escape.

Layna sent another composition close behind Vincent's, but it also burned out against the power of the shield.

"How strong is that thing?" Jareth muttered from just in front of me.

"Wait! Stop!" I cried as Vincent moved to tear another composition. "Leave the shield to me. Get ready to deal with the ropes as soon as you feel the power go down."

The captain hesitated before shoving the composition he held back into his jacket. I didn't look to see if he was retrieving another one in its place, concentrating on my own task instead.

"Take control," I cried, seizing on the power that enclosed the ropes.

The shield composition unfurled in my mind, a basic one that ignored everything other than protecting the ropes, pouring maximum power into that task.

"Protect the barge," I gasped out, twisting its purpose.

The power streamed away from the ropes, rushing downriver to encircle us instead. There was no point in letting that much power go to waste.

But a moment later I realized power still clung to the ropes. I groaned. Of course they had more than one shield around them. I should have guessed that. I would have felt it if I hadn't been so focused on speed and so distracted by the rocking boat, the chaos around me, and the terror that forced its way up my throat.

"Take control," I screamed again, this time taking the extra seconds to check for further compositions. There were three more.

"Take control, take control, take control," I mumbled, seizing all of them at once and struggling to hold them as they bucked against my mind. Whoever had crafted these protections had thrown serious power into the effort.

"There! And there!"

Vaguely I heard Cooper yelling, pointing out movement on the shore. Robed figures were pulling out yet more compositions.

"Leave them to us," Darius cried to the two captains. "You stay focused on those ropes."

He and Jareth moved, both reaching for their pockets, but I could barely follow their movements, my attention taken up with the shielding compositions that were fighting against my mental hold.

"Protect the barge," I choked out, impressing the words over all four compositions.

For a moment they resisted, and then with a mental snap, the power broke free of the ropes, rushing toward us instead.

Layna let out a wordless cry of alarm at the sudden incoming rush of power. Her hand, already holding a composition, faltered, and her other hand dove for a pocket.

"No!" I cried. "The ropes! Focus on the ropes!"

For half a breath she hesitated, and then she had the original parchment gripped in both hands again and was tearing it. A similar sound came from the front of the boat, where Vincent stood, facing the scene ahead of us.

The ropes loomed large now, spanning even higher above the waterline than I had realized from downriver. At any second, we would collide with them, our boat splintering as we were all catapulted into the river.

But Vincent and Layna's compositions hit the ropes first. The power pulverized them, disintegrating the fibers. Any stretches of rope that escaped their power went slack and fell back into the water.

Our boat rushed over them, the remaining fragments disappearing beneath the churning water raised by our passage. With wide eyes, I saw the figures on the riverbank loom large for one brief second before they flashed past in the speed of our movement. I twisted around to watch them as they began to shrink again, receding downriver.

With the rope destroyed, Vincent and Layna turned their attention to the robed figures sprinkled among those on shore. Both of them drew new compositions from their pockets, their movements mirroring those of the enemy mages. The princes had managed to prevent them from setting more shields on the rope, but they hadn't incapacitated them completely.

"Wait." I raised my voice above the sound of the water and the shouts on shore. "Don't waste your compositions. We're well shielded now. Nothing they send can hurt us. Focus on speed. We need to get past them and far out of their reach."

The two captains exchanged a look before Vincent nodded. Balls of fire flew through the air toward us, coming from the enemy mages, but my companions ignored them. Their trust warmed me, and I tested my ongoing connection to the shields I had stolen. Through the link, I could feel the enormous reserves of power that still remained, far more than enough to extinguish the fire balls beating uselessly against them. The protection would last through several more attacks, especially given less-powerful shields of our own sat beneath them, waiting to take their turn at protecting us.

Vincent and Layna withdrew new compositions in exchange for the ones they had put away, ripping them in unison. The boat lurched, picking up speed in response to whatever workings they had unleashed. Darius glanced behind us before adding a composition of his own, providing yet another burst of power to augment the existing workings. The boat shot through the water so fast I had to grab for the wood in front of me. My white knuckles gripped the bench, only just keeping me from being hurled into the water.

I crouched down between two benches, trying to find a more secure position. The rest of the group did the same, sheltering from the wind that now seemed to howl against us. The shouts of the ambush had fallen away. When I peered back downriver, squinting against the wind and blinking away the moisture it raised in my eyes, I couldn't make out the figures on the riverbank anymore.

A final attack composition reached us, only to burn out uselessly against our shields as the others had done. And then there was only the creaking of the barge, the rush of the water, and the whistle of the wind.

No one spoke, all of us crouched below the level of the hull. More minutes passed, the trees flashing by too fast to process, before the power that drove us began to fade. We slowed and then slowed again. Within minutes we were traveling at the same speed we had been using since boarding the barge.

No new shouts reached us, and no surges of power raced after us. When I surveyed the riverbank, I saw nothing but dense trees and foliage, in many places pressing right up against the shore.

I breathed a long sigh of relief and clambered up to actually sit on the bench.

"Is everyone all right?" I asked. "No one was hurt?"

"I'm fairly certain I have splinters in half my fingers," Bryony said, clearly trying to lighten the mood, "but I'm assuming that doesn't count."

She sounded relieved but also irritated. I knew how much she would have hated being forced to cower uselessly.

I gave her a sad smile. "Don't worry, Bree. I have a feeling we can expect plenty more battles where you'll have a chance to use your sword."

"Yes," Vincent said, his face and tone grim. "That was only the beginning."

CHAPTER 19

"They were waiting for us," Darius said. "And they were well prepared."

"They were waiting for someone," Cooper corrected him. "We can't know it was us specifically."

"That's true," Darius conceded, "but they didn't get all the way down here from the northern reaches of the Empire since yesterday afternoon."

Jareth threw an accusing glance at Tyron, as if he still suspected him of somehow lying about the message he'd received. But we'd all been there to see him questioned under a truth composition.

"Conall has been planning this offensive for many years," Vincent said, glancing back from his place in the prow. "I think we can assume he will have been making all sorts of preparations ahead of gathering his army."

"It was a simple yet effective ambush." Layna gazed at the water thoughtfully. "And it could have been waiting there for an extended period of time. With the ropes trailing beneath the water, and the people camped among the trees, any ships that passed would be highly unlikely to notice anything. They may have been lying in wait, just holding position until they received word from Conall that they should stop anyone trying to come north."

"We need to send word back to Kallmon." I looked at Darius. "Surely they'll be sending some of the troops north via the river."

He nodded. "That's true and may well explain the rationale for putting such a block in place. I have a small handful of communication compositions with me, and I think it's worth using one in this case. I'll make sure any forces who come this way are prepared to meet similar resistance."

Vincent shook his head. "Even with warning, they won't have as easy a time of it as we did." He looked back at me, and I looked away, uncomfortable with his words. "I don't think I'd quite grasped what an asset you'll be even before we reach Conall, Princess."

I forced myself to look back at him, glancing between him and Layna. "I'm grateful you were both willing to listen to me in the heat of the moment. We don't want to waste compositions, not when we don't know what's waiting ahead of us."

"Aye." Vincent rubbed his chin. "There's no denying we must strive for efficiency. And I can see you'll help us on that front as well." He sighed. "It's situations such as that ambush that show the value of the Spoken Mage's flexibility. Once you took down the shields, Your Highness, Layna and I wasted far more power on those ropes than was needed. A few simple cuts would have done the job. But I don't exactly keep such a specific composition in my arsenal."

"No, how could you possibly know to do so?" I agreed.

"I'm sorry I can't help in such a way," Stellan said quietly. "I may be a spoken mage of sorts, but I can do far less with my energy abilities than my mother and other power mages can do with their abilities."

"You may come in useful yet, Your Highness," Vincent said.

"We can't expect every danger we encounter to be at such a distance."

His respectful attitude toward my brother triggered a stab of guilt. I knew how the two captains felt about being the only guards on an expedition full of trainees—including four royals from two kingdoms. But they hadn't been in a position to dictate who came.

But the guilt was easily discarded. Maybe I could have fought harder to exclude my brother, but I couldn't blame myself too harshly. I might want to keep him safe, but that didn't mean I had the right to make decisions for him. How could I expect my parents to take that view toward me if I wasn't even willing to apply it to my brother?

I shook my head. Plus, as a foreign prince and a spoken mage, there was no one back at the Academy with the power or authority to restrain him against his will. He would have found a way to follow us—a far more dangerous outcome for everyone.

"How many more blockades should we expect?" Cooper asked, his focus on Vincent. "Should we leave the river?"

Vincent grimaced, glancing at Darius. "I'm inclined to say we hold the course. Unless you disagree, Your Highness? We're forewarned now." He jerked a thumb back in my direction. "And we have a weapon they can't counter. Doesn't matter how many shields they pile on with the Princess on our side. Their shields will just serve to make us safer—if I understand what happened back there correctly."

I nodded. "I'm sure there are strategies that could circumvent my ability, but they won't have had the chance to think of them or implement them before we arrive. And that's assuming Conall's people even understood what happened back there, which I doubt."

"There's every chance any further ambushes won't have even heard of our success in evading the first one," Layna said. "Not yet, anyway. I also vote for staying on the river. Speed is crucial, and we could spend days or weeks trying to hack our way through the forest."

Everyone looked to Darius, waiting for him to make the final decision. After a long moment of gazing out at the trees rushing by, he nodded his head.

"We stay on the river. We must prioritize speed. But we keep a sharp lookout for any further ambushes. I don't want to be surprised again."

"In that case," Elsie said, speaking up for the first time. "I think we could all do with some food."

She had picked herself up from the floor of the barge and began to distribute cold rations that she retrieved from both her pack and the packs of both captains. I was sure my stomach was too unsettled to eat, but when she forced food into my hand, it looked surprisingly appealing.

Silence fell for several minutes while everyone ate and gazed either ahead at the coming river, or to either side at the banks racing past. When Vincent finished his food, he brushed his hands against his clothes and exchanged a look with Layna. I couldn't read it, but she seemed to instantly understand, picking her way up the barge to take his place in the prow.

Vincent moved back a short way and surveyed us all.

"Now," he said. "While we have a few moments of quiet, we need to discuss future strategy. We were lucky to make it through that attack unscathed and without a greater waste of compositions. We were sloppy and uncoordinated—and we can't afford to be either. This group has power, but we don't have the training to work together."

We all turned to him, finishing off our last mouthfuls. He looked us over as if we were a new lot of guard recruits joining one of his squads.

"In normal circumstances, I'd want a team to train together for at least a month before I'd even consider taking them out on such a risky exercise. We don't have a month, but if we're lucky, we might have a few hours. So we need to put them to good use."

~

In the end, we had the entire rest of the day, encountering no further ambushes on the river. The first thing Vincent decreed was that the power mages share out some of their compositions among the energy mages. Even Elsie was given a few, mostly shields.

As the captain pointed out, we would fight better if we didn't need half our number sheltering on the ground without weapons. And he made it clear the energy mages would have their role to play in helping the power mages restock their supplies without burning themselves dangerously low on energy.

"So, in a sense, the compositions belong to us all," he said.

We would still only have limited opportunities to replenish compositions, however, so I was glad to discover that the two captains had brought an almost mind-boggling number with them. I suspected they represented the majority of the Academy Guards' reserves as well as the captains' own supplies. I just hoped the guards left behind at the Academy didn't feel the lack. At least we had no reason to think the fight would make it so far south anytime soon, and no doubt the guards were busy replenishing while we traveled.

I knew Layna wouldn't approve of my sharing my own personal supply of compositions, so I waited until she was engaged in a quiet conversation with Vincent before distributing a number of them to Elsie and Bryony. I still kept some, but as I explained when they tried to refuse, if I encountered a life-or-death situation, I was likely to have other ways to draw on power. I no longer needed the large stash my family had always provided.

No one gave Tyron any compositions, and he made no

protest on the matter. When I happened to meet his eyes, he gave me a wry smile. He still sat tucked into the same corner of the barge where he had taken shelter during the ambush. He had certainly made no move to hamper our defense efforts in any way. The thought brought me comfort. I had been the one to push for him to come, and I didn't want to be proved wrong about him.

The day dragged on, made tense by our expectation of another ambush, although none came. Each of the four power mages took a turn writing one of the compositions that powered the boat's momentum against the current, topping up their energy afterward with supplies from Bryony and Tyron. Once again, Tyron handed over his workings without complaint or even comment.

But when I found myself near him, he spoke in a quiet voice.

"You can stop looking at me like I'm about to bash a hole in the bottom of the boat or something. How much help do I have to give before you'll all start to trust me?"

I stared at him, struggling to form words for my indignation. In the face of my silence, he answered himself.

"But, of course—what am I saying? You'll never trust me. Not with an ability like mine." He cocked his head to the side. "Does it haunt you? Just a little? How close you've come to having an ability that would make you just as much of a pariah as me?"

"We don't mistrust you because of your ability," I snapped. "We mistrust you because of all the terrible things you've done."

"Are you completely sure about that?" he asked.

"Of course I'm sure," I told him coldly, moving away before he could speak again.

But as the day drew on, a worm of doubt entered my mind. If Tyron had turned up at the Academy and been honest about his ability, would we have trusted him? How could an ability like his ever be used for good?

And what did it mean that a small part of me still remembered the heady feeling of connecting with his energy? The same small part that sometimes itched to try wielding his ability again.

Around me, debate had turned to what we should do once we reached the edge of the forest. We would be well within the Empire's borders at that point, and if we stayed on the river, it would take us right by the capital.

We still needed to travel north, but Conall's stronghold in the northern mountains was much further east than the Abneris River, near the source of the eastern Overon River. Given his location, we could safely assume he had gathered his army from the northeastern region of the Empire.

But, as Jareth pointed out, Conall must be marching toward the capital by now, and we had no way of knowing how far he'd come. It was certainly far easier to travel by boat than by foot, and a great deal faster as well.

The decision had still not been made when the daylight began to fade. Despite the growing dark around us, we could see the trees beginning to thin out, drawing back from the riverside as their numbers dwindled. Eventually they disappeared completely to be replaced by farmlands.

But although the sun sank completely below the horizon, and the river behind us disappeared into blackness, ahead of us the glow of sunset seemed permanently fixed in place. We continued our forward progress, our attention increasingly focused on the golden glow along the horizon.

"What is it?" Elsie asked me quietly, but I had no answer for her.

As the minutes passed, I grew more and more certain that the sky was growing brighter rather than darker. I was about to question Darius, who sat on my other side, when Vincent abruptly stood and withdrew a composition from one of his many pockets.

He ripped it, and the wind, along with the force pushing us forward, instantly died away. A gentler current directed us toward the eastern riverbank, and by the time the rest of us had absorbed what was happening, we were already butting against the bank.

"Quick." Vincent jumped out onto the bank, reaching back to grab hold of the barge.

Cooper and Jareth followed him, each of them securing a different section of the boat and holding it steady against the current that was now trying to reverse our course. Elsie had already begun moving as well, gathering up their three packs, along with her own, so Stellan and I hurried to assist her. We threw the packs onto the shore before jumping over ourselves, turning back to watch Layna do a final sweep of the vessel before she also alighted.

The three men continued to hold the barge in place as Vincent conducted a hurried exchange with Darius. I couldn't follow their conversation, but it took less than a minute for Vincent to call a quiet command and let the barge go. For a moment it held its position, and then the rushing water caught it and carried it rapidly away from us, back in the direction we had come.

"What happened?" I asked, looking between Vincent and Darius. "Did you see something?"

"That light." Vincent pointed ahead of us to the glowing horizon. "I just realized what it is. We can't take the river any further."

"Well, what is it?" Stellan asked, and Cooper was the one to reply.

"It's the Sekali army, isn't it?" he asked Vincent. "That glow is coming from the lights of their camp."

Vincent nodded. "It has to be. Makes sense, too, and we should have been expecting it. The emperor will have been mustering his troops ever since Prince Darius contacted him before we left the Academy. And he'll start by setting up a defensive perimeter around the capital. Likely he's got them camped on both sides of the river."

"And we nearly sailed right into the middle of them." I shook my head. "Not nearly as bad as walking into the middle of Conall's army, but still less than ideal."

"Far from ideal, indeed," Darius said. "This is a stealth mission, and we've already been spotted by the enemy once. The last thing we need is getting caught up with the Sekalis. They would no doubt want us to see their emperor, and then who knows who he would insist on sending with us? And in the meantime, word of our presence would spread far and wide."

"And there's every chance Conall has managed to get some of his people to infiltrate that army," Layna said. "It's the sensible move, and he's had years to prepare."

Tyron nodded. "Of course he does. He's managed to recruit a few disaffected Sekalis to his cause over the years—both power mages and commonborns. Their numbers aren't large, but they're useful for such roles. Just like the ones back there." He pointed back down the river.

I frowned at him. "What do you mean?"

"The control my father can exercise isn't like what I can do. A mission like that ambush is too complicated and too distant from his and his lieutenants' direction to be undertaken by someone he's coerced. At least one—and I'm guessing more likely a couple or more—of those ambushers are following him willingly. The rest will have been coerced to blindly obey those few."

"That sounds promising," Darius said. "Does that mean his army will be disorganized and ineffective?"

Tyron shook his head. "My father will have his people at the top of the chain of command, creating the strategy and making decisions. The people he's coerced will all have been implanted with the directive to follow instructions from their superior officers. That compulsion will continue all the way up the chain until it reaches someone serving with a free mind. Armies are ideally set up for his powers. They're all about following orders, not about showing individual initiative or inspiration."

I sighed. He was right. An army set up in such a manner would be effective enough for the purpose. Conall must have known we would be hesitant to massacre his soldiers, and he no doubt intended to use that to his advantage.

"So this is where we start walking." Bryony sounded far more cheery about the prospect than it seemed to warrant.

Vincent nodded. "And our first task will be to give a nice wide berth to that army up there."

"Actually," Layna said, "I think our first task will have to be finding somewhere to hole up for the night." When Vincent glanced at her, she met his eyes steadily. "None of us had a proper night's sleep last night, and we mustn't forget that most of our party aren't hardened soldiers or guards. We'll only get ourselves into trouble if we push too hard."

I wanted to dispute her words, but I had to admit she was right. Despite the physical fitness I had gained from my years at the Academy, I felt far from ready for a long trek through the night.

Vincent acquiesced, sending Cooper and Layna to scout for a suitable spot. He had the rest of us gather into a tight huddle under a couple of trees, while he kept a sharp eye on our surroundings. His vigilance never lessened, even while he talked to Darius and Jareth about what compositions we had that might assist with evading the gathered troops in the area.

With so little time to prepare, we didn't have much fit for the purpose. The realization seemed to reconcile Vincent to a night of idleness. I suspected he intended all four of the power mages to repeat their efforts from the barge—writing up suitable compositions and then replenishing their energy with the help of the energy mages in the group.

Layna and Cooper came back with good news. They had found a small barn that appeared to be abandoned. When I looked a little skeptical, Cooper explained it wasn't uncommon for local civilians to flee when they suddenly found their homes in the middle of a war ground.

"And a barn will serve us well," he said. "Straw to sleep on, and a roof over our heads. Not to mention that it will get us out of sight."

I couldn't argue with any of that, and within minutes Layna had led us to our shelter for the night. The barn had a loft section with several windows, and Vincent organized everyone but Tyron into a roster so we could keep at least two people on guard duty throughout the night.

I was assigned to keep watch with Layna and was grateful we were given the final shift of the night. I wasn't sure if I could stay alert at the necessary level without some sleep first.

Darius and Vincent, in the first shift, seemed to have no such issues, however. And given Bryony was assigned to join them, I suspected they would be producing some compositions as well as keeping watch.

Uneasiness made it hard to settle, but I eventually drifted off, nestled against a hay bale, to the sound of their quiet whispers. I had known it would be difficult to find Conall and to evade the armies he had positioned between himself and us, but it hadn't occurred to me we would be dodging the armies of our allies the whole time as well. The Empire might be vast, but suddenly it felt all too small.

CHAPTER 20

It was Stellan who shook me awake for my turn on watch. Apparently he was to join Layna and me. And, sure enough, after giving us instructions on how to keep a proper guard, Layna pulled out a parchment and began to compose.

As dawn broke, we sighted two separate groups passing near the barn, but neither showed any interest in the building. In both cases, they appeared to be locals, walking beside carts laden high with belongings. I could only assume they were on their way out of the area as Cooper had predicted.

When Layna finished composing, she turned to Stellan. But instead of speaking a composition to gift her energy, he turned to me.

"Why don't you do it, Verene?"

"Me?" I frowned at him. "I can't give energy."

"You can give mine. It's a good opportunity for you to practice connecting with me. Better to practice now than to wait and have the first time be in an emergency when we need you to connect to me so we can both take energy at once."

Layna nodded her approval. "That makes sense."

"Unless you've connected with me before and just not

mentioned it?" Stellan looked at me curiously, no judgment on his face. "I've heard it's hard to sense from our side."

I shook my head emphatically. "No! Of course not!"

"Well, then, here's your chance." He spread his arms wide, inviting me to begin. A spear of light pierced the window, illuminating his face, telling me dawn had come and our time was running out.

"Connect," I said without further argument.

With my mother, I had been overwhelmed by her strength and by how easily I could access almost unlimited power. Stellan was a spoken mage, like her, and also able to access the energy of others, like she could, but connecting with him felt nothing like connecting with my mother.

She had long ago learned to tune out her awareness of the energy of others, as I had done. But in Stellan that awareness blazed inside him. At first, I thought maybe it was because he was younger, still new to his powers, less accustomed to the sensation. But that didn't feel quite right.

There was no chaos in my brother's mind, and the compositions he was capable of completing sprang into my thoughts fully formed and controlled. It wasn't a lack of training but rather that he felt the energy around him with an acuteness I had never experienced.

He didn't have to reach out or make any effort in order to know the exact location of everyone in the barn, and each of their energies felt distinct and unique. Without thinking about it, I knew where Elsie slept, the sense of her warm—special, in a way I didn't quite understand.

And further out, I could still feel the last group to pass us, retreating now into the distance. I knew they were sealed commonborns, four adults and three children, and that their energy was low. They must have already been traveling some way despite the early hour or else slept poorly.

But it wasn't just an awareness of the energy of others. I could see, as simply as I could see my brother's face, how to rearrange that energy. With me as a conduit, I could take it from anyone and gift it to anyone else.

It didn't matter if my eyes were open or closed, energy blazed in every direction, filling my mind.

"Stellan," I gasped. "It's overwhelming. How do you block it out?"

"Block it out?" He sounded confused. "What do you mean?"

"The energy! It's so…much."

"I don't understand. You can feel energy yourself, Verene—you told me so."

With an effort I focused my attention on his face. He looked completely bewildered.

"Yes, I can feel energy, but not like this. I've never encountered anyone who feels energy like this. It's so intense, so all-pervading."

He frowned. "I don't know what you mean. It's always been like that. I thought that was what you and Mother felt, too. And Bryony and Cooper."

I shook my head. "Not at all. I wish I could show you, but…" I frowned, thinking of Tyron. "It isn't hard to cope with? You don't feel overwhelmed by it?"

He was eyeing me warily now, as if I were the strange one. "I really don't know what you mean, Verene. Do you get overwhelmed by your powers?"

I shook my head. I did, sometimes, but not in the way he meant. "No, but then mine isn't so…present all the time."

He frowned, as if trying to puzzle out the meaning of my words. Eventually he shrugged. "Our ears can hear all the time, and our eyes can see all the time. Do you get overwhelmed by constant sight or hearing?"

"It's amazing," I said. "You're amazing." All these years, and I had no idea my brother saw the world in such a unique way.

His cheeks reddened slightly, and I had to refrain from teasing him for the flush.

"Can you not use his ability?" Layna asked. "Is there something different about it?"

"Oh, no." I had entirely forgotten the purpose of connecting with Stellan. "Not at all. I mean, yes, his ability is unique, but there's no barrier between us. Sorry."

I thought for a moment. "Take energy." I directed Stellan's ability toward myself, allowing some of my energy to flow into him.

He started, frowning at me. "What are you—"

But before he could finish, I continued. "Give energy."

This time I directed the energy I had just drawn into Stellan to flow on to Layna, along with a tiny portion of his own energy. She gave a small jolt and then grinned.

"You weren't supposed to do that," Stellan said reprovingly.

"Why not? I have little use for my own energy. At least compared to everyone else on the team. And besides, I wanted to experiment."

"It was strange," he said. "You said *take energy*, but it came out of you into me."

I nodded. "That's because while I'm connected to your ability, I'm in control, but it's still your ability and your energy I'm using. It's much less complicated with regular power mages. I use their ability just as they would, pulling power into a written composition and fueling the process with their energy. But once the process is complete, the written composition is entirely separate from them and mine to use when I please."

"I don't understand." Layna looked back and forth between us. "That felt just like other times when I've received energy."

"It was from your end," Stellan said. "But Verene was supposed to give you my energy and instead mostly gave you hers."

Layna looked at me in alarm.

"Don't worry, I had plenty to give," I said. "I just wanted to try it out. It's so easy for Stellan." I shook my head. "It's nothing like it is for Cooper, by the way."

Stellan stepped forward, his voice eager. "Do you mean the part about it wanting to return? I've been so confused about that. It seems so central to his power."

I nodded. "You're an energy mage, and you don't use power to do your compositions like Mother does, but otherwise when you draw on energy it feels like it does for her. You just absorb it, and it becomes yours to use—or, in your case, give away if you choose. It's more a redistribution than a theft—or at least that seems to be the way the energy responds."

"Thank you for the energy, whoever it came from," Layna said. "But I'm not sure this is the time for an academic discussion on your unique abilities."

I winced. "Sorry. I can get distracted when I experience something so new like that."

"Well I'm glad Stellan had the foresight to suggest you try it now, then," she said. "Because we can't afford to have you distracted in the middle of battle."

Vincent called to us from the barn floor, and we all hurried down the ladder, leaving the conversation behind us. Elsie had a basic breakfast prepared, and we ate quickly, eager to be on our way now we had managed a proper sleep.

In our absence, Elsie had also made a discovery that met with Vincent's approval. Hidden at the back of the barn was a small hand-pulled wooden cart. As she proudly displayed her find, my mind flew back to the way her presence had felt while I was connected to Stellan. If I had harbored any doubts about their relationship before, they were gone now. Stellan wouldn't let go of Elsie no matter what hardships their relationship might bring him.

"This will solve two concerns in one." Vincent slung his pack into the cart, indicating for us to do the same. "I've been concerned about the weight of the packs slowing us down, especially since none of you have experience carrying them. And we'll need to re-provision soon, which will only make them heavier. Now we can take turns pulling this while everyone else walks freely. It will also allow us to blend in more effectively. There's a significant population displacement going on right now, and another small group with a cart should be less than remarkable."

I threw my pack onto the pile, trying to keep the relief off my face. I had been determined that I wouldn't slow the group down, but privately I had been concerned about my ability to carry the pack which already felt heavier than when I packed it.

We struck off, heading almost directly east. We would need to swing north at some point, but Vincent and Darius wanted us out of reach of the Sekali army first. As expected, we passed multiple other groups similar to our own, although they generally had more heavily laden carts and moved more slowly.

By halfway through the first day, I was grateful not to have my pack on my back. My own legs felt heavy enough. By the end of the day, I was more than ready to receive the compositions handed around by Layna to ease aching muscles and heal blisters.

"We can thank Raelynn for these," she told me. "She caught me just before we left with a whole stack of them. She said we'd need them, and I can see she's right."

Even Darius accepted one, only Vincent grunting and saying he had no need. When I saw Layna hesitating by Tyron, I told her to give him one.

"We don't want him slowing us down," I pointed out, to justify what some in the group might feel was a waste.

But, in truth, while Tyron and his ability might make me feel a little queasy still, I didn't want to see him suffer. Not when he had been nothing but helpful since the moment his father sent him the message. I wasn't entirely sure if it was pragmatism or compassion that motivated me and was just grateful the two emotions were in alignment.

To our relief, many of the traveling groups of commonborns —all sealed as was the way in the Empire—had bubbles of power around them, shields they had clearly procured from Sekali mages. They might lack the power of the workings that surrounded us, but they served the purpose of making us less conspicuous.

"It's amazing," Elsie breathed when she heard me discussing the phenomenon with Stellan. "Every person we encounter is sealed. And they use compositions so casually."

"It's different in the Empire," Bryony explained, having come into earshot. "We have so many more mages."

"Amazing," Elsie repeated, shaking her head.

An idea—one which had germinated some time before— stirred, but before I had a chance to mention it, Vincent called us all back to the road from our short break.

The captain had a web of compositions surrounding us, all of them linking back to him and giving us warning when we needed to leave the road for whatever closest shelter we could find. Even moving directly away from the capital we passed numerous groups of soldiers, all heading in the opposite direction. Troops were clearly gathering from all over the Empire.

Twice we saw squads and once an entire platoon, mounted and riding hard. Each time they were heading northeast, and each time our own pace picked up after seeing them. We didn't discuss it, but we all felt the same pressure. The longer we took, the more lives and homes were destroyed by Conall.

That night we slept at the center of a dense clump of trees, and I missed the straw from the night before. No one complained, however.

Before I went to sleep, Darius drew me aside, pressing a piece of parchment into my hand in the fading light. My brows creased as I stared down at it, my eyes skimming the words. When I had read enough to understand its import, I gasped.

"Darius," I hissed. "What is this?"

He was watching me, his expression hard to read. "Last night in the barn, I removed Tyron's bindings long enough for him to write this. And only this. Don't worry, Captain Vincent and I both watched him like hawks."

"But—" I wanted to reject the composition, to thrust it back at him and tell him to find a way to safely destroy it.

My hand remained clutched around it, however. It was a powerful weapon, and I had said I would do whatever it took. I looked up and found Tyron watching us, a knowing look on his face. I promptly turned back to Darius.

"It's general and vague," Darius said, "because we don't know what circumstance might necessitate its use. That's why you have to have it. You're the only one who can adjust it after it's been worked. You can turn it into whatever we need it to be."

"I—" Once again I couldn't bring myself to actually repudiate it. "I hope it doesn't come to that," I said instead.

"As do I," Darius said, embracing me briefly. "As do I."

The next day, after consultation with Darius, Vincent turned us north. We were still a long way from the Overon River that connected the Empire and Ardann, but the captain obviously felt we had gone far enough to bypass the bulk of the emperor's forces.

By the end of the day, we had entered a different sort of landscape. Here in the north it was warmer, and spring was approaching. But the fields lay abandoned and neglected, the houses we passed looking the same.

Darius's face grew darker and darker the further we went. I

sidled up to him, positioning myself close enough on the road that we could talk.

"It's hard to see, isn't it?" I said softly.

He growled under his breath before looking down at me and apologizing. "I didn't expect to see it so soon. This isn't like that barn we stayed in or the people we passed. These people didn't choose to leave their homes. You can tell."

I nodded. "It has an eerie sort of feel. I keep reminding myself the people who live here aren't dead. We're going to free them, and then they're going to return home."

Darius looked down at my determined expression with a smile. "You always have a way of making me feel better about things."

I slipped my hand into his, emboldened by his words, and he gripped it tightly.

"I've missed you, too," I said softly.

We walked in silence for a while before I raised the question that had been increasingly occupying my mind. "How are we going to locate Conall? From the looks of this region, he must have gathered a considerable army by now. And he could be anywhere among them. Or not with them at all."

"I've been thinking about that," he said. "And I might have an idea."

"I'm glad to hear it because I have nothing."

He chuckled. "That's because you're not a law enforcement trainee. But you still played an important role in my idea."

"Me?"

He nodded. "I've never actually tried this particular working, but I've read about it. It's a composition that can be used for tracking down a fugitive, but it requires a close blood relative. And it's thanks to you we have Tyron with us."

I glanced back at him, several lengths behind us. "I hope we don't come to regret that."

Darius shook his head. "I have an increasing feeling we won't.

Even if my personal preference is that he never enters my sight again."

I looked back again to where Tyron walked alone. His earlier words rang in my head, making me uncomfortable all over again. His father had taught him their abilities were a birthright that gave them the right to use and abuse other people. Back at the Academy, it had seemed so simple when I refuted the idea, telling him we were given power to help others. But now I couldn't stop thinking about his challenge to me. With an ability like his, had there ever been a chance for a different future for Tyron?

I was walking through the Empire on a quest to stop a war because of the ability I had been given. And my brother had fallen in love with a girl whose energy shone in his amplified awareness. Despite our best efforts, was it our abilities that shaped who we became?

I shook myself, forcing my eyes away from the Tarxi. Behind him, Elsie and Stellan walked together, heads bent close and fingers entwined. Layna brought up the rear, watching them with an expression of concern. I bit my lip. Apparently Stellan had decided the time for secrecy was past. I just hoped he didn't regret that decision later.

Ahead of us, Cooper and Vincent led the way, also in quiet conversation—no doubt exchanging notes on the different methods employed by the Royal Guard and the Armed Forces. Vincent never seemed off duty, his thoughts always centered on his role as guard.

He would need to find a wife who was either incredibly understanding or equally dedicated to the same cause. I stopped myself from glancing back at Layna.

Instead I focused on Bryony and Jareth who walked directly ahead of me. As was often the case these days, they appeared to be in some sort of heated conversation. But as I watched, she looked up at him, laughter in her eyes, and he looked down into her face with a warm expression I hadn't seen him wear before.

I blinked and blinked again. Had I been so self-absorbed I had missed that development happening under my nose? Why hadn't Bryony said anything?

Somehow her silence on the matter made the situation seem more serious. If her heart was untouched, surely she would have said something.

But Bryony didn't want to be tied down, and she had always been clear about her feelings toward wearing a crown. I watched the two of them with increasing concern. Whatever was going on there, I didn't want to see my friend hurt. Especially since I was the cause of drawing her into such close association with the princes.

I was considering how best to raise the issue with her when I felt a wisp of power returning to Vincent. Darius and I both froze, just in time to hear a distant eruption of shouting and the ring of steel against steel.

"Soldiers," Vincent said unnecessarily. He looked uneasily at Darius. "We should get off the road."

Darius was still looking in the direction of the distant hubbub. "It sounds like it's in our path. We continue on."

"Your Highness," Vincent began, but Darius cut him off.

"We're not going to learn what we need to know skulking beside the road. There's a war going on in this kingdom, and we're here as part of it. We need to see what it looks like."

"And help if we can?" Vincent said with such a straight face that I was nodding before I realized his words were a trap. He would never suggest such a dangerous thing in earnest.

I quickly stopped, but he was already eyeing me with concern. "We're not here to engage in battles, Your Highnesses. That was the agreement. We complete a stealth mission to free these people, and then we let the trained soldiers deal with those who follow Conall by choice."

"Certainly we can't afford to go rushing into danger," Darius said. "But that doesn't mean we can afford to stay ignorant of the situation. I want to see what's happening—even if just from a distance. We continue on."

The captain looked like he wanted to argue, but he didn't, merely inclining his head respectfully and resuming his forward progress. I gripped Darius's hand hard, every muscle taut as the noises of battle grew closer and closer.

CHAPTER 21

When Vincent tensed and signaled for us to stop, Darius dropped my hand and reached for his compositions. I nearly did the same with the instinct of years but stopped myself. I shouldn't waste any of my compositions when I could use my voice to gather power.

Cooper was pulling the cart, and he maneuvered it off the road and into a large clump of brush. Vincent signaled for us to leave the road ourselves, continuing at a much more cautious pace. When a straggling line of trees appeared, we took refuge behind them, continuing to move along the line of the road.

We could see the struggle ahead of us now, but it was hard to make sense of what was happening given the commotion. We moved closer at a faster pace, unable to resist the sense of urgency given off by the battle. But when I nearly stepped past the end of the line of trees, Darius pulled me back.

On the road, some distance from where we stood, a desperate struggle was underway. A squad of uniformed Sekali soldiers battled against a less organized group of men and women. Several of them carried swords, but the rest wielded clubs or spears and a couple had only farm implements.

But what they lacked in organization and equipment, they made up for in determination, pushing forward again and again with wild cries. The soldiers were attempting to hold a formation, but it was obvious they were off balance, hampered by their orders not to kill the civilians they faced.

I scanned their number, my concern growing. "They don't have a mage," I whispered to Darius. "How can they manage to restrain all those people without a mage?"

As I said it, one of the soldiers made a misstep, breaking slightly from formation. One of Conall's recruits surged forward and struck the man down. A cry rose from the other soldiers, and I could feel in the air that the situation was about to turn.

"If we don't do something, those soldiers are going to kill all those people," I hissed at Darius. "We have to intervene."

I had expected him to disagree, but he merely nodded and ripped the parchment held in his hand. "Direct it, Verene."

For a brief moment, I couldn't understand what he meant, but then I grasped his intention. Whatever composition he had just unleashed wasn't a perfect fit for the situation. But I could change that.

The soldiers surged forward with battle cries, their formation forgotten, and the civilians rushed to meet them. I tried to push aside the distracting crash of battle so I could focus on Darius's working.

I didn't bother to ask him what it was for, I would know as soon as I took control of it. With two murmured words I did so, the power coming instantly under my direction.

It was a binding composition like we had practiced so many times in composition class, one that would secure a person's hands and feet, providing a lengthy binding comparative to the amount of power expended. But it was aimed at a single attacker, designed to hold them for many hours.

"Bind all of them not in uniform," I whispered, giving the power an extra shove.

The closest recruit froze in the middle of thrusting his weapon at a soldier. When he tried to move, he tripped, hitting the ground with a loud cry. Within another breath, the rest of them had also stumbled and fallen.

The soldiers pulled back, milling around in confusion and peering to all sides.

"The bindings won't last long," I said. "I had to spread the power thin to get them all."

Before anyone could reply or formulate a plan, Bryony rushed out from our simple hiding place, bursting onto the road and racing toward the soldiers, shouting as she did so.

"What are you standing around for?" she berated them. "Those bindings aren't going to last forever. Don't any of you have some real rope? Secure your prisoners!"

The soldiers, who had wheeled to face her, weapons drawn, gave a start at her words. Most of them glanced toward an older woman who looked Bryony up and down and then nodded.

"Get to work," she called. "I want them all secured immediately."

All of her soldiers except the two who were bent over their fallen comrade scurried to do her bidding. She turned her attention back to Bryony, but the Sekali girl had already fled back to us in the trees. The soldier looked around in confusion, as if she suddenly doubted whether Bryony had even been real.

"Don't do that again," Vincent said coldly.

Bryony shrugged, clearly undaunted. "I couldn't let them waste the opportunity Darius and Verene had given them. But we should probably get going now."

The sound of wheels made me turn to see Cooper puffing his way toward us, our cart behind him. Vincent must have already sent him back for it.

"We march double time." Vincent pointed away from the road and the milling soldiers. "Now."

No one pointed out we would be heading in the wrong direction, moving sideways instead of forward, and no one hesitated to obey his order. I threw a last glance over my shoulder in time to see a couple of the soldiers begin a search of the local area—presumably for Bryony.

"If that's a sign of what all the battles are going to be like, then this war is going to be a disaster," Darius said when we had made it far enough to speak safely.

"Most squads should have a mage with them," I said. "That would make a difference." I frowned. "People on both sides are going to die, though. That much is clear. We need to move faster."

As if he could hear me, Vincent changed our direction, angling us back toward the road we had been following, so we could rejoin it far beyond the battleground. If the soldiers had any sense, they would have forgotten about us and begun organizing their prisoners for transport to their main force. I suspected that would be enough of a task to occupy them without doing an exhaustive search for whoever had mysteriously helped them.

We eventually managed to rejoin our original path without encountering the squad we had assisted. But the light had started to fade, and Darius suggested we find shelter for the night. Layna jumped in to agree, and after meeting her eyes, Vincent made no protest.

Twenty minutes later we found an abandoned outbuilding, smaller than the barn we had occupied on our first night but suitable for our purpose.

In the morning, Vincent gathered us together. We were a somber group, tired from our days of travel and tense after the battle the afternoon before. The reality of the war bearing down on us had never felt so close.

"That didn't look like a planned clash," Vincent said. "I've discussed the matter in detail with Cooper, and we're in agreement that the two groups likely stumbled on each other by accident. But that tells us we're nearing the front lines of this conflict, if we haven't passed them already."

I swallowed. His words weren't exactly a surprise, but I hadn't been willing to let myself think of it in such clear terms.

"They're much closer to the capital than we were expecting." Darius exchanged a tense look with Jareth. "Just how big is this army of Conall's?"

"Impossible to say without more information," Cooper said. "But quite large enough from the look of things in the Empire. Either the situation has escalated quickly, or the emperor has been hiding the extent of the situation from us."

Bryony shifted. "Both are possible. Admitting the desertion of his people—even under compulsion—would be a significant blow to his honor."

Vincent muttered something too low for us to catch before addressing us again. "Whatever the reason, this is where we find ourselves. Which means we'll need to proceed with a great deal more caution from here."

"Are we going to try Darius's composition?" I asked.

"I spent my watch shift working on it with Tyron," Darius said. "I can't guarantee it will work, but now seems like the time to try."

He pulled out a parchment, and I looked at it curiously. It was almost a full page of words, suggesting it was either extremely complex or Darius was far from confident in composing it. My gaze focused on one section of the page before I quickly looked away, regretting my curiosity. It looked suspiciously like Conall's name had been written into the composition in blood.

I looked across at Tyron who looked calm and had no obvious injuries or wounds. I gave myself a mental shake along with the reminder that if Tyron had contributed his actual blood to the composition, he would only have needed a tiny finger prick to write a single name. It still made me queasy to my stomach, though, and I could suddenly understand why it wasn't a well-known composition.

"How does it work?" Bryony craned her neck to try to see the parchment.

"It will send power out across a broad area, searching for a specific person—in this case Conall. If it finds him, a kernel of the power will return to me to lead us to him."

Bryony rocked back. "That sounds easy."

"The reality is likely to be far from it," Vincent said in warning tones. "He's put an army between us, remember. Finding him is only one of the difficulties confronting us."

"But knowing where we're going will be a lot better than our current situation," Jareth said and received several nods of agreement.

Darius ripped the parchment cleanly in half, and I felt the power it released. It wasn't the normal rush but more of a slow and gentle trickle, pooling out around us and disappearing in every direction in the thinnest of sheets.

"That felt odd," Layna muttered, and I nodded.

"Let's just hope it finds him quickly," Vincent said. "I don't want us staying still, but I don't like the idea of wandering around aimless behind his front lines either."

"Where are we headed, then?" Stellan asked. "North still?"

Darius nodded. "Conall isn't going to be leading any charges, so it seems a safe bet that he's somewhere northeast. Of course, that still leaves a lot of ground to cover. But at least we can keep moving in that general direction."

"It would be better if we were traveling at night," Cooper said. "But not with an untrained, inexperienced force like this. We could end up getting ourselves into more trouble than it's worth."

"So we head out then," Bryony said in a subdued voice, and I caught Jareth giving her a reassuring squeeze on the arm.

"Our main aim going forward is stealth over speed," Vincent

said. "We don't want to run into any patrols—or worse, a whole force."

"But we can't move too slowly," I said. "Not given what we just saw. Every moment's delay—"

"We can only do what we can do, Your Highness," Layna said in a gentle voice. "And getting ourselves captured or killed won't do us any good."

"If we let ourselves get captured, we might get taken straight to Conall." I murmured the words under my breath, but Darius caught them, giving me a sharp look.

"Don't even think about it. If Conall has heard of you and your ability, then it's far more likely he's ordered you're to be killed on sight."

"I don't know about that," Tyron said. "I think my father would be greatly intrigued by Verene's power. He would be thinking about what he could do with it if he could keep her under his control."

Darius glared at him. "If you think you're going to trick her into getting herself captured, I can promise you, I won't let that happen."

Tyron held up both hands. "I'm not saying she should do it. I wouldn't recommend it myself."

"Good." Darius gave him such a threatening look that I stepped between them.

"I'm not going to allow myself to be captured. It's too risky a strategy, and I'm well aware of that. It was just an idle thought."

Darius turned his attention to me, the hardness in his face melting away. "I'm glad to hear it. And I meant what I said. I won't let that happen."

If I had harbored any serious thoughts of such a plan, they would have evaporated in the light of his expression. Darius would do anything to stop me being carted away by Conall's forces, and I could never put him in a position where he might take unacceptable risks to protect me. Not on purpose.

Vincent cleared his throat. "If Your Highnesses are ready, we should be moving out. We've been here long enough."

We all filed obediently out of the building, falling into our usual pairs. For a while Darius and I walked in silence while a thought squirmed uncomfortably around my brain.

"We shouldn't have run away yesterday," I said eventually, breaking the silence.

He frowned down at me. "We didn't run away. We helped those soldiers, just like you wanted. Which really meant protecting Conall's puppets."

"I mean afterward." I bit my lip. "I don't know why I didn't think of it at the time, but I could have freed those people from Conall's control. They needn't have been carted off as prisoners at all."

"You will free them," Darius said with confidence in his voice. "When we get to Conall, you'll free them all. You can't free a whole army one at a time. We have to stay focused on our mission."

I sighed. "I suppose you're right. But it's still galling. Those were the individuals in front of me, and I could have helped them."

For a moment Darius was silent, and I thought he had let the topic go, but then he spoke again.

"That's the lot of a ruler. Always having to think of the good of the many, to weigh every decision in the balance. Sometimes even to turn your back on an individual you have the power to help because helping them would hurt others. I can understand why your parents don't want that life for you."

I stiffened. We didn't usually speak of what stood between us and the decision he had handed to my parents.

"A ruler who never thinks of individuals will eventually become one who is so cold and callous he can't see individuals at all," I said. "No one is asking me to rule Kallorway. The question is whether I can be your partner. And maybe having a consort who will remind you that individuals matter would provide the perfect balance."

He looked down at me, his forehead creased. "Or would it be a constant fight, ready to drive a wedge between us?"

I shook my head. "I was raised as a royal too, remember, Darius. I understand about sacrifices and the burden of ruling. I would never hold those decisions against you."

He looked as if he was about to answer when instead we both stiffened, our eyes flying to Vincent. The captain held up his hand for us to stop, and we instantly did so, Tyron nearly running into our backs.

We had been walking parallel to the road but some distance back, beside a long ditch. Vincent indicated for us all to jump into the trench, and I threw myself in without hesitation. Not for the first time, the thought flashed through my mind that I was glad I wasn't wearing my usual white robe.

Within seconds we were all sheltering in the hole, none of us daring to put our heads up to see what was happening. The tramp of feet sounded along the road, someone calling out a marching rhythm. Still I forced myself not to raise my head, restraining my surge of curiosity.

"Which side are they on?" I asked in my quietest whisper.

I had ended up in the ditch beside Stellan, and he answered without needing to look.

"Sealed commonborns and one mage. That's all I can tell you."

"That could be either side." I bit my lip, eyeing him. "I wonder if it would be possible for you to learn to recognize from someone's energy if they're controlled by Conall or not?"

Stellan raised an eyebrow. "A skill like that might come in useful."

The sound of marching feet began to recede. Vincent stuck his head up to look in their direction, but Layna pulled him sharply back down before he had been up there even a few seconds. He glanced down our line of huddled figures, meeting Darius's eyes.

"Conall's forces," he whispered. "But they're past us now."

Darius nodded once, his face hard to read. We waited for what felt like endless minutes, the ditch growing increasingly uncomfortable, until Layna signaled we could climb out and resume our progress.

The rest of the day passed in a similar manner, our route chosen so we were always near some form of shelter. Every group that passed now was made of Conall's puppets, except a single small group of uncontrolled civilians, looking furtive and moving fast as they fled the area.

The emperor had been gathering his forces at the capital, and Conall was clearly gathering his as well, although where, we didn't know. We slept that night in another dense patch of trees, Vincent unwilling to be fenced in by walls.

Four groups passed us in the night, their torches making them stand out in the darkness. Each time, we were jerked from our sleep, woken by the guards on watch to wait in tense silence in case we needed to flee. But each time the groups passed by without stopping.

"These aren't patrols," Cooper said with certainty. "They're all on their way somewhere. Which suggests Conall doesn't know we're in the area."

When Vincent didn't look pleased by his words, he quickly added, "Although that could change at any moment, of course. We can't let up our vigilance."

As we slipped out from among the trees the next morning, I grasped Elsie's arm, telling Stellan he could walk somewhere else for a short time. He gave me an amused shake of his head and ambled off to take my place beside Darius. The prince glanced back in our direction, his face impassive. But a moment later he smiled at my brother, and the sight warmed my heart.

I forced myself to look away from them, examining my personal servant instead.

"Are you regretting coming yet?" I asked.

She looked startled. "Of course not. I knew how it would be."

"Did you?" I looked along the line stretching in front of us, all of us looking considerably wearier and more bedraggled than when we had fled the Academy. "Did any of us?"

But Elsie's eyes were focused on only one member of the line. Stellan. The memory of the way he had openly gripped her hand and stayed by her side made it easy to understand why she couldn't regret coming.

"I don't know if anyone's said it yet, but thank you," I said. "For all the meals you've prepared."

"But that's nothing," she said. "I just wish I could contribute properly, like everyone else."

I shook my head. "If you don't know the value of a full and satisfied stomach, you have a lot to learn about people. Plus, you're the one who found us that cart. We wouldn't be making such good progress without it."

She grimaced. "I can't take much credit there, since I had selfish motives. I don't think I would have made it far with my pack on my back."

"What do you think of the Empire?" I asked. "I realize it's not exactly showing to best advantage at the moment, and we haven't had a chance to speak to any locals, but..."

"I find it fascinating." She gazed around us. "From the state of the abandoned houses, they seem more prosperous than I real-ized. Even the simple farmers."

"Something we can all be grateful for." I shook my head. "We would be in trouble if we hadn't been able to forage food supplies from some of the abandoned houses."

She nodded. "It's still a strange thought that every person we encounter is sealed. I can't imagine life like that back in Ardann."

I sighed. "I wish it could be like that. But the position of commonborns has still come a long way from how it used to be. I just hope that one day soon the commonborns of Kallorway can be in the same position as those in Ardann."

"With you and Darius in charge, I have no doubts," she told me.

My eyes latched on to Darius, now talking quietly to Stellan. "I don't think that's certain." I couldn't keep my tone from turning dejected. "But even if it's just Darius, I know he won't forget the commonborns."

Elsie reached out to squeeze my hand. "Your parents will come around. I know they will."

But I noticed her eyes were on Stellan's back, and I wasn't sure if she was talking to me or to herself.

CHAPTER 22

I returned to my place beside Darius after our brief stop for a midday meal. And once again, my attention was captured by Bryony and Jareth ahead of us. Somehow I had to find a chance to talk to her in private, preferably not while we all trudged in a line, so close to each other.

I was so distracted by my friend's unexpected romance, I nearly didn't feel the thin sliver of power that wormed its way along the ground, heading straight for us. Darius responded first, swinging around to face it, leaving me to mirror his movement a second behind.

"Let me—" I started to say, but he shook his head.

"That's my composition coming back."

I stiffened. The power collided with him, wending its way up his body to settle in his palm. Now that it was still, I could feel he was right. Without taking control of it, I could sense only a vague awareness of its purpose, but it was enough to identify it.

Those behind us had stopped when we did, but it took the people in front another few moments to realize something was happening behind them. Vincent hurried down the line as soon as he realized, stopping in front of Darius.

"It's found him?" he asked, his eyes on Darius's outstretched hand just as mine were, even though none of us could see anything.

"What is it?" Bryony asked, and Jareth replied.

"Darius's search composition has returned to him. It's there in his hand."

She gasped. "So it's found Conall."

"It would appear so." Darius also stared at his palm.

Slowly the power sank into his bones and muscles, settling into his hand and reducing to the tiniest hum.

"Is it supposed to do something?" Elsie whispered from behind me. She and Stellan had drawn close, bypassing Tyron who still hung back.

"I have no idea," I admitted.

Darius flexed his fingers, looking down at them with a blank expression. "I suppose we have to try it out and see."

He began to walk in the direction we had been going, his hand held out awkwardly, and his eyes pinned to it. He had taken a number of steps when I grabbed at him, only just suppressing a scream. All of his fingers had turned black.

"Darius! Your fingers!"

"Don't worry, Princess Verene," Vincent said quickly. "That's what they're supposed to do. Try the other way, Your Highness."

Darius turned, his eyes glued to his now black hand, and walked back the way we had come. Nothing changed, and my breath came a little faster. What if there had been a mistake in the composition, and the working was destroying his hand somehow? The sight of his black fingers was certainly unnerving enough to fuel the idea.

We had been moving northeast, so Darius now turned northwest, striking away from our path entirely. I kept pace with him, my eyes glued to his hand so that three times I nearly tripped over small obstacles in my way.

"It's going away," I cried after blinking several times to be sure it wasn't my vision playing tricks on me.

But a moment later there could be no doubt. His fingers, instead of returning to their usual color, now glowed as if made of gold. Darius looked first at me, the smallest hint of triumph in his eyes, and then his gaze traveled on to Vincent, falling into darker lines in the process.

"He's to the northwest. Either he's not hiding like we thought, or his people have taken even more ground than we estimated."

"It doesn't matter which," Layna said in her steady voice from behind us. "We have our path now, and that's what matters."

But the general lift in spirits provided by the success of the search composition didn't last long. The residual power now residing in Darius's fingers might know where Conall was located, but it knew nothing of the obstacles between us and him. We wended through trees, over fences, across fields, and around houses. Every time we had to turn from our course to avoid an obstacle, I had to endure the unnerving sight of Darius's black fingers. I wasn't sure how he could bear to see his own hand that way.

It didn't matter much in the case of a farmhouse, but when we encountered a deep stream, moving swiftly, we lost several hours looking for a place to ford it. And once we even had to bypass a group of Conall's recruits who had pitched a small camp. It was the largest group we had yet encountered—a full platoon's worth —and we had to give them an enormous berth. By the time we had rejoined the correct path, the sun had sunk below the horizon.

Darius looked at his hand regretfully. "We'll need to find somewhere to stop for the night."

We had to go a short way off course to find a suitable barn, and as soon as we had chosen one, Darius pulled on a pair of thick gloves.

He grimaced a little when he caught me watching. "No one wants to look at my black fingers all night."

"How long will the power last?" I asked. "Conall may still be a long way off."

Darius frowned down at his covered hand. "It's hard to say for certain, but it should last long enough. I poured an enormous amount into the original composition." He glanced across at where the others were involved in various activities to prepare for the night. "I filled up with power from both Bryony and Tyron to do it. And then Stellan topped me up afterward."

I raised my eyebrows. I must have slept through all of that.

Once again I was sharing the last watch with Layna and Stellan. This barn had no convenient loft from which to survey the surrounding ground, and she positioned us at different windows, giving us a view in most directions.

"Vincent and I have set up warning compositions, of course," she said, "but we can't afford any complacence."

I agreed but couldn't help feeling relieved to know we weren't the only line of defense. Even with my best efforts, I couldn't see around the corner of the building, and every flicker from that direction made me start and peer into the darkness.

But nerves alone weren't enough to sustain such vigilance indefinitely. As time wore on, I became calmer, sweeping my eyes back and forth across my field of view, but not jumping at every moving shadow.

The sun hadn't risen, but dawn was beginning to brighten the sky when one of the shadows caught my eye. It moved and moved again, presumably containing an animal of some sort. I let my eyes roam quickly over the rest of my watch area, not wanting to miss something because of my fixation on the shadow.

But when I looked back at it, it was gone. Uneasiness gripped me. There had been nothing from the warning compositions, so it had likely only been an animal. My eyes flickered back and forth again, and I saw another flash of movement. My heart rate sped up, and I glanced back into the still-dark barn. Sleeping figures lay everywhere. Did I wake them and risk disturbing their much-needed rest because of my oversensitive nerves?

I looked back out the window and stifled a gasp. A spear of the disappearing moonlight had caught on something bright and reflective. I surged to my feet and stumbled backward, almost falling over a figure sleeping only steps away.

Darius came instantly awake, sitting up in one fluid motion and steadying me.

"There's someone there," I gasped out, pointing out the window with a trembling finger. "I'm almost sure."

"Wake the others." He didn't hesitate or question my uncertain language. "Get Captain Vincent."

He moved to my place at the window as I raced back into the barn.

"Quietly," he whispered over his shoulder, and I nodded back, realizing a moment later he likely couldn't see me in the dark.

I shook the shoulder of every sleeper I could find, hissing for them to be quiet. By the time I found Vincent, rustles surrounded me, and someone was already bending over him, shaking him awake. He sprung to alertness almost as quickly as Darius, leaping to his feet to stare between Layna and me.

"There's people out there, Vince," she said, her voice focused. "They're moving quietly and keeping themselves hidden."

"You saw them too?" I stared at her in relief. "I wasn't sure if I was imagining things."

If Layna had seen them, they were real. Unlike me, she knew what she was doing. Instead of bumbling around among the sleepers, she had known where to find Vincent and gone straight to him.

Vincent grimaced. "They've already got us surrounded then."

"They're a sizable force, I'd say." Darius stepped up to join us, also keeping his voice low. "And there's no doubt this is an ambush. They know we're here."

Vincent looked at Layna. "No warning came through from our compositions?"

She shook her head. "They must have disabled them."

"Which means they have a mage." Vincent rubbed his chin.

"Likely more than one," Darius said. "If they've come for us specifically, they'll have brought more than one mage, for sure."

"But why now?" Jareth asked, appearing at my side in the semi-darkness. "None of the civilian squads we passed were even on the lookout for anyone in their territory."

"My composition." Darius looked down at his gloved hand, flexing it. "It's leading us to Conall, but he must have sensed it when it found him."

"But he's an energy mage," Bryony protested from over Jareth's shoulder. "He can't feel power."

"No, but Tyron told us he has a handful of power mages on his side," I reminded her. "If he's smart—and we know he is—he'll be keeping one close for just such situations. He must have sent out patrols looking for whoever sent that composition."

"So he might not know it's us specifically." Vincent sounded relieved. "Then we can hope they've come underprepared."

"Hope for the best, plan for the worst." Layna spoke as if reciting a familiar proverb, and Vincent nodded his agreement.

By now everyone had gathered. The dark in the building had lifted slightly, and I peered around for Elsie. She remained calm, as usual, gathering our packs together in a pile in the center of the barn. When she saw me looking, she hurried over, bringing a stack of travel bread with her. She forced a piece into the hands of each of us, and I ate without thinking.

"Stellan!" I whispered when I caught sight of my brother helping Elsie dig more bread out of one of the packs.

He hurried over.

"How many are out there?" I asked. "And how many of them are mages?"

Vincent frowned, so I turned to him. "When I connected with my brother, I discovered he's not like other energy mages. He'll know exactly who's out there and where."

Vincent raised his eyebrows. "And you didn't think to mention this?" He directed his comment at Stellan.

My brother shrugged uncomfortably. "I keep forgetting Verene and Bryony and Cooper can't feel it the same way. I never knew I was different until Verene told me the other day."

"Never mind that," Darius said. "Who's out there?"

Stellan frowned, clearly concentrating. "There are twenty of them, in a rough circle around the barn. Fifteen sealed commonborns, two power mages, and three energy mages."

"Energy mages?" Tyron showed concern for the first time since he had been woken to news of an ambush. "Tarxi? My father's people?"

Stellan shrugged. "I can't tell that. They could be people like Bryony's family who live here in the Empire and have been coerced by your father just like the local commonborns and power mages."

Bryony shivered. "Thank goodness my family don't live anywhere near here."

Vincent eyed her, and I could see on his face he agreed. The last thing we needed was to stumble across someone in Bryony's family being controlled by Conall. She would never fight her own family—and I couldn't imagine fighting them either.

"They're not advancing." Stellan sounded confused. "They're just holding their circle."

Cooper, who had been flitting between the windows, keeping up a watch, was passing by as he said it.

"They'll be waiting for a signal before launching a coordinated attack."

"So what do we do?" I asked.

"Everyone get shields out," Vincent said. "But don't rip them yet. We don't want to alert them to the fact we're awake by suddenly setting off a blaze of power in the middle of the barn."

The soft sounds of fabric and parchment surrounded me as everyone withdrew compositions from their pockets.

"And I'd recommend making sure you activate shields against energy attacks as well as against power and physical ones, if you have them," Tyron said. He was staring at the closest wooden wall as if he might be able to see through it if he looked hard enough. "If any of those energy mages have come from my father, they might have nasty abilities."

"If they try anything, I'll turn it back on them," I said fiercely.

"We appreciate having you with us, Princess Verene," Vincent said, "but there are five mages out there. And who knows how many of those fifteen commonborns are equipped with compositions? You can't be everywhere and catch every enemy working. I want everyone shielded against everything—to the extent their compositions will allow."

I looked with concern at Elsie, who I knew didn't have a shield against energy, but relaxed when I saw Stellan handing her a second parchment. Our father would have ensured he was as well stocked as I always was.

"What's the plan?" Jareth asked. "Are we going to try to defeat them or punch through their line and make a run for it?"

"Defeat them," Darius said, his voice grim and his face hard, just as Vincent said, "Run."

"We fight," Darius repeated authoritatively. "We can't go after Conall with a trail of his soldiers tracking us from behind."

"Your Highness," Vincent said in a low, urgent voice, but Darius shook his head.

"We knew there would be danger," he said. "My priority is our mission, not my own safety. We can't run from this."

Several people withdrew more compositions, and I took a

deep breath. We had made it past the river ambush, and we had helped that squad on the road. We could do this, too.

I had barely completed my rallying thoughts when a loud shout from outside the barn sent birds flapping and screeching into the air. We all spun in different directions, the sound repeating from all around us. I could only imagine how it would have affected us if we had still been sleeping.

"Shields!" Vincent cried at the same moment as power raced toward us.

Ripping surrounded me, and by the time the attacking compositions reached us, every one of my companions was enclosed in their own personal bubble of power.

I had time to draw one more breath, and then the full attack hit us.

CHAPTER 23

Compositions swarmed over us as the shouts of the soldiers outside grew closer. One window smashed and then a second, arrows flying through the empty holes.

"Get down!" Layna screamed, but I held my ground. I had a shield that would block arrows, and I was willing to trust it—at least for a while.

Bryony, Tyron, Stellan, and Elsie all dropped obediently, however, and I positioned myself over them, my focus on the compositions streaming in our direction. Most of them contained pure power, meant for bludgeoning and breaking down shields. But mixed among them were several streaks of energy, just as Tyron had predicted.

"Take control!" I screamed, seizing on the closest one.

As it bucked under my command, I realized it was a sophisticated composition for draining energy. I paled. Surely these couldn't just be locals coerced by Conall. Tyron must be right about our ambushers including some of the Tarxi.

I pushed the thought aside. I didn't have time to dwell on it now. I needed to repurpose the composition before it broke free of my hold. But where to send it?

"Connect," I said, directing my energy toward my brother.

Instantly I could see the battle as he did, his sense of the energy around him much keener than my own eyesight in the dawn light. But I still had my own awareness of power as well. Unlike my brother, I could feel the power that attacked us, as well as what still lingered outside.

All of the mages and most of the commonborn attackers had shield bubbles around them just as we did. But several of them were unprotected—whether because my companions had broken their shields or because they had never had them, I didn't know. I sent the hungry composition in their direction.

It had been designed to attack one person, so I sent it after all three of the exposed ambushers, hoping it would drain them enough to disable them but not kill them. As soon as I had spoken the words to redirect the composition, I let it go, already reaching for another.

One of the mages outside dropped, his energy flickering and growing weak, although I hadn't targeted him. Several shouts came from his direction as commonborns converged on him.

I forced my attention away. Cooper must have had enough compositions on him to break through their shield and drain them. Either that, or he'd paired up with one of our power mages. My attention was needed elsewhere.

The compositions kept coming, along with the arrows, and I sank down to sit beside the group huddled on the ground. My shield had already deflected several arrows, and there was no point exhausting it unnecessarily.

"Take control, take control, take control," I muttered, drawing in as many raw power compositions as I could hold before reversing them all in an indiscriminate wave that broke over the ambushers.

"If you can take down some shields, I can redistribute the energy," Stellan said beside me, making me flinch and startle.

"Take control," I cried, unable to answer as another energy

composition reached hungrily for the people beside me. Among them, only Stellan and Elsie had energy shields, so I couldn't let any of the draining compositions make it through.

This one held the same sophistication of the earlier one, but even more power. It writhed against me, its directions specific. It wanted me and my brother. I shivered. Whatever energy mage had written this had been able to sense us and to sense we were different. Had they been out there all night, preparing for this attack?

This composition fought even harder than the last one against my efforts to twist it. I succeeded, however, sending it against the energy mage who seemed its most likely source.

As it raced toward the mage, I reached out again, taking control of his shields. Calling them to me, I directed the power to surround Bryony instead of our enemy.

With his shields gone, the composition I had sent back against him would meet no resistance. And yet, when I turned my attention back to him, the composition had dissipated. A new shield enclosed him, this one made of energy.

"An energy shield!" Stellan cried at the same moment as I registered what I was feeling. "I've never felt one of those before."

Tyron, almost flat on the ground beside my brother, cursed. "If that mage has an energy shield, then these are definitely not locals under my father's control. He only has one mage left who can produce energy shields, and he wouldn't give them out to just anyone."

"I'm taking it," I said, my voice harsh. But before I could do so, another composition hurtled toward us.

This one held enormous power, and the bubbles enclosing the others on the floor felt weak and flimsy in comparison. I seized the working, looking for somewhere to redirect its power. Two mages stood together outside the main doors of the barn, and some of our team appeared to be trying to batter down their protections. I sent my stolen power to assist.

Their shields gave way before the onslaught, overwhelmed by their own power turned against them. But I didn't watch to see what my companions planned to do now they had succeeded in their object. Instead, I reached again for the mage with the energy shield.

I felt nothing.

"Where did he go?" I asked, looking around as if I could find the missing person with my eyes alone. "He put up the shield and then disappeared."

"You stole his other shields," Tyron said. "It shouldn't be possible, but you did it. He wasn't going to stick around without the security of shields."

"Are you saying he's run for it and left all the rest of his team to fend for themselves?" Bryony sounded disgusted.

"Most likely." Tyron sounded neither approving nor judgmental, as if he was simply stating a fact of life.

I closed my eyes and reached out with my mind. Still connected to Stellan, I sought the unique energy signature of the fleeing mage. He wasn't in the immediate vicinity of the barn, so I stretched further. For a moment I thought I caught the feel of his energy shield, and then Elsie screamed.

My eyes snapped open just as I inhaled a lungful of smoke. I coughed, my eyes watering as I caught sight of red flames leaping from a nearby pile of straw. Another flame came flying through the window, carried by an arrow and deposited in yet another bundle of straw. This one went up even faster.

"Fire!" Bryony leaped to her feet.

A cloud of smoke enveloped her, and within another choking breath, I couldn't see anyone around me.

"Get out!" Vincent's deep voice, developed from long afternoons bellowing directions at new recruits, sounded above the crackle of the fire and the shouts from outside. "Everyone get out!"

Shapes emerged from the smoke, disappearing again before I could identify them.

"Elsie! Bryony!" I cried, my voice already weak from the few mouthfuls of smoke I had inhaled. "Stellan!"

The thought of my brother made me shake myself and reach down the connection that still bound us together. I found him near the door of the stables, the bright energy that felt like Elsie jogging a step ahead of him as if she were pulling him along behind her.

I stumbled after them, coughing again, and closing my eyes against the burn of the black smoke. Reaching out with my mind instead, I looked for the energy of the rest of our team, thankful that Stellan already found them all familiar.

Vincent stood beside Darius and Jareth, already out of the barn, near the door. Perhaps they had been the team working to take down the two power mages. I had no doubt the captain had grabbed both princes and forced them out at the first flaming arrow.

Elsie and Stellan were already joining them. But that was only five. I pushed my awareness across the rest of the barn. Cooper drew my attention first, his energy so bright it almost hurt to feel it. How much of our enemies' energy had he taken? And why was he standing motionless behind me, still in the middle of the barn?

I was already turning back toward him when I realized he wasn't alone. Not far from his position, Bryony was also motionless, Tyron beside her. I faltered, my eyes flying open, only to close again against the sting of the smoke. I coughed and coughed but forced my feet to hurry toward my friend anyway.

The flames had risen higher, and sweat dripped down my face from their heat. I returned the way I had come, aiming for the central place where we had all been huddling earlier in the battle. Someone else loomed out of the smoke, their hand grabbing for me, but I evaded their grasp and kept going.

I recognized the energy, and I knew if Layna managed to

catch hold of me, she would do the same as Vincent had done with Darius and drag me outside whether I wanted to go or not.

I dropped to my knees beside Bryony, taking a deep breath of the slightly clearer air at this level. I forced my eyes open despite the smoke and examined her for injury. I couldn't see anything.

"We have to get out of here," I gasped, provoking another round of coughing.

"I know, but one of the arrows got him," Bryony replied, and I realized Tyron lay flat on the ground, blood pouring from an arrow that had pierced his side.

The flickering flames revealed a face even paler than his usual white, and his breathing sounded more labored than Bryony's or mine. I gulped. It looked as if Bryony had been trying to drag him free of the barn, but she hadn't made it far.

"Go!" I said to Bryony. "You can't do anything here. I'll heal him, and then he'll be able to walk out himself."

She hesitated. "I can't leave you here."

"Yes, you can! Get out there and tell the others they need to extinguish these flames. They may not realize we're still in here."

My words drove her to action, as I had meant them to do, and she crawled away, showing more intelligence than me by staying low to the ground.

I reached for the pocket that held my healing compositions, my fingers fumbling as I searched for one that would close Tyron's wound. I squeaked when a figure stumbled from the smoke, but it was only Layna.

She reached for me, but I pushed her away, pointing at Tyron. She dropped to one knee beside us, her face and clothes already coated in ash, and her eyes red and watering.

"We have to go."

"Not without him," I said. "We can't just leave him here to burn."

While we were talking, my fingers kept moving, and I finally found the composition I needed. I glanced down at it, the red of flame illuminating enough of the words to confirm my choice.

Layna reached for me again, clearly planning to force my compliance, but I had already ripped the parchment.

"Get that arrow out!" I said in my most commanding tones, and Layna instinctively responded, pivoting to Tyron and pulling the arrow free from his side in a single movement.

His eyes sprang open, and he screamed, his body jerking. The healing composition hit him, and he groaned, a guttural sound almost as painful as his scream.

Layna didn't flinch, however. Reaching low, she scooped him over her shoulder and began to stagger toward the door. I was about to follow her when I remembered Bryony and Tyron hadn't been alone. I swerved and crawled instead toward Cooper's motionless form.

He was sitting now, curved in on himself as the flames of a nearby hay bale reached for him. The ferocity of the fire made the heat almost unbearable, and I had to shout to be heard.

"Are you injured? We have to go!"

I tugged at him, but he was like a solid rock. In the light of the dancing flames, I scanned him for injury but could see no sign of one.

The heat grew even stronger, my skin burning and my lungs protesting every heated breath. I pulled at him with all my strength.

"I can't," he panted in a voice I'd never heard before. "The fire will get me."

"No, it will get us both if you don't move!" I screamed, but he gave no sign of having heard me.

I didn't know why, but he was clearly past reason, gripped by a fear so deep it had completely incapacitated him. And I had no hope of dragging him out. For a horrible moment, the heat overwhelmed me, and I crawled away from it, desperate to escape.

But a new burst of light behind me made me stop and throw

myself back toward Cooper, beating at his arm with my jacket sleeve until I had extinguished the grasping flame. I couldn't leave Cooper there to burn. I somehow needed to snap him out of his own mind.

I gasped, my hand moving before my thoughts caught up. It flew toward my deepest pocket—the one I had hoped never to touch. The one that let me control someone's mind.

Ripping the parchment, I seized control of the composition without hesitation, propelling it toward Cooper and shaping it for one purpose only. Latching on to his mind, I removed his fear of the fire and told him to start moving.

He immediately unrolled himself and crawled toward the door. I scrambled to follow, barely able to breathe or think for the awful, burning heat and the choking smoke.

Blindly I reached out for any sort of power I could snatch.

At first I encountered nothing, but then a whoosh of power swept into the barn, and water began to rain from the roof. A moment later more power arrived, an unnatural wind springing up in its wake.

Bryony's message must have reached those outside, and they had written compositions to aid us. But the wind was only driving the smoke in swirls, making it harder to see and breathe. Ahead of me, Cooper faltered, coughing violently.

I seized at the power driving the wind, shaping it with my words. The air moved toward us, creating a tunnel that drove the smoke away from us and our path.

Cooper took a deep, shuddering breath, and clambered to his feet, resuming his forward progress at a run now. I pushed myself up as well and hurried after him.

We burst out of the barn on a gust of fresh air, wet and covered in soot and ash. I almost collided with Layna who stood beside a still-groaning Tyron. There had been no time for a pain relief composition.

Stooping over him, I saw his skin had closed over, his wound healed. I tried to straighten again, but his hand whipped out and caught my arm, holding me in place.

"Thank you." His eyes pierced into me, their pale blue intense with the power of deep glaciers and rippled ice. "Thank you for not leaving me to burn."

"Don't thank me." I pulled my arm free. "Layna was the one to carry you out. And I wouldn't have even known you were injured if it wasn't for Bree."

"Perhaps." His voice was rough and low from smoke inhalation. "But you stayed, and you saved me. Despite who I am. You didn't have to do that."

"I wasn't leaving anyone to burn." I shuddered. "Not even you. And there's something else I have to tell you, too." Unexpected excitement gripped me. "You're wrong about your ability, you know."

"What do you—" He cut himself off, his eyes seeking out Cooper, who was bent nearly double, drawing long, shaking breaths. "You used my composition," he breathed.

I followed his gaze to Cooper, the rest of our surroundings catching my attention before I could reply. Smoke still swirled lazily into the sky, but the flames seemed to have been extinguished.

With a start, I remembered we had been in the middle of a battle when the flames erupted. But no enemies appeared from the gathering dawn to strike us while we were vulnerable, and no new compositions sped through the air to beat at our shields.

Layna had stationed herself right beside me, her back straight and manner focused, despite her dreadful appearance. But even she didn't find any enemies left to fight.

"It's finished, Princess," she said, catching my confused expression.

I nodded slowly, exhausted and relieved. Someone—Cooper, I now suspected—had incapacitated one of the energy mages early on, and the princes and Vincent had dealt with the two power mages. With the one I had sent fleeing, that only left one other mage. Perhaps it wasn't so surprising those first out of the barn had already defeated our remaining enemies.

Darius appeared beside me, sweeping me into his arms despite the state we were both in.

"Verene! You're all right! Vincent pulled me out before I knew what was happening. I would have gone back in after you, but he and Jareth restrained me."

Fury blazed in his eyes, and I could easily see how our remaining attackers had fallen before him. I let myself rest in his arms.

"We all made it out. That's what matters." I reached out with my mind, counting the reassuring burn of nine familiar energy signatures around me.

Reaching out further, I counted my way through the people who still lay dispersed around the barn—many of them with energy so low it flickered only faintly. When I finished, I rubbed the side of my head and started again. I was still confused from the smoke. But once again, I counted only eighteen.

I stiffened in Darius's arms, and he drew back to look at my face in concern.

"There are only eighteen of them!" I cried, despite my aching throat. "One fled during the battle, but where's the other? He might still have compositions, or—"

Darius shook his head, silencing me. "I think your missing attacker is there." His voice sounded resigned, bordering on dejected, and I followed his pointing finger in confusion before sucking in a sharp breath.

One of the enemy soldiers lay sprawled in an unnatural position, his eyes wide in death. Another soldier sat beside him, groaning softly and cradling one leg.

"We killed one," I whispered. "We're supposed to be avoiding hurting them."

"They nearly burned you alive." Darius's eyes looked black in the increasing light of the morning. "We did what we had to."

I bit my lip. I knew he was right, but I still struggled to accept it. Had the man had a family before he was unwillingly dragged into this war? Parents who loved him? Children who depended on him?

"I'm freeing them all," I said with determination. "Right now." I looked up at Darius. "We can't be dragging prisoners across the Empire after Conall."

Darius didn't argue, and I didn't stop to wonder if it was because he agreed or because he saw in my eyes it was something I had to do. He stayed close beside me as I made the loop around the still-smoking barn. At each person, I stopped, connecting with them and searching their energy for the small hole left by the segment stolen and held by Conall.

When I found it, I took control of the working that held the cancerous hole open, pulling their missing energy back with none of the subtlety I had employed so long ago with Matthis. Defiance filled me as I freed one person after another.

Let Conall feel what I was doing. Let him know that his attempt to capture or kill us had failed, and that we had the power to rip his people from his control. Let him know that we could free his army, and we were coming for him.

Only when we reached the rest of our team, still stationed at the front of the barn, discussing our next move, did I realize I had freed all eighteen of them. The process had left me more shaken than I wanted to admit.

Having connected with Conall's working, I understood what he had implanted in these people. His control was triggered only when they received a command from one of Conall's people, and then they were helpless to do anything but obey it. And like he had with Matthis so long ago, he had included a second command, a pressure to obey with an unthinking ferocity. It was a truly sick control, especially since he had gathered all adults in his path, not bothering to look for those who could effectively fight. They were mere bodies to be thrown between him and his enemies—and if they were bodies his enemies would hesitate to kill, all the better, from his perspective.

"These are all people coerced by Conall." I met Tyron's eyes. "So the energy mage who ran must have been their leader. It looks like he was the only one with a free mind."

"And he used it to abandon his people without warning them to flee themselves." Bryony sounded furious.

"These aren't his people," Tyron said from where he still lay on the ground. "His people are the Tarxi. These soldiers are just pawns to serve his purpose."

"You talk like you know him." Darius regarded the newly healed energy mage with narrowed eyes.

"I don't know for sure. But I have a strong guess. I suspect that was either Adair or Cormac."

"And they are?" Darius hadn't relented in his manner at all.

"My father's closest and most powerful lieutenants. Adair is the one who can create energy shields, and Cormac can take energy. But he's incredibly powerful and has had decades to perfect his skills. He's the one who can leave a hidden composition inside someone to trigger at a particular moment and drain their life."

He looked and sounded disgusted—hardly surprising given such a composition had been left inside him and would have killed him without my intervention.

"Good," I said harshly. "If he sent them then that must mean he's scared. He knows someone is coming for him. I'm sick of hiding. We need to take this fight to him."

"But how many people will die in the process?" Jareth asked, his eyes on the body of the dead soldier. "And at our hands."

I looked at him, concern in my eyes, and he met my gaze squarely.

"That could have been me, Verene. That man is exactly the

same as me—forced by a power he couldn't resist into doing terrible things he never wanted to do." He looked haunted. "And I was the one to kill him."

"Given the chaos of that battle, I'm surprised more didn't die," I said.

"No, the rest of you were restrained." Jareth sounded disgusted with himself. "I was the only one to lose control. And an innocent person lost their life because of it."

Bryony stepped up beside him and slipped her hand into his.

"This isn't your fault, Jareth," she said fiercely. "Don't you dare carry this. That man's death is a tragedy, but it's not one that rests on your shoulders. The blame belongs with Conall."

I nodded. "It certainly does. And if we don't find him and undo all his compositions, then many more people will die. And soon."

CHAPTER 24

While I had been releasing the soldiers from Conall's grasp, and the others had been debating, Elsie and Stellan had slipped away. They returned with news of a nearby stream where we could all clean up.

"And our packs survived, thankfully," Stellan added.

"We have Elsie to thank for that. As soon as we realized we were in the middle of an ambush, she dragged them right into the center of the barn, which turned out to be away from any of the bales of hay."

"They're covered in ash," Elsie said, "but the contents are intact."

Layna wouldn't let anyone leave for the stream until she had given us all a healing composition for smoke inhalation. I looked at her suspiciously as I took it.

"Are you going to say that Raelynn gave you *ten* compositions for smoke damage?" I asked her.

She shook her head. "She gave me two, and I copied them. Healing isn't my greatest strength, but I'm competent. You needn't fear it will hurt you by accident."

"Stellan," I called, and my brother came hurrying over. "I

think we could do with some energy redistribution."

He glanced at Layna and then over his shoulder at Cooper, understanding lighting his eyes.

"Sorry," he said, "I should have thought of that myself."

"You were busy," I said, not having meant to criticize him. "But Layna wrote those compositions that just healed us all, and I, for one, am incredibly grateful." I took a deep breath of the cool air without erupting into coughs. "And Tyron has just had a major healing," I added as an afterthought.

I hesitated before continuing. "If any of the enemy soldiers seem dangerously low on energy, you'd better top them up as well. When they wake up, they won't be enemies anymore."

Stellan quirked an eyebrow at me but shrugged and began muttering the words of his composition without protest.

Layna watched him with knitted brows.

"This doesn't sound like a good idea," she said. "Prince Stellan can't have enough energy for so many people. I'm not near enough to collapse to need any extra."

I shook my head. "He's not giving away his own energy. Stellan's greatest gift is his ability to redistribute energy between anyone. You wouldn't be able to feel it, but Cooper is bursting at the seams with energy. It's a wonder he can stand still. And since he has a normal energy ability, all that energy he stole is going to break free any minute and return to all its owners. But this way Stellan gets to control how much goes to who."

Cooper looked up at the sound of his name. He seemed to have recovered physically, but his expression was haunted.

"My memory is a little hazy, but I froze in there, didn't I? And I nearly got you killed in the process."

"It wasn't your fault," I said. "You weren't yourself." I bit my lip, hesitating. "Have you been in a fire before?"

Pain flashed across his face as he slowly nodded. "When I was a child, my home burned down. I was trapped inside and nearly died. Even when I was pulled out, I would have died from the burns if a healer hadn't seen the flames from afar and come running. I'm just fortunate we lived in a big enough town that we had a resident healer. I've been terrified of fires ever since."

"That's understandable," Layna said, in a surprisingly gentle voice. "Some fears go too deep for reason."

I nodded. It was exactly the same realization I had experienced inside the barn, and her words rekindled my earlier excitement. With so much happening, it was hard to hold on to any one thought, but I couldn't wait to share my idea.

Cooper turned to me before I could speak, however. "You saved me, Verene. Thank you."

I shook my head. "I'm sorry there wasn't time to ask your permission, but you were too heavy for me to physically drag out."

"What did you do?" Layna looked between us. "How did you get him out?"

"She used one of my compositions." Tyron stepped forward to join us, his expression inscrutable.

I nodded, turning to him. "You thought your ability couldn't be used for good, but I used it to save Cooper's life. And even without the emergency, you could help him—and others like him. With their permission, you could take away the fears that grip and debilitate them long enough for them to face those fears and overcome them."

I turned back to Cooper. "Just like you worked out a way to use your ability for good."

He nodded slowly, clearly considering my words. "It might work," he said at last. "Theoretically, at least." He cast Tyron a doubtful look, and I knew he would be unlikely to trust Tyron enough to let him work a composition of his own. But that knowledge didn't dampen my enthusiasm.

I looked defiantly at Tyron. "Now do you believe me? We're never forced by our abilities to seek power over the good of others."

"Always determined to cling to your ideals, Princess," he said lightly, but I could see my words had shaken him.

"It's time we were moving," Vincent called, drawing us all back together.

"What do we do with the soldiers?" Cooper asked, shaking off the lingering remnants of his fear and shame, and refocusing on the task ahead of us.

"Leave them," Vincent said. "Tyron and Princess Verene seem convinced the mage who got away is especially dangerous, so I don't want us hanging around here any longer than absolutely necessary."

Cooper looked at me. "You're completely confident they're free? If we leave them unrestrained, they're not going to come after us?"

I nodded. "They were all being controlled by Conall, but I've freed them from his compositions now." I looked across at the man with the injured leg who still sat beside his dead companion, a confused, glazed look in his eyes. "But we can't leave without healing him. It wasn't his fault he was fighting us, and we were the ones to do that to him."

Vincent looked less than happy at my words, but Layna gave him a loaded look, and he merely nodded once.

"I'll take care of it," Layna said. "And check none of the others need healings."

I nodded at her gratefully and went to take my turn at the creek Elsie had found. Given the chaos around us, it seemed far too soon to be moving on, but smoke from the barn still spiraled into the air, and I could understand Vincent's desire to be away.

Darius had already discarded his glove, and his composition was still working, his fingers an unsettling black. It didn't take him long to have us back on the right path, though. Our direction seemed to have changed slightly, bearing back toward the west.

"He's on the move," Vincent muttered.

"Could his lieutenant have already made it back to him with news of the attack?" I wondered aloud.

"If he's that close we'll be on him sooner than I'd like," Layna said from behind me. I raised my eyebrows at her, and she continued. "We need to put some distance between us and that barn, but we also need time to regroup before we're plunged into another conflict."

"I thought we were trying to avoid conflict," Stellan said.

"That was before Conall knew we were coming." Layna sounded unhappy. "It's going to be harder to avoid now."

We all moved at pace, despite our weariness and the unpleasant smell of smoke which hung around our packs, clothes, and hair. But when we passed the first burned out shell of a house, I realized not all the smell was emanating from us.

A little further on, we found an entire village burned out. Everything was cold and silent. The damage was clearly several days old, so we didn't stop to look for survivors. I could only hope they had all either fled before this happened or been co-opted into Conall's army.

"What's happened to the children?" I asked Darius, seized by a sudden horrible thought. "If Conall has stolen all the adults for his army, what has he done with the children?"

"He's just ignored them, from what the emperor could determine. Now that we're working together, the emperor has admitted a couple of villages' worth of people disappeared some time ago. Conall may not have been ready to mobilize his full army at the time, but he wanted some troops to keep close. The authorities only discovered the situation because the children all came wandering alone into the next closest village."

"But..." I looked around at the increasingly desolate landscape, dotted with blackened tree trunks, destroyed buildings, and torn up fields. "This isn't a couple of villages. The children would have so far to travel to find anyone who could help them. What if..."

"We haven't seen any children," Darius reminded me. "Not traveling alone or…" he grimaced and swallowed, "dead either. Which hopefully means the emperor got enough warning to implement his plan."

"He had a plan?" I brightened. Of course he would have. I should have realized that. He wouldn't just abandon his empire's children.

"As soon as he got word Conall was mobilizing the people he had entrapped, the emperor was going to send in targeted missions to retrieve the children left behind. Their primary goal would have been speed and avoiding Conall's forces. We thought there would have to be an initial period of some chaos before the people had time to reach the gathering point and start receiving proper orders, and that was the window to get in and get out."

As we continued to move forward, following Darius's glowing hand, we saw more and more burned-out buildings, surrounded by ravaged countryside. Conall's incursion was much further into the heart of the Empire than any of us had been expecting, so it wasn't surprising when we passed the abandoned detritus of a past battle.

This one looked bigger than the one we had intervened in on the road, and I counted three bodies before I turned my face away, burying it in Darius's shoulder as we hurried past. The emperor's soldiers must have done their best to follow orders not to hurt Conall's makeshift force, or there would have been more bodies, but it was a sickening reminder that some death was inescapable in such conflicts.

The fire of anger in my belly roared higher at this evidence that Conall's forces were under orders to simply leave the bodies where they lay, as if the lost lives had no meaning. Tyron had said these people were only pawns to Conall and the Tarxi, and he was obviously correct.

I glanced back at Conall's son, wondering what was in his mind as his eyes dwelt coolly on the abandoned bodies. He still wore clothes streaked with blood, but between the healing and the energy from Stellan, he moved as easily and quickly as the rest of us.

It might have been my imagination, but he seemed to be sticking close to me. I didn't appreciate it, since the sight of him still made me uneasy, the conflicting feelings of the past and present overlapping into a confusing mosaic. For more than two years he had been a friend and year mate, only for him to become my greatest enemy. But what was he now? I had risked my life to save him from that burning building and insisted that Stellan restore his energy as well.

I could say I'd done it for strategic reasons or just basic humanity. But I wasn't entirely sure either was true. Tyron had helped us more than once now, and it confused the matter—reminding me of when we had been friends. He claimed that being free from the constant use of his ability had changed his perspective, and having felt his ability for myself, it was easy to believe. Sometimes I even wondered if he welcomed the bonds we had given him since they made it impossible for him to give in to the siren call to use his ability.

But those thoughts only reminded me that Tyron believed it was impossible not to wield the power he had been given. He was utterly twisted by his father's beliefs, a willing participant in a plan that had already led to so much death and destruction. He didn't deserve my compassion.

But a voice in the back of my mind couldn't let even that thought rest. Was that the point of compassion? Was it only given when deserved?

Perhaps he caught me watching him because Tyron spoke to me, although he had been silent since we left the burned barn.

"Do you think you could take control and disable an energy shield as easily as you can a power one?"

I shrugged. "I don't see why not. It's just another type of

energy composition, and my ability doesn't seem to distinguish between power and energy workings."

"That's good," he said.

"Why?" I looked at him curiously. "Are you worried about Adair?"

"My father has double warning now. He knows we're coming, and he knows we're powerful. We won't get to him without getting through Adair and Cormac first."

"We can do it." I injected confidence into my tone.

Tyron glanced sideways at yet another burned out home. "For the sake of the locals, you had better hope that proves true."

"And what of you?" I asked. "What do you hope for?"

His eyes focused back on me, surprise in their depths. "I don't know that I hope for anything. But if you're asking me what I would wish for if given a chance…I suppose I would wish for the ocean."

"The ocean?" I stared at him.

"The chance to live a free life somewhere near the seashore. To wake up every morning to the crash of the waves and the salt on the wind—and no thought in my mind of empires or kingdoms or thrones. There's something so vast about the ocean. It makes it easy to put everything else into perspective."

I frowned. "Tyron, there's a way for you to use your ability for good. You should have hope. But I don't know that—"

He shook his head quickly to cut me off. "Oh, I know the impossibility of such a life. My crimes in Kallorway are too great, and I can see now that the life my father offered never included freedom. He never even took me to see the ocean, you know, not even when I was a small child." For a moment he was silent. "As I said, I do not hope."

I winced. "I'm sorry," I said softly.

"Yes." He looked at me with a quizzical expression. "As much as it surprises me, I do believe you mean that."

I shrugged. "It surprises me as well, to be honest."

"Having a unique ability sets us apart." His eyes moved past me to Darius. "Other people can't understand that—no matter how powerful they are."

"My mother understands," I said, talking mostly to myself. It was probably what drove her to try so desperately to protect us—even from our own decisions.

She understood because she had been faced with the same dilemma. Some had believed her gift too powerful to ever be safe. But she had proved them wrong.

I looked sideways at Tyron. I had felt so excited at the realization of how his ability could be used, but was it too late for him to ever use it in such a way? Did he have it in him to resist the more sinister applications and win the trust he would need before anyone would let him attempt such a thing?

And why did I care so much? Was it merely that we both had unique abilities? Or was all my compassion for him just a desperate attempt to cover up my own weakness—to cover up the fact that I, too, had felt the siren call of his ability and the power it could wield.

A fresh wave of smoke hit my nostrils, distracting me. We skirted a clump of surviving trees to find a farmhouse so recently destroyed it was still smoking. Fury ripped through me. It didn't matter what abilities I had to use, I would defeat Conall.

Vincent called a stop, gesturing us to huddle close together.

"Someone's near," he said. "And for all we know, it could be an entire army. Is anyone out of shields after that ambush at the barn?"

Both Bryony and Cooper admitted they were, and Vincent handed them new shields. When he looked at me inquiringly, I shook my head. My family had provided me with ample supplies.

"We have Verene, and she should be able to take down Adair's energy shields," Tyron said. "But until she does, remember that only physical attacks will work against an energy shield. Throw rocks at them, but don't waste your power trying to bind them or anything like that."

Vincent looked at him for a moment before nodding his head. "True. But not all of us will be able to sense the presence of an energy shield." He glanced around the group. "So we'll be relying on our energy mages to let us know if they're in play."

"Of course," Bryony said. "It would be nice to feel like I'm helping in some small way."

"Don't underestimate your contribution," Vincent said, somewhat to my surprise given his usual focus on the task at hand. "We've needed to write ourselves a number of compositions on this journey so far, and it normally wouldn't be possible to do so while traveling in the manner we have been. It's only been achievable because of the highly unusual number of energy mages among us."

Bryony flushed with pleasure, and I beamed at the captain. He was an even more effective leader than I had realized.

"But for now," Vincent continued, "I want Prince Darius and Princess Verene with me. Everyone else is to stay with Layna. Head back to that surviving group of trees and take shelter there until we return."

Jareth looked as if he wanted to protest, but he glanced at Bryony and kept silent. She was the one to ask what Vincent intended to do.

"We're scouting a short way ahead to see if we can find the soldiers who set that fire." He jerked his thumb in the direction of the smoking building.

"And you want me to help you scout?" I asked, taken by surprise. "Are you sure you don't want Cooper instead? He's the one with training in such activities."

"You're the most powerful among us, Princess," Layna said seriously. "If the three of you walk into the middle of a squad, Vincent and Prince Darius will need you to help get them out."

I blinked. I still wasn't used to thinking about myself that way.

"You should take me, too," Tyron said.

I turned to stare at him.

"Not that I'm particularly useful, given the way you have me bound. But my father's followers will all recognize me. Seeing me will give them pause, and it might buy you crucial time."

Vincent and Darius exchanged a look.

"I think we should take him," I said. "He makes a good point. And he might have some insights to offer on whatever we find."

"Or else he might give our position away and walk back into his father's open arms," Vincent said.

"You're forgetting he's bound," I said. "And besides, with the amount of help he's given us at this point, I suspect his father's reception might not be so very warm."

Darius turned to look appraisingly at Tyron before looking back at me. "I trust Verene's judgment. He can come."

I swallowed. Now that I had convinced them, I suddenly had less faith in my judgment than Darius did.

Vincent didn't waste further time in debate, ordering us to move out. I followed behind Darius and Tyron, Vincent bringing up the rear, a watchful eye on everything.

We moved faster and more quietly with only four and soon began to hear sounds that seemed out of place in the deserted landscape. We exchanged looks, no one talking as the hubbub of voices and movements increased.

"That's not a squad," Darius whispered, and Vincent nodded in silent agreement.

Our path led us up a slight incline, the ground sloping upward toward another surviving clump of trees. We moved slowly, inching our way up until we could shelter among the vegetation.

I had wondered if Vincent would ask us to climb one of the trees to gain a view of the landscape ahead, but as soon as the land crested, our view cleared. We didn't need to climb any trees to see that below us spread a vast army, encamped in a confused mass of tents and bedrolls that lay open to the sky above.

CHAPTER 25

For a moment silence gripped us all as we took in the sight ahead of us. Northward, everywhere we looked was filled with the army.

"So many," I whispered.

We knew Conall had been binding people to his cause over many years, but it was different to see the reality of it spread out before us.

"There." Vincent pointed at a cluster of tents in the middle of camp. They were larger and more luxurious than any of the others we saw, and a whole collection of flags flew from the tip of the grandest. "I suppose he considers himself a real commander."

I gaped at the distant tents in dismay. "I don't care how much power and energy we have between us, how are we ever going to get through so many people to reach him?"

Vincent stroked his chin. "How close do you need to get, Princess?"

I grimaced. "I don't actually know. I haven't had much reason or opportunity to practice with distance within the Academy walls."

"I don't suppose you can reach him from here?" Vincent's voice sounded hopeful.

"I can try." It didn't seem likely, but I couldn't see any reason not to at least attempt it.

"Are you sure?" Darius asked quickly, directing the question at Vincent. "Tyron could feel her presence when they connected. If she attracts Conall's attention before she finishes freeing everyone, he might come after us. And we only have the four of us here."

"I won't try to release anyone," I said quickly. "I'll just check if he's within range."

Darius didn't look entirely convinced, but after a moment he nodded. Tyron just looked at me curiously, as if he was interested in whether or not I could achieve it, but otherwise uninvested in the outcome.

I reached out across the tents, missing the acute awareness I had experienced during the time I was connected with Stellan. If I couldn't reach Conall now, it might be worth bringing Stellan back with us and trying again.

When I opened my mind to my energy senses, I was nearly overwhelmed by the sheer numbers in the camp. But my time connected with Stellan's ability seemed to have increased my own natural senses, and I could easily distinguish between power mages, energy mages and sealed commonborns. All three types of combatants littered the camp, although the commonborns were in far greater number, of course.

I skimmed over the top of them, reaching for the tents in the middle, expecting to find a knot of energy mages. But I felt nothing.

I strained and strained again. Still nothing. Sighing, I shook my head.

"It must be too far. I can't feel him at all."

Darius frowned, and I wished I didn't have to disappoint him. But rather than saying anything, or even turning back the way we had come, he instead turned west. He walked several steps, staring intently at his hand. Nothing happened that I could see, and Vincent pulled him back just before he emerged from the cover of the trees.

Again, he didn't speak, merely turning east and repeating the exercise, this time with Vincent trailing close behind. But this time Darius stopped himself just inside the tree line. When he turned back in our direction, his face held an expression of triumph.

"I think you can't feel him because it's all for show."

Vincent raised an eyebrow. "An army that size is good for a lot more than just show."

"No, I mean those tents in the center of the camp. The flags. I think Conall wants us to think he's there. But I don't think he's with the army at all. It's subtle, but I'm fairly sure my hand is directing us east again from here, not into the camp."

"That sounds like Father," Tyron said. "It seemed unlike him to make himself so obvious—especially when he doesn't know your range."

"Should we go back and get the others?" I asked.

Vincent stroked his chin again before shaking his head. "We scout a little further and make sure His Highness's instinct is correct. I couldn't see any change in the hand myself."

"I've spent a lot of hours staring at it," Darius said, not sounding offended.

"We'll know soon enough." Vincent gestured for us to start moving. "But we need to get off this hill before we do anything else."

I wouldn't have called it a hill myself, but I had no desire for us to expose our presence even at the top of a small incline such as this. We retraced our steps to the point we could no longer see anything of the camp, and only then turned east.

We were fortunate Conall's forces weren't a proper army, full of trained soldiers. We could never have moved so freely in such close proximity to them if they were. If they had a system of sentries, it must have been a poor one because we saw no one.

Darius wasn't the only one staring at his hand now. It was hard to be sure if the color was actually changing or if it was merely wishful thinking on my part. But as we progressed further west, the change became clearer. It was definitely growing more gold.

Darius experimented with small changes in direction, determining that it wanted us to head northeast. We didn't completely comply, however, still needing to skirt around the edge of the army.

But it seemed the majority of the troops stretched further westward because we reached the edge of the camp sooner than I expected. Darius's composition continued to lead us northeast, however, moving further and further from the camp. After a while, I dropped back to walk beside Vincent.

"Should we be turning back yet?" I whispered. "How far should we go? It's clear Darius is right, and Conall isn't in that camp."

"There!" Darius pointed ahead, interrupting before Vincent could respond.

We had just rounded a clump of rocks that thrust up from the ground, avoiding a small collection of partially burned homes that butted up against them. Fields stretched around the destroyed houses, the ground torn up and desolate. Only a small number of trees had escaped, standing in a few clumps some distance away. One such grouping shaded a small collection of tents, nestled between two of the now abandoned fields.

From this distance, there was nothing about these tents to distinguish them from any others, but Darius's hand was glowing brighter than I had yet seen.

Tyron immediately tensed. "We're too close," he said, although we were far enough away that any occupants of the tent would be unable to hear our voices.

"Is it him?" I asked, just as a combined wave of power and energy hit us from the rear.

Vincent moved faster than seemed possible, responding while I was still spinning around to stare behind us at the apparently empty landscape. Had the composition he was tearing already been in his hand?

Another layer of shields sprang up around all four of us, even as our precautionary shields crumbled under the onslaught.

"Darius!" Vincent shouted, and more tearing came from where Darius stood, now at my rear.

But the power he unleashed didn't cling to us and neither did it seek out our attackers. Instead it went streaking off into the distance.

Before I could ask its purpose, however, another wave of attack compositions raced toward us. And these ones didn't come alone.

A squad of commonborns burst out from a hiding place within the rocky outcropping, jumping down onto the clear ground and running toward us. War cries ripped from their throats, and they all held swords aloft.

Darius, Vincent, and I also drew our swords. But even as I readied myself to meet the oncoming attack, a part of me noticed there was no such sound of drawn steel from Tyron. My heart sank into my stomach. He was an expert swordsman and would make a valuable ally in such a situation. But it seemed he did not mean to aid us.

I couldn't spare any further thought for him, however. The first of the commonborns reached Vincent who had stepped forward ahead of the rest of us. Darius leaped forward to join him, and I nearly did the same. But before I could, the incoming compositions crashed against our new shields.

They made me falter, frowning. I had drawn my sword out of instinct, but I would be more help dealing with the compositions than wielding my sword alongside the others.

"Take control," I cried, seizing on the first composition that my awareness touched.

A working to drain energy came under my command, showing the same sophistication and strength as the ones I had encountered in the barn.

"Cormac," I muttered. "It must be."

The energy swirled, seeking to push into my own and steal it away. I turned it against the unshielded commonborns who had almost overwhelmed Darius and Vincent, felling three of them with the single composition.

My lips curled up in derision. If the Tarxi mages had attended the Academy and trained in the arena, they would know it was poor strategy to leave their swordsmen so undefended—even if they didn't care for their well-being.

But while I was distracted by that composition, the others had broken against our shields, wearing them down so low I could barely feel the flicker of power around us. Vincent and Darius both fought furiously, somehow managing to hold off all seven remaining soldiers between them. Neither of them had time to think of compositions.

I thrust both hands into my pockets, pulling out a pile of shields that covered both energy and power. I ripped them just as more compositions rushed toward us.

"Take control, take control, take control," I said, grabbing at all of them at once.

But I immediately realized my mistake. They were all different—two power compositions and an energy composition —with different purposes. They careened around within the grasp of my energy, pulling against my control, and over-whelming my mind. My awareness of each of their different purposes overlapped, confusing the quick thinking I desperately needed in order to twist them. At any moment I was going to lose control of them altogether.

"Reverse," I cried in desperation, throwing my command over

all three at once. It wasn't an effective use of the power they represented, but it was the best I could do.

The compositions streaked away from me, moving not toward the battling squad but back toward the rocks. The mages weren't among the soldiers, then. I reached for them with my senses but had to stop when yet more compositions bore down on us.

Vincent and Darius struggled, clearly hampered by their efforts not to kill any of the soldiers. Vincent had a long gash down one arm, and Darius appeared to be limping. If I couldn't use this next set of compositions to help them, they would be in trouble.

My hands scrabbled to tear another shield, shoring up our protection so I could afford to let most of the compositions hit us. I ignored the power ones, seizing on an energy composition. Sure enough, it was a working to drain energy.

I sent it against the soldiers only to realize the mages had recognized their mistake and activated a shield around their commonborns.

"Take control," I screamed, as my stolen composition attempted to reach the first of the soldiers. It bounced off the shield, reaching for the next soldier as I pulled the shield away from all of them, wrapping it around Vincent, Darius, and myself instead.

The composition I had sent collided with the last few soldiers, making three of them falter, although it didn't send them crashing to the ground this time, having already expended some of its energy against the shield.

The new shield around us did nothing to slow the ferocity of the fight, and I realized why I hadn't immediately recognized its presence. It was an energy shield. Adair then. Either they were both among those rocks, or they had supplied the mage who was.

A soldier sidestepped Vincent, rushing toward me instead, and I only just got my sword up in time. He thrust with wild abandon, but he no longer had the advantage of numbers, and my blade danced along his, twisting his aside and out of his hands. He pulled back with a startled cry, and I whispered a quiet apology as I sliced across the tendons on his sword arm.

He screamed, grabbing at the gushing wound as he fell back. If we survived this ourselves, one of us could heal him. But for now, I needed him out of the battle.

More compositions hit us while I was distracted, but the new shield I had stolen from the soldiers protected us. It wouldn't last forever, though. I dropped back again, trying to give myself more room so I could focus on the compositions. But I didn't dare go too far, or I would step out of the circle of our shields.

"Tyron?"

The surprised cry made me turn, looking up at the rocks instead of searching for a new composition to control. Tyron stood there, fully exposed, looking down at someone out of my sight—the source of the call.

"How did you get here?" the same voice asked.

But Tyron didn't answer, looking at me instead.

"Verene?" he called, his voice low but carrying across the noise of battle.

His eyes pleaded with me, and I didn't need him to say more to know what he was asking. He wanted to be let free of his bindings.

I glanced at Vincent. I knew what the captain would say.

But he wasn't the one with my abilities. I needed to make my own decision, and I needed to make it now.

"Take control," I muttered, seizing the composition that bound Tyron.

I had never connected with it before, and for a moment I was distracted by its complexity. But I had no time to waste. Now that I was concentrating in that direction, I could feel the energy of two mages, hidden from my view. I thrust the composition toward one of them. Unable to feel power, he didn't even seem to notice as the bonds wrapped tight around him.

I looked back at Tyron. He was already frantically scribing something on a piece of parchment. He finished and looked up, his eyes finding mine. For an awful moment, I thought I had made a terrible decision. But he made no attempt to use his newly completed composition to attack me. He wanted something further.

For a brief moment I felt only confusion, and then I remembered his earlier words. He had asked if I could disable an energy shield. He must have known Conall's lieutenants would be sheltering beneath one.

"Take control," I whispered, reaching for the shield I knew must be there. Sure enough I found it and thrust it around Tyron instead of the two men currently under its protection.

As energy mages, they felt this working, letting out cries of alarm. With the two of them distracted, the stream of attack compositions had stopped. I glanced back at Darius and Vincent to find them both now locked in single battles. Their victory wouldn't take long.

When I glanced back toward Tyron, he had disappeared from sight. With the sound of the soldiers diminished, I heard the faint sound of tearing parchment from the rocks. I braced myself for more compositions, but the rush of energy didn't move in my direction.

Instead, it latched on to one of the enemy mages, and a second later I heard an enraged cry. I looked toward Darius and Vincent again, but they no longer needed my help.

Racing forward, I leaped onto the first of the rocks. Slipping and sliding, I scrambled across the rough, uneven surface, trying to reach Tyron and the two mages. I clambered up a particularly jagged peak only to pause at the top, staring down the other side.

Tyron stood back, watching as one of the men attacked the other with his bare hands, his face twisted with rage. The one being attacked had clearly been taken by surprise, and he looked up at Tyron, shock on his face.

"What have you done?" he asked as he leaped away from the other mage.

The movement nearly sent him tumbling down between two rocks, but it also gave him time to draw a long knife from within his robe. The other mage continued to charge forward, undaunted by the weapon, but the knife-wielder didn't strike at him.

Instead, he jumped across a gap in the rocks, only just evading his enraged companion. His hand flashed downward as he struck at Tyron instead. His face lacked the blind rage of the other mage, but the cold anger in his eyes made my stomach clench.

Tyron didn't quite dodge far enough, the knife biting at his recently healed side. He swayed but didn't go down.

The mage pulled the blade back to strike again, but he had turned his attention from his companion for a moment too long. The pause had allowed the man under Tyron's control to seize a large rock.

The knife-wielder realized his mistake and spun to face him, but the enraged mage was already upon him. His arm moved faster than seemed possible as he brought the rock down with full force on the knife-wielder's head. His knife flashed out again, piercing the chest of his attacker, but he was too late to stop the stone.

Both of them fell, their bodies collapsing and sliding down the rocks, staining them red. I could feel the energy draining out of them, but it was Tyron I hurried toward. When the other mages had fallen, he had sunk slowly to the ground himself, and I dropped awkwardly to kneel beside him.

"Hold on." I pushed my hand into one of my pockets.

But my reaching fingers slowed as I looked again at his wound and realized how similar it was to the one he had sustained in the barn. I wasn't a healer with a healer's case of compositions. I had only the ones my family had provided for my own use. And I had already used the composition Tyron now needed.

I gulped. Perhaps there was another one close enough to suit the purpose? One I could modify after I had worked it. My mind raced through my supplies, trying to remember which healing compositions I carried on me.

"Tyron, I don't—" I could hear the frantic note in my voice.

He smiled at me, his hand fluttering weakly toward mine although it couldn't quite bridge the distance.

"Don't worry, Verene." His voice sounded unnaturally soft. "Maybe it's for the best. I wanted freedom, and we both know I wasn't going to get it in either Kallorway or serving my father. You took your aggressive ability and managed to use it for good. But it's too late for that for me." His eyes held mine. "Just think, Verene. Even if all my crimes were pardoned, what sort of future could I have with an ability like mine? Better it dies with me."

"You're forgetting what happened back at that barn." I looked back in the direction I had come, my view blocked by the rocks. "Darius will have the sort of composition we need. If you can just hold on long enough for…"

But Tyron's blood spilled from him faster and faster, and he shook his head. His face no longer held even a hint of color, but he still managed to curl his lips upward as his eyes moved toward the bodies of the two mages.

"No. There's no time. I will be free, as I wished. I'm just glad I took those two with me." His voice turned sour. "Cormac hid a death composition in me, but I was the one to get him in the end."

With a sudden spurt of strength, he reached my hand, squeezing it tight. "But my father remains. You must promise me you will kill him for me, Verene. Promise me!"

I froze, unable to make my lips speak the words. These could be Tyron's final words, and he was using them to call for more death. And yet still my compassion for him remained. How awful to reach the point where you thought death was your only escape.

The horror of it was eclipsed only by his delight at taking others into death with him—regardless of who they were. Conall had warped Tyron, and in recent weeks I had wondered if he might be on the path to redemption now that he was free of his father. But he showed no remorse for his actions—past or present. He had helped us because he preferred our bonds to those of his father, not because he had begun to see a different way.

But perhaps it was not too late. Determination filled me, and I pulled out a healing composition almost at random. Ripping it, I flicked the power toward Tyron, seizing control of it and directing it to stop the bleeding and seal the wound.

"Verene!" A welcome voice called my name seconds before Darius's familiar figure appeared at the crest of the rocks.

"Verene," he said again, almost falling in his haste to reach me. "Are you injured?"

I shook my head, staring down at my red hands. I hadn't even realized I'd been trying to stem the bleeding by physical means.

"No, it's Tyron's blood." I looked at Tyron's chest, moving up and down with shallow breaths, and met his confused gaze before turning to Darius. "I've healed him, but I had to twist a working to do it, and I'm no healer. I don't think he's properly healed inside. But I'm hoping this will be enough to last until we can get him to a real healer."

Darius nodded, his gaze traveling further to take in the bodies of the two Tarxi mages.

"Did he do that?"

I nodded. "He took control of one of them and set them to fighting. It was…"

I faltered, and Darius wrapped his arms around me. I leaned into him, shivering slightly.

I lowered my voice so Tyron wouldn't hear. "He thought he was going to die, and he was glad of it—and glad to take them with him. It was awful. He's been helping us, so I was hoping he was starting to think differently, but…"

"It's true that he's helped us many times," Darius murmured. "And yet, while you've been hoping for his redemption, I've been questioning our trust in him." He looked down at me. "But you were right in this. You freed him, and he didn't turn against us—in fact, he helped us. So perhaps you're right to hope as well. You've saved his life. Perhaps in time he'll develop regret for his past actions."

I sighed. "I hope that's true. But redemption is a painful process, and I'm not sure Tyron has the hope he needs to drive him through it."

Darius's arms tightened around me. "Then we will have to find a way to give it to him. Everyone should have hope."

For a moment I let myself lean into him and absorb his strength. Then other familiar voices reached us.

"You called for reinforcements," I said to Darius, not bothering to make it a question. That mystery working he had unleashed at the start of the fight must have been a communication composition, calling for the rest of our team.

He nodded. "With their help, we've easily subdued the squad we were fighting. But we still need you to free them from Conall." He glanced at Tyron. "I'll send Cooper and Jareth to carry him down. Others have need of you now."

CHAPTER 26

*B*ryony and Stellan were almost as horrified by the blood coating me as Darius had been, but both calmed right down when they heard it belonged to Tyron. Elsie asked nothing, simply holding out a water skin and helping me rinse my hands under its clean flow.

Vincent gave me a hard look when I admitted I had freed Tyron's bindings, but given how it had turned out, he refrained from expressing his disapproval. Instead he turned his attention to the tents which still sat untouched on the other side of the field, as if out of reach of the turmoil and commotion of the recent battle. If Conall was in one, he either hadn't heard us, or he was hiding.

"It's not over yet," Vincent said. "We don't have Conall." He turned to Darius, his eyes dropping to Darius's power-infused hand. "Do we know if he's in one of those tents, or did they just belong to those lieutenants of his?"

I turned away from them, moving toward the soldiers they had subdued instead. After the recent practice at the barn, it didn't take long to connect with each of the ten, searching their energy for the working Conall was using to control them. To my horror, I found most of them had several connections to him, and reversing them seemed to take more effort, as if the control was more deeply embedded.

When I finished, I looked up with a grimace. Layna and Jareth stood close by, so I beckoned them over, gesturing at two of the men.

"Those two aren't connected to Conall."

Jareth glared at the two of them. "So they were serving him willingly?"

I shrugged, uncomfortable. "They must have been, as hard as that is to believe."

"We should expect to find more of his loyal people now that we're so close to him," Layna said. She pulled lengths of rope from her pack, handing some to Jareth. "We'll secure them for now and come back for them after we've dealt with Conall."

But the man whose tendons I had cut turned at her words. Stellan had used a composition to heal him, and he looked both alert and angry.

"We'll take them in hand, Sir," he said. "If you don't mind. All we need are directions to where the true Sekali army is gathering. Handing these two over to the emperor's justice will bring me a great deal of satisfaction."

Another of the freed soldiers stepped up beside him. "Conall came for us years ago. He wanted servants and guards always at hand, so he used that awful power of his to bind us to him. None of us could go further from him than twenty yards, unless he ordered us away on some particular mission. And while our minds remained our own, we were compelled to obey any direct order he gave us. We haven't seen our families for three years. Do you know where they might be found?"

"Are you from one of the first villages to be taken then?" I asked, horror for their plight gripping me. "I believe your children made it to the next village and were taken in. They'll likely have all been evacuated by now, though. The emperor's forces were rounding up the children and getting them out of the battle zone."

"Long live the emperor," the first said with a reflexive bow, the second promptly mirroring him. "And thank goodness for the Spoken Mage."

"The Spoken Mage?" I asked quickly, unable to resist asking for news of my mother.

The speaker nodded. "Since we were bound to that monster's will, he didn't hesitate to speak freely around us. So, between us, we've managed to keep updated on how his war efforts are progressing. He was enraged when the Spoken Mage joined the emperor's forces far faster than he expected. She alone has been keeping Conall's army in check, stopping them from sweeping on the capital." He glanced at the man beside him. "She has single-handedly held back an entire army, maintaining a vast barrier all the way along the front lines. It doesn't hurt Conall's soldiers, but they haven't been able to break through it yet, either."

The other man shook his head. "It seems impossible. I would like to see for myself if one person can perform such a feat."

"She's not doing it alone," I said. "The emperor must have vast legions lending her their energy to maintain such a composition." I frowned. "It's a simple strategy, but only a short term one. The emperor won't stand for Conall burning everything on his side of the line, as he seems determined to do."

I glanced at Layna. My mother was giving us time, as she had promised. She must have been furious that I had fled with such minimal protection—and taken Stellan with me, too. But she was giving us the time we needed to complete our task.

One by one, all eight coerced members of the attacking squad joined us. I glanced at Stellan. Their quick recovery must be thanks to his efforts at redistributing energy.

Layna gave them directions as best we could, and they fell to arguing over the best path to the front lines. The first of them remained separate from the conversation, however, taking the ends of the ropes that bound the two traitors' hands with another bow.

"I would offer to stay and help you go after that monster, but…"

I quickly shook my head. "No. You have a family who haven't seen you in years. Go, and I wish you smooth travel from here."

He bowed again to all of us before tugging sharply on the ropes and dragging the traitors to their feet. Within minutes the ten of them had disappeared from sight.

Darius turned from contemplation of the distant tent, his hand blazing. "Can you feel him now?"

I reached with my mind. Gasping, I pulled back.

"What is it? Are you all right?" Darius was at my side instantly.

I took a deep breath. "He's so powerful. His energy blazes. But it also feels…"

"Sick?" Stellan asked beside me in a quiet voice. "Wrong? It's been sickening me since we arrived. I've never felt something so twisted before."

I gulped, placing a reassuring hand on his arm. With his heightened awareness, he must have felt Conall's presence as soon as he arrived. Whereas I had been tuning it out. No wonder Stellan had been so quiet.

"Are you sure about this, Verene?" he asked, his voice still subdued. "Do you really want to connect with…that?"

I shivered. "No, I don't want to."

Everything in me shied away from the idea in horror. I only hoped I could force myself to do it when the moment came. The first time I had encountered one of Conall's workings, my inner self had tried to pull away from making any sort of connection with it. But the feel of Conall himself was a thousand times worse than a single, small working. What if I couldn't make myself do it?

"I don't want to," I repeated, "but I have to."

"Do you?" Tyron asked in a soft voice.

I started, unaware that he had approached. He limped slightly and clutched his side, but his eyes were piercing.

I frowned at him. "I'm not abandoning our mission now. I'm not leaving Conall to defeat the Empire and turn his sights on Kallorway and Ardann."

"No, of course not," Tyron said. "That's not what I meant."

His voice dropped low, and I moved closer to him in an effort to catch his words.

"What do you mean, then?" I asked.

"You keep thinking your ability is the only way to reverse my father's workings, but there's another way. He also has the power to reverse them himself."

I shook my head impatiently. "Conall is never going to reverse his own workings."

"Not voluntarily." Tyron met my eyes steadily. "But we have a way to change his mind—to change it to whatever we want."

"*Your* ability," I breathed, my eyes widening.

He nodded slowly. "I seem to have lost my pen. But if you give me one, I'll write you a composition right now. You can take it into that tent over there and end this right now."

He chuckled grimly. "It would be a fitting end to have him destroy his life's work himself. He certainly didn't have any hesitation to destroy his own son."

I chewed on my lip, my eyes drilling into him. Could his suggestion work? I had trusted him enough to release his bindings. Surely it was only a small step further to give him a pen.

Somehow, while we were talking, we had drifted a few steps away from the rest of the group. I glanced back at them now, all of them having joined the conversation between Darius and Vincent except for Elsie who was preparing some food.

"If something goes wrong with your composition, then I'm back to being our only hope. So I have to be the one to face Conall, even if it is with your working. Given that, I'm not sure

Captain Vincent will agree to your involvement. He doesn't trust you enough. He'll suspect you're setting me up for capture."

"I may not love you, Verene," Tyron said, "but I hate my father. I didn't trek all the way here to rejoin him."

I swallowed. I had heard what Tyron believed to be his dying words, so I knew he spoke the truth. But could I convince the others?

I glanced at them again, coming to a quick decision. Pulling a pen from an inner pocket, I handed it to Tyron.

"Write quickly."

I positioned myself to shield him slightly from view, listening tensely to the scratching of the pen against parchment.

"Done," he said after a moment, thrusting the finished composition at me.

I scanned it slowly. It appeared to be just what he had said it would be—a composition to convince his father that he wanted to release every person he held entrapped.

"All I ask is that you take me with you," Tyron said. "I want to see his defeat with my own eyes."

"I wasn't planning to get that close," I said.

Tyron frowned. "But you're using my working now. And the closer you are, the more effective it will be." He glanced toward the tent. "You can sense energy, so you can tell he's alone in there. We don't need to fear physical danger from confronting him."

He looked at me. "With my father's ability, he's never needed to use physical means to subdue anyone."

I weighed him with my eyes. Tyron was driven by emotion, and he clearly wanted the chance to confront his father in person. But that didn't mean his words weren't true. It was hard to hold on to all the information I had understood while connected to Tyron's ability, but from memory there had been some factor about distance.

"Your father can sense energy, too," I said. "He'll know we're coming. He must already know we're here, although he continues to hide away."

"Another reason to take me with you." Tyron looked again toward the distant tent. "He knows my energy well enough to recognize me. As far as he knows, I still haven't triggered the death composition he had Cormac hide in me, which means I haven't betrayed him. He probably thinks of me as nothing more than a prisoner. If he feels me approaching with only one other, he'll be more curious than threatened. He might think I've escaped in the chaos."

I raised an eyebrow. "You want us to go alone?"

Tyron shrugged. "The rest of them got you this far. That was their purpose. From here, the battle is yours."

I considered his words, looking for the flaw. I could find none. He was right that no one else could help me at this final stage.

A reckless energy filled me. I had been waiting and fearing this final confrontation for so long. It was time to stop thinking and act. One way or another, it would all be over soon.

"Very well." I glanced again at the huddled group behind us. "Let's go now."

Tyron grinned, keeping pace with me as I strode toward the tent that housed Conall. But we weren't even halfway across the field when someone called after us.

"Run," I said to Tyron, gripped by an idea.

I took off racing, Tyron at my side still. Pounding feet sounded behind me, but we had a head start, and I pushed myself to go faster still.

Let Conall feel his son's energy racing toward him, pursued by a clump of enemies. It was better this way—he wouldn't have time to analyze the situation.

And once I had worked Tyron's composition, gripped tightly in my clammy hand, he would be under my control and it wouldn't matter if the rest of our team piled into the tent behind us. In fact, I preferred it that way.

Now that I was actually racing toward Conall, it was easier to think of ways in which Tyron's words might prove untrustworthy. Now that I was no longer trying to convince myself they were true, I feared they were deceptive. I wanted backup in case anything went wrong.

My breath rasped in and out of my throat, all my focus narrowing to this moment, this final confrontation. But a loud clamoring made my head spring up. Back behind the burned houses and the rocky outcropping, distant figures had appeared, yelling as they charged toward us.

Conall's continued absence now made sense. Darius hadn't been the only one to call for reinforcements, and Conall had been hiding in his tent until they appeared.

I faltered. It was hard to gauge their numbers from here, but it looked like multiple squads. My friends would need my help.

But Tyron looked back at me, his eyes burning, and I picked up speed again. The best way to help my friends was to stop Conall. Once he had released the people under his control, this army would cease any attack. I couldn't stop now.

Tyron had also lengthened his stride again, and he burst into the tent two steps ahead of me. I barreled in after him, one of our pursuers almost at my heels.

I heard Tyron say, "Father," and then several things happened at once.

A ripping sound filled the tent, and a blazing wall of immense power slammed around the canvas, enclosing us inside with Conall. A gravelly voice spoke Tyron's name, and then another parchment ripped in half. I screamed as the composition in my hands burst into flames. I dropped it as the words disintegrated, the energy they had contained burning up with them.

My jacket began to smolder, and I ripped it from my back,

flinging it to the floor as every composition it contained burned along with the one from my hands.

"Impossible!" I gasped, shaking my stinging fingers.

A rough laugh made my head spring up, my gaze latching on an older, scarred version of Tyron. He stood in the center of an austere tent, containing only a bed, a small table, and two chairs. His light eyes bore into me, their expression frightening, not least because there was something inexpressible wrong with them, some hint of the twisted interior lurking behind.

"I have been preparing to take my rightful place for decades," he said. "Banished in the mountains, there is plenty of time for experimentation, Princess."

I gulped, my eyes flying to Tyron. Had he tricked me, then, after all?

But no. Hatred and anger radiated off Tyron's tense body as he stared at his father. He clearly hadn't known about Conall's defensive measures.

"I've been curious to meet you," Conall continued. "Your name comes up a surprising amount for a girl who apparently has no power. And here you are again. I'm going to enjoy commanding you to spill all your secrets."

Despite my fear, a small spark of triumph filled me. All the secrecy had been worth it. Conall knew enough to fear me—although he hid that concern behind carefree words—but he didn't know what I could do.

Tyron stepped forward. "Adair and Cormac are dead. I killed them."

For the first time I saw Conall falter. Had he not been able to feel their deaths at this distance? But he recovered himself swiftly.

"You're a disappointment, Son," he said.

The calm Tyron of our journey disappeared, strong emotion gripping him as he faced off with his father. But I only listened to their conversation with half an ear.

Tyron's presence had succeeded in distracting his father, as we had hoped it would, and Conall clearly didn't consider me a threat. But with the rest of my team blocked from entering the tent, and all of my compositions destroyed, I wasn't sure how to proceed. And every moment I delayed was another moment my friends were left fighting for their lives against Conall's army. I had to do something.

I could take control of the barrier itself, but it contained an enormous amount of power. What would I do with it? I couldn't twist it to replace the composition of Tyron's I had lost—the barrier's original purpose was too disparate. And once I had pulled it down, Conall's attention would be back on me instantly.

Despite myself, my legs shook at the thought. Now that I was so close to him, his energy burned in my mind with terrifying intensity. He held not only his own energy but thousands of stolen slivers from others, the cumulative effect both over-whelming and sickening. The composition from Tyron had burned away, but my stomach roiled just from standing near Conall. I wasn't sure I could force myself to connect with him. I needed to replace the composition I had lost. And maybe that was still possible.

My main advantage right now was that he thought me trapped and helpless which gave me a small window to take advantage of his distraction. Stooping to the ground, I thrust my hand into my still smoking jacket. Somehow the compositions had burned without taking the material of the jacket with them, and it gave me hope that Conall's working had been extremely directed. If it had targeted only compositions…

Yes! My questing fingers found intact parchment. His compo-sition hadn't touched the blank sheets of parchment I always carried with me. I pulled out a pen and one sheet, angling my body to keep them out of Conall's sight.

My stomach heaved, every nerve and muscle tense. My mind screamed at me to run as far as I could from the unnatural energy in front of me. But I forced my legs to stiffen and hold their ground.

"Connect," I whispered in the quietest possible voice, reaching for Tyron.

After so many times doing the same thing back at the Academy, I connected easily with his familiar energy. The faintest tremor showed he felt my presence, and his voice raised in volume as he continued to argue with his father.

The feeling of power I had wrestled with back in Kallorway washed over me. How easy it was going to be to reach out and make this terrifying man bow to my every whim. I could make him do anything I wanted. He would be powerless before me.

The thoughts made me pause, afraid. It was just like Tyron described—I was helpless before the nature of his ability.

I shook myself. No. I was still in control. I had said I would use any ability necessary to save my kingdoms, and I had meant it. I would use Tyron's ability to reverse Conall's evil, but no more. Whatever Tyron said, it was possible to show restraint, to use even his ability only for good. It was our choices that formed us, not the ability we had been given.

My hand flew across the page as I recreated the composition I had lost. Only as I was writing the final words did I realize the error I had made in my haste. Instead of adjusting the words that sprang so readily to the fore so that the working would connect with me, I had written it so that it would connect with Tyron.

I bit my lip, reaching for a fresh parchment.

"What are you doing?" The threatening words made me freeze.

Slowly I looked up to find Conall bearing down on me. There was no time for further compositions—no time even for hesitation. I ripped the parchment in my hand.

Tyron let out a wordless yell of triumph as the working reached for his father, connecting the two of them. Conall hesitated, looking back toward his son, his face twisting in confusion.

"What…I don't understand. Why…"

"You want to release all those people," Tyron said, in a calm, friendly voice, as if it was a reasonable suggestion. And then he continued on in the same tone. "And then you want to end your life."

I gasped.

"Tyron! No! That isn't what we came here to do!"

Conall cocked his head to the side, his brows lowering as he regarded me curiously. He swayed, his expression confused, as a visible battle raged behind his eyes.

Tyron reached me in two long strides, clamping his hand over my mouth.

"Silence," he hissed. "Do you want to help my father break out of my hold? It may not be what *you* came here to do, but you must know my father will not be allowed to live. Not after his crimes. And I want to be the one to kill him."

"His punishment is for the three crowns to decide," I said, my voice muffled against his hand. "This is wrong. I wrote that composition, and I didn't write it for this."

Tyron made an impatient sound in his throat. "You must know I overlaid this direction on the earlier composition. I was never letting him walk away from this."

"No." I shook my head, pushing his hand away from my mouth. "You know your ability can be used for good in more than one way. Forcing your father to peaceably reverse the hold he has over so many people is one of them. But twisting his own mind to betray him to his death is an evil use of your power, no matter what his crimes. Forget about him. Don't do this to your-self. You can choose to turn your back on your old ways and start forging a path toward new trust."

For a moment, I thought my words had swayed him, but then he shook them off.

"Stay silent, or my father won't be the only one to die here."

Someone slipped through the flaps of the tent, ripping me

from Tyron's grasp. I staggered and nearly fell, but Darius held me steady, his furious gaze spearing into Tyron.

"Touch her again, and I'll make you regret it."

"Where did you come from?" I asked, leaning into him, my body trembling. I had been so consumed by fear of Conall, I had missed the presence of another energy behind me.

"I was just inside the barrier when it went down," he said. "But all my compositions burned up. I've been waiting and watching for the opportune moment to intervene."

"Tyron!" I shouted, my attention ripped away from Darius.

Conall's energy writhed and twisted in a nauseating way, at constant odds with the stolen pieces of others' energy. It was a sickening backdrop to every interaction in the tent, and it masked his efforts to break free from Tyron's hold.

Perhaps it was because of his splintered, broken self that Tyron's ability couldn't properly latch on. Whatever the reason, I only realized what was happening when the energy snapped free.

Tyron felt it as well, spinning at the same moment as I shouted his name.

But we were both too late. His father already had a blade in his hand, and he plunged it straight into his son's heart.

CHAPTER 27

Tyron's eyes connected with mine for one brief moment, and then he fell and didn't get back up.

I screamed, but Darius already had me whisked behind him, his sword in his hand.

Conall paid no attention to his son, instead drawing his own sword with an amused look on his face. I couldn't help glancing at Tyron's still body before looking back at Conall. My stomach heaved, and my knees wanted to buckle, but I straightened my spine and refused to give in to either sensation.

"Prince Darius," Conall said, the amusement sounding in his tone. "I was wondering when you were going to stop skulking outside the door and show your face. How convenient of you to come to me. I was planning to take your throne next, after I've dealt with this so-called emperor."

Darius merely narrowed his eyes and gripped his sword more tightly.

"You won't be able to protect her with a mere blade," Conall said. "Surely you know that."

"I can try," Darius said, his voice stone cold and just as hard.

Conall shook his head. "You're even more of a fool than I

expected. So much power, and yet you're going to just throw it all away. You had a kingdom worth of people willing to place themselves between you and me in order to protect you, and yet here you are."

"My strength is exactly why I'm standing here," Darius said. "It was given to me so I can protect the people I love, not use them."

Conall barked his harsh laugh. "So says the fool just before he dies."

"Maybe," Darius said. "But I'm not dead yet."

Conall shrugged. "You soon will be. As will everyone who refuses to bow before me. I was chosen to rule—gifted with a power greater than any other."

"It's not our strength that makes us great," I said, stepping around Darius. "It's our choices. It's holding on to hope, and making the right choice, even if it's hard. In the end, Tyron couldn't see that. He was given a way to use even his ability for good, and he still chose to use it for evil." I took a deep breath. "And there is one person with a power stronger than yours. Me."

Conall sneered at me, but I could see a whisper of doubt behind his eyes. It didn't matter, though. My speech had achieved its purpose. It had given me the courage I needed to speak a single word, although everything in me screamed not to do it.

"Connect," I said, and forced my energy forward into the twisted black energy at Conall's core.

He let out a great bellow, the sound one of outrage.

"What are you doing?" he cried. "This isn't possible! Get out of my mind!"

But I barely heard the words. Distantly I felt Darius push me back behind him again, but I no longer had any real sense of my own body. Instead I was consumed in a maelstrom.

I could only assume Conall's mind still functioned—he couldn't have conceived and executed this plan otherwise. But there was no such order or reason left in his ability. It sucked me in to a black landscape, my mind screaming for release as his energy tried to wrap around mine.

I had never felt anything like it. Tyron had sensed my presence in his mind, but his father's energy actively tried to seize me. It wanted to incorporate me into its own twisted labyrinth of energy. How much of the energy that clung to Conall was actually his own? He had stolen from thousands upon thousands, leaving a piece of himself behind to maintain the hold, and he was now more a patchwork of others than himself.

But each of the fragments was too small for cohesion or order of its own. And many of them fought him, struggling constantly to be free, pulling against his mind and will from the inside. Tyron had no doubt been right, and there were older layers that had gone dormant, but the top ones were plentiful enough to overwhelm me.

Conall's intellect might remain, but he couldn't be sane. No one could resist such a chaotic onslaught for so long and remain stable. Already I could feel the darkness in him eating at me, slowly stripping away pieces of my energy.

I screamed, almost tearing myself free in mindless terror at the feeling of losing any part of myself to this awful place.

A distant voice called my name. Darius. I calmed. Darius was here with me, protecting me. I could find my way home when I was ready because he was my anchor. I would always find my way to him.

But the darkness still clawed at me, and the futility of my mission made it hard to breathe. Another piece of me was peeled away. I wrestled it back before Conall could sink his will into it, but already he was pulling another portion free.

I couldn't remain here long enough to free so many people. It would take days to do so. I grunted as I reclaimed another stolen piece of my energy. Even if I was physically and mentally capable of keeping up the effort for long enough to free every person trapped here, I couldn't afford to stay that long. Above all else, I couldn't let Conall get control of my ability. With me under his control, he could break through even my mother's shield.

For a moment black despair shot through me, the emotion an opening at which Conall's darkness leaped, trying to worm its way through. But the distant voice reached me again.

"You can do this, Verene. I believe in you."

Darius sounded strong and sure. I grasped hold of his certainty and made it my own.

In the fight with Conall's lieutenants, I had given a single command to three different compositions. Those three had nearly overwhelmed me, but they had been so different. These were all the same—and I had managed multiple similar compositions in the past, even if I had drawn them in separately. Could I do it now with thousands upon thousands?

Conall's energy tore at me, ripping two chunks free at once and leaving me scrambling to retrieve them. There was no more time for thought. I had to act.

"Take control," I said, my own voice sounding strange and disconnected.

My energy reached out, and I directed it toward every writhing sliver of foreign energy that tore at the inside of Conall's ability. My own energy latched on to them, revealing with sickening clarity the composition Conall had used so many times to ensnare so many. My mind expanded as it tried to keep pace with my ability's achievement.

There was no time or space for subtlety. "Free!" I screamed as I broke every one of the countless compositions, erasing the commands he had embedded, and sending a flood of writhing energy racing back toward its rightful homes.

For the briefest second there was calm inside Conall's ability. And then the backlash hit, his own energy ricocheting free from all those thousands of minds and rushing back into him. It was energy that wanted to seize and control, and the only target left was me.

It reached for me with greedy intensity, and I gasped and panted as I tried to hold it back. I could feel the dam of my energy breaching, however, holes appearing, when I suddenly sensed sluggish movement from the deeper layers of Conall's ability. As if in response to the frantic activity, the older compositions were stirring. I had seized only the ones that still fought, forgetting the thousands of older ones that lay dormant beneath them.

My mind shied away from the idea of trying to seize control of those compositions as well. I was still connected to a backlash of energy I couldn't contain, struggling to redirect Conall's released compositions. I could only hold so much, and I was already at my limits. The anchor of Darius's presence receded from my awareness as I struggled to hold on to myself.

But did I need to take control of them? The thought speared through me like lightning. I had all this seething energy, needing to be directed toward something related to its original purpose.

"Free them all," I gasped out, pressing down with my will on the bucking energy and directing it against the remaining, untouched compositions anchored in Conall's ability.

It fought, tearing at me and howling through the chaos of his energy.

"Free them all," I repeated through my teeth, bearing down with every bit of strength I had left.

Suddenly and completely, the energy submitted, reaching for the thousands of dormant compositions. Conall's own energy, now turned against him, freed them in a great tsunami. The energy I directed against him fought the energy he had been using to keep them bound, the two burning out against each other until there was nothing left inside him but emptiness and silence.

I floated for a moment, untethered, trying to remember myself. And then a frenzied, frantic voice shouted my name.

Darius. Darius was waiting for me.

"End connection," I choked out and pulled myself all the way free.

I opened my eyes and looked up into Darius's frantic face. I appeared to be cradled in his arms now.

"Thank you for bringing me home," I whispered, and then my mind retreated into the calm, cool darkness of my own self, and the world faded away.

CHAPTER 28

When I came back to consciousness, I couldn't immediately tell how much time had passed. Darius's arms no longer circled me, but when I struggled up to a sitting position, I found Elsie sitting watch over me.

She smiled at me, but the worry in her eyes was stronger.

"What's going on?" I looked around.

I sat against one edge of the rocky outcropping, facing toward the distant tents. The canvas sides of one of them had collapsed inward, the structure destroyed. People moved in and out of the others, milling in all directions and spilling out across the fields.

"You freed them all," Elsie said. "So they stopped fighting. But now there's just chaos."

We were tucked away in a quiet pocket beside the rocks, but the open ground did look chaotic. And I couldn't see the rest of our team.

"Why do you look so concerned?" I asked, fear making my voice sharp. "And where's Darius?"

She bit her lip, eyeing me as if she feared I was too weak for bad news. I pulled myself to my feet.

"Tell me! What's happened?"

"Everyone got separated in the fighting. I was sheltering here among the rocks, and Stellan was protecting me when everyone suddenly stopped fighting. Darius appeared out of that tent, carrying you in his arms. At first I thought you were—"

She cut herself off, her voice wobbling slightly before she managed to steady herself and resume her story.

"He brought you to me and Stellan, and the others began to gather to us, too. But Jareth didn't come."

"Jareth?" I spun around, scanning the crowds of people around us. "Where is he? He didn't…"

I turned back to her, and she shrugged.

"I don't know. Darius and Stellan and the others went searching for him and left me here to watch over you."

I tried to stride forward, only to sway and grasp at Elsie for support. I moaned softly.

"My head feels so strange."

"Of course. Here, let me help you." Her gentle hands guided me back to sitting before offering me a fresh water skin.

I gulped from it gratefully before giving her a weak smile. "You're starting to make a habit of this. Clearly I shouldn't attempt any great feats with my ability unless you're there to help me put myself back together afterward."

She shook her head. "Somehow I think you're going to keep amazing everyone, whether I'm here or not." She hesitated. "I'm sure Jareth just got separated in the fighting. Once it stopped, he probably got held up helping someone, or…"

I nodded. I wanted to go racing off to look for him, but clearly I was in no fit state to do so. All I could do was accept Elsie's attempts at comfort.

"I didn't see you this time," she said, clearly trying to keep me calm and stationary, "but I remember last time. I can't describe what it's like to watch you, locked in battle in your own head."

I blinked at her. "Not in my head, really. In someone else's usually."

I continued to scan the people around us, finally noticing a single, unmoving figure. Layna stood a short distance away, clearly on guard duty. So I had more than one loyal friend watching over me.

I wanted to call to her to go and join the search for Jareth, but I knew it would do no good. Instead I looked back at Elsie.

"Conall?" I asked cautiously, half afraid of the answer.

"Dead," Elsie said in a quiet voice. "Darius told us he just dropped dead. But Stellan said Conall's energy had been… fighting itself?" She sounded uncertain of her words. "He said it was diseased and twisted, and then it turned on itself. It just… consumed him. And when it had finished, it was burned completely away." She gulped. "He thinks you pulled free just in time."

I swallowed at my narrow escape. Having seen the inside of Conall's energy and ability, I couldn't be surprised at the news. He had twisted himself far beyond the point of recovery.

"Over here!" Cooper's voice rose above the general hubbub of the freed soldiers. "I've found him!"

I surged back to my feet, and this time, Elsie hurried to support me. Together we moved toward Cooper, my shuffling feet slowing us down.

He was behind a spur of the rock, bending over someone tucked into a deeper crevice than the one that had sheltered me and Elsie. I wasn't close enough to see behind him, but I could see the expression on his face when he turned back toward us. I stumbled, my head and hands going cold.

Darius appeared, and Cooper shook his head, his face white.

"I'm sorry," he murmured. "I don't think…"

But it wasn't Darius who shouted a protest at his words. The anguished cry came from Bryony. She sprinted toward us, shoving aside anyone in her path. She reached Cooper only steps behind Darius and didn't hesitate to push both of them out of her way.

"Nonononononono." She dropped to her knees beside the body that I still couldn't see clearly past the tight gathering of people at the mouth of the crevice.

"He's still alive," she cried. "It's not too late."

Cooper grimaced, shaking his head at Darius. Darius thrust his hands into his pocket before horror washed over his face as he remembered all his compositions were destroyed.

But Bryony's fumbling hands produced a parchment, ripping it clean through.

Energy washed out of the composition, flowing into Jareth. Bryony was trying to give him strength to hold on. I looked to Cooper, willing him to somehow produce a powerful enough healing composition to save Jareth.

But both Cooper and Darius stood still, staring down at Bryony and Jareth. Surely they wouldn't have given up. I frowned.

Before I could open my mouth to spur them on, however, a smile broke over both their faces.

"Why are you all looking at me like that?" a familiar voice asked from behind them.

Gasping, I pulled Cooper to one side so I could see past him and into the crevice. Bryony still knelt, tears streaming down her face, although she was now smiling down at a bemused Jareth.

He pushed himself up to a sitting position and gave us all a quizzical smile.

"Why are you all looking like I've just come back from the grave?"

Darius laughed and pulled him the rest of the way to his feet. "Apparently Cooper hasn't learned as much from the healers as he thinks he has. Either that or someone gifted Bryony an extremely powerful healing composition."

He glanced back at me, gratitude in his eyes, and I could see he thought Bryony's composition had come from me.

Cooper was shaking his head. "I've never been so glad to be wrong in my life."

But my own gaze was fixed on Bryony.

"Bree…" I breathed, and she looked up, meeting my gaze. She shook her head sharply, and I shut my mouth. She didn't want me to say anything, and I wouldn't. For now.

No one asked any more questions, too relieved at Jareth's recovery and our success to pursue the matter.

Layna had followed us, and the others quickly gathered as well. While everyone else had been searching for Jareth, Vincent had been using a powerful communication composition to contact my mother. She had reported that the combined forces of all the allies had now gathered, so she was going to lower the barrier. The troops would disperse into the occupied areas to restore order.

"We won't be the only place in chaos with all those people suddenly restored to their own wills," Elsie murmured to me.

"Not all of them," I said sadly, thinking of the bodies we had passed and the one we had left behind at the barn.

"No." For a moment she looked downcast before brightening. "But it could have been a lot worse. From what Vincent heard from your mother, the strategies the Armed Forces developed after working with the trainees were highly effective. Despite the barrier, there were clashes, like the ones we encountered, but our forces were largely successful in restraining Conall's soldiers. So your efforts at the Academy were worthwhile."

I raised my eyebrows. "You knew what that was about? Back at the Academy?"

She chuckled. "All the servants were talking about the strangeness of it, so it wasn't exactly difficult to work out."

Stellan stepped up to speak to her, and I turned to look for Bryony. Jareth had pulled her to her feet, tucking her into his side, but Darius drew him away, and I took the opportunity to give my friend a hug.

"Don't think you're avoiding talking about this," I whispered in her ear.

She nodded slightly before giving me a second squeeze. "Later. When we're alone." Her voice brightened. "But never mind me! I'm just glad you're alive."

"As are we all." Stellan turned from Elsie to grin at me. "You did it, Sis."

I shook my head. "Elsie tells me you think I got out just in time. I've never been more glad of anything. It was horrible inside there, Stell."

He gave me an awkward hug, including Bryony because she still hadn't let go of me.

"I can imagine. I was worried for you."

"But you did it!" Bryony cried, even more of her normal buoyancy returning. "So we can forget about the awfulness of the experience and focus on the result. You freed Conall's army and saved us all." She beamed. "My best friend! I knew you could do it."

I grinned back at her. "It's true that you never lost faith, Bree. I'm lucky to have you for a friend."

She flushed, but another voice speaking my name kept her from answering.

Bryony, Stellan, and Elsie all drew back, as if recognizing Darius's greater claim. He strode over, pulling me to my feet so he could wrap me in his arms.

"You're all right. Thank goodness you're all right." He buried his face in my hair as I clung just as tightly to him as he was holding on to me.

"Only thanks to you," I said. "You were my anchor."

I pulled back a little so I could see his face, noticing in my peripheral vision that the others had moved back even further to give us space.

"I only survived that because of you, Darius. You helped me find my way back because you are home to me. You're so worried about my giving up my home to come to Kallorway, but in these last four years, you've become my home. I don't care what my parents say, although I believe they'll come to understand. I could never go back to my old life in Ardann now."

Darius drew a deep breath, his eyes drinking in my face. He leaned forward to press a kiss against my hair.

"You were right all along, Verene, and I was a fool not to see it."

I smiled up at him, not sure what he meant but delighted all the same.

"I've spent most of my life keeping myself under the tightest control, striving never to make a single misstep. And then Tyron came along and made me turn my back on everything that mattered. I thought my inability to fight free of him meant I was weak." He shook his head. "I didn't know how to let myself fail. I worried it meant I wasn't strong enough to protect you. But I was wrong."

I reached up to touch his cheek, but he kept talking. I let him get it all out, taking in his words greedily, my heart singing.

"No one is infallible. No one's judgment never fails. I second guessed myself constantly with Tyron after what he did to me. And yet, when it mattered, I trusted your judgment, and you turned out to be right. That's what I should have realized from the beginning. In moments when I can't trust myself, I can look to you. If we're going to rule a kingdom together, then we have to trust each other. Together we're stronger than we are apart."

"Are we going to rule a kingdom together?" I raised my eyebrows, fighting to keep the grin off my face. "I think you've skipped a step."

For the briefest moment he frowned down at me before a broad smile broke across his face, and he dropped to one knee.

"Princess Verene of Ardann, will you do me the honor of

becoming my queen and ruling Kallorway at my side? You're intelligent and loyal and fierce and beautiful, and far more than I deserve. But, selfishly, I hope you'll say yes and let me—and my kingdom—keep you forever."

I pulled him to his feet. "Of course I'll say yes. I never wanted to rule a kingdom, but from the moment I met you, everything in my life began to change. And now I can't imagine any other future than by your side."

He pulled me back into his arms and placed the softest and gentlest of kisses against my lips. I pushed up onto my tiptoes, pressing my mouth against his, and he deepened the kiss. His arms tightened around me, and fire raced up and down my spine.

But sudden cheers broke through the moment, making us both pull back sheepishly and turn to our audience. Bryony was the one making the racket, but Elsie and Stellan looked just as pleased. Even Layna, several steps behind them, was grinning from ear to ear.

"Oh, hush," I told Bryony with a laugh. "You've already told me you knew everything was going to work out once today."

"Of course I knew it," she said with the familiar twinkle in her eye. "But that doesn't mean I'm not happy to see it come true."

Vincent appeared behind Layna, watching us with a slightly indulgent expression. But when he spoke, his usual focus remained strong.

"I want to get moving. We've achieved what we came for, and there are three armies whose job it is to mop up after us. These people have been freed, and that's all we can do for them. They'll need to wait for the rest of our forces for anything else. Right now, I have four royal charges in the middle of a foreign empire with only two royal guards between you. I'm sure you'll understand when I say I would sincerely like to be moving back in a homeward direction."

I had been hoping we would head for the imperial capital to meet up with my mother, but I couldn't argue with his concerns.

Darius had already sent the location of Conall's body to the emperor, and Vincent wanted to be gone before the emperor's troops arrived.

"Not that I think they'll do you harm," Vincent clarified. "But I won't rest easy until we're back behind the Academy walls. And if the emperor insists you come to his palace to meet with him—as he likely will—there will be no refusing."

Darius let out a long, weary sigh. "I am more than ready to be home." He glanced at Jareth. "And I would like to return as soon as possible. Despite our great-aunt's reassurances, I don't know what sort of chaos I might be facing, given my defiance of the Mage Council. It's best that I keep my absence as short as possible."

And so we began the return journey. With the release of Conall's captives, there were groups moving in every possible direction, so we easily blended in. We evaded three groups of Sekali soldiers, and one group of Ardannian ones, before we encountered three squads of Kallorwegians.

Vincent had no problem revealing ourselves to them, and within hours of doing so, we had proper transport arranged and an appropriate honor guard for the king-elect.

It felt strange to travel in style inside a carriage after our stealthy flight through the Empire, but I was glad to rest my weary feet. I sat at the window, taking in everything we passed. The Sekalis were wasting no time in getting the rebuilding underway.

We even passed one village just as two squads of soldiers turned up, escorting three carts full of local children. The screams and cries of joy as parents were reunited with their offspring warmed my heart for the rest of the day.

I needed moments like that to balance against the tears I couldn't help shedding when we passed fresh graves in burned fields, or people picking through the wreckage of what had once been their home. Moving swiftly in a carriage somehow made the scale of the devastation seem even larger.

But everywhere we saw soldiers—keeping order, transporting civilians, helping to rebuild, directing the endless streams of traffic.

"If only those were the only roles the Armed Forces were ever called on to fulfill," I said to Darius with a sigh. "I would like living in such a world."

He smiled down at me, his arm tucked around my waist as it so often was these days. "Then we must build that world, you and me."

I reached up for a quick kiss, only pulling away with a chuckle when I caught sight of my brother's disgusted expression.

On our first night on the road, I seized the opportunity to get a moment alone with Bryony.

"Cooper has been working closely with the healers for years," I said. "And he said Jareth was beyond healing." I shook my head. "You're just fortunate that in all the panic, no one else noticed that composition you worked was an energy composition not a power one. They think you worked a regular healing composition that I had given you in case of an emergency."

"And you'll let them keep thinking that?" Bryony asked.

I nodded. "Of course." I hesitated. "Although Darius..."

"You can tell him," she said. "I wouldn't expect you to keep a secret like that from him." She paused and then finished in a rush. "And he's going to be my brother, anyway."

I squeaked and gave her a hug. "Jareth proposed?"

"On the way to confront Conall," she said. "But you know how I've always felt about being royalty. I cared about Jareth, but I wasn't willing to commit to becoming a princess." She drew a shuddering breath. "Until I saw him dying on the ground. And then I knew that I would give up more than my freedom to have the chance at a life with him."

I pulled back, scanning her face. "You don't regret giving him some of your energy? Even though it's gone now forever?"

"Of course I don't regret it," she said, her ready smile curving her lips. "Jareth's life is worth far more than the portion of energy I had to sacrifice to save him."

"I didn't know you carried a healing composition around with you," I said. "I should have noticed your energy was lower from the minute you wrote it."

"I didn't carry one around before. But that first night after the trip up the river…" She shrugged. "I decided it was worth the sacrifice to have one ready. After that we were traveling constantly, so you probably thought my energy was lower from the exertion."

I leaned forward and embraced her again. "I'm delighted for you, Bree. Well, of course I am! What could be better from my perspective? This might even make it easier for Mother and Father to accept the situation—knowing I'll have you with me. And Kallmon has lots of shops, just like you wanted." I hesitated. "But do you think you can be happy with a life at court?"

Bryony shrugged. "I've reconciled myself to that. I could never be like you and Darius—with the court masks and all the control. I wasn't raised to it like you were. But Jareth has shown me there are different ways to approach the issue. He chose a different path from his brother, hiding behind his charm and social nature instead, and it's a path I can live with."

She grinned. "Plus he's told me we can escape to the coast whenever it gets too much. Great Aunt Mildred has promised to leave him her part of the estate down there, so he'll always have a refuge from 'the snake pit of the court.'"

I laughed. "That sounds like her." I embraced my friend again. "We always said we were family, and now we will be."

"Yes!" she exclaimed triumphantly. "We're upgrading from cousins to sisters."

It wasn't until two nights later that I had the chance to speak to Layna in private.

"I still need to officially ask you if you would accept the position as my personal guard once I become queen of Kallorway," I said. "I can't imagine having anyone else watching over me."

Her eyes flew to Vincent, standing some distance away, and I smiled when I saw he was watching us closely. "And I know I'm not the only one who'd like you to come to the capital with us."

For the first time, I saw her flush.

"Please say yes," I said. "I really do need you. I might be sure about marrying Darius, but starting a new life as queen in Kallmon still feels overwhelming."

"Of course I'll stay with you, Princess," she said quickly. "I already told you so at the beginning of the year."

"Thank you," I said, trying to put all my gratitude into the words. "I'm fairly sure Dellion means to have the position if you don't take it, so you're saving me in more ways than one."

Layna chuckled. "I heard about that. But she then informed me she had set her sights on your first child, so I'm not sure you're in the clear yet."

I shook my head. "I can't believe I'm going to say this, but I might even trust her for that role when the time eventually comes."

Darius came over to join us, and I flushed, wondering if he'd heard me discussing our future children with my guard.

"Has she said yes?" he asked.

I nodded, and he smiled and thanked Layna himself. "I'm glad for Verene's sake, of course, but also for my own. I'm grateful you've found Kallorway to your liking."

When she moved away, I shook my head at him. "I don't think it's *Kallorway* she finds to her liking especially."

Darius chuckled. "No, of course not. But I can't mention that yet. I'll bet you anything you like Vincent hasn't said a word. He'll be restraining himself, convinced she's going to leave after you graduate. It won't take him long to speak up now you've officially offered her the position, and she's accepted."

I turned and wrapped my arms around his waist. "Anything I like? How about a kiss?"

He laughed down at me. "You don't have to bet me for those. I'm quite happy to freely distribute them."

He pressed his lips to mine, proving his words with actions, and I gave a happy sigh. I had fought so hard for a future with Darius, and it was already everything I had dreamed.

CHAPTER 29

Vincent's own squad of royal guards had traveled up the Abneris and were waiting for us where the river met the forest with a boat big enough for us all. The honor guard we had requisitioned were relieved of their duty as escorts and instead sent to the imperial capital with formal messages for the emperor.

He had sent Darius an invitation to the imperial palace, and Darius's reply promised he would visit after his coronation. There were imperial soldiers stationed on the river, but they didn't try to stop us. Instead they bowed low whenever we crossed their path, making it clear that by stopping Conall, we had won ourselves great favor and honor in the Empire.

The knowledge brought me pleasure, but not for my own sake. This would clearly be a new era of cooperation between the Empire and Kallorway, and I already had an idea of one way I wanted to use the new connection.

In the boat on the journey home—a journey that went a great deal more smoothly than the one in the other direction—I found a chance to talk to Elsie and Stellan.

"From what I've seen and heard, we've all won ourselves

honor among the Sekalis for what we achieved back there. It's not just me. So I'm wondering…what did you think of the Empire? Or at least what we saw of it?"

"It was amazing," Elsie breathed. "I wish we could have seen more of it."

Stellan frowned at me. "What are you thinking, Verene?"

"I'm thinking that *both* of you just won positions of honor and prestige in the Empire. And I'm thinking that among the Sekalis, commonborns aren't looked down on in the way they are in the southern kingdoms. In fact, the Empire considers our treatment of commonborns to border on barbaric. So, from their perspective, what could be more enlightened than a southern prince marrying a commonborn—not one like Mother, but one without power?"

"Are you suggesting we abscond to the Empire?" Stellan asked, a crease between his brows.

"Of course not! You're my brother, and I'm fully ready to love Elsie as a sister. I don't want you to end up causing some sort of royal incident. I'm suggesting you would make excellent Ardannian ambassadors to the Empire. In that role, you could turn your marriage to an advantage—and you could live somewhere Elsie won't always be disparaged and looked down on. And if Aunt Lucienne can't see the truth of that, then you can be Kallorwegian ambassadors to the Empire."

Stellan stared at me. "That might actually work! I'm not saying Aunt or our parents will love the idea of us getting married, but this could go a long way to reconciling them to it."

"Especially Mother and Father," I said. "They don't look down on commonborns, they just want to know we have the chance at a happy future. So we have to convince them there's a possibility for you and Elsie to be happy together."

Stellan lurched forward and wrapped his arms around me. "You're the best sister in the world, Verene." He pulled back and grinned at me. "And I don't just say that because you're my only sister, and you're about to become a queen."

"I do my best," I said modestly, before laughing. "The truth is, it should be me thanking you for bringing Elsie into my life. I can't imagine not having had her with me these last two years."

Elsie smiled. "You've saved us in more ways than one, Verene. And we won't ever forget what we owe you."

"Steady on," Stellan said, "or she'll get big headed."

Elsie rolled her eyes. "Ignore him, Verene. He's grateful, too."

"I just want you two to have a fair chance." My eyes drifted to Darius. Now that I was so happy, I wanted to spread that happiness around to everyone else. I couldn't help it.

He looked up and caught me looking, his serious expression melting instantly. It was hard to even remember all those years when he had kept himself so carefully hidden behind his icy mask. The mask still made appearances, especially when he was completing some official function, but it wasn't his only face anymore. And I couldn't be more pleased.

Arriving back at the Academy felt peculiar. After everything we had endured, everything we had achieved, and everything I, personally, had won, it was strange to see the Academy looking just as we had left it.

Apparently word of both the threat we had been living under and our subsequent triumph had beaten us home. When we stepped into the entranceway, it was crammed with both trainees and instructors, all of them wanting to thank and congratulate us.

Dellion pushed her way to the front, our other year mates trailing behind.

"I knew I didn't want any part of what you four were up to," she announced triumphantly before wrinkling her nose. "I have no desire to go trekking in secret through the mud of the Empire."

I grinned, strangely endeared by her predictability. "An understandable feeling. I've had better experiences."

She narrowed her eyes. "Then why can't you stop smiling?" Her eyes flashed to Darius. "Oh, don't tell me you've finally stopped falling over yourselves and managed to get officially betrothed?"

"Verene has accepted my proposal if that's what you mean," Darius said, a little of his old stiffness in his voice.

I just laughed, however. "We have, indeed. So don't worry about any wrinkles in your own future plans."

"I'm not worried," Dellion assured me. "You were the only two who didn't seem to realize your own inevitability."

Frida and Ashlyn pushed past her to offer their own congratulations, Frida whispering that she and Armand had decided to be open with their families.

"It seems like the opportune time," she said. "I can see what you meant now, and I think you're right. If our families can't come together at a time like this, they never will. And we can't let their old-fashioned prejudices stand in the way of our happiness. There's to be a new king on the throne, and it's time for them to embrace the new, united Kallorway."

"Bravo." I embraced her. "If it helps, you can tell them that you have our approval."

"If Royce can change his mind, they can," Armand said quietly from her side.

"Royce?" I looked around. "Where is he?"

"He went home to take his parents to task for not throwing their full support behind Darius after the news was spread about the Tarxi." Ashlyn shook her head. "I couldn't believe it when I heard he'd left."

"He has a thick skull, but eventually we got through to him," Dellion said with a note of satisfaction. "And I've actually heard he managed to convince them, too. He told them their family had always supported the crown, and they weren't going to stop now."

"Unless they wanted to be branded as traitors," Ashlyn added gleefully. "So that convinced them. Who knew Royce had enough spine for that?"

I shook my head. "I'm glad to hear it. It's long past time Kallorwegians came together." But my eyes sought out Dellion with a silent question.

She leaned close and whispered quietly enough that the others couldn't hear. "Don't worry, he hasn't changed that much. He still hates you as much as ever. But Darius reminded him how it feels to be back on the side with all the power, and he wasn't willing to give that up. He might hate you, but he knows it wouldn't serve him to challenge you. Especially not now."

Before I could reply, Isabelle pushed in to our small circle, surprising me by throwing her arms around my neck. "I've been sick with worry ever since we discovered where you'd gone. I'm so grateful you all made it back all right."

She pulled back and looked behind us. "Or at least, most of you did." She hesitated. "Tyron…?"

Her face told me the other trainees at last knew the truth about not just the Tarxi, but also our former year mate.

"What does it matter what happened to him?" Dellion's eyes flashed. "He was a traitor, lying to us this entire time."

"He's dead," I said. "But he wasn't all bad. He helped us greatly, even if he did it for his own selfish reasons."

"He was bad enough," Dellion muttered, and I could see Bryony nodding out of the corner of my eye.

I considered arguing, but what could I say? They were no more wrong than I was. Tyron had chosen to believe he was a slave to his ability, using it as an excuse to choose power and anger and hate. He had spent nearly four years at the Academy, but he hadn't been able to see the examples it offered. Examples that had inspired me—like Cooper, who had found a way to use his aggressive ability for good. I had already decided to suggest Duke Francis offer Cooper a permanent teaching position, and I hoped he would accept. There was no reason he ever had to go back to the Armed Forces.

Returning to classes felt almost impossible, but Isabelle told us the remaining soldiers had left the Academy, and arena battles had been put on hold. And Cooper told us we had officially completed enough field work to not need discipline classes for the rest of the year. So we had very few classes to attend, anyway.

Bryony, at least, was delighted with this development since she told me she needed the time for wedding planning. She had decided she would mitigate the horrors of a royal wedding by joining ours and turning it into a double wedding, and I had promptly made her official wedding planner.

Somehow, despite being stuck at the Academy, she seemed to have contacts at all the finest shops in Kallmon and was soon buried neck deep in plans. Seeing her only made me congratulate myself on my excellent good sense in turning the whole event over to her.

When word reached me that my parents had arrived at the Academy—having traveled straight from the imperial capital—I wasn't sure if I was more excited or nervous. I still rushed down to meet them, though.

To my relief, my mother burst into tears at the sight of me and wrapped me in such an enormous hug, I thought she might never let go.

"Oh, thank goodness," she said when she finally let me disentangle myself. "You don't know how it does my heart good to see you in one piece. Now I just need to lay eyes on your brother." She looked around the entranceway, but he had yet to appear.

"You aren't angry?" I asked, still a little nervous.

"About what?" my father asked. "That you went storming off to face Conall with a bunch of trainees and your younger brother? Or that we hear you're now officially betrothed to Kallorway's king-elect?"

I regarded him warily. Was that a note of humor in his voice? "Both?" I asked.

He gave me a hug of his own, and then put his arm around my mother's shoulders. "Your mother swore that if Darius brought you back from the Empire in one piece, she would give her approval for your marriage, so you can stop looking so nervous."

My eyes widened, and I looked between them. "Really? You approve?"

"Approve might be going a tiny step too far," he said. "We'd prefer not to lose you to another kingdom. But if the two of you can keep each other alive while defeating what might be the greatest threat either of our kingdoms has ever known, then clearly you belong together. Even we can acknowledge that."

"What you did, rushing off like that, terrified us," my mother said. "But it was necessary. You made a measured response to the situation at hand. We might not like the necessity that forced you into it, but we can respect it. And we certainly won't hold it against you."

"Since you made it home in one piece," Father interjected, and I laughed and wrapped them both in another hug.

"I'm so happy," I said. "I can't wait to tell Darius."

"Lucien sent this," Father said, holding out a sealed letter. "And his love."

I accepted it, tucking it into a pocket to read later.

"We also heard you're going to have Bryony to keep you sane," Mother said, as I had predicted she would. "It helps to know you'll have a friend by your side and watching your back."

I glanced between them. "Is that the only couple you heard about?"

Mother frowned. "What do you mean?"

"She means us," Stellan said from behind me, stepping forward to face them, his hand firmly wrapped around Elsie's.

She followed a step behind, clearly being dragged forward by his grip.

"You?" Mother gasped, falling back a step, her hand flying to her throat as her eyes darted between Stellan and Elsie. "But—"

Stellan held up a hand. "Hear our story before you say anything. I wouldn't want you to say something in shock you end up regretting."

Our father's eyebrows shot up, and he exchanged a look with Mother. I couldn't read everything that passed between them, but when he turned back to Stellan, he nodded.

"Very well, Son. We'll hear you out. I hope we can learn lessons, even at our age, and after what's happened with your sister, we won't rush into any hasty judgments."

Stellan threw me a grateful look, while Elsie flashed me a terrified one. I shot her a reassuring smile. They had worked on their arguments, and I believed they would be able to convince our parents. Especially after they had just given their approval to me and Darius.

"Why don't you come up to my suite," Stellan said. "We can talk about it there."

"Would you be willing for us to join you?" an unexpected voice asked from behind us.

We all turned to see Duke Francis standing side-by-side with Zora. My parents blinked at them both, looking slightly confused.

"Certainly," my father said with a respectful inclination of his head. "If you wish it."

I stared at Zora, though, my mouth slightly open.

"I thought you said you were happy to stay here, ruling over your own domain?" I couldn't help but ask.

Zora glanced at the duke, who nodded supportively. "And so we were until I started to spend time with young Elsie. Not that we intend to leave the Academy." She shot me a look. "Unless you and the soon-to-be-king wish to be rid of us."

"No, of course not," I said quickly.

She nodded with satisfaction. "I thought you'd be more loyal than that. We don't have any plans to leave, but we're done hiding. If our example can help bring happiness to young people such as Elsie and her prince, then it's wrong of us to keep ourselves hidden."

"Wait…" My mother looked back and forth between Zora and Duke Francis. "Are you saying you're—"

"Married, Your Highness," Duke Francis said. "Very happily, and for many years. My old friend, Mildred, could not have sent me a greater treasure when she sent Zora here."

"Mildred?" I suddenly remembered the strange conversation between her and Zora just before we left. "She was the one who sent you to the Academy?"

Zora nodded. "We're old friends, Mildred and I. At the time, she said it was a good position for me—a promotion from my role as her personal servant. But she admitted many years later that she actually thought Francis and I would be a good match."

"*Mildred* not only knows about your marriage but approves?" I still couldn't wrap my head around it.

"She approves of our marriage, but not of our recent decision to openly acknowledge it," Duke Francis said.

"That's why she came in person to stick her nose in—like the interfering busybody she is," Zora said, but there was affection lurking behind her disgust. "She should know me well enough to know I wasn't likely to be intimidated by any of her arguments."

"She cares about you," Duke Francis said softly, looking down at his wife with love in his eyes. "I can understand that."

"Be that as it may," Zora said implacably, "times are changing, and it won't do to let ourselves be trapped in the past. Not when it means letting others suffer unnecessarily."

My parents exchanged a look.

"Clearly there's a great deal for us all to talk about," my father said. "By all means, please join us." He gestured for Zora and the duke to precede him up the stairs, and the six of them disappeared toward Stellan's suite.

I retreated to my own rooms to read my older brother's letter. I scanned the words quickly and then read them again more slowly. Finally I gave a soft sigh. It was a very Lucien type of note.

But I was glad he had reached out, even going so far as to apologize for his actions over the summer. We would never again be the boy and girl who used to play together and eat at the same table, but we would love each other in our different ways, and we would always be brother and sister. And one day, he would sit on the throne in Ardann, and I would sit beside Darius on the thrones of Kallorway. Together, we would bring a new era of peace and friendship to our two kingdoms. I just hoped Stellan and Elsie could be part of that as well.

I didn't see Stellan again until he appeared in the dining hall for the evening meal. One look at his face told me everything I needed to know.

"You convinced them?" I asked, sitting beside him at the second year table. "Tell me everything."

"They were impressed by your suggestion about the Sekalis," he told me. "They're already making plans for me to talk to Uncle Jasper, and to Uncle Julian and Aunt Saffron. They've promised to make my case to Aunt Lucienne, too."

"Poor Aunt," I said with a smile. "It's a good thing she has Lucien since she's going to lose both of us."

"Speak for yourself," Stellan said hotly. "If she gives her approval, I'll fight for Ardann as hard as I can while an ambassador."

"Good," I said. "Let her see that fire, and she'll have to agree." I sighed. "The only sad thing is that I'm going to lose Elsie. I don't know how I'll ever replace her."

"At least we should have some more sealing ceremonies soon," Jareth said, coming to sit across from us. When Darius and

Bryony joined us as well, delighted whispers broke out among the second years at having such illustrious company at their table.

I frowned. "Why? Don't tell me you've found more traitors?"

Darius shook his head. "Not here. But the Kallorwegian forces in the Empire were responsible for apprehending a number of mages who were following Conall by choice. The emperor has graciously said we may keep them as prisoners of Kallorway rather than handing them over to him. They're doing the same thing for Ardann."

He glanced down the table and lowered his voice. "He knows we need the sealing ceremonies more than the Empire does. And he's inclined to be generous given our discovery that it was one of his mages who betrayed us all to Conall."

Bryony raised an eyebrow. "It was a Sekali?"

Darius nodded. "The emperor started moving too many troops, too early." He shrugged. "The wrong person found out why he was doing so. We just have to be grateful it wasn't someone who knew about Verene's ability and our full plans."

"The emperor's desire to make amends is excellent news for us," Jareth said. "There couldn't be a better way to begin your many reforms on behalf of the sealed commonborns." He glanced at me and Bryony. "Darius isn't wasting any time. He's already contacted the Mage Council and turned the emergency war edict that allowed commonborns access to compositions into a permanent law. Sealed commonborns can freely purchase and use compositions now."

"So the Council have forgiven you, then?" Bryony asked.

Darius grinned. "I'm officially betrothed to Verene, and I've won great favor with the emperor. I'm sure they'd like to be angry, but they don't dare."

I chuckled. "The four of us are going to keep them on their toes."

"Good," Darius said. "They need it."

"And they might even be a little grateful that with our return, Great-Aunt Mildred has returned to her retirement at the coast." Jareth chuckled, slipping his arm around Bryony's waist. "I've promised to take Bree down for a visit at the first opportunity."

I laughed. "That's taking a gallant blow for the team, Bree. I can't imagine she's feeling too generous after being roundly put in her place by Zora."

"Oh, no," she assured me. "I love Great-Aunt Mildred. I think I'm going to be her one day."

I shook my head. "No, no, you're far too good-natured."

"Am I?" She grinned up at Jareth. "I did forgive Jareth, so maybe you're right."

"Who could resist forgiving me?" Jareth asked, laughing back down at her.

I grinned across the table at Darius. After four years we had finally found our happiness. In weeks we would graduate, be married, and be crowned.

And then our real challenges would begin. But now that I knew I would have not only Darius, but also Bryony and Jareth by our sides, I couldn't wait to meet our challenges head on.

EPILOGUE

I smoothed my white trainee robe for the last time as I gazed out at the extensive audience. So many people had wanted to witness our graduation that the ceremony was being held in the arena instead of the dining hall as was the usual custom. I had heard all the details from Elsie, who had helped Zora with the preparations in her role as my personal servant.

"You have to continue as a trainee, despite all that's happened," she had pointed out in the face of both my and Stellan's protests. "I want to honor my commitment and finish the year as well."

Of course I had to accede to her wishes, despite my fear she was actually thinking of me and not her own preference—a suspicion that was reinforced when I discovered she and Stellan were waiting to make a formal announcement about their relationship until Midsummer. The delay seemed like yet another kind effort not to undermine my moment.

But I wouldn't have minded someone stealing some of the attention. I hardly needed more given the suffocating weight I had been carrying since our return from the Empire. Although, on second thought, perhaps she truly did prefer to wait and change her status on her return to Ardann. She had a close enough view of the pressure I was under.

My eyes latched on to Duke Francis, in position slightly to the side of the assembled graduates. While he stood alone now, he had entered the arena with Zora on his arm, the head servant looking magnificent in a gown of soft, pale green decorated with intricate patterns of darker green embroidery. It was a subtle yet effective nod to the dark green uniforms of the Academy servants, and eyes and whispers followed her every movement. I only hoped the public shock over their relationship would soften the ground for Stellan and Elsie in a few weeks.

Zora sat in the front row of the arena seating with the highest ranked guests. My eyes slid along the other occupants, fastening on my family. My parents sat together, their broad smiles reflecting in their eyes as they looked proudly back at me. They were flanked by my brothers, although neither Stellan nor Lucien were currently looking in my direction. I had half-expected Aunt Lucienne to come herself given the import of our graduation and the ceremonies immediately following it, but she had sent Lucien as her representative.

As soon as he arrived, he had pulled me into a hug that included a whispered apology, and I realized she had done it for my sake. When she traveled, the crown prince remained behind in Kallmon to govern in her absence. By staying herself, she had allowed my brother to be here. It was a fitting decision. Today was about a new generation.

The Sekalis had sent not only Princess Kalani but an enormous retinue of officials—a mark of honor and respect for our service to the Empire. And, of course, the entire Kallorwegian Mage Council was in attendance.

I had half-expected to see Mildred as well, but Zora said she was still sulking after having her unsolicited advice so roundly rejected. Of course, her letter to Jareth had expressed a different sentiment. Something about how the last thing she wanted to do was travel anywhere near the capital when every fool in the kingdom was flocking there en masse.

Duke Francis stepped forward to begin the ceremony, clearing his throat for attention. The arena fell unnaturally silent as all eyes focused on us. Several of the trainees shifted uncomfortably, but I had a lifetime of experience when it came to such functions. I easily maintained my attentive expression, even as my mind wandered.

Captains Layna and Vincent were equally well-disciplined, their faces impassive as they scanned the crowd from their position only a few steps away from the line of white-robed graduates. At the completion of this ceremony, we would no longer be trainees, and the old rules would no longer apply. Even here in the Academy, they would be our personal guards, shadowing our every move.

I suppressed my instinct to take Darius's hand, forcing my eyes not to slide sideways to where he stood beside me. We had fought so hard and endured so much to make it to this day. And for all the moments of both joy and terror, there had been even more of sheer boredom. We could make it through a little bit more.

My heart fluttered at the thought of the other ceremonies still in front of us in the next two days—ceremonies that would be anything but boring. In just a few minutes we would be fully qualified mages. Meaning it was finally time for Darius to be crowned king.

The Mage Council had intended an immediate coronation in the capital, but Darius had declared he would be crowned with his queen by his side. Which meant our coronation would happen directly after our wedding.

A small, impatient movement from my other side made me smile. I wasn't the only one getting married in two days. Just as Bryony had stood by my side through four years at the Academy, she was ready to join me in my commitment to Kallorway as well. Jareth couldn't have chosen a better bride—for his sake or mine. Knowing I would have both of my best friends with me took away all the fear of a new home. Because in two days I was not just getting married, I was also beginning a new life as both a queen and a Kallorwegian.

My eyes shifted back to my family. They had already assured me that our love for each other would be unaffected by the enormous changes in my life. And with them as inducement, I would dedicate myself to ensuring Kallorway maintained a good relationship with my home kingdom.

Duke Francis's tone changed, and I recognized his speech was coming to an end. It had been full of the usual congratulations and exhortations for the future with only the most veiled references to either the status of some of this year's graduates or the dramatic happenings of the past four years. Tradition must be upheld.

At his signal, five of the ten members of the Mage Council stood and walked across the arena floor to join us. Each of them carried folded squares of material, and all of them nodded respectfully toward Darius before taking their places a few paces to one side of the Academy Head.

He called Duchess Ashten, Head of the Wind Workers, forward and then spoke the formal words of graduation, directing them to the trainee standing closest to him.

"Isabelle, I hereby declare your mage training successfully completed. As you receive the privileges of your status as mage, remember your duties and responsibilities to your discipline and your kingdom."

Isabelle stepped forward, her eyes on the duke as she replied with quiet grace. "I thank you for your training, and I will remember."

She turned to Duchess Ashten who spoke the next of the rote words. "Isabelle, we welcome you into the wind worker discipline." She shook out the material in her hand to reveal a blue robe.

Isabelle bowed to her new head of discipline before accepting the robe and slipping it over her head. "I pledge myself to the wind workers."

Duchess Ashten nodded her acceptance of the new mage's words and, since Isabelle was the only wind worker trainee in our year, turned back toward the stands. Isabelle trailed behind to take up a reserved seat immediately behind the duchess.

Next, Duke Francis called for Duke Rennon, Head of the Creators, to step forward. As he took his place, he gave a small nod to his two nephews. Armand looked far too nervous to acknowledge his greeting, but Wardell grinned back at him.

Duke Francis called both of them forward one by one to recite the words of graduation and accept their orange robes. When Duke Rennon had led them both back to the stands, Duchess Callista took his place to receive Ashlyn and Frida, the two grower trainees. Both girls looked excited, casting giddy looks between those of us who remained and the crowd of observers. I smiled at them both, remembering the way four years had transformed their initial wary distance into friendship. While we would never be close in the way I was with Bree, I knew I would welcome the sight of their faces at court.

I couldn't say the same of the next trainee to graduate, however. As Royce—the sole Armed Forces trainee—recited the necessary words, I strove to keep any sign of emotion from my face. Royce's loyalty would always be conditional, and we would be wise to keep a close eye on him.

As the only member of the Mage Council remaining, General Haddon didn't wait to be called before striding forward to Duke Francis's side. I suppressed a head shake at the subtle message conveyed by the proud old man. He might have pledged himself to Darius's rule, but that didn't mean he would forget decades of command and maneuvering. He had been a daunting opponent, and I hoped he would prove an equally effective ally.

Jareth had trained in the Royal Guard discipline, but only Dellion was called forward by the general. She looked regal with her enviable height, her hair braided and wrapped around her head like a crown. As she walked toward her new discipline head, I remembered my initial impression of her nearly four years ago. I had observed then that she moved with an elegant, predatory grace, and that hadn't changed.

In fact, all the traits I had sensed in her then had proven true—practical, determined, elegant, connected, skilled, ambitious. And yet, in the intervening years, my thoughts about her had changed. Somewhere along the way, we had become allies. And what a difference it made to my impression of those traits to anticipate them being used on my own and my family's behalf.

When the gold robe slipped over her head, she gave a single, triumphant look back at the four of us remaining. I met it with a broad smile. She had declared that court was her chosen place, and she already looked like she belonged there.

When only Jareth, Bryony, Darius, and I remained with Duke Francis, he looked toward the stands. Zora rose solemnly to her feet, a pile of material in her hands. A brief wave of murmurs, quickly suppressed, swept the stands. Neither Zora nor the duke gave any sign of noticing the crowd's reaction as she crossed the dusty floor to stand beside him.

He called Bryony forward first, and this time his words varied slightly.

"Bryony, I hereby declare your mage training successfully completed. As you receive the privileges of your status as energy mage, remember your duties and responsibilities to your kingdom."

Bryony repeated the same thanks and promise the rest of the trainees had made and turned to Zora.

"Bryony, we welcome you to Kallorway," Zora said, handing her a purple robe.

A brief shiver ran through me as Bryony accepted the robe and spoke the required words. "I pledge myself to Kallorway."

And then it was my name being called. I moved forward, the crowds forgotten, although whispers had once again broken out among them. I glided along, not feeling the ground beneath my feet, as I focused on the Academy Head.

Before starting at the Academy, I had dreaded graduation, anticipating a ceremony that held more farce than meaning. Becoming a qualified mage meant less than nothing for someone with no ability.

How much had changed since then.

Now the words held more meaning than I could have imagined. Not only was I now truly qualified, but I was also pledging myself and my immense powers to the service of a new kingdom.

Somehow, despite all the impediments before me, I had discovered and mastered my abilities—and along the way, I had found a home and a purpose. As the purple robe settled onto my shoulders, my eyes sought Darius.

Our gazes locked as I said, "I pledge myself to Kallorway."

The burning fire in his eyes made every past difficulty and future risk worth it. In a moment, he would step forward as the last to graduate, the traditional words turned on their head. Instead of welcoming him to Kallorway, as she had done for me, Zora would declare Darius qualified and ready to rule. It was time for us to leave the Academy behind us and begin the rest of our lives.

NOTE FROM THE AUTHOR

Did you miss the adventures of Verene's mother, Elena, when she attends the Ardannian Academy as a commonborn and becomes the Spoken Mage? You can read the whole series now, starting with Voice of Power.

Or for more fantasy, romance, adventure, and intrigue at a very different sort of mage academy, try A Mage's Influence, set in a whole new world and starting with Seeds of Glory and Ruin.

Two sisters. Two seeds of power. One Mage's Guild, and an unprecedented new power—but which sister does it belong to?

To be informed of future releases, as well as Hidden Mage bonus shorts, please sign up to my mailing list at www.melaniecellier.com.

And if you enjoyed Crown of Power, please spread the word and help other readers find it! You could start by leaving a review on Amazon or Goodreads or Facebook or any other social media site. Your review would be very much appreciated and would make a big difference!

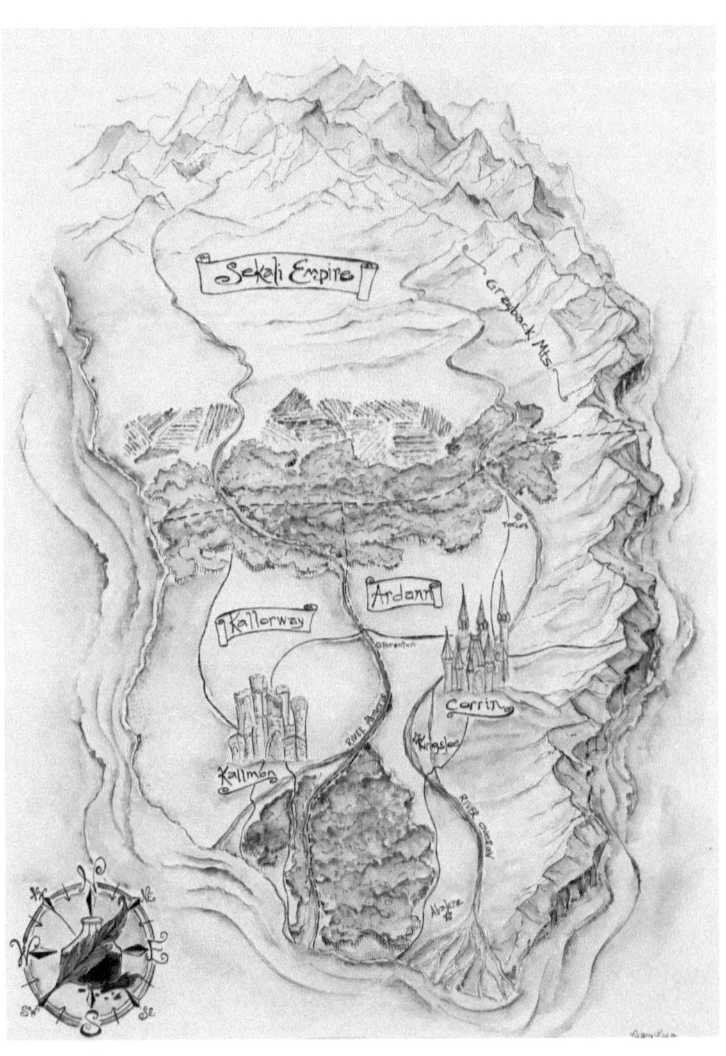

Sekali Empire
Greyback Mts
Ardann
Kallorway
Corrin
Kallmon
Obrenton
Kingslee
River Ausis
River Oresav
Torlos
Abylere

ACKNOWLEDGMENTS

I'm so grateful to be finished with another series. Each series feels like a special achievement—something beyond the sum of each of the individual books. I hope you enjoyed getting to know Verene and Darius, and joining them as they saved their kingdom and started to rebuild Kallorway. The idea for this series has been in my head ever since it helped shape the end of the Spoken Mage series when the idea popped into my head to pair the (apparently) powerless daughter of the strongest mage alive with the powerful son of a weak, sealed king.

And I'm so grateful to everyone who helped me along the way. Verene's journey turned out to be more difficult than I had anticipated, but it was rewarding to see it come together in the end.

A big thank you to Marc, Mary, Rachel, Greg, Priya, Katie, Deborah, and both my parents. Your support, feedback, and enthusiasm help keep me going.

And an enormous dosing of love to my adorable children who keep me from entirely losing myself in the computer. You make every bit of stress worth it, and I thank God for you constantly, as I thank him for his ongoing grace.

ABOUT THE AUTHOR

Melanie Cellier grew up on a staple diet of books, books and more books. And although she got older, she never stopped loving children's and young adult novels.

She always wanted to write one herself, but it took three careers and three different continents before she actually managed it.

She now feels incredibly fortunate to spend her time writing from her home in Adelaide, Australia where she keeps an eye out for koalas in her backyard. Her staple diet hasn't changed much, although she's added choc mint Rooibos tea and Chicken Crimpies to the list.

She writes young adult fantasy including books in her *Spoken Mage* world, her *Mage's Influence* world, and her various *Four Kingdoms* and *Kingdoms of Legacy* series that are made up of linked stand-alone stories that retell classic fairy tales.